She Flew the Coop

ALSO BY MICHAEL LEE WEST

Crazy Ladies

She Flew the Coop

A NOVEL CONCERNING LIFE,
DEATH, SEX, AND RECIPES IN
LIMOGES, LOUISIANA

MICHAEL LEE WEST

HarperPerennial
*A Division of HarperCollins*Publishers

HarperCollins books may be purchased for educational, business, or sales promotional use. For information please write: Special Markets Department, HarperCollins Publishers, Inc., 10 East 53rd Street, New York, NY 10022.

First HarperPerennial edition published 1995.

Designed by George J. McKeon

The Library of Congress has catalogued the hardcover edition as follows:

West, Michael Lee.
    She flew the coop : a novel concerning life, death, sex, and recipes in Limoges, Louisiana / Michael Lee West. — 1st ed.
       p.   cm.
    ISBN 0-06-018348-9
    1. City and town life—Louisiana—Fiction. I. Title.
PS3573.E8244S48   1994
813.54—dc20   93-49505

ISBN 0-06-092620-1 (pbk.)

95 96 97 98 99 ❖/RRD 10 9 8 7 6 5 4 3 2 1

For my father and mother,
Ralph Joseph Helton and Ary Jean Little Helton

This grotesque adventure is ours. We must live it. Death is absurd also.

—JEAN ANOUILH, *ROMEO AND JEANNETT*

That was the spring when all of Limoges became unhinged, as if a huge hand descended from the sky, shaking every house, flinging innocent husbands and wives, even young girls, into the wrong beds. It was 1952, leap year, coming on the heels of a hard winter. Someone traced the craziness back to the Neppers, but I personally think it's a sign from Revelation. You can look it up.

—ANONYMOUS SHOPPER, GALLERY STREET, LIMOGES, LOUISIANA

LIMOGES [20 alt, 905 population], lies in the extreme northeast corner of Louisiana. The town is situated 1.2 miles [as the crow flies] west of the Mississippi River, on a five mile stretch of oxbow lake. Two-lane highways feed into Limoges [the "s" is silent] from north, west, and south, but in the east no bridge crosses the water. The town dead-ends at the levee. To reach it you must cross the river at Vicksburg, turn right at Tallulah, and travel 42 miles north on Highway 65, following the grassy levee, past pecan groves and row crops—cotton, soybeans, and rice. Just beyond the WELCOME TO LIMOGES sign is a corridor of pin oaks [planted in 1865, by Scott Abolitionists and, so the legend goes, French pirates]. Long before the levee was built, the bottomland was so waterlogged that these early settlers bored holes in coffins so they would sink. In West Limoges, [R on Geranium] is the Yellow Fever Cemetery, where monuments tell the story of the epidemic. During the summer of 1878, hundreds died, and many Limogeans fled to adjoining parishes, returning after the first frost in late September when the mosquitoes were killed. The business district [R on Gallery] features cobbled roads, filigreed iron balconies with wooden ceiling fans, and storefronts painted salmon, brick, sea foam. It's worth the trouble to stop at Butter's Cafe [corner of Hayes and Sparrow] for coconut chess pie and the best coffee north of New Orleans, or Nepper's Drugs on the Square [L on Lincoln Avenue], with its old fashioned soda fountain. Ask the counter girl to make you a pecan praline soda or a banana pudding sundae, with crushed vanilla wafers and caramel sauce—your choice, 25 cents, still the best bargain in Louisiana.

—FROM WPA GUIDE TO LOUISIANA

Prologue:

Spring Fever, It's Catching,

Run for Your Life

∾

In this day and age, with our boys dying in Korea and the Russians building A-bombs, our own American teenagers are going wild. They are hard to love. But there is a bright spot: If they don't die in car wrecks or some other tragedy, they generally grow into nice people, the same as you and me.

—Reverend T. C. Kirby, pastor, First Baptist Church, Limoges, from his sermon, "What to Do When You Can't Do Anything: Today's Young People," March 1952

On the first warm Saturday in March, while geese flew north and crawfish filled the bayous, Olive Nepper turned against Jesus. She was sixteen years old, a teenaged Baptist, the only child of Henry and Vangie. Thanks to the delicate nature of her upbringing, the renunciation seemed like the crime of crimes. Ashamed and heartbroken, she stood in her mama's kitchen and swallowed a whole bottle of rose poison. Even though she'd mixed it with orange Nehi, the taste, not to mention the act itself, was a letdown. She'd already done so much worse.

The town had seen its share of tragedy, like when old Mr. Walker fell off his John Deere and the bush hog sheared over him. They said you could fit what was left into an egg carton. And last Halloween the Bodeen twins threw a sackful of kittens into the Mississippi and accidentally drowned themselves. Misadventures happened, and so did love snarls, but hardly anyone committed suicide (unless you counted Luther Cross when he got caught for back taxes).

One of the busybodies, a Methodist who wished to remain anonymous, observed that Olive couldn't have picked a better season—if you were going to poison yourself, spring was the time to do it. When it came to burials, the ground was too hard in winter, not to mention cold, and delta summers were renowned for being deadly. March was just right for a funeral, cool and breezy, the landscape flushed with blooming dogwoods and quince. The air around Limoges seemed pinkish, almost tinted (later, some would say *tainted*).

It was leap year, a warm, dizzy spring after a brittle, pipe-shattering winter. Old-timers sat around the courthouse watching folks run errands in short sleeves and cotton dresses. They shook their heads. *The worst isn't over*, they cautioned. *Time's still left for a killing frost*. The Yellow Fever Cemetery, on the corner of Geranium and Washington, was so colorful it almost hurt the old-timers' eyes. Almost any time of day they'd see ladies setting out Ball jars full of jonquils. The town itself seemed like a woman—pretty yet wasteful, unaware of all dangers. The Limoges Year-Round Garden Club, for instance, had planted 905 daffodils along the cemetery's cast-iron fence, one for each person in town, and in another few weeks tulips would bloom. The president of the club, Mrs. Harriet Hooper, openly called the cemetery a Garden of Eden, the perfect site for picnics; the old-timers thought it was more like a florist's shop without the fancy chill. Everyone agreed it was just too pretty to last.

The poisoning occurred on a sunny morning, eighty-five degrees, not a cloud in the sky. All over the parish, women stood in their backyards, gossiping over crepe myrtle hedges, hanging up cold, dripping-wet linens on clotheslines. High above them kites flapped like pinned butterflies. A yellow kite snapped loose and veered west, over Geranium Street, over the cemetery, toward the First Baptist steeple. It was the tallest landmark in town, taller than the Presbyterians', even. The kite smacked against the steeple, then slid down, following the slope of the roof, bumping along the shingles. It drifted to the front yard, startling a flock of pigeons; they flew up, a dark spill against the flat blue sky.

Below, the church door swung open, banging against the bricks, and Olive Nepper ran out. She clattered down the steps, then jumped over the kite. The minister stepped from inside and watched her run across the yard. He was young for a man of God, with long sideburns and a cleft in his chin, but his eyes were old, small-lidded and blue. "Olive?" he called out.

From the sidewalk, Olive turned. Stepping backward, she hooked her ankle into a rusty croquet wicket. She toppled over, skidding against the bumpy concrete. Her dress ripped at the waist, exposing a white cotton slip. Good, she thought, lifting one skinned palm. Maybe I jarred something loose. From the porch, the minister frowned. Her ponytail had come undone, and blond hairs fell over her eyes. She scrambled to her feet and dusted off her knees. The reverend lifted one finger as if to call her back, but she shook her head, then took off running again.

Two maiden sisters, Mamie and Meredith Marshall, spotted the girl and called out to her. They were staunch Methodists, on their way to the cemetery to say hello to Mother and Daddy and to set out some fresh lilacs. "Is that Vangie's child?" said Mamie, gripping her sister's arm. "Olive? Olive Nepper?"

The girl whirled around and wiped her eyes. "Yes, ma'am?"

"Well?" Mamie stepped closer. The child was a Baptist, which explained a lot, but *still*, her behavior demanded further explanation so the sisters could savor it later, when they weren't so preoccupied with grave-tending. "What's the matter, child?"

"Ask him." Olive pointed to the church. The sisters turned just in time to see Reverend T. C. Kirby dart inside, the heavy walnut door catching the tail of his jacket. Before he jerked it through the crack, the cloth protruded like a black tongue. The sisters gasped and turned back to Olive, who had taken off again, running down Geranium Street, a speck against the yellow bells and azaleas.

"Reckon what's happened?" they whispered, looking back at the church. The sisters shook their heads. You could never figure what a Baptist would do—always so goody-good, but seething inside with sin. Yes, indeed. Seething. "One of these days," said Mamie, "this whole town'll see the light and cross over to First Methodist."

"Amen," said her sister. "But we'll need a bigger church." By the time they'd reached the corner of Geranium and Washington, they were castigating the Presbyterians and Lutherans. They'd clean forgotten Olive Nepper, who was a whole two blocks away. She turned down Lincoln Avenue, passing through sun, then dappled shade. Her house was two blocks east on Cypress Street, which dead-ended into Lake Limoges, a five-mile oxbow.

She cut through Oak Street, down the side lawn of the Beaulieu Funeral Home. Through the blooming azalea hedge she saw her own backyard and a corner of her house, white with pink shutters. She moved without thinking—her mind was still with the reverend. All her life she'd read the Bible and recited prayers at her bedside. She'd been raised to believe that prayers were like wishes. If your wants were sincere, the Lord would provide. Reverend Kirby assured Olive that she was a very sincere girl, and he would provide what the Lord did not. Now she felt betrayed by all men. Since Jesus was a man, and probably a Baptist, too, she held Him responsible. After all, He'd led her straight to the Baptist church and Reverend Kirby.

She fit herself through a gap in the azaleas, scratching her forearms, and tumbled onto the grass. Straight ahead was her mama, Vangie, kneeling in the rose bed, waving enormous clippers. Olive's daddy, Henry Nepper, was always warning her to tread softly around her mother, hinting that Vangie had a weak constitution, coupled with a childhood injury that had knocked her senseless. Olive looked past her mama, past Cypress Street, where Lake Limoges spread out green and sparkly, between tree stumps and wooden docks. A man in a straw hat stood on the third dock, gripping a fishing pole.

"Drat these weeds!" cried Vangie, rubbing a red dot on her wrist. Her mama's hair was gray and curly, like sphagnum moss, and disciplined into braids. She looked old before her time. Her heart-shaped face was starting to sag on either side of her chin. Olive darted behind a pecan tree, hoping her mama hadn't seen her. She dug her fingers into the bark, then peered around the trunk. Her mama was eyeing the dead limb of a prized floribunda. Over to the right, near the property line, was a chain-link kennel where her daddy's spotted hunting dogs slept in a strip of hot sun. If they started barking, she'd never slip into the house. She twisted her neck, looking back at the kitchen windows, hoping Sophie Donnell wasn't inside. Olive normally looked forward to Sophie's cleaning days—she always left behind a surprise: caramel squares; a coconut cream pie with five inches of meringue; bacon-deviled eggs on a cut-glass platter. She'd taken care of Olive for sixteen years, and she had an uncanny way of sniffing out trouble.

Olive wiped her eyes on her sleeve, then lifted her dress. Her knees were smeared with dried blood, and her hands were still stinging. She uncurled her palm and stared down at her lifeline. The bottom half was rubbed raw. That, too, seemed like Jesus' fault. She peeked around the tree. When her mama leaned forward to snap off the limb, Olive darted toward the house. She eased open the screen door and stepped into the pink-and-white kitchen. The room was empty. Light streamed through the windows. Breakfast dishes were stacked in the plastic drainer, beads of water still clinging to juice glasses and coffee cups. Several of her daddy's shirts were draped across the ironing board.

"Sophie?" she called out, then held her breath.

Silence. Just the drippy faucet and whirring icebox. She sat down at the table and cradled her head. No one knew the truth; she was polite and prissy on the outside, man-crazy underneath— and there were precious few to choose from in Limoges. Last year she'd advertised in *Pen Pals of the South*, and every morning when the mailman dropped letters in the box, she ran outside to snatch them. One day the mail arrived when she was frying bacon, and she took the letters straight to her bedroom, forgetting the smoky skillet on the burner. She spread the envelopes on her bed and looked at the postmarks—Atlanta, Charleston, Mobile, Lake Charles. She smelled smoke, remembered the skillet, and raced into the kitchen, screaming *fire fire fire!* While her mama ran next door screaming for help, flames leaped to the curtains. After the neighbors doused the fire, Vangie turned on her daughter. "How did you let this happen?" she cried. "Don't you know your daddy will kill us both?"

Olive had been afraid of that. She walked outside, straight into the lake, and tried to drown herself. When the cute undertaker pulled her out of the water, she bit his hand. That's how much she didn't want to face her daddy. Home disasters could really provoke Henry Nepper. Small wonder that she couldn't face him now. She marched straight to the sink and opened all the cabinets. Hunkering down, she knocked over bottles and grabbed a can of rose poison. She took out a funnel, sifted the powder into an orange Nehi, and shook the bottle, using her thumb as a cork. Then she began to drink. With every swallow, she imagined her mama's nasal voice, instructing in the fundamentals of gardening: Herbicides worked from the taproot, strangling the plant, but insecticides killed the pest that fed on the leaves. These potions, she knew, must be measured with care; too little would have no effect, too much would sink to the marrow and kill.

She gripped the Nehi bottle with both hands and looked through the kitchen window; the sun darted behind a cloud, throwing forsythia and haw bushes into shade. All around her the air was acrid, making her eyes water. She had no intention of dying, but a deathbed wouldn't be half-bad. Reverend Kirby could hold her hand, saying, *Sorry, sorry.* The poison burned her throat. She wiped her mouth, then carelessly set the bottle in the sink, sloshing orange soda. If she had more time, maybe she could have thought of a more appetizing method, but all that came to mind was a Boris Karloff movie, where the monster had pulled the lever after Dr. Frankenstein warned him not to, blowing up his bride and the castle. "As if castles have self-destruct levers," she told herself and rubbed her lips with the heel of her hand.

First thing, she had discarded the notion of telling her mama. Olive had gotten herself into this trouble; she'd trusted the wrong man, believed his every word. And it was a sorry day when you couldn't trust a preacher. Her mama wouldn't understand about young girls getting into fixes. She'd said plenty of times that no man bought the cow if he got the milk free. And the reverend had enough to open his own dairy. T. C. Kirby had come to Limoges two summers ago, during a revival. He stood at the podium, one lock of hair falling into his eyes, and sang "Just As I Am." People

got up from the pews and poured down the aisles to rededicate
their lives. Even Olive's own mama elbowed her way through the
crowd, as if in a daze. Vangie Nepper stood in front of the whole
congregation, in front of all those visiting Baptists from Epps,
Oak Grove, and Lake Providence; in front of all those friends and
strangers, she cried her eyes out. Later, she said there was just
something *unusual* about Reverend Kirby, and it wasn't because
he'd traveled with the Billy Graham Crusade. Harriet Hooper,
who'd also rededicated her life, said, "It's almost like he's on a
first-name basis with God."

When their regular pastor died of food poisoning, the congregation asked Kirby to stay. After all, singing preachers were hard
to find—most had gravelly voices like they'd been eating too
much parakeet grit. But a preacher who could make grown people laugh and cry was a rare bird. In the two years he'd been at
First Baptist, the membership had swelled. They had the crème
de la crème of Limoges: the Cheniers who owned the barge lines;
the Fondrens of Empire Gas; the Hobarts from Guaranty Bank
and Trust; the Galliards/Neppers of Galliard Gin; the Glass family
who sold John Deeres in the whole Louisiana delta. Since T. C.
Kirby started preaching, the Baptists had even stolen a few choice
Methodists, peeving the Marshall sisters.

Olive's mama thought T. C. Kirby was the finest minister in
Louisiana—not that she was a good judge of people. Vangie was a
self-taught home economist, an expert in canning, recipe reduc-
tion, and horticulture. After a canasta party, while Olive and her
mother were washing dishes in mother/daughter aprons, Vangie
turned to Olive and said, "You may not realize this, but you're
being raised to host glorious parasites."

From the living room, Henry Nepper rattled the newspaper
and called out, "You mean host *parties*, don't you?"

"That's what I said." Vangie looked at her daughter, wrinkling
her forehead. "Didn't I?"

Vangie had cooking, gardening, and hospitality down pat, but
she was also an armchair expert on death. Everyone who lived on
Cypress Street had a sensitivity toward death—their backyards
faced the rear of Beaulieu Funeral Home, a whitewashed brick
with columns and stained-glass cupolas. One hundred years ago
it was a Greek Revival mansion; now it was a mausoleum, a glorified motel for the dead. It was disconcerting to see caskets carried in and out, empty or otherwise. Years ago the women on
Cypress Street revolted and planted an azalea hedge, but only
enormous trees, like willows and pine, would have blocked the
old mansion.

"At least they won't have to carry me far," Olive thought, laying her head on the counter. She'd lost her virginity—it had been

dangling by a hair anyway—on a youth-choir trip to Lookout Mountain, Tennessee. Reverend Kirby had driven the bus, with no other adults present; he had insisted. "These kids are good as gold. I won't have a bit of trouble." Olive had chosen a seat directly behind him and spent the whole trip gazing at his ears, admiring how the sun turned them pink and transparent. It was the first time she'd been away from her mama and daddy, the first time she'd seen mountains. Shortly after they crossed into Alabama, the reverend turned and smiled. "How we doing back there, Sister Nepper?" he asked. Thrilled that he'd singled her out in front of the others, she blushed all the way to Birmingham. Like a fool. He was probably laughing at her right now; he'd threatened to write a sermon about her.

Now she wished she'd stayed in Limoges. Not fifteen minutes ago, when she'd told Reverend Kirby about her condition, he'd raised his eyebrows and said, "Well, I'm sorry, just real sorry, but it's your word against mine. And God's." He riffled through his night table and took out a comic book, *Victims of Vonnatur!*

"What about those afternoons at the parsonage? And that one time in the belfry?" Her eyes filled. "You said you'd marry me."

"Did I?" He turned a page. "Why, I don't have a recollection of that."

"You took advantage of me!"

"But I never penetrated," he said fiercely. "At least, not much."

"Then how'd I get your baby inside me?" She pointed to her stomach.

"You're sure it's mine?"

"No, it's a *Victim of Vonnatur!*" She slapped the comic book from his hands. "Of course it's yours!"

"Does it have my name written on it?" A vein pulsed in his neck. "Do you have a witness? Somebody who saw us together?"

When she didn't answer, he raised his eyebrows. "I'm not the only man in Limoges. You could've laid with anybody."

"I just laid with you, and you know it. A preacher should own up to his actions."

"But I don't have to own up to yours."

"I'm telling my daddy!"

"You go right ahead, Sister Nepper. Just go right on. The other day he was saying how proud he is of you. What a good girl you are, and how much he loves you. How he's counting on you to go to L.S.U. and be a teacher. Go ahead and break your daddy's heart, Sister Nepper. I'm sure he'll get over it sooner or later, if the shock don't put him in the hospital."

"He'll make you marry me!"

"Not if I leave town, he can't. I've left other places in the dark of night, and nobody's caught up with me yet. My name is clean as a whistle."

She fled from the church, but his voice was trapped inside her skull like bees scratching at a shut window. He wasn't going to marry her. Even if her daddy believed her, she'd still be disgraced. No college would accept a woman who carried a baby on her hip. Certainly no *man* would want her. And that's all she really wanted out of life—a man, a baby, and a color-coordinated kitchen. She looked around the room for something to throw—the pink canisters? The Mixmaster? A can of poison?—but decided it would make too much noise.

"Sister Nepper, my foot," she cried and kicked a chrome step stool, stubbing her toe. She limped out of the kitchen and picked up a snow dome from the TV set. The whole house had an empty feel to it, which suited her just fine. She turned into the hall, limping over the rose-strewn carpet. As she walked, she shook the dome. It was a souvenir from Lookout Mountain, and it showed two miniature people standing on Lover's Leap, a lip of bone that slanted into a gorge. Reverend Kirby had called it a cleft, but the word hadn't meant anything to Olive. "It makes me think of wedding nights," he confessed, but she still didn't get it. She'd bought the dome with baby-sitting money, thinking it would look pretty in the rectory when she was Mrs. Kirby, a bona fide Baptist wife. "Even if he marries me," she thought, "I'll still be disgraced." She supposed they could move; a church in Texas or Georgia would be nice. Someplace bigger, where no one knew them. The new congregation wouldn't count months; they would accept her baby as full-term, legitimate.

She knew exactly when she'd conceived this child—not on the trip to Chattanooga and not in the rectory, but in the tall, white steeple of First Baptist. It was late January, too cold to undress. Freezing air blew through the arched windows. She remembered how heavy he felt and how the wood floor squeaked beneath her. She looked over his shoulder, into the narrow, pitched roof where the bell hung above them. Pigeons flew in circles, disturbed by the lovemaking. When Olive squinted, they looked just like angels. Later, when Reverend Kirby stood up and turned, she saw that the back of his sweater was splattered; white commas stood out against the red wool. She didn't have the heart to tell him—how could she word it? "Pardon me, Reverend, but you might want to change your sweater?"

"Why?" he'd say, looking down at his spotless front.

"Well, a bird has shit all over you." (There was no other way to say it—"dookie" and "pooped" just didn't have the same ring.) She had to admit, the whole thing had weird symmetry. While the reverend deposited one thing, the pigeons deposited something else. Except for the birds, everybody got a souvenir.

No matter how hard she shook the dome, the people never jumped. She turned it upside down, and the couple stood on their heads, fine grains of rice collecting in the curve of plastic. Or maybe it was real snow. She couldn't tell. She'd never seen any in her whole life, just freezing rain and frost. Inside the globe, the teeny people were trapped in winter. Here in Limoges death had four seasons, like Princess Summerfallwinterspring on "Howdy Doody." If Olive had to live in a snowglobe she would choose summer—long afternoons at the country club pool, the scent of chlorine rising from blue water, the concrete walls cold as tombstones.

She flopped down on her bed, causing the box spring to creak, and held up the dome. The walls looked distorted through the plastic. It was her childhood room, pale blue, fourteen by fifteen, with a ceiling of hand-painted clouds. Aunt Edith, who lived next door, had painted them seven years ago when she came to Limoges as a war bride. Edith was from New York City, the only genuine Yankee in town. She'd married Zachary Galliard, Vangie's only brother, in 1945. There was talk—especially among Galliards—that Edith had maneuvered Zachary into marriage, but Olive hadn't believed it. She adored Edith. Uncle Zachary, though, perpetuated the rumor. After all his bachelor years, he seemed to enjoy his status as a pursued man. "I saved her from starvation," he'd joke at family gatherings. "She lived in Murray Hill, a third-floor walk-up. No bigger than Mama's biscuit porch. The littlest rooms I ever saw, with roaches big as hamsters."

"It was lovely," Edith would say, pinching his cheek. "It was an artist's studio."

"Only if the artist was a pygmy." Zachary laughed and swatted Edith's bottom. Then he bent her over backward and kissed her in front of his mama and everyone. Last summer, on the hottest day of the year, a blood vessel ruptured in his brain. He died instantly—with Edith on top of him, if you believed the rumors. Harriet Hooper, who had the longest tongue in Limoges and lived two doors down from the Galliards, swore it was true, but she was the kind of gossip who could dig graves with her mouth. Like all troublemakers, no one paid her any attention.

Olive set the snow dome on her stomach, watching it rise and fall with her breathing, then she looked up. When she was a small girl, those clouds had looked real. She pictured living in New York City, where the wind blew between skyscrapers, dusty air speckled with voices, old women speaking in tongues. Sometimes she imagined the air moving in circles, as if caught inside a glass jug. New York seemed as foreign as snow. She imagined a warm October afternoon, with light falling like strained pear juice, the cypress turning red along the lake. She'd wheel the newborn baby down the sidewalk, with all the neighbors looking on. They'd lean together and whisper. "Who's the daddy?" Harriet Hooper would demand, peering close to examine the baby's features. The child, Olive was certain, would resemble a miniature reverend, clutching a Bible rattle.

There was no escape from Harriet, and there was no escape from this baby. Gossip would be ferocious; they'd lap up everything like starving people sitting down to a meal. She imagined her body stretched out like a kite, her skinny legs trailing down. She wasn't the first girl to have a child out of wedlock, but she would probably be the last. Women in Limoges would set her up as an example. "It ruined her," they'd say. "Poor Olive Nepper. No decent man will touch her with a ten-foot pole."

She blinked at the gauzy blue ceiling. Poisonings were delicate things. Life, death, sex—even conception—it was all in the timing. She wasn't sure how long she was supposed to lie here. When she got good and sleepy, she'd fling the paperweight through the window. It would shatter on the patio. Her mama would look up, startled, and say, Olive? Did you do this, Olive? Probably now would be a good time, only she couldn't lift her arm. When she opened her mouth to scream, all that came out was a whisper. Mama. Maybe she was already dead—but no, she was breathing, because that stupid paperweight bobbed up and down.

Waiting to die, she reasoned, couldn't be too different from waiting your turn in the doctor's office. Waiting for the snow to settle in the gorge. She guessed the baby was the size of a jelly bean, a grasshopper on a rose leaf, a tiny figure in a snow dome. All the bedroom windows stood open, blowing in coolish air, ruffling her venetians. The back of her mouth tasted bitter. From outside, voices moved through wind and sun, weaving through trees and telephone wires. She heard a dog bark, listened to children running down the sidewalk, music rising up from a scratchy record player. Tomorrow was Sunday. If she woke up, she'd walk to the Catholic church on Sparrow Street. She was drawn to the idea of veils and holy water and pretty black beads with crucifixes. Also, the Catholic Jesus seemed different, a little less handsome than the Baptist version, but serious and noble. The noise fell away, and she saw herself rising into the clouds, high above the backyard. She could see far into the future. Her mama would stand next to her rose beds, turning her face up to the sky. The baby would fall through Olive and land into Vangie's outstretched hands, slippery and red, its mouth opening like a bud. All around her the wind blew and blew, sending spring across the delta, and she drifted between clouds, waiting for the voices to sing her back to sleep.

Cantaloupe Pickles

From the kitchen of Harriet Hooper

Peel & cube: 1 cup cantaloupe
Soak: in 1 cup vinegar overnight
Boil: 1 cup sugar and 1 cup vinegar for each cup fruit
Add: fruit. Skim off foam.
Add: 1 teaspoon salt
1 tablespoon whole allspice.
Boil hard for 10 minutes. Cool. Pour into sterile jars and seal.
Yield: 1 Pint

In the old days we called these "Can't Elope" pickles and avoided them like the plague so we wouldn't be old maids!

Down to Earth

❧

Gardens come and go, but I find myself getting attached to certain perennials. My tulips are bridesmaids with fat faces and good posture. Hollyhocks are long-necked sisters. Daffodils are young girls running out of a white church, sun shining on their heads. Peonies are pink-haired ladies, so full and stooped you have to tie them up with string. And roses are nothing but (I hate to say it) bitches— pretty show-offs who'll draw blood if you don't handle them just right.

—Vangie Galliard Nepper, from her "Garden Diary," March 1952

Vangie Nepper

I've always loved dirt. It's dark and moist like a lump of chocolate cake in your hand. You think it will taste sweet, but it's bitter as gall. My daddy, Major Galliard, grew cotton, and he used to say that soil was the basis of his life. Mama always laughed and said, "I thought Jack Daniel's was." The drink killed my daddy, but the soil remained firm and cool beneath my knees.

High above me, over Lake Limoges, a plane droned in circles. It made a slow loop, crawling along the backside of the sky like a bug caught inside an overturned glass bowl. I heard the noise and looked up, shielding my eyes with pruning shears. I knew the pilot from the way he drew out a check mark, his signature jettison. Sometimes the sky was slashed all over the delta, the marks widening into V's. Emmett Welch was the best crop duster in north Louisiana.

Today, though, it was too early for dusting. He was up there because he loved it. My daddy believed that sitting in a cockpit was like praying. The whole sky was his church. Sundays used to hurt Mama—all the other husbands sitting with their wives, fanning their sweaty babies. Daddy would be somewhere above us, his plane chewing up the blue, flying so low the stained-glass windows trembled.

My daddy taught Emmett to fly in 1922, a day that broke my heart. Emmett was a bowlegged kid working at Galliard Gin. His poor old daddy got gassed in World War I, and his mama ran off to Shreveport. Daddy was known for hand-picking his pilots, mostly orphans, training them himself. Emmett Welch had gray, close-set eyes that took in everything. My daddy knew that look. There was precious little he didn't know. He'd fought in every war that came along, even World War I. He was too old for the second one, but a crony pulled some strings with the recruiting office in Monroe. Major Galliard, they called him. A veteran who'd never seen action. Still, he had a chest full of medals, awards for perfect attendance and cleanliness. But he was an unsung hero when it came to picking pilots. He called Emmett into the knotty pine office and said, "Boy, get you some goggles and climb up in that cockpit and wait till I get ready. I'm gone teach you to fly."

I'd been sitting under my daddy's wide oak desk, carving my initials into the wood with a straight pin. I looked up, and my eyes met Emmett's. Behind him, a crowd was gathering, sweaty men with bits of cotton sticking to their necks and arms. Emmett turned back to my daddy. A rotary fan riffled through papers on his desk. "Sir?" Emmett shuffled his feet. "I ain't never been no higher than the water tower, and I didn't even climb all the way up."

"Climbing ain't like flying!" Daddy narrowed his eyes, a startling shade of turquoise, a Galliard trait. "Didn't get scared, did you, boy?"

"No, sir." Emmett shuffled his feet, glancing over his shoulder at the men. "Had to pee."

"That's good. Because you're going real high today, boy. Real high."

"Teach me, too!" I crawled out from under the desk and threw myself on Daddy's arm. My eyes filled. I worshipped him; I followed him everywhere—down to the fields, the gin, and even backwater cabins where he bought whiskey. But he refused to let me ride in the plane. My brother, Zachary, was eighteen months older, a thin, solemn boy who clung to our mother. Zachary was sickly, prone to asthma, chest colds, and nightmares. The Major was bitterly disappointed. I tried to be both son and daughter to him, but he was naturally prejudiced against girls. The single time he'd tried to take my brother flying, Zachary hid under the porch. When Daddy pulled him out, Zachary went berserk. He kicked, hollered, and arched his back. He screamed for Mama, screamed for Jesus. Then he ripped away and lunged for the wooden glider; he climbed up the chains and held on like a sloth. "It's just a little old plane ride," Daddy said.

"I'll die first," Zachary said. He sucked in air and then held it, pursing his lips until his eyes bulged. Mama cried, "Oh, my baby!" She stepped forward, but Daddy grabbed her wrist. Now he was 100 percent the Major, watching everything with fierce blue eyes.

"He'll suffocate!" Mama cried.

"Let him," the Major said. Zachary's face swelled up like an eggplant, dark and shiny. One hand fell away from the chain, then the other. He fell to the porch, banging one eye on the corner of the glider. He came to in Mama's lap; the eye was purple, starting to swell. It made him look pitiful.

I thought of all this as the fan blew over my daddy's desk, wafting over to the sweaty men in the hallway. I looked up at my daddy and said, "I'm old enough to go flying. And I'm not scared."

"The hell you ain't," the Major growled. "Your mama'd skin me. Anyhow, gals can't fly."

Emmett blinked; behind him a trickle of laughter rose up.

"But girls can ride, can't they?" I looked up into my daddy's eyes. Then I lowered my voice so Emmett and the other men wouldn't hear. "I won't tell Mama."

"Hell," he said impatiently, waving one hand. "Come on, then. Get you some goggles and come on."

As soon as we lifted off, Emmett peed his pants. I was delighted until Daddy accused me of the crime. "No, no!" I cried, pointing to the stain on Emmett's crotch, but the wind ate up my words; it rushed into the cockpit, sucking my hair out of the leather helmet. Daddy just laughed. Behind his back, I knew people thought he was ridiculous. It hurt me to see him march in parades, smiling like a four-star general, waving to old ladies and children. He wore his medals everywhere, even to oversee his fields. From a distance he resembled a little dictator, Stalin or Mussolini.

"Hell, let's cross the river!" he hollered. "Just to say we been to Mississippi and back." Below us was nothing but cotton, a field of clouds, miles in all directions. *Get your head out of them clouds, Vangie!* old Della used to say. She was our cook until she passed and her daughter took over. My mama never turned her hand in the kitchen. She was a Hughes from Port Gibson, Mississippi; she'd been a debutante at Newcomb and married Daddy after her first semester. Marriage to a Galliard man meant babying him. She did all of the Major's work—planting, cultivating, studying fungicides, hiring and feeding gangs, calling up the exchange for daily prices. Gossiping with the planters' wives. "My daddy is a cotton king," I bragged to the pickers' children. Mama overheard and said, "No, your daddy gallivants. He lives for parades and flying. Too bad he isn't a pigeon."

Now Emmett's plane veered south, toward Legion Field, and disappeared to blue. I turned back to my roses, snapping off a sucker. I hadn't seen Emmett in ages, not since my daddy's funeral. We buried him with all of his medals. "The delta grows anything," he used to say, "but it's particularly susceptible to rice and cotton." And weeds, too, I thought, looking sideways at my garden. Weeds the size of beanstalks, with long, difficult roots. All I could do was chop them down, maybe sprinkle a handful of lime. Somebody from the garden club gave a talk about weeds and pests; through the centuries, they said, frugal women preserved their gardens any way they could. In Europe they steamed the soil, long enough to cook a medium-sized baked potato. I remember how Mama worried about boll weevils and pink bollworms, reading off names of chemicals, while the Major sat on the porch sipping whiskey from a coffee cup.

"Don't you go spraying arsenic on my cotton," he said, walking to the edge of the porch, holding the cup in two fingers. "It leaves a film in the soil. It just about ruined Europe. You can't use arsenic, no ma'am."

"Who said I was using it on cotton?" Mama said.

The sun was a powerful distraction. It hung above me like a pot of boiling butter. Like the Major used to say, there's hotter places than the delta, but the Mississippi River saturates everything. It literally takes your breath away. Today's heat was not a good sign. I glanced toward the street, hoping to see Sophie Donnell, the lady who looked after my house on Tuesdays and Saturdays. She'd been with us since Olive was a baby, 1936 to be exact. I mopped my forehead with the edge of my apron. It was just too hot to think. And noise, my Lord. Next door, Harriet Hooper started playing another Ethel Merman record, a voice that matched her own, like she'd sucked too many sour balls. I set down my shears and stood, looking up and down Cypress Street.

The sidewalk was empty except for Fanny, Dr. Phillip Le-Gette's girl, riding her bicycle. Last winter her mama died, hadn't been in the ground four months when the doctor started dating Miss Waldene Wallace. We all thought Dr. Phillip would fall for a nurse, but Waldene was a beauty operator. They were married last June, and Reverend Kirby preached the wedding. Shocked everybody. You could see why he fell for her, though. Waldene was a pretty thing, with long curly blond hair, even if her eyes were a bit small. Now she was expecting a baby, five months along, throwing up every morning. This had to worry Fanny. Her mama died trying to give the doctor another child. Margaret Jane LeGette started bleeding in the night. When Dr. Phillip woke up, she was ice cold. Pale as the sheet she was lying on. Later, after the funeral, they had to burn the mattress.

When Fanny saw me she rang her little bell, then skidded to a stop. She straddled the bike and yelled, "Howdy, Miss Vangie! Olive home yet?"

"Not yet, sugar." I shook my head. "She went to town."

"Which part?"

"She didn't say. Check back later."

"Yessum." Fanny climbed back on her bike. It was way too big. My heart just ached for that child. Here lately, Olive acted like she was too old for Fanny. Even Harriet Hooper made sly remarks about Olive being too grown-up, chasing boys. "Have you ever heard of a magazine called *Pen Pals of the South*?" Harriet asked a few months ago. "I think your Olive's got an ad in it."

"There's nothing wrong with pen pals," I said.

"There is when you're advertising for boyfriends." She swelled up. "Convicts and all kinds of rascals read that magazine."

"It's not a crime to write a letter."

"It is when you're sixteen years old!" She made a face, then stalked off. Later, when I confronted Olive, she said, "I'm just doing some chain letters is all. With other Baptist kids. I hope that's all right, Mama." She smiled the sweetest smile.

Teaching a child manners was like training beans to run up a pole. The Bible said as much. They need a little help, a little firmness in the right places. From birth until age fourteen, my Olive was a perfect, if pious, little angel. Choir, GA's, perfect attendance in Sunday school. Cried her little eyes out when she learned that Baptists didn't have nuns. That was what she wanted to be, an orphanage nun, which scared her daddy. Henry was a confirmed Baptist. Then, shortly after her fourteenth birthday, she turned moody and mean. I bought her a box of Modess and a little book called *You're a Young Lady Now*, hoping we could read it together. Olive said, "Oh, Mama. You're about two years too late."

"No!" I was heartbroken.

"Check my closet if you don't believe me."

Well, I did. Behind the plastic wardrobe bag were boxes and boxes of Modess, more than a grown woman could use in her lifetime. I backed out of the closet and said, "How did you sneak these into the house?"

"Don't you want to know how I got them *out*?" she said crossly. Then she reached out and took my hand. "Poor mama. You don't know the world is turning."

Probably I still didn't. This morning, Olive left the house before breakfast. She said she had to run an errand, an important secret errand. "What for?" I pressed. Olive looked at me with calm, unblinking eyes, blue as my own, and said, "Mother's Day. It has to do with Mother's Day."

"But that's a whole two months from now."

"Mama, I'm in a hurry." Olive rolled her eyes. She grinned, showing all her dimples. "Can I go now, please ma'am?"

That's my girl, I thought. Polite to the very last second. I really couldn't complain, even if she didn't always make up her bed. Fanny LeGette was a good girl, too. A bit mischievous, but well behaved. Way down on the sidewalk she pushed off with one foot and steered her bicycle, the handlebars wobbling. She rode past Harriet's house, then veered into her own driveway.

I glanced back at the sidewalk, but it was empty. The sun pushed down on my head, and I headed toward my kitchen, think-ing a cool glass of water would taste so nice. When I stepped inside, the air smelled of beans and also something tart, making my nose itch. Even before I reached the sink, I saw the mess. On the counter stood a Nehi bottle and a can of insecticide, what I used on my roses. The porcelain sink was splattered with orange pop. All the cabinet doors gaped open. I didn't have a recollection of making this jumble—I was the tidiest person in the world—but I had an idea who did: Henry Nepper, registered pharmacist, the man who dis-pensed everything from penicillin to Modess to chocolate sodas. He was the last to leave, taking his own sweet time shaving and trim-ming nostril hairs, leaving them laid out on the sink like dead fleas. Who's he primping for? I thought (but did not say). Why, you'd think he was getting ready to fill prescriptions for President Truman or Rita Hayworth.

A person could get real mad, but not me. My mama's voice lived inside my head: "It's your duty, Vangie, to make things nice—a blue checkered cloth on the picnic table, a jar of Queen Anne's lace, paper lanterns strung up in the trees." She would probably expect me to clean up Henry's nose hairs, too, and never ask the first question. From the hallway, the phone started ring-ing. Thinking it might be Olive—maybe she wanted us to shop together?—I ran to answer it. "Hello?" I said, but no one was there.

"Hel-*lo*?" I said again. More silence, then a click. I frowned at the receiver, then slammed it against the cradle. Two, three times a week this happened. The calls started last September, and some weeks were worse than others. When I complained to Henry, he said, "A prank, a child's prank. Nothing to worry your head about."

Nothing bothered Henry. Two summers ago, a Peeping Tom had tormented nearly every woman in Limoges, even me. The worry went out the top of my head. One evening I looked out the bedroom venetians, straight into the eyes of the pervert himself. I ran screaming into the living room. "Oh, hell. It's your imagination," Henry scoffed. "It's wishful thinking." Turned out it was one of the Draper boys from Lilac Street. His people sent him to military school in Tennessee. He couldn't have been more than twelve or thirteen.

The phone chimed again. I snatched it up and shouted, "Hello!" Then I paused, straining to hear background noises, anything to help identify the caller. Then I cried, "Who *is* this? Why are you calling me? Why won't you say something?"

After I hung up, I got madder and madder. It galled me to think someone would worry me this way. People like that were freakish, Peeping Toms from afar; instead of closing your venetians, you had to take your phone off the hook. I lifted the receiver, laid it on its side, then walked briskly to the kitchen. The room still smelled of red beans and chemicals, but I'd have to clean it later. My nerves were ruined. I grabbed a glass from the cabinet, filled it with water, and drank. The room was so quiet, I heard the liquid falling into my stomach, like I was watering flowers down there. Henry was always accusing me of having a fertile imagination, but that was the wrong direction. Probably somebody in this very town had lily-of-the-valley growing in their stomachs. What slipped into the body, however innocently (a child eating daisies, maybe), came back to haunt you. The Major used to make me and Zachary spit out watermelon seeds for this reason.

I walked toward the back door, pushed open the screen, and stepped into midday heat. A fresh Ethel Merman record was playing. I didn't know which was worse, the annoying calls or Ethel, but I chose Ethel. The screen door slammed behind me. I walked over and picked up my shears. Then I headed into the deepest part of my yard and began hacking weeds. My garden was *L*-shaped, divided into sections—flowers and vegetables. The French grew cabbages right next to tulips, but I kept everything separate. Just as the Lord knew every hair on my head, I knew my plants. Flowers were a kind of luxury, I supposed, but vegetables were the backbone of any garden. They're almost like family:

Okra reminded me of baby boys, whole bushes of them; they grew next to cucumbers, dirty old uncles who peed in front of the aunts. Me, I was a pumpkin rotting in the sun, turning mushy on the inside, waiting for someone to carve me a face and light me up with candles. Smiling when I'd rather not, all gap-toothed.

I hated to say this, but as much as I loved Olive, she reminded me of lettuce. She was born all frilled at the edges—easy to grow, easy to wilt. The doctor said it was a hard, troubled labor, and I suspected she took after Henry's side of the family. His mama's name was Olivia, our baby's namesake. Mrs. Nepper reminded me of squash with blossom rot, the whole plant shriveling until it's no more than a yellow streak in the dirt. She had real bad nerves. In 1932, she threw herself into a freshly dug grave and broke her hip, and it wasn't even a blood kin's funeral. Later, she died of a bone infection. During her last days, she was suspicious of everything— me, Henry, the doctor. She thought we were putting rat poison in her food. When she listened to the radio, she confused the announcers with the apostles. "I'm not listening to Judas the Betrayer," she'd say, blinking at me and Henry. "Change the dial. Hurry now, try to find one of the fishermen, James or Andrew."

My sister-in-law, Edith, who's from New York City, would be Silver Queen corn, tall and graceful, but you had to shuck her to reach the good stuff. And then you had all those little hairs to deal with—her northern ways, the barriers she put between herself and others. And last but not least was Henry. He put me in mind of a sugar beet, an under-the-ground sort of man, red-faced and messy to fool with. Best served with vinegar and lots of pepper. Sometimes, though, I thought he was like hot pepper jam. You spent all morning chopping jalapeños and bell peppers, skimming foam and ladling, and all you ended up with was three little half-pint jars. Hardly worth the trouble, if you asked me.

Last July Fourth, which was also our twenty-third wedding anniversary, I invited the neighbors (even Harriet and Leonard Hooper) to a cookout. Well, Henry had a fit. "This will cost a fortune!" he yelled. "Why didn't you check with me? Don't you go fixing anything fancy, Vangie. Let them eat hot dogs, just plain old wieners!" To tell the truth, I knew he'd act this way, but I wanted things to be nice. Food is a hobby with me, even more than gardening, but it is harder on my poor body. I baked a pork tenderloin, sliced it Texas-style, and then made a barbecue sauce from scratch. The recipe got wrote up in the newspaper—it was that mouth-watering. I fixed potato salad, slaw, deviled eggs, baked beans, and fresh string beans from my own garden. Olive baked a white sheet cake. She spread it with seven-minute vanilla frosting, then decorated it to look like a flag—blueberries for the stars, strawberries for the stripes. It was so pretty I took pictures with the Kodak. Cab Beaulieu, the next-door undertaker, cranked ice cream under the mimosa tree. Down by the azalea hedge, watermelons jutted out of three galvanized tubs, ice sliding down the green hulls.

After the party was over, Henry went into the house and shut the door. He did not speak to me for three days. He was raised poor, and it twisted his notions about money; I was raised to make sure my husband's house stayed clean and comfortable, to provide all the nice little extras that men generally don't think about. Henry thought flowers were frivolous, yet he praised me for growing our own vegetables. I prided myself on keeping the altar at First Baptist supplied with roses, and the pastor with zucchini (come summer, my garden tended to explode). "Miss Vangie," said Reverend Kirby, "you are a saint. Jesus will reward you." I didn't know about *that*, but between gardening and striving to be meek, I hoped I had heaven covered.

My mama always hinted that breadwinners had to be pampered or something awful would happen. I never figured out what—maybe they wouldn't stay breadwinners. Maybe he'd lose his pharmacy and end up planting cotton on my family's derelict farm. It had been vacant since they all died. I married Henry and raised our daughter the same way my mama used to sew a dress without a pattern. A simple but classic design, no stripes, sleeves, or buttons. Just an A-line with a single zipper. Now I saw gaps and loose strings. All my fault, of course, but it was much too late to rip out the seams. What's done is done. I had everything a woman could want—don't get me wrong, I wasn't ungrateful—but it seemed like less. The Lord said what is twisted can't be straightened and what's missing can't be counted. He claimed the pure in heart shall see God.

The Lord said a lot of things.

Meanwhile, I found ways to soothe myself. That was the main reason I threw myself into house and garden, you see. To take my mind off Olive acting so distant. To forget about the telephone. And maybe to show off a little. I didn't mind dirt or biscuit dough under my fingernails the way some women did—as long as it wasn't both at the same time. There is nothing better than taking potatoes and onions out of your own backyard. Peel, then fry in bacon drippings. Heap on French bread. Add catsup, lettuce, and pickles, and you've got yourself a meal, a fried potato sandwich. As my daddy said, soil is the basis of everything.

Like all the yards in Limoges, ours was deep. A bit narrow, but who said you could have everything? Our front lawn was pure glory, a cushion of Saint Augustine and pink roses, the same shade as our shutters. After you crossed the street, the lake started, with big cypress trees growing in the water, rotten stumps jutting up, sun beating down on everything. Henry called it his own personal Elysian Fields. Sophie Donnell said she thought heaven would be like the French Quarter, where she lived while Burr was in Angola, the state penitentiary. "I'd pick up free oysters at the market, then walk over to Morning Call for free coffee and cream doughnuts. Next, I'd go sit with my Jesus at the Saint Louis Cathedral, licking powdered sugar off my fingers."

Me, I didn't know as I'd like all that commotion, although the gardens at Longue Vue House would be nice. I remembered when my daddy took me and Henry to the Roosevelt Hotel in New Orleans. Sophie Tucker was singing in the Blue Room, and they had a great big wooden floor that rolled out for dancing. I hoped heaven would be just like my front yard—a lake with lily pads, mosquito hawks floating, then lifting up like crop dusters.

Now that Olive was all grown, I didn't know what to do with myself. You could build your life around one single thing, like a view or a child, but that was risky. You had so much to lose. Maybe Henry had the right idea—he spread himself thin. Every morning except for Sundays, he left at seven-thirty. He opened his drugstore, poured a cup of coffee, and after he read the *Times-Picayune*, he started filling prescriptions. He might as well have worked in New Orleans or even New York. He never came home for lunch. Five o'clock sharp he reappeared, ready for his supper, unless he had a meeting. Henry was real big on organizations.

I always saw myself in a home economics classroom, teaching young ladies everything from butter curls to skinning tomatoes (drop in boiling water, and the skins will slip right off). Of course you had to go to college to do that; they just wouldn't let you walk into a school and teach, even if you knew your subject inside out. All these years I'd taken care of Henry and my baby girl. I worked in the yard and clipped coupons and recipes from the *News-Leader*. I sewed curtains and Easter dresses. Sometimes I felt satisfied, sometimes I didn't. When I told Mama how I felt, she acted like I was talking crazy. "This is your *husband*," she said, squeezing my hands until my knuckles ached. "The father of your child. I don't want to hear another word about it."

The Major was no help. His mind had turned dusty. He'd sit on the veranda, gazing at the fields, and say, "The history of gardening is the history of America. Beans equals Food equals Life.

It's just that simple." Mama would wring her hands and say, "He's been like this all week. Going on about Sir Walter Raleigh bringing crops to the New World. As if he'd *been* there, standing right next to the colonists."

The only time I got to see them was when Henry carried me to the farm on Sundays. I never learned to drive, so I walked to town and bought groceries at City Market. Sometimes I popped in on Henry, but he always got flustered. Claimed I was a distraction, making him lose count of pills. "I run a life-or-death operation here, Vangie," he told me. "It's not like your silly recipes. I can't mix up teaspoons and tablespoons. Pharmacy is an exact science, Vangie. Exact. Hell, I could *kill* somebody."

Lord forgive me, but sometimes I'd like to kill Henry Nepper. A time or two I'd come real close to fixing him a tainted mayonnaise sandwich, sweetened with sugar, but the urge always passed. I've heard of women who lost their grip. (Henry's mama was a case in point.) One day I'd forget and call Henry a sugar beet, and he'd carry me down to Mandeville, where they sent his mama twice. They'd lock me up and shoot electricity in my brain—the latest thing for nervous breakdowns. It didn't seem possible, but once upon a time Henry recited poetry on my daddy's porch, the glider's rusty chains screeching like cicadas. " 'O why do you walk through the fields in gloves,' " he'd say. " 'Missing so much and so much, O fat white woman whom nobody loves?' "

I'd laugh and say, "Now say my poem, say mine." I thought he was somebody special, spouting out poems with the fervor of an evangelist.

"That is yours," he'd joke.

"It's not. Besides, I'm not fat."

"You'd better not be." Then he'd get serious. " 'The leaves fall early this autumn, in wind,' " he'd say, placing one hand over my heart, barely touching my breast. " 'The paired butterflies are already yellow with August.' "

I heard Sophie before I saw her, singing "Marching to Zion," her voice blotting out Ethel Merman's. Sophie was a heavy-set woman with skin the color of pecan shells. Two stubby braids curved down the center of her head. She plodded toward the garden, swinging a wrinkled Maison Blanche bag. When she saw me, she stopped singing and called out, "Didn't mean to be so late. I had to fix Burr's supper ahead of time. You know how he is."

I nodded, but I'd just as soon pretend that Burr Donnell didn't exist. He was the only person I knew who'd served time in Angola. Sophie swore up and down it was manslaughter, but how could you know for sure? After all the things he'd done to her, I suspected murder. I tried not to look at her bad eye, the one he put out six years ago. He threw a firecracker in her face and broke open the pupil, at least that's how Dr. Phillip explained it.

Sophie set down her bag and pulled the shears from my hands. "Lord, look at this mess you made. You can't chop weeds unless you want them to grow back double. You got to dig up the roots. Here, let Sophie fix it for you." She poked the shears into the ground, bending the weed, exposing its roots. The muscles in her arms moved beneath her skin like tiny fish beneath dark water. There was no voice on this earth like hers. She was with me the night Mama died; she hugged me and sang to me, and by morning I knew my mama would be all right as long as a big, black woman was in heaven with her. They could sing together and keep watch on all of us back home.

"Miss Vangie, you nothing but a sissy, a halfhearted sissy. Chopping these weeds. That's what trash do, too lazy to pull. Or else they got a pure-dirt yard."

"Maybe that's what I need."

"You'd just as soon die."

"I would *not!*" My lips curved into a smile. Sophie's spirit was something to behold, but it kept her in trouble with Burr and a few of her other day jobs. She cleaned the funeral home and three houses on Cypress, including Harriet Hooper's. Next door, Harriet passed in front of a window, and a moment later I heard her shuffling records.

"Lord, save us all," Sophie said, rolling her eyes. "If I owned me a talking machine, I'd listen to Muddy Waters, what Burr plays on the ukelele." She drew in air, and it came out music: *"Well, I'm leaving this morning/sure do hate to go."* Ethel Merman sang louder and louder, blotting out Sophie, and I knew Harriet was playing with the volume, trying to irritate us.

"I was just thinking." I crossed my arms and glanced at her house. Curtains streamed out of the Hoopers' windows like they were trying to escape. "If Harriet was a vegetable, what would she be?"

"A *what?*" Sophie stopped digging weeds. She cut her eyes back at me. "Why you ask that?"

"Well, I just wondered. Would you say she's kind of like an acorn squash?"

"No, ma'am. *I* wouldn't say that." Sophie scratched her chin and looked thoughtfully at the house. The Merman record ended, and there was nothing but she *s-s-s-t* of the needle on the seventy-eight, hissing beneath dust that Sophie probably left on purpose. "Some people, though, they might say onion."

"She makes my eyes water, sure enough."

"And she shape like one." Sophie bowed her arms. "Like this, with a twisty, pointed head."

I laughed, and my hand disappeared into the folds of my apron. "Let's go inside before the onion hears us," I said.

"Hallelujah," Sophie sang out, loud as she could, looking straight up at the sky.

Waking the Dead

❧

Yes, we saw Olive Nepper run out of First Baptist, with that preacher just a-staring. He wasn't saving any souls. That's not his job. If there'd been Baptists in Sodom and Gomorrah, it would've burned up a whole lot sooner.

—THE MARSHALL SISTERS, CALLING PEOPLE ON
THE TELEPHONE, MARCH 1952

Afternoon light slammed into the narrow house, slashing through the venetians. In every window lint boiled in the air. The women moved in and out of it, bending and stooping as they changed sheets. They peeled back white linen that still smelled of backyard sun. Henry slept on his side, and Vangie slept on hers. You could lead a horse to water, but you couldn't make him drink. And if you tried, the horse swore he was a gelding.

"Might as well change Olive's sheets, too," Vangie said, stepping out into the hall. Now that Sophie was here, with her chatter and busy hands, Vangie had forgotten about the mysterious caller. She replaced the phone on its cradle, then walked into Olive's bedroom. Light fell through half-raised venetians. All the windows were pushed open, but the air smelled sour, faintly of baby vomit. She hunkered down, gathering bouffant skirts that were scattered about like balloons.

"Miss Olive? You still sleep?" Sophie said, stepping into the center of the room.

"Why, she's not here," Vangie said, pivoting on her heels. Even as she turned, she knew something was wrong. There, on the bed, lay her baby girl, her legs bent at funny angles. A paperweight was balanced on her chest, a souvenir from Chattanooga. She looked dead in a rumpled sort of way—as if she'd fought it, hard.

From the hallway, the phone started ringing, and Vangie's first thought was murder. Someone had climbed through the window and rape/strangled her daughter. Then left her kitchen a mess—fixed himself a Nehi, plundered in her cabinets. Left her baby for dead. "No!" Vangie shrieked. She threw down the skirts, hurled herself across the bed, and lifted Olive by her shoulders. The girl's head snapped backward, her throat bowed. The paperweight rolled onto the bed, snow swirling inside the dome. "Wake up, baby! Tell Mama what happened." She glanced up at Sophie. In her mind's eye she shouted orders, knew exactly how to save her baby, but her throat was tight. Her whole neck seemed to shrink. She drew in a ragged breath and tried to drag Olive off the bed.

"Miss Vangie, stop pulling on her. You'll break her neck."

"We've got to get her to the hospital!" Vangie's eyes shifted back and forth. She sat up on her knees, pulling Olive against her.

"Should I run next door and get Miss Edith? Mr. Cab and Israel?" Sophie leaned across Vangie and lifted Olive's chin. "Lord, this is bad. Look how her eyes rolled back inside her head!"

"Let me see." Vangie sagged forward. Sophie pushed back the girl's hair, then lifted both lids, revealing white eyeballs, small as guinea eggs.

"Like somebody looking at my Jesus," Sophie said, pulling Olive into her arms, rocking backward.

"No, it's not, it's not!" Vangie was breathing so fast, her nose felt numb. Her whole body tingled. Then she pitched forward with a little cry, flopping across Sophie and Olive. As she fell she had a sense of failing as well, but she couldn't remember who or why or how. She thought she might be dead. Then she saw the strangest thing—two souls lifting, mother and daughter souls borne upward by baby parakeets, fluttering against the cloudy ceiling. The only thing missing was harp music. From far away, someone kept calling her name: *Miss Vangie say something please talk to me.*

Hush, she thought. *Hush or you'll confuse the parakeets, they'll return our souls to the wrong bodies.* The room filled with a whirring sound, then it slowly began revolving, picking up speed like a carnival ride. A breeze lifted the curtains, rattling the venetians. In the hallway, the phone stopped ringing.

"Miss Vangie?" Sophie lifted her head. She was pinned beneath Olive, and Olive was pinned beneath Vangie. There was one thing to do, Sophie thought. Take the girl and run through the azaleas. Run to the funeral home and bring her to Israel and Mr. Cab. They'll know what to do. Undertakers know the difference between dead and alive and what eyes rolled back in the head means. *I'm leaving I'm leaving child I ain't coming round here no more.* One thing at a time, one step at a time, pick this baby up and run. Run like you're running to Jesus, and leave Miss Vangie to her white-lady dreams.

But first she got to move the white lady. She shoved Vangie's hips, meaning to free Olive, but she pushed a little too hard and Vangie started rolling. The paperweight smashed against the floor, leaking water and plastic snow. Then she fell. It was such a large sound in such a small room that everything vibrated— Olive's china dog collection, Doll-of-the-Month figurines, ballerina pictures on the wall, even the windowpanes.

Still, Miss Vangie slept on. She dreamed Olive was trapped in the highest branch of a locust tree and no ladder in the world could reach her. Vangie felt her feet lift from the ground. She looked down, astonished, and the top of her head thumped into a branch. Why, she could float up to Olive and save her. All these years she'd had the ability to levitate, but she'd been scared. She'd feared gravity. Oh, but now she could fly. Her daddy would be so proud, but her mama wouldn't say a word, didn't believe in praise; only criticism, Sunday school, and a part-time job raised a child right. O fat white woman why do you walk through the fields in gloves when your daddy can take you flying, missing so much and so much? In her dream, she was talking a mile a minute, words spilling out like crop dust, she couldn't stop talking, this fat white woman whom nobody loved.

A green-eyed Jesus appeared wearing a white robe and brown sandals. He had long brown hair that looked freshly permed— why, Vangie even thought she smelled the curling solution, so bitter it made her eyes water. She told Him she had planted by the almanac. Lettuce, sugar beets, and pumpkins. A perfect garden except for weeds growing past the clouds, all the way to heaven.

I sure wish You hadn't invented dandelions, she told Jesus. *They're strangling my garden. Can't You do something?*

I help those who help themselves, Vangie. He handed her the hoe. Here, chop them down.

I'm chopping. But please O please don't let the parakeets loose.

Sorry, sorry. They're already gone.

Nepper's Drugs:

Catching Mr. Henry with

His Pants Down

∾

My marriage to Vangie is dead. I'm just waiting for the funeral.

—HENRY NEPPER, PHARMACIST, TALKING TO DEEDEE ROBICHAUX, COUNTER GIRL, IN THE STOCKROOM OF NEPPER'S DRUGS, MARCH 1952

Israel Adams

Miss Olive ain't dead, she's breathing, but Mr. Cab say, "Hurry and load her into the hearse, boys." So we carry her out, me and Twilly. All around us womens is yelping and carrying on, standing in they backyards hollering, *What's the matter? What's happening?* Every hunting dog for three blocks howls and bays, answering back. Me and Twilly, we don't say nothing. We're licensed, certified embalmers at Beaulieu's.

On the way to the hospital, Miss Olive stops breathing twice. Each time, I reach down and shake her. "Don't you die on me," I cry. "Don't you go and die." Her lips are swolled up, circled in blue. Epiphany Parish Hospital is barely five blocks away, but the hearse crawls down Lincoln Avenue.

"Go faster, Mr. Cab," I say. "Faster!"

"I'm mashing the floorboard!" Mr. Cab hollers. He veers into the parking lot. I see Dr. Phillip LeGette waiting with two orderlies, a little one and a big one. They all got on white smocks.

"Twilly, you help them carry her inside," Dr. LeGette say. Then he walks over to the hearse and puts one arm around Mr. Cab. "I just talked to Edith, and she says they found some poison in the kitchen."

"Poison?" Mr. Cab's eyes get big.

"In an orange Nehi. And Olive drank every last drop." Dr. LeGette pauses. "Now, listen to me, boy. Listen to me good. I need your help. Henry's liable to have a fit when he hears this. He could kill himself, or even somebody else, trying to get here. You hear me, boy?"

"Yessir."

"So I want you to drive down to his store and carry him back here." He squeezes Mr. Cab's shoulder. "Break it to him gently."

"What am I supposed to tell him?" Mr. Cab lifts both hands.

"You'll know. You're good at dealing with hysterical folks." Dr. LeGette slaps Mr. Cab's shoulder, then he struts off toward the hospital.

"I don't think this is a good idea," Mr. Cab calls out, but Dr. LeGette, he keeps on walking, his white coat flapping in the breeze. Then he dashes up the concrete steps, jerks open the door, and disappears inside the hospital. A smell of rubbing alcohol drifts out, reminding me of the embalming room back at Beaulieu's. Mr. Cab turns back to me.

"You hear what he said, Israel?"

"Yes, sir. I sure did."

"It's a goddurn shame about Olive. A goddurn shame."

"Yes, sir. A tragic shame."

"Wonder why she drank poison? Of all things." Mr. Cab whistles, then glances at me. Like I got all the answers. Before I can nod my head, he barrels on. "If Henry goes berserk, I might need your help."

"Yessir." I look down at my skinny brown arms. Don't look like they can wrassle much of nothing, but I'm strong for a old man. In this line of work I've seen growed men lay on the floor and squall. Beat they heads. Sometimes I got to help Mr. Cab with the crazy living folks. Still, I was hoping to get out of this. Mr. Henry is square-shaped, with a belly that look stuffed, soft like a cream doughnut with too much sweet stuff inside, leaking out the edges.

"Coming, Israel?" Mr. Cab climbs into the hearse and starts the engine.

We park on Gallery Street, next to the courthouse. Three old mens is whittling, shavings piled up around they feet. They look up when we climb out of the hearse and step up onto the curb. Because of flooding, the town was built high, making the roads look like shallow ditches. Sometimes even a levee won't hold back the Mississippi, and we got two between us and the river. Sunlight beats hard against my old head, pushing me down until I walk more spraddled than usual. We cross the street and head toward Nepper's Drugs. A little redheaded girl is blocking our way, turning one cartwheel after the other on the cracked sidewalk, her pigtails swinging like red ropes.

"Let's get this over with," say Mr. Cab, turning back to look at me. When he faces the sidewalk, the little girl knocks into him. She falls down and skids on her hands and knees.

"Oh, sugar! I didn't see you." Mr. Cab reaches down to help her up. "You all right?"

"Yessir," the child say, taking his hand. "Sorry, mister." She give him a toothless smile. Her hair is shiny red in the sunlight, with strands sticking up like important wires.

"Sure you're not hurt?" say Mr. Cab.

"Nope." She brushes off her legs.

"I haven't seen you before," he say. "Whose child are you?"

"DeeDee Robichaux's," she say. "And Renny Robichaux's, but he's crippled. He's a war hero, did you know that?"

"I sure did." Mr. Cab gets this funny look on his face.

"My name's Billie, but I ain't no boy." The child points at Nepper's Drugs. "My mama works in there, for Mr. Henry. Her name's DeeDee. You know her? She'll fix you a soda if you want. I get to eat here free, but you got to pay."

"No, sugar. That's all right." Mr. Cab smiles down at her.

"See you later, mister." She takes off running, spinning into another cartwheel. Mr. Cab stares after her a minute. Then he shakes his head, walks up to the glass door, and pushes it open. A little bell tinkles above his head. We step inside. Two big fans churn up the air, flipping sale banners. Straight ahead is a glass-and-wooden balcony where Henry mixes medicines. It's empty. One customer, a man wearing a polka-dot bow tie, sits at the pink marble counter, eating a slice of lemon cake. DeeDee Robichaux, the counter girl, ain't nowhere to be found. The cashier, Miss Mary Byrd, perches on a wooden stool, eyeing us suspicious-like. She a old maid with yellow eyes and papery skin. "What can I do for you, Mr. Beaulieu?" she asks, straightening her glasses.

Mr. Cab walks over to the checkout counter and spreads his hands on the counter. I can tell he's trying to be polite so nobody won't push the panic button. "Miss Mary." He nods. "How you today?"

"Hot and irritable. You?"

"I've been better myself." He glances down the aisle, then looks back at Miss Mary. "You seen Mr. Nepper lately?"

"Back there." She rolls her eyes.

"Back where?"

"Stockroom." She lifts one claw finger and points toward a swinging door. The flesh on her arm shakes. "But I wouldn't go in there if I was you."

The bow-tied man at the counter squeaks around on his stool and looks over at us, the coffee cup raised halfway to his mouth. I don't recognize his face. He looks like a traveling man to me. Mr. Cab motions for me to follow, then we head down the aisle, pushing open the door. The stockroom is a dusty place with wood shelves, high ceilings, and light bulbs hanging from wires. Another big fan beats up the air, making a noise like a airplane. Behind a shelf of calamine lotion and hydrogen peroxide, I see something move, like a deer dashing through trees. Then I hear a woman giggle.

"It's big as a zucchini," she say and giggle again.

"That's all?" a man say. Sounds just like Mr. Henry.

"A gourd?" The woman carrying on like she at a party.

"Why, you're trying to insult me." The man laughs. "Take another look, you silly thing."

Mr. Cab shakes his head and gives me a look that say, *Ain't that something?* He turns the corner, and I'm right behind him, like a burr under a dog's tail. Then he stops walking. There, in the narrow aisle, is the woman, DeeDee Robichaux, her dress peeled down to her waist, with big titties jutting out. Mr. Henry's trousers wrinkled around his ankles. The woman's hand stuck inside his boxer shorts.

"Afternoon, Henry," Mr. Cab say, cool as cellar air. Acting like that woman ain't there. He looks at all the shelves like he's aiming to buy something—saccharin bottles, tooth powder, box of Ronson lighters. DeeDee Robichaux's mouth drops open, and I see silver fillings in her back teeth. Before she can pull out her hand, Mr. Henry steps backward, dragging her with him.

"What you doing back here, Cab?" he ask, pulling up his trousers like it's nothing. The girl breaks loose and runs down the aisle, hiding in the rest room. The wooden door slams, causing the shelves to rattle.

"Can we go in your office, Henry?" Mr. Cab spreads his hands apart. "I have to tell you something."

"I know what you're going to say, and I can explain about DeeDee," Mr. Henry begins.

"I don't care about that." Mr. Cab holds up one hand. "What you do is your business."

"Well, I don't want you getting the wrong idea." Mr. Henry leans against a shelf full of dusty vaporizers and wooden potty chairs with duck decals. "I was just checking a mole on that young woman. She's been after me to look at it. Says it's growing."

Mr. Cab looks down at his feet, scratches his ear, then looks back at Mr. Henry. "I've come with some bad news, and you'd best be sitting down when you hear it."

"News?" Mr. Henry straightens up, looking from me to Mr. Cab, like it's just now sinking in where we come from. I got Beaulieu Funeral Home embroidered on my shirt. "What's happened?"

"Let's you and me just walk—" Mr. Cab tries to put his arm around Mr. Henry.

"I don't want to walk anywhere." Mr. Henry throws up his hands, pushing Mr. Cab away. "Tell me *now*. Is it one of my dogs? They didn't get out of their pens, did they?" He shuts his eyes. "Please don't tell me they got hit by a car."

"No, not your dogs, Henry." Mr. Cab exhales slowly. He is calm for a young man, would've made a good doctor. He puts one hand on Mr. Henry's shoulder. "It's Olive."

"Olive?" He snatches Mr. Cab's lapels. "She got hit by a car?"

"No, not a car."

"Then, what?" He lets go of the lapels. "Just spit it out, tell me!"

"She's . . . " Mr. Cab hesitates, and I hope he won't tell the truth. The way Mr. Henry acting, he might rush out the store. A car could mow him down, and then poor Miss Vangie have a double tragedy on her hands.

"I really don't know," Mr. Cab say. "They found her unconscious."

"Unconscious!"

"You need to talk to Phillip." Mr. Cab lifts his arm, turning his watch up to the ashy light that's seeping through the stockroom windows, a nervous habit of his. Like time be running out, running like water through the levee. "Let me drive you over."

"Where?" Mr. Henry's eyes narrow.

"The hospital."

"Hospital! Just how serious is this?"

"I don't know." Mr. Cab sighs. "Maybe she just fainted."

Mr. Henry's eyes skitter toward the ceiling. "Did she fall and hit her head?"

"It's possible." Mr. Cab draws in a deep breath.

"But not real hard, you don't think?"

"I can't really say." Mr. Cab wrinkles his nose, shakes his head. Like he's talking to a child. "Let me drive you over. I'll bet Olive's already waked up. Waiting for her daddy."

"Whew! You scared me for a minute." Mr. Henry give a short laugh, then rubs his bald spot. Behind him, the bathroom door creaks open. The girl pokes her head out. When she sees me, her eyes narrow and she slams the door. The lock clicks. Shoot, I think. Ain't looking at you, girl. All the trouble you cause.

The mens drive off to the hospital, and I walk back to Beaulieu's. I don't see how Miss Vangie will hold up to the gossip. She reminds me of my youngest granddaughter, Peony, who is five years old and her mama still dress her every morning. Peony just lay there in the bed, lift her arm and let her mama thread it through the dress. Then lift her other arm. "You keep on doing that," I told Marilyn last Christmas, "and you going to end up with a growed baby on your hands."

"The baby can *be* babyfied," said Marilyn. All her girls name after flowers, but they live too many miles from me. Marilyn married herself a well driller, and they live in Hilda, Texas. Got them a windmill in the front yard. She writes letters about her flower girls, and I see them growing tall in my mind. She's got Daisy, Iris, Camellia, Poppy, and little old Peony. Marilyn was my and Miss Hattie's only child. We lost Miss Hattie ten years ago last Thanksgiving, when her kidneys give out.

My white cotton shirt soaking wet when I reach the funeral home. I go inside and stand under the ceiling fans, holding out my arms. Beaulieu's got air conditioning, but it ain't turned on. Not many businesses has it, just Hibernia Bank, Majestic Theater, and a few diners. Mr. Cab bought two boxes last summer, and we sit them in the window. He said it's the coming thing, not to mention being good for business.

Twilly is in the morgue, what Mr. Cab calls our procedure room, working on Mr. Elmer Barnes, a fifty-two-year-old schoolteacher who passed with brain cancer. People's dying younger and younger, seems like. And of worser things.

"How Miss Olive doing?" I ask Twilly, coming around the table. Mr. Barnes all stretched out on a repose block, and his skin has turned waxy blue.

"Touch and go."

I never think much about what I do for a living until it's time to embalm a child. And Olive, she just a slip of a girl, sixteen or so. Like my old grandmama used to say, "People is more fragile than you might think."

"Doc says she in a coma." Twilly glances up. "Did Mr. Henry take it bad?"

"I reckon. Even though we catched him spooning a lady in the storeroom."

"Customer?" Twilly looks shocked.

"No, that counter girl of his. Miz Robichaux." I rub the top of my head. "There they was, Mr. Henry with his pants dangling. Grabbing on her titties."

"Lord have mercy." Twilly shakes his head. "He don't seem the type to have sweeties. Always look like he'd be shamed to be naked in front of a lady."

"Ain't that the truth?" I say, thinking about the size of Mr. Henry's belly.

"But Mr. Cab, *he* the type to womanize."

"Shoot, the womens womanize *him*."

"Yeah." Twilly throws his head back and laughs. "He's got the widow womens trained. Bringing *him* food, calling him on the phone. Reckon he'll ever marry?"

"Maybe when he's old. Like us fools."

"Hand me that basin, fool." He grins, points to the metal shelf. "And that bottle next to it, right there."

I reach up and see that he's chose Tru Lanol fluid for Elmer Barnes, what comes in sixty color shades—a special pink, that's good for womens and children. Keeps the skin velvet soft. You got to consider these things. If you die of jaundice, the embalming fluid turns you green, but if you die of carbon monoxide poisoning, you keep a healthy glow all your own. Drowning victims is worse of all—we call them floaters. A body will keep for twenty-four hours unless it been opened, but once a body hit the water, it starts rotting. I've saw many a corpse pulled from the Mississippi and Bayou Maçon, with crawfish stuck to they mouths and rectums. In the olden days undertakers burned gunpowder to hide the smell, but nowadays we just stick them in the freezer. After four hours or so, the skin freeze and they stop stinking.

Two famous peoples asked not to be embalmed—Franklin D. Roosevelt and Queen Elizabeth. They say the queen's body bust open before they got her in the ground. The main reason you embalm is so you won't bury somebody alive. I don't want nobody, not even Twilly and Cab, fooling with my dead body. When my time comes, just stick me in a pine box and be done with it. I don't want nobody cleaning my teeth with Bon Ami, shining them up with clear fingernail polish. Here at Beaulieu's, we got more stuff than a beauty shop. Behind me is shelves of sprays, fluids, oils, powders, creams. We got plaster of paris to replace limbs. We got eye cement, Armstrong Face

Former, and a Edwards Arm and Hand Positioner. It's right sickening.

"Hey, you awake?" Twilly waves the trocar at me.

"Yeah." I rub my eyes.

"Then come help me do this poor man. I ain't got all day, and I'm getting hungry."

Walking the Floor Over You

(At Epiphany Parish Hospital)

Suicide is a sin, no matter what religion you are. It's right up there with lust, greed, pride, and sloth. Not to mention gluttony and gossip. I don't partake of any of it, thank you very much, because I am a fifth-generation Baptist. And you can put that in your pipe and smoke it.

—MRS. HARRIET HOOPER, OVERHEARD IN NEPPER'S DRUGS (EATING A BANANA SPLIT)

Dusk washed over Limoges, dense purple air that smelled of the river. Women moved inside houses that bloomed yellow light. They set out dishes, tumblers, forks and knives. Set out platters of fried catfish, bowls of black-eyed peas, sweet slaw, rice and gravy. They pulled corn bread from the oven and turned it onto a plate, burning their fingers as they cut and buttered, steam rising into their faces. All over Limoges, men, women, and children joined hands around kitchen tables and said, "Heavenly Father, we thank You for this food we are about to receive."

"Amen," the women said. Some of them knew the Neppers personally and had sent over food, with their names taped to the underside of bowls. They wished they could do something more than offer a rump roast or raspberry layer cake. They'd gossiped and speculated (not the same thing, mind you) over back fences and clotheslines. Rumors hung in the air like crisp linen, the fabric's shape distorted by prevailing winds.

Epiphany Parish Hospital sat on the corner of Jefferson and Delphinium, a *U*-shaped building, red brick with dozens of casement windows. Pecan trees grew in symmetrical rows, almost like headstones. Behind one window, where a plaid curtain sucked against the screen, Olive Nepper slept in a metal bed. The bed had been painted so many times, the color flaked off like lichen, sifting to the tile floor. The upper half of the bed was covered by a clear oxygen tent. All around her the walls were sap green, a shade reputed to be soothing to invalids. If Olive were to open her eyes, she would see two pictures hanging on the far wall, the images slightly blurred by the plastic tent: Harry S Truman waving from his new balcony and a young mother sitting in a rocking chair, holding a blond, curly-haired baby. In her other hand was a scroll:

> *If polio comes to my community,*
> *I will not let my children mix with new groups.*
> *I will not let my children become chilled.*
> *I will not let my children become fatigued,*
> *because chilled or overtired bodies*
> *are less able to fight polio.*
> —THE MOTHER'S POLIO PLEDGE

A nurse stood by the windows, pulling the dingy cord of the venetians, adjusting the angle of light. Olive drew in shallow breaths, dreaming of her childhood, and just outside the door, in the waiting room, Dr. Phillip LeGette put his arms around Henry and Vangie, explaining that he had done all he could for little Olive. The rest was in God's hands. He'd explained this over and over the last two days, but the Neppers weren't listening.

"How many times did she stop breathing?" asked Vangie.

"Twice," Dr. LeGette said, holding up two fingers, hoping Vangie would finally understand. "Once on the way here and once in the emergency room. She might have aspirated some vomit—that just means she breathed it into her lungs. I've pumped her stomach and injected her with Atropine. That's just a medicine, Vangie."

Vangie nodded.

"And she's under the oxygen tent. I've got fluids running in her vein—that's what that tube is—so she won't dehydrate." He pulled a plaid handkerchief from his pocket and wiped the back of his neck. "I don't understand why she hasn't come around."

"Just answer me this," said Henry. "Does she have brain damage?"

"Like I said, I just don't know." Dr. LeGette spread his hands. "When they stop breathing like that . . . I won't know anything until she wakes up."

"*If* she wakes up." Vangie bit down on her knuckles.

"Of course she will," cried Henry. "Won't she, Phillip?"

"We just have to give her time. Why don't you folks go on home and get some rest? I'll call if there's any change."

"Oh, I couldn't leave." Vangie looked sideways at her husband. "But you go on. I'll stay."

Henry's eyebrows moved up and down; he was tempted, but he could tell by Vangie's voice, the way it screaked up at the edges, that she didn't mean a word. She expected him to keep vigil right along with her, day after day, hour after long hour. As if he didn't have a store to run. People were counting on him to fill prescriptions, because Phillip LeGette certainly hadn't stopped writing them.

"No," he said, shifting his weight from foot to foot. "I'll stay too."

"Suit yourself." Dr. LeGette stuffed the handkerchief into his pocket, flipping up his white smock. "I'll have the nurses bring you some fresh coffee."

"But what made her do this?" Vangie squeezed the doctor's arm, wrinkling his sleeve. Her eyes were red-rimmed and filmy, her face a queer, greenish tint that matched the walls in her daughter's room.

"*Made* her? Can't you stop saying that?" Henry stared at Vangie, then turned back to Phillip. "It could've been an accident, couldn't it?"

"Well, yes." Phillip scratched his head. They'd asked this, too, a hundred times.

Vangie looked up into the doctor's eyes, her brows slanting together. One side of her hair was mashed flat, the other bent into a grotesque braid with wild gray sprigs. She looked as if she hadn't slept in days. "You've known Olive since she was big enough to fit in a shoe box," she said. "Surely Olive wouldn't try and take her own life. There's just no reason for it. None at all."

Henry groaned, then shut his eyes.

"I really can't say." Phillip sighed. This was the truest fact of all their lives: No one could really say. A round-faced nurse came to the door, her shoes squeaking on the tile. "Doctor?" she said.

"Yes?" Phillip LeGette turned. The nurse stepped over and whispered something in his ear. Henry and Vangie leaned forward, but the nurse's voice was too low.

"Thank you, Abigail." Phillip turned back to the Neppers, who were gaping at him. Vangie's hands were clasped under her chin. "I'm just going to check on Olive," he told them. "Nothing's wrong, it's just routine. Why don't you go on home? Even a few hours will rest you."

"I can't." Vangie's hands dropped. She started pacing up and down the tile floor, glancing back as Phillip walked into the room. He shut the door, leaving her to stare at patterns in the wood grain.

"I can't believe she'd do it on purpose," she said again.

"The more you say it, the more gossip you'll stir up. Is that what you want, Vangie?" Henry stared until she shook her head. Then he sat down in one of the green chairs, running his thumb along his jaw, feeling sharp whiskers. He needed a shave, but it would have to wait, like everything else. "We need to tone this down," he said.

"I know, honey," Vangie said. She walked over and slumped into the chair beside him. "I know."

"What I think is this: She was thirsty and in a hurry, and she thought she was making a soda. And that's all in the world it was."

"She'll tell us when she wakes up." Vangie stared at the door, drawing in a deep breath. "She'll tell us everything."

Henry rubbed his cheeks. He was still mortified that Cab and Israel had caught him in the stockroom with DeeDee. It wouldn't take long for the gossip to swing back to Vangie. That's all Limoges was good for—rumor spreading, a kind of oral newspaper that circulated over back fences and in spotless kitchens, while matrons sipped chicory coffee and nibbled cake. It was like a smell, a rich, strong cinnamon smell. And it always seemed better coming out of someone else's kitchen.

He could just imagine what was being whispered by old Mary Byrd, his cashier since 1934. She knew enough to hang him. And if Harriet Hooper found out, she would take it upon herself to break the news to Vangie. "Dear," she'd say, her tiny eyes black and shiny, like doodlebugs. "Dear, I have some unfortunate news about Henry. A little bird told me he's been slipping around behind your back, leaving worms in someone else's nest."

Limoges had its good side, too—nothing like a tragedy to make the women cook. Waldene and Edith had brought hot meals to the hospital the last two days, individual plates of fried pork chops, meat loaf, rice, fried apples, beans, slaw, chocolate chess pie, and corn bread. The food was packed into a wicker basket, swathed in tinfoil, with a large Thermos of sweet tea.

They'd even sent little Fanny over with napkins, packets of sugar, and lemon wedges wrapped in waxed paper. And the ladies from First Baptist had stopped by the house with a picnic ham, potato salad, and coconut layer cake. Canned beans from somebody's garden. A box of jelly doughnuts from Ralph's Bakery. A whole pan of pit barbecue (not as delicious as Vangie's), with corn fritters. Reverend Kirby had visited twice a day, clasping their hands and whispering prayers that brought a tear to even Henry's eye. Even Sophie, their day help, did her part: She took it upon herself to clean and air Olive's room, pointedly leaving her pay under the sugar bowl. Just like she was part of the family, which was the key, in Henry's opinion, to keeping quality help—letting them think they're somebody special.

Now Henry sat up straight, causing Vangie to lean over and stare. He drew in a deep breath, wondering if Olive might have heard about him and DeeDee Robichaux. She was an only child, his baby girl, and this might have been her way of making him choose between his family and DeeDee.

"Is anything wrong, Henry?" Vangie's hand slid into his lap, heavy as a stone, and touched the inside of his knee.

"Just worried is all." Henry flinched and briefly closed his eyes, thinking of DeeDee's light touch, her long red nails scraping down the backs of his legs. Sometimes he thought Vangie was blind, seeing what she chose, letting everything else hover in the air and float into space. Or maybe she didn't know what to look for, thank God.

His eyes blinked open, and he stared at her hands, the skin rough and cracked from gardening, the nails short and unpolished. Year by year she had widened, grown square in the hips from eating too many mayonnaise-and-bacon sandwiches. And her hair was prematurely gray. He vaguely remembered that her fortieth birthday was coming up, not that they were in the mood to celebrate. Not that they'd *ever* really celebrated. They'd been married twenty-four years, and the first eight were childless. Here lately, or maybe a little longer than lately, it killed him to think of rolling over in bed, pulling up her flannel gown. The puckers in her big legs fit his fingers like dents on typewriter keys, like pecking out names on prescription labels. His mama had big legs, too—the medicine they gave her in Mandeville made her eat— and she used to say, "Shakes like jelly, but jelly don't roll." Then she'd laugh and wiggle her arms. It used to scare Henry to death. In a few years, Vangie might be doing the same thing—eating and having nervous breakdowns.

"I wonder if Parish Hospital is good enough for a coma," said

Vangie, laying one hand on her cheek. "Maybe we should've driven to Vicksburg?"

"Phillip knows what he's doing."

"I don't doubt that, not for a minute, but a larger hospital is bound to know more about poisons."

"Do you want me to talk to Phillip?" He flattened his hair, smoothing his bald spot and averting his eyes.

"No, I guess not. I'm sure Olive'll be all right. Forget I said anything." Her hand dropped to her side, rustling against the cotton skirt. Closing his eyes, he imagined DeeDee's sweet-scented neck, the silk of her dress as she pulled it over her head. He smelled her on his hands. Sometimes he dozed in church, dreaming of entering her tight little body, squeezing her bottom. Then Bessie Freeman would fire up the organ, and he'd snap out of the dream. He'd have to drape the mimeographed program over his erection—imagine, something like that happening in church! He hadn't spoken to DeeDee Robichaux since Olive's collapse (he'd stayed at the hospital), but he could see her face clearly. She'd be expecting him to call. She'd be waiting.

His life was divided into light and dark, things he could reveal and things he could not. Truth and consequences. That was what being unfaithful meant to Henry Nepper. It was hiding your love away, if you could call it love, and promising the moon when it wasn't yours to give. He wasn't stupid. Women wanted you to hold them and say how pretty they were, how you couldn't live without them. It wasn't always the handsome man who got into a lady's britches, it was the good liar. The man with the straight, guileless face who said, "I'll love you forever. You're my everything." Women would put up with a lot, hoping to hear the four magic words: "Yes, I'll leave her."

He loved DeeDee Robichaux's body, and what it did for him, but he had strong feelings for Vangie. She reminded him of ornaments on a Christmas tree, the ones you'd had for ages. They'd lost their sparkle, the color had worn off in places, but it would break your heart to throw them out. A man couldn't help looking at new ornaments now and then. He could hold one up to the light and imagine how pretty it would look on his tree. But that didn't mean he had to buy it. He wouldn't dream of divorcing Vangie. Why, it was unheard of in his family, worse than insanity, even. Most all the time, though, he pictured DeeDee—what she did to him in the dark, the car rocking back and forth—and yes, he'd admit it, he wondered what he'd do if Vangie died. Accidental drowning in Lake Limoges was his favorite method, followed by a tumor of the brain.

Now he glanced over at her and said, "I'm just going to stretch my legs." He pointed down the green-tiled hall. "I'll be back in a heartbeat. I just need to go home and shave. I feel like I haven't bathed in a month."

"Fine." Vangie's voice sounded forced, high-pitched. "You go on."

"You don't mind?"

"No," she squeaked.

He looked into her eyes and knew she was lying. She expected him to sit with her, neglecting his personal hygiene. Her world would end if he didn't stay. His mama, Olivia Nepper, had been the same damn way, always fretting over things that couldn't possibly happen. She had a mortal fear of door-to-door salesmen. According to her, the Watkins/Fullerbrush/McNess men were peddling more than extracts and brushes: They were looking for victims. "Why, Mama?" Henry would ask her. "Why do you think that?"

"Because I saw how he looked at me. I just *know,*" she would say, shredding a paper napkin in her lap. "I *feel* it in my bones. He'll be back, so you might as well just go on and call the police in advance. There's going to be bloodshed tonight. If not mine, then somebody's."

Olivia Nepper, Lord rest her, had been a highstrung lady in a town that didn't tolerate peculiar women. Whenever she kissed her husband or Henry, she left scarlet marks, like deformed butterflies. It was hell wiping them off, too. Even at her funeral, when she was laid out at Beaulieu's, she looked clownish. "Don't end up like that," he told Vangie.

"But Henry," she said, "we'll all die sooner or later."

"No! I meant all painted up. Promise me you'll keep your face bare."

Now, looking at his wife's pale, freckled face, he couldn't help but think of DeeDee's pink lips and long eyelashes. Makeup seemed natural on a natural beauty. Apparently this blessing had caused her trouble. One night after they'd made love in his Rambler wagon, DeeDee raised her arms above her head and sighed. "It's so hard being a beautiful woman," she said.

He believed her.

Now he reached over and patted Vangie's hand. She needed a hug, but he could not bring himself to wrap his arms around her. It took all his effort to lean over and peck her cheek. Her arms lifted, reaching to pull him closer for a real embrace, but he stepped backward.

"Can I bring you anything from home, Vangie?"

"No." She gave him her best long-suffering look, wrinkling her forehead and frowning. "I'll just stay here in case Olive wakes up."

"Well, okay. See you later." He headed down the empty hall, the clap of his shoes rising behind him. He knew she was watching. As he walked past the nurses' station, he felt them watching, too, and he wanted to assure them that he loved his child. He'd fight anyone who claimed otherwise, but his mind did not work like Vangie's or any other woman's. His life was partitioned—pharmacist, Rotarian, father, hunter, fisherman, husband, member of Phillip LeGette's class at First Baptist, and, more recently, adulterer. Everything was separate, in little boxes. If women could learn to do this, they'd be content. It was no different, Henry thought, than the way they organized their kitchens, keeping all the knives in one drawer, the potato masher in another. You'd think they came by this organization naturally and would use it as a guideline for marriage, motherhood, and club meetings. No, they had to mix everything up and stay miserable, always one breath away from a nervous breakdown.

The man who kissed DeeDee Robichaux's navel wasn't the same man who filled prescriptions, or drove his wife and daughter to church, or led the Pledge of Allegiance at Rotary. Every role called for different moods. When Olive was a baby, he never felt the urge to hover the way Vangie did. They'd waited so long to have her, but still, he didn't fret about leprosy when the child got a diaper rash. Vangie excelled at worrying. It really got on his nerves. Henry's motto was Why Worry About Something That Might Never Happen? Everyone in the family seemed to think that it went back to a childhood accident. When Vangie was ten, she'd fallen out of a wagon, smashed the back of her head, and stopped breathing. Zachary revived Vangie by blowing air into her mouth. Still, it was days before she came to her senses. She didn't know her own name and told everyone that she thought it was Clementine. Her mama used to tell that story at the supper table, even after Vangie was married.

Henry traced all her problems to this accident. Otherwise how could he explain the things she did? For no reason at all, she'd turn moody and harp at him to *take out the trash stop snoring quit stealing the covers pay attention to me I'm talking*. He was a patient man. Having Olivia Nepper for a mama had taught him to be lenient with women. All those years ago when Vangie struck the ground, she possibly *had* damaged a lobe of the brain responsible for judgment, disposition, and self-reliance, not to mention intelligence. For example, after her mama and daddy died, she refused to sell her half of the homeplace—twenty-five hundred acres in north Epiphany Parish. Even Zachary went crazy. "You've *got* to sell!" he bellowed. "This is ludicrous!"

She refused. After Zachary died, his half of the property went to Edith, who would never push Vangie. The Galliards' old house sat empty, with swallows making nests in the brick chimneys and mice scratching inside the walls. All that land, and Vangie wouldn't even agree to tenant farmers planting cotton and soybeans.

"We're missing out on a fortune!" Henry had told Edith, hoping for sympathy.

"It's Galliard land," Edith said. "It's Vangie's home."

"Zachary was a Galliard," Henry reminded her. "He wanted to sell."

"Vangie's different." Edith had shrugged. "She loves that old house. You can't take it away."

Henry gave her a shrewd look, but he didn't say anything. He could wait. He knew what he was doing. Everything Vangie owned was in his name, and together they owned plenty. The years between 1947 and 1951 were prosperous for his pharmacy. Last September he bought a turquoise Rambler wagon and 150 wooded acres near the Arkansas line—both were bought without consulting his wife, which made her sullen for days.

"What do you need land for?" she'd said. "We've got twenty-five hundred acres in north Epiphany."

"That's Galliard land," he said, smirking. "This belongs to me. It's Nepper soil."

He'd bought it for speculation, but he also pictured the dogs running in the woods, beggar lice hanging on their fur. "Want to go out for a spin?" he asked Vangie, holding up the Rambler's keys.

"Oh, I suppose," she said, sighing. "But I can't see myself in a station wagon. I wish you'd checked with me. I had my eye on that creamy yellow Buick."

"But you don't even drive!"

"Only because you said it's not safe."

"It's not."

"This isn't New Orleans, or even Baton Rouge." She folded her arms. "I could learn."

"You?" He laughed. "Don't be ridiculous. You'd kill yourself."

"I would *not*." She opened the turquoise door and climbed inside, then looked back to make sure he was following. "Are we still going?" she called out.

They drove to the end of Cypress, then turned left on Lincoln, circling toward the Square. He admired the car's reflection in shop windows, the whitewall tires and thick chrome bumpers. He ran his right hand over the plaid upholstery. Vangie kept yapping about station wagons, and how they were meant for big families. Then she started in about Alma Perkins's funeral, which was that afternoon. "I can't believe you've bought this car, and you can't even drive me to the cemetery."

"I've got to work, Vangie."

"But you're your own boss, just like Leonard is. He's driving Harriet."

"Then catch a ride with them."

"I'd rather walk." She shot him a glance. "You know how Harriet grates on me."

"She grates on everybody."

"Except Leonard. That man is a saint."

"No, Harriet's just got his balls in her pocketbook."

"Henry!" She narrowed her eyes. "I know what's wrong. You just don't like funerals."

He ignored her and kept driving. On the corner of Lincoln and Geranium a red squirrel darted in front of them, bumping against the front tire. Vangie screamed and made him stop. She flung open the door and ran out, her heels stabbing into the asphalt. Henry climbed out. The squirrel was lying on its back, its tiny paws curled. "Look, it's breathing," Vangie pointed. "It's alive! Oh, Henry! Pick it up for me."

He walked over and hunkered down. The squirrel was unconscious but perfectly intact, not a mark anywhere. Vangie tearfully insisted on putting it in the back of the station wagon. "The poor, poor little darling," she said.

"Hell, it's probably crawling with fleas," he growled, but picked it up and carried it to the back of the car, setting it on the greenish blue carpet that he'd special-ordered to match the metal.

When they got home, Vangie said, "I guess you'll have to walk to the store."

"What do you mean, walk? I've got a brand-new car."

"But the squirrel. You'll be inside the store, and the poor thing might suffocate."

"I'm not taking it to town with me."

"Then where can we put it?" She glanced over at the dog pen, where Checkers and Dot were sleeping on smooth-packed dirt. "I'll just get a box."

"How long will *this* take?" he cried, exasperated.

"I don't know! At least a few of your precious minutes!"

"You don't want me to take the car, do you?"

"I never said that." She turned and looked sideways at the Rambler, fingering the tip of her braid.

"Oh, hell." He put his hands on his hips and stared up into the trees. Then he rubbed the back of his neck. "Okay, I'll leave it here. You won't start it up or anything?"

"Heavens, no."

"Well. I guess it's all right." He headed for the sidewalk, then turned around. "Just don't forget that squirrel!"

"I won't!" She blew him a kiss. "See you later, darling!"

Henry trudged the three blocks to the store. It was mid-September, and a hot, sticky sun burned above him. Vangie was trying to run his life, maybe even ruin it, taking away his pleasures one by one. His money had bought that car—he didn't see why he couldn't drive it. Why, he wouldn't be surprised if she turned the Galliard land into a sewing-and-Bible retreat for her friends. He pictured middle-aged women running about in pedal pushers and rag curlers, weaving potholders on the front veranda. Women who couldn't drive, who'd never earned a penny and were proud of it. The Rambler would stay parked, its white-walls deflating.

He pushed open the door to his pharmacy and sat down at the counter. Pretty little DeeDee Robichaux glided over with a glass of lemonade, made with crushed ice, grenadine, and long-stemmed cherries. "Just what I wanted," Henry said, smiling. His eyes swept across DeeDee's narrow hips. He had completely forgotten the squirrel, Vangie, and his brand-new Rambler.

Later he pieced it all together, and he could have kicked himself for drinking lemonade while Hiroshima was taking place three blocks away. Vangie told him how she'd come outside with a blue Madame Alexander box. She peered through the rear glass of the car. The squirrel was running along the dash, against the windshield. It leaped through the steering wheel, then dove under a seat. Bits of turquoise fluff sprang from the passenger side. She had to get that squirrel out before it scratched the upholstery. She just didn't know how to capture it. Halfway to Edith's, she remembered Alma's funeral. All of Cypress Street was at the cemetery—where she should be, except she'd lost track of time.

She strode back to her yard and stopped next to the dog pen. She called out to Checkers, the ninety-pound male, and lifted the latch on the gate. "Come on, boy," she said, clucking to him. As she shut the gate, Checkers leaped into the air, his head momentarily level with hers, then bounced onto the grass. The female, Dot, ran around the pen, then she stood on her hind legs and bawled. Vangie lifted the Rambler's hatch, then snapped her fingers.

"Fetch!" she told him. The dog scrambled into the backseat, his nails digging into the carpet, picking up the scent. Vangie slammed the door and stepped back. Within seconds, the frantic squirrel jumped onto the dash and raced alongside the windows, pursued by Checkers. The car rocked back and forth. The squirrel dove under the front seat, and Checkers lunged forward, digging into the carpet. Vangie stepped back, one hand to her lips. She just knew the squirrel was chewing to the springs. Particles of upholstery flew into the air. Stuffing bubbled from the cushions. From the dog pen, Dot threw herself against the chain-link fence, causing the poles to sway. Her bark sounded like a man's scream. Vangie fled inside, to call Henry. "Help!" she screeched into the phone.

"Vangie?" Henry said. "What's the matter?"

"The squirrel!" she sputtered. "Checkers!"

Then she hung up, missing the cradle, and mashed her finger with the receiver. The last thing Henry heard was a blood-curdling yell from his wife. He ran out of the store, onto the sidewalk, rushing past startled pedestrians. He imagined Vangie sitting in the hammock, gently reviving the squirrel, and Checkers leaping over the fence, into Vangie's lap, biting off the squirrel's head. He imagined blood and fur splattered on his wife's pink-gingham dress.

When he finally got home, he saw Vangie beating on the car's window, shouting, "Stop! Heel, Checkers! Sit! Oh, for heaven's sake, stop!"

Dot paced back and forth in the pen. When she saw Henry, she tossed her head back and bayed. "Help!" Vangie threw out her hands.

Henry ran up to the Rambler. The interior was shredded. Bits of turquoise fabric floated in the air like confetti. "Goddammit," he said and flung open the door. The squirrel shot out, followed by Checkers, who was covered with fluff. The squirrel raced up a tree, and Checkers hurled himself against it, standing on his hind legs and yelping.

"What did you *do*, Vangie?" Henry yelled. Stuffing drifted out the open door, floating toward the azalea hedge.

"Henry, don't be mad," she sobbed. "The squirrel came to and was running around like crazy. I didn't know how to get it out!"

"And so you did what?" he said, prompting her.

"I got this idea." She laid one hand against her cheek, her eyes spilling over.

"Oh, goddammit, Vangie!"

"I told Checkers to fetch it." Vangie nodded, tears running down her cheeks.

"Why didn't you just open the goddamn door?"

"I didn't think to."

"No, you didn't *think*." He slammed the door, then turned to glare at her. "Why didn't you get Cab or Israel? Or Edith?"

"I tried! Nobody's home. They're all at the cemetery."

"Goddammit!"

"Don't you take the Lord's name!"

"Should I take yours? Just look at my car, my brand-new car!" He ignored her tears and strode back to the pharmacy, where DeeDee Robichaux was waiting with a fresh pitcher of ice-cold lemonade, and a good bit more.

There was a courtesy phone in the main lobby, hidden behind a row of plastic philodendrons. Henry picked up the black receiver and dialed 452, DeeDee's number. She lived with her aunt, a short woman with a heart-shaped head who owned Butter's Cafe on the corner of Hayes and Sparrow. The aunt also helped take care of Renny Robichaux, the paralyzed war hero. DeeDee's little girl answered on the fifth ring; Henry cleared his throat and said, "Billie? May I speak to your mother, sweetie?"

"Sure." She banged down the phone and screamed, "Mama? Telephone!"

He strained to hear footsteps from DeeDee's house, the flat, splayed sound of her aunt's oxfords, or (God forbid) the squeak of Renny's wheelchair. He pressed the receiver to his ear but heard only a faint scratching on the line, like sand blowing across glass. Finally DeeDee picked up the phone, breathless, and said, "Hello?"

"Darling?" He squeezed the receiver.

"Oh, Henry! I've been so worried. Is she any better?"

"No. Still in a coma."

"I'm so sorry." She paused. "You wouldn't believe how many people have come to the drugstore, asking if there's any news. Me and Miss Byrd said we didn't know the full details—was that all right? I mean, it's true. We don't know."

"You did good, DeeDee."

"I've been so worried. Are *you* all right?"

"Not really." His eyes filled and he pushed his fingers into the sockets. No one had bothered to comfort him—no, he had been the one to administer sustenance, bolstering Vangie, translating medical terms and procedures so that her pinhead brain could understand. "Can I see you tonight?" he asked. He held his breath, thinking he heard a click on the line.

"Did you hear that?" he asked.

"Hear what?" DeeDee yawned.

"That click."

"No." She giggled. "You're *always* hearing things."

"I don't hear it now." He scratched his throat. "Listen, can you meet me in a few hours?"

"Tonight? Well, it'll take some doing."

"Let's aim for seven o'clock. Remember where I picked you up last week? Say you're going out for cigarettes." He reached down to adjust his male parts, which were straining inside his boxer shorts. "Make up something for me."

"I'll be there."

"Thank you, darling," he said, but she'd already hung up. He stroked the phone, wishing he could reach inside and grab her.

"Henry?" said a voice. "Henry Nepper?"

He turned, expecting to see a customer, but the lobby was empty.

"Henry?" the voice said again. "I know you're there, Henry."

He held out the phone, listening to the voice push out of the tiny black holes. He stared at the receiver, then lifted it to his ear.

"Who's this?" he said.

"Never you mind," the voice snapped. It sounded familiar, but Henry couldn't decipher which hen it belonged to. He thought of all the women in Limoges who flocked to his store for cosmetics, magazines, and prescriptions, but he couldn't match the voice to a face.

"You ought to be ashamed of yourself," the voice hissed. "Carrying on like this. With your child lying one step from the grave and your wife tore all to pieces. Why, I'd like to slap your face!"

"Slap your own," Henry said. "You've got the wrong party. This is *not* Mr. Nepper."

The Things They Leave Behind

$\backsim$

Cooking is soothing and predictable, the way life isn't. 1 cup self-rising flour + 1/2 cup milk + 2 heaping t. mayonnaise will always equal dinner rolls. Bake in greased muffin tins, 400 degrees till brown.

—Vangie Nepper, wife, mother, Baptist, and gardener (not in that order)

Vangie Nepper

The whole time I was piddling in my garden, worrying about prank telephone calls, my baby girl was in the house, slipping into a Nehi coma. "Didn't you even check her room?" Henry said over and over. "Didn't you even *notice* when she came back from her errands?"

"No." Tears streamed down my face, but I was mad enough to hit him. Not that I would.

"Well, there you go," he said, lifting one hand like he'd solved a mystery.

"If it makes you feel better to blame me," I said, "then be my guest."

"Don't start with me, Vangie," he warned. "Not when you let our only child drink poison."

"I didn't exactly mix it for her!"

"Don't start," he said, shaking his head. "Don't you start."

I'd just as soon live at the hospital, so I didn't have to listen to him. He kept her bedroom door shut, but I knew what was inside. The stuffed French poodle from Christmas 1939. Asthma medicine, a jug of marbles, and her own personalized Bible. Her closet bulged with dresses and crinoline petticoats. We gave her the world on a silver platter, and now she was laid out flat at Parish Hospital. Anybody who'd lost a loved one could tell you that the worst was what they left behind. After my mama's stroke, I went back to her house and saw her shoes on the back porch. Looked like she'd just stepped out of them. The leather was stretched and splayed. I didn't see how a pair of shoes could out- last the person who wore them. For months after she died, I walked around like a clumsy ghost, bumping into walls.

Now I walked the same way. I was bruised and spotted all over like old bananas. When somebody asked me a question, I had to think and think. It was real upsetting. Meanwhile, I had to take care of my family—what was left of it. First thing of a morn- ing, I put on coffee. While it perked, I fixed breakfast: scrambled eggs, bacon, grits, biscuits drizzled with butter and cane syrup. "Seems like I'm forgetting something," I told Henry, pouring cof- fee. His eyes swept over his plate, then he stabbed his fork into the eggs, steam coiling around his chin.

"Sit down," he said. "You're making me nervous." Then he shoved the eggs into his mouth, his eyes closing. I make good eggs. (The secret is to start with a clean pan. Drippings will blacken scrambled eggs to pieces.) I nibbled a biscuit and sipped coffee. I was not much of a breakfast eater—at least not in front of Henry. Something nagged at me, something I should have been doing, but I couldn't put my finger on it.

After breakfast, Henry carried me over to the hospital and let me out on Delphinium Street. I passed through the lobby, then went straight to Olive's room. After I got settled, I brushed her hair and fanned it out on the pillow. Phillip LeGette said it was perfectly okay to move her head. I was scared to, but he swore it wouldn't hurt a thing. So I was just a-brushing and talking up a storm, like the nurses said to, and who should walk in but Reverend T. C. Kirby. "I thought I'd find you here," he said, smiling. "Is she any better?"

"The same." I picked up a blond curl, draped it over my palm, and brushed the ends. He had been good to come two, three times a week to pray with us. He watched for a minute, then he said, "I just finished going over the bulletin for this Sunday, and I noticed your birthday is today."

The brush froze in my hand. Birthday? I thought. *Me?* Then it hit me, March 26. Yes, that was my day, all right. It seemed unfair for me to get a year older when Olive wouldn't be there to help me blow out my candles. You couldn't hardly blow out forty in one breath.

"Did you forget?" said the reverend.

"Forget?"

"Your birthday."

"I sure did. I've had so many, I've lost count."

He laughed, then took my hand, and we prayed over Olive.

Around two o'clock Edith stopped by with a cake she and Sophie made, coconut layer. "I didn't stick in the candles," she said, setting the cake on the metal table.

"Thank goodness." I hugged her.

"I'll sit with Olive today. Why don't you go home and rest?" She pulled up a chair, opened a green bag, and lifted out a sketch pad.

"I hate to leave," I said. I was also a little afraid that she'd try and sketch Olive; this coma was not something I wanted to hang on my wall.

"I know, but it's your birthday." Edith smiled, showing two slightly crooked eye teeth that would look ugly on anyone else. It gave her a mysterious air. "You're exhausted, Vangie. Go, I insist."

"But she might wake up." I glanced over at the bed. Olive's eyes moved behind her lids, as if she were watching us talk.

"I'll call. I mean it. Now go."

I kissed them both, Olive and Edith, then I picked up the cake and walked home. It was sunny and warm, with a mild breeze smelling of the river. I hated to leave my baby lying in that hospital, but at the same time I felt starved for sleep. When she was real little, I'd hire me a sitter and sneak out of the house. If Olive saw me go, she'd climb the screen, hollering out, "Mama! Mama!" I'd feel guilty, like I was stealing from her, but at the same time, happy to swing my arms back and forth, free of her wiggling weight. I'd go to the drugstore and have a Coca-Cola, watching Henry mix elixirs. Other days I'd go to the quilting bee at the church; we sewed a different one every year to raffle at the Pecan Festival.

The farther I got from the hospital, the lighter I felt. It felt good to move my legs, to get the blood pumping. I knew Edith would watch over my baby. Olive considered her to be a second mother, but she was my best friend. Most Limogeans assumed she was unsocial because of how she stayed in that house and painted. Zachary loved people, so she'd clean up her studio and invite twenty for Sunday brunch. Only she'd serve mimosas, when nobody drank that early. Or she'd cook up Yankee-tasting food. Every New Year's Eve she made her famous alcoholic eggnog and filled her house with guests. She'd turn out all the lights, except for dozens of candles. Zachary switched on the hifi. As Nat King Cole sang "The Christmas Song," Edith danced with every man, one hand circling his neck, the other holding a glass of Scotch that she and Zachary had driven one hundred miles to buy. If anybody complained, Edith said, "This is a party. If you don't like it, there's the door. Hit it."

She was sincere; she'd tell you exactly what she thought, if you were bold enough to ask. Her version of "truth" wasn't always acceptable to God-fearing Limogeans, though. She'd hoped her Saturday-night soirees might loosen up the town, but all they did was loosen tongues. This was the one thing about Limoges that nobody could change—people were too "polite" to be honest, but they'd slip around and gossip behind your back. With Edith you always knew where you stood. Phillip LeGette once said she would just as soon kiss you on the lips, man or woman, as look at you. Zachary laughed and said, "Hell, you mean she'd just as soon kiss your a_ _ as look at you."

When I got home, the house was hushed, almost like a church on Saturday evening. I set the cake on the counter, then pushed open the kitchen window. A breeze stirred the curtains. I laid out bacon in a cold skillet, then turned up the stove. I was craving me a mayonnaise-lettuce-bacon sandwich (nobody's tomatoes were in yet), just what my hips didn't need. Music drifted in through the window. Harriet had a right to play Ethel Merman full blast, but I had a right not to listen. Why didn't she ever play the Andrews Sisters? The noise was so shrill, my teeth vibrated. While the bacon sizzled, I prayed for her record player to break. A neighbor like Harriet made it hard to be 100 percent Christian.

A long time ago the Marshall sisters lived next door. They'd still be here, but their Aunt Josephine, another old maid, died and left them her house on Gallery Street, the one with the Grecian columns. Harriet and Leonard moved in five minutes after the sisters moved out; as soon as the moving truck rumbled out of the driveway, here came Harriet and Leonard, like they'd been watching with binoculars. It was October 10, 1935, and I'll never forget because I was six months along with Olive. I brought the Hoopers a chicken-and-rice casserole and a pan of corn bread. Harriet pulled me into her kitchen, past boxes stuffed with newspapers, and gave me the grand tour. I'd seen the house dozens of times, but I didn't have the heart to tell her. I acted like it was all new.

Harriet was five years younger, so I'd missed her at Limoges High. She'd married tall, stoop-shouldered Leonard, who ran his daddy's dry goods store on the Square. She opened a box and showed me her china patterns, crystal, silver, and everyday pottery. Now and then she darted over to the phonograph to slap on a fresh seventy-eight record. This was before the days of Ethel Merman, so she played Kate Smith and Sophie Tucker.

She peered into my eyes and said, "You've got such a pretty face. It's a shame you've let yourself go."

"Why, I'm having a baby," I said, insulted.

"You are?" Her eyes skipped to my stomach.

"I'm due in January."

"Oh."

She never said another word, not congratulations, how wonderful, or kiss my foot. Every day, as soon as Henry left for the store, she'd call me up and tell me to drag the phone to the window so we could talk and wave. This got old real fast. Most irritating of all, she had an eye for people's flaws, and her tongue was sharp. Everybody knew Margaret Jane LeGette was a pack rat, but Harriet called her a lazy pig. She hinted that my brother Zachary didn't like the ladies (it was years before World War II and Edith). She even insinuated that old Mr. Beaulieu had a thing for corpses. I shuddered, wondering what-all she said behind my back.

Five, six times a day she'd call. If I couldn't talk, she'd knock on my door and try to draw me out of my house. It got to where I was afraid to check the mailbox or go lie down in the hammock, because she'd come running out of her house. The only way to avoid her was to pay attention to her routines. If she watered her grass in the evening, I'd water mine the next morning, before she'd had her coffee. When the Marshall sisters lived next door, Margaret Jane and I used to visit back and forth, but Harriet's jealousy put an end to that. She said we were leaving her out, that we didn't like her. We didn't, but how can you say it? Once Margaret Jane and I happened to run into each other on Gallery Street. We went into Henry's store for iced coffee, and she said, "I almost feel like we're doing something wrong, talking to each other. Like we're leaving her out on purpose."

This was true. Harriet drove us all crazy, and I started avoiding her. I got to where I wouldn't answer the phone, and my mother had to call down at Henry's store to make sure I hadn't gone into labor. Harriet caught me at the mailbox and said, "What's the matter? Have I done something wrong? Our friendship is real, real important to me."

Now, how can you tell a person they're a pest? I couldn't. So I broke a commandment and lied. I looked her in the eye and said,

"I hate to run, but I've got something burning on the stove." My supper was already done, tuna-macaroni salad, and when I sat down to eat, it stuck in my throat because I am not a liar by nature. A few days went by, and Harriet tried another tack. She called me up and complained about Henry's dogs, saying they barked all night. This simply wasn't true. They howled on occasion, but mostly they were well behaved. She took to walking past the pen, deliberately teasing them, meowing and hissing; I heard her. When they'd yelp she'd march straight over to my house and bang on my door.

"Listen to your stupid dogs!" she'd yell, then stand back, waiting for me to deny it. I saw right then that she knew she was wretched, but she couldn't do a thing to stop herself. I saw that she wanted to be loved and petted and bragged on. The most popular wife in town, the one everybody sought out. When she saw it wasn't going to happen, it broke her heart. After a while, I guess, she got over it. She knew what she was, and she began to play it up the way some old ladies seem to work at being weird—collecting newspapers and cat food cans, whole rooms full of junk. Only with Harriet, meanness was all in the world she had.

Even after my baby was born, Harriet called at nap time and said, "Did I wake Olive up?"

"Yes," I said impatiently. "If you could just call after four o'clock. She's awake then."

"Oh, I didn't know." Harriet clicked her tongue. "So when does she take naps?"

"In the mornings, from nine until eleven, and in the afternoons, from two to four."

I should have kept my mouth shut, because from that day forward, she called at nine-fifteen, ten after two. Sometimes the shrill ringing would throw Olive out of a dream, and she'd cry until I fetched her. That was Harriet for you, devious where she could have been kind. I didn't know if being childless had made her this way, or if her personality had soured her insides. Henry always thought Leonard might be sterile, but I suppose we'd never know which twin had the Toni.

When I thought back to the Marshall sisters, and what good neighbors they were, it made me want to move. Henry wouldn't hear of it, and all these years I'd suffered with Ethel Merman. Suffered through Harriet spying through her venetians and her swooping down on me when I just wanted to pull weeds and be alone with my thoughts. A good, virtuous neighbor was worth her weight in jewels; oh, yes, she was far better than rubies.

I gobbled my sandwich and set my plate in the sink. Henry's

Field & Stream was on the counter, and I wondered if he'd forgotten my birthday. I wished Reverend Kirby hadn't reminded me, because if Henry forgot, I'll just be honest, my feelings would be hurt. I'd been so heartsick, I wanted to be fussed over, to have him put his arms around me and say, "You're older but better, Vangie. Like good hoop cheese."

But he'd probably forgotten. We hadn't been ourselves, what with Olive's condition. Hospitals were hard on the healthy, too. What I normally did was start reminding him a few days beforehand. I'd let little things slip. "Last year for my birthday, we had yellow cake with chocolate icing," I'd say. "Do you think I should make chocolate-on-chocolate or pure white?"

Usually that was enough to get my point across. He knew me, and I knew him. We married when I was sixteen years old. Girls married younger in those days. Seemed like all my friends had their silver patterns picked out. I'd gone to nearly a dozen weddings, watched my friends transformed by white frothy netting and organdy. I'd gone to gift teas, kitchen and linen showers; back at their houses, the dining room tables were full of presents, each one bearing the donor's name, as if it were a museum piece. Goblets, salad forks, iced-tea spoons, china teapots. Sheets, towels, skillets, cake pans. Salt well, sugar tongs, tablecloths. Here in Limoges, if nowhere else, the brides came fully equipped. That made all the difference to Henry Nepper.

I know the Bible says to be frugal, but Henry goes too far. For all his charity work, he is not a compassionate man. He skimps on everything—hugs, kisses, and grocery money. He denies this, of course, but I know better. A long time ago we were going on a vacation to Biloxi, a whole week at the Buena Vista, and the evening before we left, it poured rain. As I heard a knock at the back door. Olive was in her high chair, banging a spoon. I turned on the porch light and liked to fell over when I saw who it was— Sophie, her jaw red and purple, swelled up double, and one eye looked sewn shut. Cuts all over her face and neck like she'd been scratched.

"Burr's on a rampage," she said. "I didn't know where else to go."

I pulled her inside and reached behind me, jerking off the tablecloth, sending the sugar bowl crashing to the floor. Then I wrapped the cloth around her and guided her to a chair. Her hose were bagged around her ankles, and her legs were shaking. My heart just went out to her. I lived such a placid life—maybe not happy, but safe from some crazy man whopping me upside the head. From the high chair, Olive kept beating the spoon on the tray. She was thirteen months, in yellow ruffles and plastic pants. I kept a satin bow in her hair to match her outfits. "Da?" she said, banging the spoon. "Da-da!"

I turned and saw Henry standing in the doorway. He ignored the baby and glared down at me, nodding his head at Sophie. "What's she doing here this time of night?"

"What's it look like?" I said.

"Excuse us, Sophie." He grabbed my arm and pulled me out of the kitchen, into the hall, all the way to his study. "Now, what's she doing here?"

"Burr's beat her again," I said.

"I can *see* that." He sighed. "It's not our problem, Vangie."

"Yes, it is. She's bleeding. I need to call Dr. Phillip—"

"We're leaving in the morning." Henry squeezed his eyes shut, then opened them. "Don't you start something. I mean it, Vangie."

"But what if her jaw's broken?"

"Oh, it's not."

"Can't we just stay home tomorrow? Just to see if she's all right?"

"No!"

"Please, Henry. She's desperate."

"Are you crazy? Delay my vacation on account of some nigra woman?"

"Then she'll go with us."

"Like hell she will!"

"You've got to let her come. Burr might kill her."

"If he finds out she's here, he's liable to kill *us*." He rubbed the top of his head, pushing on his forehead until it wrinkled. "I doubt the Buena Vista'd let nigras stay there. And who's going to pay for all her food? Me, I suppose. Leave it to you to ruin a man's vacation, something he's saved and worked for all year."

"You've got plenty of money," I snapped. "My daddy made sure of it."

"You're nothing but a little fool. That's all you are." He threw up his hands. "I'm sick of you. Do what you want."

But Sophie wouldn't go. I wouldn't have either, if I were her. I suspected she'd overheard Henry. Instead, she asked if she could stay at our house for a few days. "Until Burr calms down," she said. "Stay as long as you like," I said. A week later, we rolled into the drive. My roses were in full bloom, and beneath them the soil was black and moist where they'd been freshly watered. I walked into the house, Olive on my hip, hollering, "Sophie? Sophie?" But even as I hollered her name, I knew she was gone. The house had an empty feel to it. On the kitchen table was a spice cake with an inch of caramel icing, studded with pecans. Next to the cake was a note with her spiky printing: *Gone back home this morning. Burr's OK now. Sweet as this cake I make you. Love, Sophie.*

I looked around the room. All the windows sparkled. The baseboards had been wiped clean. In the hallway, the hardwood floors gleamed, as if they'd been brushed with honey. "Come inside and see what Sophie did!" I cried, walking into the yard to find Henry. Olive's fists were tangled in my hair. Henry stood next to the roses, smoking a cigarette. His dogs yelped, throwing themselves against the fence, but he wouldn't look at them. Red cedar shavings were scattered all over the pen's enclosure.

"Look, she's even cleaned out the pen." I pointed to the chain link enclosure. I drew in a deep breath. "It smells wonderful, Henry. Like the cedar closet back home."

Henry walked over to the pen, taking a long drag on the cigarette. The dogs leaped against the chain link, kicking up red shavings. "Hell, what'd she put cedar in here for?"

"To make things nice." I walked up to the fence, trying to uncoil the baby's fingers from my hair; Olive held on tight, yanking my head back and forth.

"Nice, hell." Henry unlatched the gate. As soon as he stepped inside the pen, the dogs were all over him, kicking shavings around his shins. Henry clapped his hands and yelled, "You idiots, *hush*!" The dogs slithered around him, heads dropped low, but their tails whipped against his legs.

"She didn't mean any harm," I told him.

"Hell, I'll never get rid of this shit." He kicked a chunk into the air. "And I don't care what Burr does to her. In the future, you stay out of it. That woman is never staying in my house again. Do you hear me, Vangie? Do you hear me?"

I caught myself gazing into the backyard. It hadn't rained in weeks, and my roses and tomato plants were limp. Even the crickets screeched in parched voices. Next door, a screen door flapped and Harriet strutted out of her house holding on to Leonard's arm. Today was garden-club day, and she wouldn't miss it for the world. She wore a brown dress with yellow rickrack and her mother's cameo earrings. She was just chattering away, barking out orders to Leonard. He nodded and gripped her elbow. When they reached the car, he helped her inside. The whole time Harriet never stopped talking. As soon as they drove off, little Fanny LeGette climbed down from the great big pecan tree in Harriet's backyard. She ran over to her house. A minute later she came back hugging a mason jar. I couldn't tell what was inside, but it looked like brown sausages all mashed up against the glass.

I wondered if her stepmama had sent her on an errand. *Here*, Waldene probably said. *Take these sausages over to Miss Harriet*.

Fanny squatted next to a haw bush, then crawled inside. She'd just turned twelve—a little old to be a tomboy, and too young to keep up with the likes of Olive. Right after Fanny's mama died, the child caught a baby bird and then dug up the Hoopers' side yard looking for worms. She did it at night, so there weren't any witnesses. Harriet told me all about it, asking if I'd seen anything. "Maybe it's gophers," I said.

"A gopher named Fanny." Harriet snorted. "I know all about that baby bird. Tonight I'm going to lay awake and catch her digging. Then we'll just *see* what happens to that bird!"

I never heard another word out of Harriet. And she never caught the person who snapped off all her daylily buds, either. Harriet worships her daylilies—it's the only flower she will tolerate (and she's president of the Year-Round Garden Club). When she started screaming, I came running. She pointed to a pile of tight green pods and said, "Look at this, just look at this!"

"Why, they're all broken!" I cried.

"I just know it's Fanny LeGette." Harriet narrowed her eyes and glanced toward the LeGettes' house. "Yesterday I caught her cat doing his business on a pink lily. 'If you can't keep Mr. Peepers out of my lilies,' I told her, 'then I will. In fact, you'll never see that cat again.'" Harriet sighed. She picked up a pod and held it to her cheek. "And now all my precious lilies are beheaded! And of course I can't *say* anything to Phillip LeGette. He's just buried his wife. He has no idea that Fanny is running wild."

"But did you see Fanny do it?" (You could tell my brother was a lawyer.)

"Oh, no. She's too sneaky."

"Don't worry so much. I'll help you plant more daylilies."

"When?" Her eyes blinked open. "Today?"

Later, I saw Fanny pushing a doll buggy down the street. "Say hello to my baby, Miss Vangie," she said. I leaned over and stared into the eyes of Mr. Peepers. He was wearing a ruffled bonnet and a half-chewed doll gown. He looked absolutely furious.

"Is your baby good?" I asked.

"No, he's got ants in his pants."

"Oh, my. That's a bad thing to have, isn't it?" I patted Fanny's head. Inside the buggy, Mr. Peepers let out an indignant meow. "By the way," I said. "Wasn't it a shame about Miss Harriet's daylilies?"

"An awful shame." Fanny looked at me sideways.

"Wonder who'd do such a thing?"

"Well, I don't know. But I'd *say* it was a little girl with a cat? A cat who liked to poop in daylilies? So maybe the little girl thought if she got rid of the daylilies, then Miss Harriet wouldn't get rid of the cat."

"It makes perfect sense to me."

"Well, I've got to be going," she said airily. "It's time for my baby's nap."

Now I stared at the Hoopers' back door. It gaped open into shadow, and I knew Fanny was up to something with those mason jars. Olive was too self-righteous to commit crimes, but Fanny reminded me of myself. How I used to be. Somewhere inside me was a girl who went flying with her daddy and refused to sew dresses. I liked to think my mama forced me to be a lady, but I only had myself to blame. "You'll never get a husband unless you can make biscuits," Mama used to say.

"Maybe I don't want no husband," I said. Then I saw Henry Nepper at a church picnic, so round-faced and cute, with a football scholarship to L.S.U. Daddy hired him to paint the veranda, and Mama chased me out of the house. She said it would hurt my female parts to smell the fumes. Down by the ditch, I picked up a jay feather and put it in my pocket. The afternoon sky sagged low like a bleached sheet on a clothesline. When I finally walked back to the house, Mama was in the front room, playing "Alice Blue Gown" on the piano, singing as loud as she could. I crept around back and saw Henry kneeling by a bucket, rinsing off his paintbrushes. He wasn't wearing a shirt, just black cut-off trousers. He had the prettiest back—not that I'd seen another, but I just knew his was the best in the parish. As he scrubbed the brushes, muscles moved between his shoulders. There was something sweet about the curve of his neck, a boy's neck. He turned, saw me staring, and jumped back against the pail, spilling it. White water ran between his legs. His hands went to his chest, covering the dark hairs.

"Your mama told me not to take off my shirt," he said, blushing, "but I got hot. You'd better not look."

"Oh, all right!" I said, turning around, but of course I had already seen plenty. Inside the house the piano banged shut. A minute later Mama was standing at the screen door, all grainy against the mesh. She did not look happy. Later she said, "Don't you get any ideas, Vangie. He's not what I had in mind for you."

"Why not?"

"Because he comes from a bad family."

"His daddy's a housepainter. That's perfectly respectable."

"It's a far cry from what we're used to. Anyhow, he drinks and goes round to juke joints."

"Lots of people do that." Like Daddy, I thought.

"Yes, but his mama's not right." She tapped her temple. "In the head."

"Why, she's as nice as she can be!"

"Then explain why they found her naked in her front yard that time." Mama's face looked pinched.

"Because," I said, rolling my eyes, "she was taking a bath and she thought some man was trying to break in. So she climbed out the window. Then she couldn't get back into the house 'cause it was locked."

"Then explain why that poor Watkins man was arrested?" Mama put her hands on her hips. "I happen to know he spent three whole days in jail before Olivia Nepper admitted she hadn't been attacked. The poor man hadn't even set *foot* in her house. She thought he looked like a rapist. Explain all that."

"Henry can't help what his mama does," I said. "He's got a full scholarship to L.S.U."

"Well, I don't see how. Considering what he's from."

"He wants to be a doctor."

"A what?" Mama drew her lips together, absorbing this new information. After a minute she said, "You really think he'll make a doctor?"

"I certainly do."

"Then ask Della how to cook. She's had three husbands in less than ten years. If anybody knows the way to a man's heart, it's Della." Della said the secret to being a good cook is patience, a willingness to experiment, and a garden in your backyard. (She also said two of those things applied to marriage, but she told me to figure that out myself.) She taught me to can tomatoes, to make vinegar from nasturtiums. I learned the secret of pot likker: Add chicken stock after cooking your turnip greens.

Once I got Henry Nepper in my mind, I longed to be his bride the way I'd once longed to fly. My mama and daddy still thought he was beneath me, but they liked the idea of having a doctor in the family. They took me to Memphis, rented a suite at the Peabody, and bought me a wedding gown fit for a princess. When I got back, Henry and I were sitting on the side veranda, drinking lemonade, planning our honeymoon. It was mid-June, just after dusk, but the temperature was still in the low hundreds. "The only thing I ask of you," I told him, "is that you'll never be like my daddy." This took a lot, to be disloyal to my darling daddy, but I wanted to get things straight with Henry. The Major was the best daddy in the world, but he just wasn't a good husband. His lady friends had notorious fights. Sometimes the police would drive up to our house and ask to speak to Major Galliard.

"Do you know a Wanda Jones?" the officer would ask.

"Hmmm," the Major would say. "Name sounds familiar. Why?"

"Well, she's been knifed. Cut to pieces at Ike's Lounge."

"No! Is she dead?"

"Afraid so. And we're holding Shirley King on charges. She's why I'm here. She said you'll make her bail."

My mama never heard anything. She made a point to be upstairs sewing, ripping out hems, when the police came. She came from a long line of suffering women. They believed if Jesus could turn the other cheek, so could they. Besides, a divorce was scandalous, equal to murder or insanity.

That night on the veranda, Henry took a big swallow of lemonade and said, "You don't have to worry. I'm going to be a doctor. I'll never plant cotton."

"No, I mean have other women."

"Shoot, I'll never do that."

"But if you ever did?" My eyes filled. "I'll flat leave you. Or kill you one."

"That day'll never come." He reached into his glass and fished out a chunk of ice. He traced it around my neck, then reached inside my blouse and drew an *X* over my heart. I felt water seep into my brassiere. I squirmed away, fanning my skirt across my legs.

"Listen," he said, pushing his mouth against my ear. "'Let's have one other gaudy night.'"

"Gaudy?" I leaned back. "Is that a poem or a kind of mosquito netting?"

"No, it's William Shakespeare."

"Do I know him?"

"Vangie! How'd you ever get to be a high school senior and not hear about Shakespeare?"

"Maybe 'cause I was double-promoted?" I shrugged. "He could've graduated before me."

"Oh, Vangie. What am I going to do with you?" Henry laughed and pulled me against him. We started kissing. His breath smelled like lemons.

"Let's do it," he whispered. "Let's go all the way."

"Can't you wait till our wedding night?"

"No."

"Well, I can."

"Then rub me like you did the other night."

"No!"

"Come on, baby. Please? I need it bad."

"No, you don't."

"Vangie, come on. You know what the French say? You can't make an omelet without breaking eggs."

"What's that supposed to mean?" I drew back. "That you're no different from scrambled eggs?"

"Damn," he whispered, rubbing between his legs. "I can't *stand* it."

"Don't cuss," I said in my mama's voice. But I slid my hand up his leg, then opened his zipper. "This is the last time," I said. "I mean it, Henry. The very *last* until the wedding."

We had a great big ceremony at First Baptist in Limoges, July 4, which was Henry's idea. "So we can start off with a bang," he said, but I was such a fool I didn't get it. I had me ten brides-maids, all dressed in ashes of roses. Mama and I decorated the church with huge bouquets of Queen Anne's lace and gladioli. Now, if you don't think that is pretty, then you don't know much. Afterward we drove to the Ozarks for a honeymoon, in a mountain cabin overlooking a great, big green lake.

First thing, he carried me into the bedroom and laid me down on the creaky mattress. He started kissing my neck, one hand twisting up my dress, the other mashing against my new white bra. Then he shucked off his trousers and reached for my panties, working so clumsily I helped by kicking them off my ankles. As he rolled on top, pushing me into the mattress, I closed my eyes. Surely Mama and Della had gone through this, women everywhere went through it, it was something we had to do. After all we'd done on the veranda, I still didn't know it would be like this. I tried to tell him I had a brand-new gown in my suitcase, but he stuck his tongue between my teeth and fumbled between my legs. It was over before he could get it all the way inside. He moved his hips a few times, causing the headboard to bang against the wall, and started moaning. He lay on top of me, my dress bunched up around my chin, and breathed into my hair.

I didn't know why, but he seemed to lose interest in me that first week. He'd go off fishing, leaving me alone in the cabin, then at dusk he'd walk up with a string of bluegill for me to fry. "What other man," he said, "would bring you home the best fish in the Ozarks?"

Right then I made up my mind to make the best of things. I found an Audubon book, and I learned to identify birds. I taught myself the difference between oak and hickory leaves. The lady we rented the cabin from taught me how to fry frog legs. First, you cut off the hind legs close to the body, then rinse them in cold water. You strip the skin like you're pulling off gloves, then chop off the feet. The real secret is soaking them in ice-cold water, adding the juice of one lemon. Roll the frog legs in flour. Dip in egg wash (3 eggs thinned with milk), then roll in cornmeal. Fry in hot oil till golden brown, about 10 minutes on each side. Serves 6.

I heard about a woman in Memphis who killed her husband with this recipe, except she put ground glass in the cornmeal. They said she crushed up all her mason jars. Then she dipped the frog legs in egg, rolled them in the sparkly meal. The woman didn't eat a bite. She drank iced tea and sucked on the lemon, watching her husband chew, waiting for his insides to fall out. And they sure enough did.

When we got back from Arkansas, it was time for Henry's college to start. We moved on down to Baton Rouge. I threw myself into housewifery—cooking, cleaning, gardening, organizing my cupboards. The Major paid all our bills, so Henry could apply himself to his studies. Me, I spent a lot of time exchanging recipes with the other wives, who were always pregnant. They complained about being so poor, having to suffer while our husbands sat in classrooms filled with coeds. Some of the women were bitter—they'd gotten pregnant in college and were forced to marry men they weren't sure they loved. "How do you keep from getting pregnant, Vangie?" they asked me. I just smiled. I had my own cross to bear. It seemed to me that all over the South, women were making beds and then having to lie in them forever.

Henry's grades were not what we'd hoped for, so he applied to pharmacy school in Jackson, Mississippi. After he graduated, we gave away our shabby furniture and moved back to Limoges. We never discussed living elsewhere. It didn't occur to us. The Major bought us a house in town, on Cypress. Then he set Henry up in business, and I joined all the clubs. The years flew by, and I still didn't have me a baby. People stopped asking me and Henry about the pitter-patter of little feet. And I seemed to get a sick headache every single time one of the ladies at church had a baby shower. I just knew I was barren as Abraham's wife, Sara—but even she gave me hope (she didn't have her first child, Isaac, until she was about a hundred years old). Just when I was on the verge of starting a prayer chain, Henry said we needed to see a doctor.

We drove over to Jackson, to the medical center, and a specialist put us in separate rooms. He asked personal questions. Things that made me blush. He wanted to know how long Henry stayed erect. Fool that I am, I thought he meant good posture. "No, no!" said the doctor. "Erect, as in penis. How long does it stay . . . hard?"

"Let me think." I rolled my eyes. It wasn't any of his business. I worried that he was one of those rape-stranglers you hear about. If nothing else, this visit was an education. I tried to remember the act of love. It was messy. Seemed like I was changing the sheets and bathing all the time. "Twenty seconds?" I said.

"Twenty?" He raised his bushy eyebrows. "Are you sure?"

"Well, maybe just a teeny less. I'm not real mathematical, you know."

He took blood from my arm and told me to take my temperature every single day before my feet hit the floor, and to return in two months. "We can adopt," Henry said when we got home. "I still love you, Vangie. You don't have to bear my child."

Come to find out, I was fine. Fit as a fiddle. And Henry had plenty of sperms. The doctors were puzzled, so they took us into separate rooms and quizzed us again. The problem turned out to be Henry. "Mr. Nepper is a premature ejaculator," the doctor explained. "He's not getting his sperm into the proper place."

"And where's that?" I asked in a tiny voice. I wasn't sure I wanted to know.

"Inside you, Mrs. Nepper, not *on* you." He patted my arm. "Technically, you are still a virgin."

I suppose they talked to Henry, too, and two months later I was pregnant with Olive. No one was any prouder than Henry.

I made the bed, straightening the ruffled shams and pink Dutch-doll quilt. I had a whole cedar chest full of quilts, but my favorite was made up of Bible verses that my grandmother's Sunday school class sewed in 1903. My least favorite was a burial quilt that Emmaline Beaulieu left me when she died. Cab brought it over after the funeral. "Mama wanted you to have this," he said and laid it in my arms. It felt scratchy and smelled of mothballs. To tell the truth, I didn't want it, not with all those dead Beaulieus embroidered in the squares, some with velvet tombstones, but how do you say no?

A basket of clean laundry sat on the floor. I started putting it away, sliding out Henry's sock drawer. He'd messed it up something awful. Everything was tangled, and way in the back, the socks were pooched over something. I lifted the snarl and saw a long blue-velvet box. I picked it up, creaked it open, and stared down at a diamond wristwatch. It was the prettiest thing I'd ever seen, expensive and delicate, with a sterling silver band. Feminine. Printed on the box was Cox's, a jewelry store in Vicksburg, Mississippi, forty-five minutes southeast. In a whole other state. We hardly ever ventured to Vicksburg anymore, and I couldn't recall Henry going by himself, especially when he hated to put miles on his car. I held the box, trying to explain it. It just wasn't like Henry to go to all this trouble for a watch. Also, I didn't like the idea of him crossing the Mississippi in secret; if he did that, what else would he do?

Then it hit me. I had accidentally stumbled on my own birthday present. I was so shocked, I lost my balance and rolled backward, my rear end hitting the floor. I felt terrible for having opened the box. It was like seeing into the future when half the joy of life was being surprised by it. I pictured Henry fastening the watch on my wrist, and I felt a rush of tenderness. He had never, in our whole married life, bought me a piece of jewelry. Even when we got married, he couldn't afford a diamond, so Mama just gave me one of hers. *"Don't you let him get away with this, Vangie,"* she said. *"At least make him buy you a new setting."* But I just laughed and said, *"Oh, Mama. Things like that don't matter to me. I'd be happy wearing a paper Roi-Tan band."*

Now I just wanted to hug his neck. All these years I'd thought he was too stingy to be thoughtful. I slipped the case back into the drawer, stuffing the socks back over it, then hurried into the bathroom. Seemed like a good idea to freshen up a bit and then walk to the store, bringing a wedge of Edith's cake. I put on a blue shirtwaist dress that hides my hips. Then I cut two big slices of Edith's cake and wrapped them in foil. All the way to town, I hummed "How Great Thou Art." I pushed open the glass door, listening to the bell jingle, and stepped inside. My eyes swept past the men at the counter, past the dark-eyed girl who poured coffee into thick white cups, past women browsing on the cosmetics aisle, past Miss Byrd at the checkout. I spotted Henry up in his loft, filling prescriptions. I marched straight down the aisle, carrying the cake high, and climbed into the upper room. Henry looked up, did a double-take, then dropped a giant bottle of blue pills. They ticked against the tile floor.

"It's just me." I smiled and held up the cake. "I brought you something."

"Yes, I can see that." He swallowed. "Is anything wrong?" Then his eyes got big. "Is Olive better? Did she wake up?"

"No, honey. She's still sleeping. I just came by to say hello. And bring you a little snack. I didn't mean to alarm you." I set the cake on the counter, then knelt down to collect the pills, not that he'd use them in a million years. Nepper's Drugs stood for quality.

"Did you leave her by herself?" he asked.

"No, Edith's with her." I reached under a shelf and flicked out three pills. Then I stood up and dumped the medicine in an ashtray. I glanced down into the store. The dark-eyed counter girl was watching us. She looked at me full in the face before she went back to pouring coffee, which bothered me in a way I didn't understand.

"Can I buy you a Cherry Coke?" I poked my elbow into Henry's belly, denting his white smock.

"I wish I had time, Vangie." His eyebrows drew up, and then he gestured to the pills and bottles scattered about. "But I'm swamped. You'd think there's fifty doctors in Limoges instead of two."

"Well, I won't keep you," I said, hoping he'd stop me from leaving. "I guess I'll be running along."

"Sure, thanks for stopping by." He sighed and rubbed his bald spot. His eyes swept out into the store, hanging on something for just a second.

"Can you get off early tonight?" I asked. "I'll cook us a special supper. We haven't eaten a meal at home since, well . . . " I broke off and swallowed hard. "I can cook you some spaghetti."

"I've got a meeting tonight. It's local businessmen." He reached into the ashtray and picked up several pills, holding them up to the light.

"But you've got to eat sometimes, don't you?"

He shot me a look, then dropped the pills. "I can't help these meetings, Vangie."

"But it's my birthday!" Then I bit my lip. I didn't mean to say this, not with that diamond watch sitting in his dresser drawer, but it just popped out. Self-pity would do that every time. "I just thought we could have a meal at home for a change," I said. "I'm so tired of eating at the hospital, balancing plates on my knees. Aren't you?"

Henry just stared.

"Anyway, I myself forgot what day it was." I let out a high, rickety laugh. "Reverend Kirby had to remind me. So don't feel rained on. We've all been under a strain, honey. The biggest in the world."

"I didn't let it slip by." He reached across the counter and tapped the square page, March 26. *Vangie's B-Day* was written in red pencil. He held out his arms. "Come here, old woman. This day's not over yet."

When I stepped out of the loft, I felt twenty-five, not forty. I smiled at Miss Byrd, who grinned back, showing all her teeth. She even nodded the way people do in church, causing her tight curls to shimmy. I turned to acknowledge the brown-eyed girl, but she kept her eyes averted. Her name kept sliding right out of

my mind. It was impossible to keep track—counter girls came
and went; only Miss Byrd stayed. When the girl glanced up, I
smiled. She did not smile back. Sometimes the counter girls were
friendly; sometimes they seemed to hate me. This woman,
though, had a hard life. Her husband was a crippled veteran, so I
supposed she carried grief deep in her heart, same as me. Plus,
she had a little girl to look after.

I headed down Gallery Street, toward City Market, planning
the menu in my mind. We would have spaghetti and meatballs,
nothing fancy, but I'd make the sauce from a roux. A lemon chif-
fon salad would be nice. A jar of summer beans, garlic French
bread, iced tea. Or maybe I'd open a bottle of Christmas sherry. It
wasn't every day that a woman turned forty and got a diamond
wristwatch. I couldn't wait to show it to Olive. Wherever she was,
locked up inside her dreams, I knew she would be proud.

Aerial View of Limoges

❧

Patient remains in deep sleep. No apparent distress. No complaints.
Skin warm and dry. IV dripping normal saline. Oxygen tent in place.
Vital signs normal: Temp: 98.7, Blood pressure: 120/78. Pulse: 72 &
regular. Respirations: 12 & regular. Mother snoring at bedside.

—ABIGAIL POTTER, R.N., FROM HER NURSE'S NOTES, OLIVE
NEPPER'S CHART, GRAVEYARD SHIFT

Six miles north of town, Emmett Welch's plane skimmed over the
old Galliard place, the fields empty except for last summer's
weeds and volunteer cotton. The plane dipped over a row of dried
stalks, stirring up dust the way some people gossiped. Fine particles hung in the dry air, a shimmery veil that distorted Emmett's
view. Heat combined with distance made everything look peculiar. It hadn't rained a drop since the first of March, and farmers
were beginning to talk about droughts. This morning, before he
started up his plane, crickets emitted a shrill noise, the sound
swarming in the air like radiation.

Everyone predicted the summer of '52 would be long and
crazy-hot as only Louisiana summers could be. You had to be
stouthearted to live here. Not too many weeks from now, Emmett
would be sweeping over the fields, poison seeping from his wings,
just a smidgen left over from spraying cotton across the river.

At Legion Field he heard it all: cotton prices, weather predic-
tions, and hell, yes, gossip. This one swallowed poison, that one
was sleeping in the wrong bed. It was one durn thing after
another. The Major wouldn't have liked it. Now that he was gone,
Emmett worried about Miss Vangie the same way he worried
about the crops—some things were beyond his control. Some
things were just not his. He wanted to say, *Miss Vangie, if there's*

anything I can do, just anything at all, say the word. He was
beholden to the Major forever, and Vangie was the only living
Galliard, so he was beholden to her, too. There must be a way he
could help, but he wasn't a talker. Never was, never would be. He
was a flyer, just like the Major.

He circled over Limoges, then tipped toward the lake. From
this altitude the town reminded him of bins in a dime store, the
streets no more than glass dividers holding everything together.
All these houses with people stuffed inside, listening to the radio
for updates on Korea, polio, and the Rosenbergs. They were
arrested for being spies, and now there was talk of electrocution,
maybe next summer. As Emmett flew above the Square, old-
timers, no bigger than fire ants, sat around the courthouse, talking about the big question: Dwight D. Eisenhower or Adlai
Stevenson. And just the other day President Truman had seized
the steel mills to prevent a strike. The talk would no doubt turn to
the Russians and Red Chinese. If it wasn't one enemy, it was
another. Even at Legion Field they talked about treason and electrocution. Why, the world could pop apart like a pressure cooker
with the metal weight pulled off too soon. He'd seen that happen,
too. In Mrs. Galliard's own kitchen the summer Vangie married
Henry. Black-eyed peas shot into the ceiling like bullets, and the
Major laughed like crazy.

The plane made a *T*-shaped shadow over trees and rooftops,
over Lincoln Avenue and finally Lake Limoges. He flew so close
to the water that the surface ruffled. When you're dusting, the
farmers wanted you to fly low—if they didn't see cotton hooked in
your wheels, they called you chickenshit. As he curved back
toward Cypress Street, he saw Miss Vangie coming up the sidewalk; he'd recognize the Major's daughter anywhere. She seemed
to be looking thoughtfully at the Hoopers' house, or maybe she
was looking at him. From this distance, it was hard to tell.

Way down below, Fanny LeGette stood in Miss Harriet's cool
green backyard, looking up at the sky, watching the plane curve
over Lake Limoges. The noise was loud as Mr. Hooper's Cadillac—for a second it had confused her, and she worried that she
might be caught trespassing. She was relieved to see the crop
duster. If the Hoopers saw her right now, how would she explain
this mason jar? Inside were two baby chicken snakes that she'd
sent into premature hibernation—cooled for one half hour in her
stepmama's icebox, then dropped into the jar like long, limp
strands of licorice. She started to unscrew the lid, then hesitated.

She wouldn't be doing this, it was purely evil, but Miss Harriet had gone too far. Yesterday, Fanny had hunkered under the

Hoopers' forsythia bushes, pretending to be a spy; the Hoopers were really Red Chinese sent to wipe out Limoges. Months ago, Reverend Kirby said if the Russians came to America, they'd burst into all the churches with machine guns and ask everyone to leave, except for the Christians. Then they'd start shooting. After the sermon, Olive clasped her hands under her chin and said, "I hope the Russians don't come to our church."

Fanny agreed. She wasn't so sure she'd lay down her life for Jesus. "They'll probably shoot us all," she said. "Christians or not."

"Why?" Olive looked puzzled.

"'Cause nobody in Limoges speaks Russian," Fanny said. "They'll just get inside the church and talk gibberish. For all we know they could be saying, 'Leave if you *love* Jesus. Stay if you want a bullet sandwich.'"

"I hadn't thought about that," Olive said, chewing her lip.

Fanny crept toward the Hoopers' house, dodging bees in the forsythia. Playing Communists was no fun by herself. She needed Olive, even though Olive had gotten prissy before she went into the coma. She settled against the house, directly under the Hoopers' living-room window, and waited for the enemy to reveal themselves. It didn't take long. "There's more to this so-called coma than meets the eye," Miss Harriet told her husband. "I think Vangie did it."

"Oh, she wouldn't!" said Mr. Leonard.

"You don't know her like I do. I'll bet she gave Olive too much paregoric, and now they're all covering for her."

"She worshipped that child."

"Maybe that's why Olive's in that coma. It's a sin to worship anything but Jesus. That's why I worship nothing."

"Oh, Harriet."

"Well, it *is*. And I'll tell you something else—Phillip LeGette doesn't know a coma from a hole in the ground. I wouldn't let him doctor a snake."

"You hate snakes, Harriet."

"Yes, but if I had a snake, I wouldn't let Phillip touch it. Furthermore, his little Fanny is a future criminal. Truth be told, *she* probably suffocated Olive. Don't look at me that way, Leonard. She'd do it in a heartbeat if she thought Olive stole her Madame Alexander dolls."

"Well, she is a little devil," Mr. Leonard agreed.

"Phillip just won't face up to it, and Waldene doesn't care—it's not her daughter. She's got one of her own about to be born. Another rotten little LeGette to meow in the street and ruin my day. I wish they'd move. I just wish they'd *all* move!"

Fanny sat inside the forsythia, her arms clasped around her knees, tears streaming down her cheeks. It didn't take long to hatch out a plan. Now she opened the jar and arranged the baby snakes across the back steps. Then she stood back. When the snakes woke up, they'd head into Miss Harriet's kitchen. Fanny held the empty jar to her chest, then ran across the yard, into her house.

"Are you all right?" asked her stepmama from the doorway. She held a damp dishcloth.

Fanny blinked. She tried to think of something that would keep Waldene busy. "Can you fix me a peanut-butter-and-bacon sandwich?"

"I swear, you eat like a *hog*. I just hope you don't get chubby." Waldene rolled her eyes, then walked into the kitchen. Fanny crawled up into the window seat and waited for her sandwich. The bacon was sizzling when the Hoopers pulled into their driveway. Mr. Hooper got out of the Cadillac, then hurried around and opened his wife's door. They walked toward the back of the house, and a minute later the screaming began—whether it was Mr. Leonard's or Miss Harriet's, it was impossible to tell. The noise seemed to rise over Cypress Street, over the lake, clear to the Mississippi River like something airborne.

There Is a Balm in Gilead

❧

WANTED—I'm a young woman searching for a job. A job that entitle housework, cooking, or babysitting. I'm available anytime. Tell Mrs. Hawley at City Market your name and directions to your house and when you want me to come.

—LIMOGES *NEWS-LEADER*, CLASSIFIEDS, MARCH 1936, PAGE 9

Sophie Donnell

The snakes put Miss Harriet in the hospital. She lays up in room 23-A, just down the hall from Olive, making the nurses wait on her hand and foot. Better them than me is how I look at it. Meanwhile, back at her house, mens tearing the place apart. Hammering, sawing, carrying out walls. Ripping out baseboards. "Why you doing all this?" I ask them.

"Fumigation," they say. "If there's one snake, there's fifty."

"Found any yet?"

"No, but that don't mean they ain't here." Then they cut a hole in the wall and shine lights down inside it. I run myself ragged trying to keep sheetrock swept up. It's the latest thing for houses, but I hate it. Fine white powder, gritty as Bon Ami, covers every table and china doo-dad. The record box and all the records look like they sprinkled with confectioner's sugar. It gets in my hair, ears, and even inside my shoes. Looks to me like snakes would be better, long as they wasn't poison. I'm just glad I only have to come here on Wednesdays.

One day I see Mr. Leonard downtown, and he says Miss Harriet's starving, won't eat hospital food. "The poor little thing's just wasting away," he says. I think, *Mmmhum, I got to see this for myself.* So I cook a batch of chicken and dumplings, rice, and corn bread sticks. I wasn't going to, but once I got started cooking, seem like I couldn't stop. It was like the old days when I was raising all of Burr's kids and my own little boy. I cooked aplenty. Still would if I could. It soothes me in a way I can't explain.

When I get to the hospital, Miss Harriet is sitting up in bed wearing a yellow nightie. Got frothy lace at the neck and wrists. Got a matching gown and slippers, what she call her ensemble. All she needs is a big neck bow and long ears. Then I can stick her in a Easter basket and pass her off as a rabbit. "What you doing in this hospital, girl?" I say.

"It's shock," she tells me. "The shock of all those snakes."

"Yes, ma'am."

"I *do* hate all reptiles, Sophie. Hate them with a passion."

"Yes, ma'am."

"What have you got in that sack that smells so *good*?" She reaches for the food. Me and Mr. Leonard watch her lap it up. She loves my cooking. Long time ago, I put okra in her gumbo, and she like to went crazy. "I'd just as soon eat dirt," she said, wiping her mouth. "I got to get this taste out of my mouth. Where's that nice fresh cup of coffee you promised me and Mr. Hooper?"

I went outside and dug up some fresh dirt and put it in the coffee grounds. I knew it was wrong, the baddest thing I ever done, but I'd had all I could take. Miss Harriet say, "This is the best cup of coffee I ever had in my life."

Now I look over at her. She hollering to the nurses, making them fetch a jar of milk so she can crumble in the corn bread. "This is Louisiana caviar," she said. The nurses lift their eyebrows. Say, "Yeah."

Lined up on her table is half of Nepper's Drugs. Lavoris, Dr. Lyon's tooth powder, jar of cold cream, Jane Horton assorted chocolates. There's a dozen roses in a milk-glass vase. A card say: Love, Leonard. Nothing like the flowers for Olive, and no visitors neither, but Miss Harriet is so pleased. She don't know she ain't popular. Makes me smell every last rose, then screeches, "Don't you *dare* touch your nose to the petals!"

She don't look sick to me. Says, "Crank down this bed, Sophie. Help me with these slippers. Hand me that lipstick. My hair's pooched up something awful. Can you tease it down?"

I ain't no beauty operator, but I pick up the brush and try to fringe the curls. Mr. Leonard excuse himself and walk out into the hall to smoke. Looks for Mr. Henry or whoever he can find, anything to escape Miss Harriet. This, too, she don't see.

"Now, help me into that wheelchair, Sophie." She wiggles her fingers. "The nurses keep fussing at me to walk, but I'm just too weak." She leans hard on my arm and takes baby steps. Falls hard into the cane chair, causing it to roll back; it mashes against my toes. My shoes are thick oxfords, so it just pinches. I don't say nothing. Just take hold of the handles and push her into the hall. She's heavier than she looks, and she looks stocky. I grunt just a little, feel sweat gather at the back of my neck. She waves at people like she's the Queen Bee of Limoges.

"It's time for you to take my blood pressure," she warns the nurses. "And bring me a fresh pitcher of ice, too, while you're at it."

"Yes, Mrs. Hooper," they say, rolling their eyes.

"Make it snappy. I can't run the halls just to make your job easy."

We turn a corner. The door to Olive's room is closed. It has been closed ever since Harriet got put in Parish Hospital. A sign says:

IMMEDIATE FAMILY ONLY
ALL VISITORS CHECK AT NURSES' STATION
THANK YOU

"Now why in the world would they do that?" Miss Harriet points at the sign. "They're trying to hide something, I'll bet you. Only people with secrets try to hide themselves away."

Me, I just look at the door, thinking Miss Harriet don't know what she talking about. I came to work for her the same year Miss Olive born. I was in the Hoopers' lime green kitchen (what I call slime green), cleaning up the mess. She always leave a big one. That morning, I filled the sink with hot soapy water, then eased in the iron skillet. Miss Harriet screamed, "What do you think you're doing!"

"Cleaning your skillet," I said.

"Why, it's seasoned. You supposed to wipe them out. Don't you know any better?"

"Yes, Miss." I nodded. "Got me one just like it at home."

"Then why're you trying to ruin mine?"

"Miss, you can't wipe out burnt food."

"Don't you sass me, girl, or I'll call Mr. Leonard."

She's always threatening me, saying she's going to call the police. She never do. Now she nudges my arm. Says, "I don't have all day. Let's get cracking. Wheel me down to the lobby so I can see who's coming and going. Unless you got something better to do."

"Yes, ma'am," I say, but she don't get it. I got plenty better to do, but I wheel her down to the lobby like she's a little old crippled white lady. We wait for people to walk through the double-glass doors, but it's getting near supper time. Through the big windows, the sky gets bluer and bluer. One of the nurses leaves out the front door. Say to me, "Sophie, don't you ever go home?"

"Oh, she likes it here." Miss Harriet waves her hand, then winks at the nurse. "You know how it is with them. It's not like they've got a regular life or anything. Do you, Sophie?"

I can't answer. If I was to open my mouth, the police would be called and they'd lock me up. Throw away the key. So I shut my eyes. Think, Heart, keep beating. Don't jump out of my chest and thump her on the head. I do have a life. I got one bigger than hers. It's stout and painful, but it's all mine.

Later, when some new nurses bring the supper trays, I slip off. Hear Miss Harriet crying for me, telling Mr. Leonard to chase me down. I turn the corner and knock on Olive's door. "It's me," I say. "Sophie."

From the other side, I hear footsteps. Then Miss Vangie cracks open the door. When she sees it's me, she gives a little cry and pulls me inside. Says, "I'm so glad it's you."

"I almost didn't knock," I say. "That sign put me off."

"It wasn't meant for you," she says. "I hated to put it up, but Harriet would be in here every second."

"I'm surprised you're keeping her out." I look over at Olive. A plastic tent is draped over her, and her hands lay on top of the sheets. All around her are flowers—on the floor, lined up in the windows, on the wooden dresser. The most you've ever seen.

"Harriet's already slipping notes under the door." Miss Vangie points to a pile of papers. She runs her hands through her hair. It's unbraided, falling in gray strands around her shoulders. Looks like it ain't been combed in days, and there's blue circles under her eyes. I lift one paper. It say,

> Dear Vangie,
> I don't mean to be a bother but I have to know the answers to a few things. Do you have snakes in your house?
>> Check one
> ——Yes   ——No
> Also: How about your yard?
> ——Yes   ——No
> Just slip this back under the door and I'll have Leonard pick it up later. I am looking forward to your swift reply, as you know I am not in good health. Thank you.
>> Your neighbor,
>> Harriet

By the time I get home, Burr's gone, and I know my Jesus is looking out for me. A full moon is on the rise, a fisherman's moon. Catfish will be biting good. Burr will run lines all night, and then come home eat up with chigger and mosquito bites. The deeper we get into spring and summer, the worse Burr acts. It's from the heat—nothing but a misery. Me, I'll be dressed and gone, working in town. I won't have to listen to him scratching and hollering for coal oil to rub on the bites. If he was here now, he'd want me to kill a hen and fry it. I'd spin her around the way Burr used to crank our engine. He'd want slaw, hoecakes, rice and gravy. When it's just me, I eat what I want. Sometimes I carry a pan of corn bread to the porch, eating with my fingers, listening to the frogs in the bayou. Oh, Lord, I get so happy, I want to dance around the house. Or else roll up my dress and wade in the bayou. Hot summers nights I lay me down and bathe. If it's coolish, I heat a kettle and pour it into the trough (I keep fresh water sitting there all day, drawing in heat, but Burr leave it scummy dirty). Take me a long, soaking bath. Wash that man right out of my hair like the gal sings on Miss Harriet's machine. I'll lather with French soaps Miss Edith give me, what I keep hid under the bed. A woman ought not to be this happy without a man.

Tonight I got me a hankering for beaten biscuits and raspberry jelly. Some days I can eat two dozen, but Burr say they takes too long to make. And they ain't so easy. You need lots of time, a tree stump, and a mallet. Some folks cover up the stump with a clean rag or waxed paper, but I don't. Just wipe your stump clean. Mix 3 3/4 cups flour, 1 t. salt, 1/8 t. baking soda. Then rub in a hunk of shortening. Slowly add 1 cup milk. A hollow biscuit bowl is good to use. The dough should feel stiff. Knead till smooth, and shape into a ball. Put ball on a tree stump and beat it with a mallet. Shape into a ball again and beat flat, the same way he beats me. Roll into a ball, feel his hands all over me, God did not mean for a man to do this to a woman.

Keep doing this—shaping and hitting—over and over till the dough blisters, about one half hour. Sometimes he beats me till my skin is tight. I just lay there on the floor, let him move me any way he wants. Feel his hand thumping thumping, *I'll shape you yet, woman. I'll straighten you out.* Just roll out the dough, cut into circles the size of half-dollars (a half-pint jar lid works best, but you can use a cookie cutter if you like). Then lay flat on the pan. Keep working the dough, rolling and cutting, until there's nothing left. Bake till brown, about thirty minutes. After a little practice, you'll know when your biscuits should come out the oven. You'll know when they've had enough.

Tonight I take my dough ball, carry it outside to the stump, and whack it with the mallet. Way off to the bayou I hear a dog bark. A hoot owl hollers. The night feels cool on my arms. The dough feels like a part of my body that's broke off. I pretend I live all by myself, happy as can be, maybe a few cats for company. Imagine being able to eat jelly and biscuits if that's all you want. Imagine being that free. Two, three times a month I can count on a whipping. Come to work and can't see to clean, got bruises up and down my side like somebody been marching. Marching to Zion. I believe with all my heart that I bring on these beatings. I egg him on, fight back, say *You no-good nigger, you son of a bitch*. Of course he strikes back. Of course, he does. If I could get hold of my tongue and not sass, then I would not get hurt.

Once Miss Vangie bought me and her matching white sandals and dresses printed with sailboats. "Where you get them clothes?" Burr hollered. "Where you get them shoes?"

"Miss Vangie give them to me."

"Don't you lie to me." He balled up his fists. "Ain't no white lady give you something new. Some man buyed it."

Next time I saw Miss Vangie, I handed her the shoes and the dress. Said, "Miss, I'm sorry. I appreciate it so much, but my husband won't let me take this." One side of my face mashed in, the other size oozing. My arm hitched up like a broken tree.

All my ladies, even Miss Harriet, they ask, "Sophie, why do you stay?"

"I don't know what you mean," I tell them. It shames me to explain. They don't see how it is. All those years I stayed because I loved him and because I thought he'd change and because I was scared and had no money and because it was easier than leaving and because I had no place to go and he was so pretty and he played the ukelele like Muddy Waters and we had kids to raise and he'd pick wildflowers and take me canoe-riding down Bayou Maçon, the mist rising up, swallowing us whole. I stayed for all these reasons, but how do you explain?

So I'd look at those ladies, those kind women bringing poultices for my busted eyes and lips, and I'd say, "I fell off the porch."

Afterward, he lays his head on my lap and cries like he's the one been beat. He digs his fingers into my legs and holds on. Says, "Baby, I'm sorry, I didn't mean it. I'll never lay a hand on you again."

And you want so bad to believe. So you try and you try and you try, and then you're old and everything's the same—there's still no money and noplace to go. You're still here, you're alive, and you see there never was anyplace you could run. Mama died not too long after I married Burr, and my sisters, they all poor like me. They would have took me in, but I knew I'd be one more mouth to feed. Truth be told, my pride was bigger than my hurt— I'd just as soon died as let them know what-all he done to me.

So I'd look at my ladies and answer them back with music. Just start humming and singing, filling my chest and letting the pain come out in hymns. *There is a balm in Gilead,* I'd sing. The good Lord knew what He was doing when He made music. I just don't think He was paying full attention when He made Burr. A hard life makes for a hard man sometime. Burr lives on the river, and he fight it like he fight me. Sometimes he brings mens home and they play the banjo. Says to me, *Listen to this song, Sophie baby. Come here and sit by me and listen.*

Long time ago, years ago, a white man strung up Burr's mama in a smoke shed and beat her till the blood dripped on the dirt floor. Beat her till she matched the hogs hanging from the rafters. All because she talked with her eyes to a picker. "Pickers and house nigras don't mingle," the white man said and laid her back open with a razor strap. It was 1905. White man give her ten cents a day for mopping, waxing, shining, stirring, kneading, baking, washing. Wiping dirty faces of the white lady's children, sometimes feeding them from her own breast. She had ten kids of her own, and another hanging on her titty wasn't more than a tick sucking her blood.

Burr's mama fell sick in the white lady's kitchen. A vein busted in her leg, and she bled all over the floor. She saw what was happening and tried to wrap herself with an oilcloth. That's how they dragged her out, with the back of her head hitting each wooden step. Then they laid her on the ground. She was still alive, but they left her there in the boiling sun, with green flies swarming and the whole dizzy world spinning.

"She can lie here till her people come in from the field," the white lady said. "She has gone and ruined my kitchen."

Burr's mama died on a Tuesday, but they had to wait till Sunday to bury her. It was the only day people could get off work to dig the grave and have the funeral. At the end of planting season they all moved south, to work the sugarcane. Burr's daddy, his grandmama, and all ten kids. Four months later, Burr's daddy married a high-strung woman, somebody to braid hair and fry breakfast and do the wash. Sweep out the yard. Fifteen months later Burr's daddy died, and the stepmama she took off. Soon as they lowered his coffin into the hole, that woman was gone. She got into a car with Alabama tags, and they never saw her again.

The grandmama was too old to raise tomatoes, much less ten kids. The oldest ones didn't want to be saddled. They took off too. Burr went into the Mississippi Delta with his sister Clynell. He was seven year old. Picked cotton fourteen, fifteen hours a day. Picked beans, okra, corn, and strawberries for five cents a quart. He grew tall and strong. Fished when he could, brought Clynell bass, crappie, bluegill, turtles, frog legs. Stayed up all night running trot lines. By then Clynell have four kids and her husband always beating up on them. Taking out his grief, holding Burr's head in the water trough until the bubbles stopped. Then yanked him up, water streaming down. When Burr was thirteen he took off. He was his own man, and the whole river was his and all the frogs and fish and turtles and animals that came to drink. The river was his home.

Me, I had a sweet life. I was born in Natchitoches, the youngest of three daughters. Mama had a child before and after me, but they got lung fever and died. All my life Mama did days work. Daddy was a farrier. Shoed everybody's horses until the Depression and folks had to let their horses go unshod, or else found somebody in the family to do it. Daddy went round selling figs door-to-door, ten cents a bucket to white ladies. Sometimes they'd make him sit all day on the back steps while they rustled up their money. Just let him sit there, like they hated to pay him after they took the figs. In 1931, the day after Easter, he was carrying two buckets and just keeled over. Just dropped to the sidewalk, not a mark on him, figs rolling everywhere. They said his heart give out.

Not six months later, Mama took sick with rheumatism and had to give up her days work. She would sit on the porch and rock, her fingers and knees swelled up double. My sisters took over Mama's houses. The oldest sister, Mary Annie, left her kids for me to watch. She was a widow. I'd get the little boys to pick figs, and we'd peddle up and down the streets. Sometimes we'd go to Front Street and search the bricks for lost pennies and dimes. Sometimes we'd walk by Cane River Lake on the grassy banks. In some places cotton grew nearly to the water. Years back the Red River up and left its channel and carved out a new one, five miles from Natchitoches. They built dams at both ends. Turned the old channel into a lake clearer than what used to be.

Then Burr Donnell come to town. Shift my life like a riverbed. Lord, he was handsome. He stood up in church and said he was a widower with two boys and a little old girl. Said they was from Mississippi and come over here after his wife died. Then he started coming round, sitting on the porch with Mama.

We couldn't figure which sister he was sweet on. I didn't see how he could study about love when he'd just buried his wife. Then somebody said she'd been dead three years. Like that made it all right. "If my husband died," I said, "I'd never remarry."

"Huh." Maroon snorted. "You'll never *get* married. "

Everybody like to fell over when they saw it was me he wanted. Little old ugly me with gap teeth and crooked toes. I'd be inside sewing, and he'd stop in front of our house, open the gate, and walk up to the porch. Say, "Where's that little one at? The one you call Sophie?"

I got up from the machine and looked out the window. "Probably she gone," Maroon said, rolling her eyes. She was two years older than me, but she got polio and one leg shrunk up. It made her mean, even though her face was so pretty you had to be careful when you looked at her. It was like you was falling in.

"I got a song I wrote for her." Burr rubbed his ukelele. "Tell her I come to play it special."

My big sister Mary Annie grabbed my arm and pushed me out the door. Then she stood in front of it so I couldn't run back in. I stood there blinking at them—Mama, Mary Annie, Maroon, Burr, and his kids.

"Miss Sophie! There you are!" His whole face lit up. Maroon twisted her mouth, then limped over to the glider. He commenced to playing and singing the prettiest song I ever did hear. I didn't know what he wanted with me, but whatever it was, I wasn't letting him have it. I'd seen how men sidled up to my sisters, making promises and sweet eyes. Next thing you knew they was gone. Mary Annie said that nobody wanted a wife with times so hard. The Depression changed us all. Whenever I got a hankering for something, I pretended like I didn't want it. This way I could ease my mind. Once Mary Annie and me seen a picture of Sonja Henie, and we got it in our heads we wanted skates. Mama laughed and said, "Where you going to get some ice in Natchitoches, you crazy girls?" I made myself think about bloody knees. A cold hard froze lake cracking open, sucking me down. Mary Annie, she don't think of nothing; she cried for them skates.

When Burr finished singing, Mama sent my sisters into the kitchen for ice tea. I got up too, but she grabbed my dress and yanked me back to the chair. Then, rubbing her wrist, she looked Burr Donnell up and down. "How'd you end up in Natchitoches?" she asked.

"Oh, just drifted from river to river," he said.

"Cane River ain't no river," I told him. I was feeling sassy. "It's a big old lake."

"Lord, yes," he said. "The very biggest."

"So how'd you get here?"

"I just did. We was on our way to Texas, and this seemed like a good place to stop."

"Well, it's not."

"I think it is."

I looked him square in the eyes, trying to see if he was lying. I couldn't tell. Then he smiled. Lord, he was pretty—big old eyes and dimples deep enough for you to put a finger inside. But I knew you couldn't trust no pretty man. I was scared he'd leave me with them kids and run off, chasing womens and rivers. A lady mama used to work for, that happened to her.

"You're awful quiet, Miss Sophie," he said, grinning at me.

"No, I'm just sick of looking at your face."

"Sophie!" Mama cried.

"And," I said, "you don't smell too good." I got up and went into the house, leaving Mama squawking, hollering for me to come back and apologize. From then on, when he came round, he reeked of cologne. He always brought Mama a string of catfish or a mess of greens wrapped up in newspaper. Made his kids carry them. Then he'd get to bragging on Mama. Said she made the best butter he'd ever tasted—how'd she do that?

"Same as anybody," Mama said. "Out of clabber."

"Yours is something special, though." He leaned forward. "And your buttermilk can't be beat."

"I always add a pinch of soda to my buttermilk—cuts down on the sourness."

"Is that a fact," he said, then turned round and smiled at me. I was real suspicious; why he like me? I wasn't pretty like Maroon, and I wasn't shapely like Mary Annie. Both my sisters had mens hanging round the house, but nobody ever came to call on me. Burr would sit on the porch with Mama, sipping tea, letting his kids play hide-'n'-seek, waiting for me to show. Whole hours went by. He ignored my sisters when they pranced by saying, "Mr. Donnell, you want more spice cake? Want me to freshen your tea?"

"No, thank you," he'd say. "No, thank you."

One night he left, and Mama hollered for me to get myself downstairs. "You have broke poor Burr Donnell's heart," she said.

"How?" I hung back in the shadows. "I don't even know him."

"He wants to marry you."

"Why?"

"'Cause he love you."

"He's lying." My eyes filled. "He don't love me. And you can't make me marry him. He's nothing but an old river coot. He won't stay round here."

"He's a fine man, a real fine man." Mama nodded. "Handsome, too. Did you hear him playing the ukelele for me?"

"No."

"Then you missed something good. I always said you can trust a man who plays the ukelele."

"Then you marry him."

Mama raised up from her chair and slapped me so hard she hurt her hand. She grabbed her wrist and moaned. With those swolled hands of hers, I knew it had to hurt. "But Mama," I said, squeezing back tears. "He's too *old* for me. Besides, he's a widower with children. Three routy children. I don't want to saddle myself with that!"

"Why not?" Mama settled back in her chair and propped her wrist on her lap.

"It's too hard, that's why."

"You let him slip by, and you'll be sorry."

"No, I won't!"

"You will when there's no food to go around. You will when I'm dead and you ain't got no husband."

He kept coming around, but I hid upstairs. Told everybody I didn't love him and nobody could make me. My sisters took turns bringing him pie and ice tea, then slipped back into the kitchen, holding their breaths, waiting for him to ask after them. I could hear them clear up to my room, so I know Burr had to hear, too. "He's got a thing *this long*. I seen it through his pants," they whispered, hopping on one leg with their fingers crossed. "Ooooo, I'll bet it'd bust you wide open!"

"How's Miss Sophie?" he said.

"Same as yesterday." Mama laughed a little.

"Think she'll come out?"

"Maybe."

"I'll just play a song, and maybe she'll get curious." He put the ukelele in his lap and started tuning it, playing sour cords. Then he began humming. When I couldn't stand it no longer, I crawled on the roof and listened. I scooted way down and leaned over, catching a glimpse of him. His eyes were closed, but his fingers whisked up and down the ukelele. Out in the yard, his children ran in circles, throwing pecans at each other. I shut my eyes and said, "Lord, take me now, just take me."

Burr kept coming and coming. It was like the more I wouldn't see him, the harder he had to try. I'd lay on the roof and listen to him sing and talk. "She just shy," he told Mama.

"But I'll bet she sweet." Mama agreed with everything and then turned right around and told more lies. Said how much I love and swoon over him.

He believed every word. He blushed and preened.

"You needs a wife," she said. "Your kids needs a mama."

"Yes, ma'am. It's a hard life."

"I got me some other girls," Mama said, nodding toward the house. "Sophie, she think too much. Some girls think until they wear they insides out."

"Yes, ma'am. I know." He paused. Took a long swallow of tea, then set the glass on his leg, leaving a damp circle. "You think Miss Sophie fixing to come out in a minute?"

"Why you keep asking me that?" Mama acted like she was mad, but she was enjoying every minute.

"You think she will?"

"Don't look like it to me."

"Then I'll just wait a while longer," he said.

Mama rocked for several minutes. Then she said, "Mr. Donnell? You been saved?"

"Saved?" Burr raised his eyebrows and lifted his hand, smoothing the back of his head. "A couple of times. I sure have."

"How many?" Mama stopped rocking.

"Well, one time I fell off a boat south of Memphis. Two mens dragged me out the river with a cane pole. Another time I got heat stroke cutting cane—"

"No, no!" Mama waved one hand. "I mean *saved*. As in Jesus Christ, your personal Savior."

"Ohhhh." Burr rubbed his chin. "*That* kind of saved."

"Well?" Mama cut her eyes at him. "Have you been?"

"I don't recall that I have." Burr's forehead wrinkled, like he was trying to remember something. "No, ma'am. I guess not."

"No girl of mine marries a man who ain't been saved."

"I can do that."

"No need to unless Sophie come down." Mama laughed. "Your glass is empty, Mr. Donnell."

"It is?" He lifted the glass. "Well, it sure is. I've done drunk it up."

"Do you want more?"

"If it ain't trouble."

"You, Maroon!" Mama hollered, and a second later, almost too fast, my sister limped out the door. "Fetch Mr. Donnell another glass of tea."

As soon as Maroon left, Mama said, "Now, she a good one. She had polio, but she still a pretty thing."

"Yes, ma'am."

"She'll come out here and sit with you."

"That's awful nice, but I'd just as soon wait for Sophie."

"Don't hold your breath. She stubborn."

"Yes, ma'am." He laughed. "I like stubborn."

Maroon opened the screen door, and I scooted farther down the roof. I watched her hand Burr the ice tea, then she stepped back and clasped her hands. "Want anything else?" she asked him.

"Well, would it trouble you to see what Miss Sophie is doing?"

Maroon's eyes narrowed. Then she walked to the edge of the porch and looked up into the mimosa tree. I was afraid she'd see me, so I scooted back, and my bare leg scraped against the tin roof. Maroon's head jerked up. Her mouth fell open, and she pointed up at me, her eyes two little slits. "Well, if this don't beat all," she said. "Sophie, what you doing up there? Spying?"

Inside the house, I heard Mary Annie and her kids running to look out the window. I scrambled up the roof, but the hem of my dress caught on a nail and yanked me back down. I lost my balance and skidded down the roof, the rumpled tin banging against my bottom. And then I was in the air, headed straight toward the mimosa tree. I fell splat into the branches, shaking down a film of pink fuzz.

Mama and Burr gaped up at me. Even his kids stopped throwing pecans to look. I took a strong breath, climbed down, and walked straight into the house, like this was something I did every single day.

"That's some girl," Burr said, laughing and shaking his head. "That's some *fine* girl."

Next day he came with flowers. Day after that he came with candies. He came with his children dress up all wrong, and that's what finally got to me. I braided my hair and put on a blue-flow-ered dress. Walked down the stairs, straight outside, and sat down in the glider. I wouldn't look at Burr to save my soul. The little girl's hair was all tangled. I got a comb and started working real easy, telling her how pretty she was going to look.

"Ain't that the truth," Mama said. "You listen to Sophie, now. She knows how to fix up little girls."

The little boys peek through the porch rail. From the corner of my eye I see Mama and Burr grinning. Next thing you know, I'm a bride, but first Mama made him get dunked in Cane River Lake. We had us a big picnic, food laid out on quilts—fried chicken, potato salad, devil eggs, three kinds of slaw, sliced ham, red velvet cake, lemon meringue and chess pies. Burr's children dress up in white, wading out in the river, mud squishing between their toes. Somebody was playing the harmonica, somebody else shaking cowbells. Both my sisters was dancing barefoot. I looked over at Burr and took his hand. He gave me a smile that was so pretty I had to shut my eyes. A hankering washed over me so strong it almost felt like pain.

They is nothing better than biscuits and jelly made by your own hand. I don't even fix me a plate, eat straight from the pan, licking butter from my fingers. Then I go outside to wash. Crickets screeching like something after them—a bunch of bad boys with jars. I dip water into a pan, splash it on my face, and let it drip down my neck. Then I hold up my hands. Burr used to fit my palm up against his and say, "Look how little!" Now they big-boned with short, thick nails. The backs of my hands are scarred, cuts and grease burns. My whole body seems to have growed like it knew it needed extra. Everything on this earth always changing, trying to stay alive, trying to be what it thinks you want, even your own self.

I pour the dirty water through a lattice trellis where I got lemon trees planted. After years of getting drenched with sudsy water, don't you know my lemons taste soapy? I go back inside the house and change into one of Miss Harriet's old gowns, one of Hooper's finest. Slide under the cool sheets, pull up the scrap quilt. If he ain't here tomorrow, I'll fry me some cabbage. First, take you a iron skillet and fry some bacon. Cut your cabbage into hunks, and lay in the skillet. Heat and stir till it's all brown. Crumble bacon on top. Serve with corn bread and beet pickles.

I sing myself to sleep, but all around me is the voice of my Jesus, loud and clear. This is a voice I need to hear when I lay me down to sleep. He says, *There is a balm in Gilead, oh, Lord, yes, to make the wounded whole. There is a balm in Gilead to heal the sin-sick soul. If you can't preach like Peter, if you can't pray like Paul, Just tell the love of Jesus, And say He died for all.*

Hallelujah.

How It Spreads

◣

*Remember the time Olive Nepper went with us on that youth
hayride? She was the only Baptist, so naturally she stood out. Timmy
Johnson's cousin invited her. I forget his name, but he was blue-eyed
with a hair-lip scar. Anyway, on the way back, Olive pulled a blanket
over their heads, but you could see them wiggling under the wool. All
the Methodist girls passed the word: "Psst! When Olive comes up for
air, lets all stare her down!" So when she pulled off the blanket, straw
was sticking out of her hair like those spokes on the Statue of Liberty.
All her lipstick was kissed off. "What y'all staring at?" she said. I
spoke on behalf of all the Christian youths. "Nothing," I said, narrowing my eyes. "We're looking at* nothing."

—MARY FRANCES MARSHALL, NIECE OF MAMIE AND MERE-
DITH, M.Y.F. MEETING, MARCH 1952

Olive Nepper's room faced Delphinium Street, and all afternoon
boys rode bicycles up and down the sidewalk, causing old ladies to
holler, "You devils! Look out, or I'll tell your mamas!" Sometimes
the women walked in the evening—"Walking off pie," they said, but
they loved to look inside the hospital. The windows showed relatives sprawled out on chairs, nurses whisking by with blue plastic
trays. It was the next best thing to owning a television.

Through Olive's window it was possible to see everything: all
the vases of daffodils, redbuds, and hothouse roses; the get well
cards taped in crooked rows along the wall, next to the picture of
President Truman; the bumpy yellow-and-cream afghan folded on
a vinyl chair, next to a wrinkled *Collier's*. A log-cabin quilt, made
by Vangie's Grandma Galliard, was folded on the bed; a metal
table held a pan of steaming water and a tiny bar of Ivory soap. A
thick-wristed nurse crossed the room and drew the curtains.
Then she dropped a rag into the water. Her name was Nurse Abi-

gail Potter, and for some days now she had been bathing Olive with considerable suspicion. There was something disturbing about the fullness of the girl's breasts, mapped by crooked, blue veins—a classic sign of pregnancy.

"Surely not, she's only sixteen," Abigail Potter muttered. Then she lifted Olive's gown and palpated her pelvic bone. She felt a lump, all right, the size of a lemon.

"Oh, I don't believe this!" She tossed the rag into the pan. Drops of gray water sprayed across the table. Abigail hurried out of the room, walking past the girl's mother, who was slumped over in one of the green vinyl chairs, and headed toward the nurses' station.

"We've got a problem," she told Nurse Clayton, who followed her back to Olive's room. Miss Clayton made a cursory examination, then looked up at Nurse Potter.

"Looks like three, maybe four months," she said. "But it could be two. Especially if it's twins. You'd better call Dr. LeGette."

Nurse Potter rushed out to the nurses' station and called the doctor, her face swollen with importance. The other nurses crowded around her. "The Nepper girl's pregnant," she crowed, then rushed down the hall. She smiled at the girl's mother, taking in her wrinkled shirtwaist dress and saggy jelly-roll stockings. "We're almost through bathing her," Nurse Potter said and shut the door. She was an old army nurse and had never adjusted to civilian life. It seemed to her that the rest of the world would benefit if they adjusted to *her*.

Behind the door, she heard Mrs. Nepper's timid knock. She ignored it. One thing they didn't teach you in nursing school, she thought, was to be quick and slippery with patients' families. She learned that at the veterans hospital, when she was responsible for seventeen sick soldiers, all with mamas, daddies, wives, and cousins. It was sickening, all those people. She learned to smile and say, "Visiting hours are over." Then she'd glare at the assorted relatives until they backed out of the ward.

Now she sagged against the door and cleared her throat, getting Nurse Clayton's attention. "What a pity," she said. "Sixteen years old and pregnant."

"Either that or a tumor," said Nurse Clayton, looking down at Olive, whose eyelids were stitched with tiny pink veins, like a sleeping bird.

"Her daddy fills my prescriptions." Nurse Potter crossed her arms.

"He fills everybody's." Nurse Clayton sighed. "Wonder if the poor little thing even knows she's pregnant?"

"Poor thing, my foot!" Nurse Potter stepped over to the bed. "She ought to be spanked."

"Bet that's why she drank the poison."

"Could be. You know what's next, don't you? Dr. LeGette's got to break the news to the Neppers."

Nurse Clayton rolled her eyes. "Sure hope I ain't around to hear."

"Me neither."

"The poor child's in a fix."

"Lord, she's *been* in one," Nurse Potter said. "Unless you call a coma a picnic."

"Wonder who the daddy is?"

"No telling. Could be anybody. Probably some boy she went to school with. It's always something like that. Let's hope she don't die before we find out."

"Oh, hush. You're awful." Nurse Clayton scowled, then straightened her uniform over her broad hips. "We'll find out. Nurses find out everything."

"I don't know." Nurse Potter shrugged. "Sometimes we do, sometimes we don't."

From the iron bed, Olive's forehead wrinkled. Her eyelids fluttered, and she saw scuffed green walls. Two angels in white gowns were arguing, their wings folded on their heads, which seemed a brilliant evolution. Then Olive's eyes closed and she drifted. Her body was light as paper, wafting in sweet air. She returned to a cold morning in December, contrary weather for northeast Louisiana. It was Sunday. She sat in the second pew at First Baptist. Sleet hit the stained-glass windows like rice poured into a bowl, but the ground was too warm for it to stick. Someday she wanted to live in a place where it snowed and *stayed* on the ground.

The reverend looked straight at her for the better part of the sermon. When the organist played "Just As I Am," her fingers stabbing ivory keys, T. C. Kirby's voice pierced Olive's heart. She looked at the blue-eyed man, and everything fell silent, sucked up into the heat of his glare, as if he were the Lord Himself, calling His sinners home. He spoke of love, redemption, and forgiveness.

It was his talk of love that got to her. She thought about standing up, working her way down the aisle, defying her mother to dedicate her life to Jesus for the fifth time in six months. ("It's getting to be a habit with you," Vangie had complained.) Just as she uncrossed her legs and started to rise, a wide-hipped girl beat her to it. Little Waynetta Dawn Hooper, Harriet's niece. Waynetta waddled down the aisle toward the altar and collapsed against the reverend.

"Yea, brethren," he said, grasping the girl's chubby arms. "Be washed in the blood of the lamb. Walk forward and renew yourself in Christ almighty. Walk forward into love and salvation."

The hairs lifted on Olive's arms. Then T. C. Kirby stared at her. "Don't be afraid," he said, "Come on up. No one is looking."

Every afternoon she walked over to the parsonage to discuss the upcoming choir trip to Lookout Mountain. She and Reverend Kirby drank tea laced with honey, and he told her about his dream of being a famous evangelist, bigger than Billy Graham, even. "I was born on a chicken farm," he admitted, "but I was meant for indoor work." He held up his hands. They were smoother than Olive's, and when she touched him, she thought it was like sticking her hand into a bowl of warm peaches. He leaned across the kitchen table, sliding his hand under her hair, and pulled her toward him. She clung to him, digging her fingers into his shirt.

He led her into his dusky gray bedroom and gently pushed her onto the narrow bed. He pulled off her shoes and socks and kissed the backs of her knees. Then he lay down beside her, running one hand up and down her arm. "I have fallen for you, Olive," he whispered. "I want to kiss you so bad, but you mustn't tell. I'll have to leave Limoges if this gets out."

She nodded, then licked her lips. "I won't tell."

They crushed their hips together through layers of cotton, leaving her sweaty and breathless. Then he pulled back, blinking. "We've got to be extra careful," he said. "Or we'll make a baby. Has your mama talked to you about this?"

Olive nodded, then shook her head. "She hasn't told me a thing," she confessed.

"Well, that's all right. Babies are real simple to avoid. I just can't spill my seeds in you."

"Seeds?" she asked, thinking of her mama's nasturtiums and zinnias.

"I've got them deep inside me." He unzipped his trousers, pushed them down, and guided her hand to his erection, sucking in air when her fingers circled him.

"Do you want to see these seeds?" he said, smiling when she nodded.

"Then squeeze me." He grabbed her wrist, jiggling it up and down. She watched his face as he ejaculated into a tea towel. His mouth opened and his eyelids fluttered, briefly shutting out his gaze. The towel, she knew, was washed and ironed every Thursday by volunteers from the church. A bachelor preacher was a delight to the ladies, and Reverend Kirby was well tended by his flock.

On the choir trip to Tennessee, hidden from the others, he pulled down her panties. When he kissed her, she felt something swing inside her chest, like a wrecking ball. When he reached between her legs, she thought, *No, don't touch me there mama said never let him don't you know it's wrong?* As he moved on top of her, she was filled with a deeply ingrained, almost biblical sense of shame. *This is nasty, this hurts.* It was not at all what she'd expected, but it was irreversible, like stepping off a bridge, plunging into fast water. What's done is done. You can't go back and change it, the way you can in dreams.

Afterward, he quoted from the Bible, explaining how Onan spilled his seed. How she had saved him, Kirby, from the shame of self-love and gratification.

"They weren't talking about sunflowers," Olive thought.

"I'd just as soon Vangie not know," Henry told Phillip Le-Gette. They stood outside Olive's room, in the green-tinged hall where cafeteria workers pushed carts full of steaming blue trays. The air smelled of roast beef, gravy, corn bread.

"I don't advise that." Phillip jammed his hands into the deep pockets of his lab coat. "If Olive comes out of this coma, how will you explain a baby? And even if she doesn't wake up, Vangie's bound to find out. She's got eyes. Olive will be showing before too long."

"Wonder if she got raped? Some boy could've forced himself on her and she was scared to tell us. Goddammit, I'll kill the bastard."

Phillip lifted his shoulders and glanced down at the floor, counting specks in the tile.

"I'm just protecting her for a little while," Henry said. "As long as I can. Vangie might go crazy if she thinks her baby was. . . . What if your Fanny was lying up in that room?"

"You're asking something I can't answer." Phillip's brows puckered; he didn't want to get caught in the middle, between husband and wife.

"She's better off, believe me," Henry was saying. "If she knew our little girl had been you-know-whatted, well, she'd lose her mind. You know how Vangie is. She's almost like having another daughter."

Phillip let this pass. He scratched the side of his nose. "What'll you do when the news gets back to Vangie?" he finally asked. "And just about everything comes to light in Limoges, sooner or later."

"Not everything." Henry lifted his chin, then a smile creased his face. "Remember when Olive was just a tiny thing, and Vangie used to bring her up to the store and set her in a drawer? Do you remember that, Phillip? We used to laugh and say she was raised in a drawer."

"I do remember."

"Is she ever going to come out of this coma?"

"All we can do is keep her in the oxygen tent for now, to help her breath better. And wait."

A nurse with a black moustache and thick wrists came to the door. "Dr. LeGette? They're ready for you to scrub in OR."

"Thanks, Nurse Potter. I'll be right there." He turned back to Henry and spread his hands. "I've got an emergency appendectomy waiting in the operating room. A little bitty boy. Let me know if you change your mind."

"I won't," Henry said. He left the hospital, climbed into his Rambler, and drove to his store. His mind switched gears, and he turned back into Henry the Pharmacist, dispenser of cough syrups, purgatives, tonics, and banana splits.

This same spring, the community was stricken with *Haemophilus influenzae*, a particularly virulent strain that settles in the lung and bone. When Nurse Abigail Potter finished her shift at Parish Hospital, she sneezed five times before she reached her car in the gravel lot.

"Must be my allergy," she told herself, reaching in her purse for a Kleenex. Ash trees were budding, and the air was thick with pollen. By the time she got home, the backs of her calves were starting to ache. She walked stiff-legged to the mailbox and waved to Imogene O'Neal, who looked smart in her winter-brown suit with the square buttons, bought on sale at Hooper's. Imogene knew she'd look snazzy at the Jesters for Jesus meeting down at First Baptist.

"How's things at Parish Hospital?" Imogene called out.

"Terrible," said Nurse Potter. "Flu's everywhere. We had to do an emergency appendectomy on a four-year-old boy. And you *won't* believe this, but the Nepper girl is pregnant."

"No!"

"I'm not lying. That's why she tried to kill herself."

"Henry Nepper's girl is *expecting*?" asked Imogene, her bottom lip trembling. Thoughts tossed in her brain like ripe blueberries. She thought she'd burst before she got to First Baptist, where Harriet Hooper had promised to save her a seat.

"She's expecting something, all right." Nurse Potter nodded.

"P-r-e-g-n-a-n-t?" Imogene twirled a button on her jacket. After three boys and one miscarriage, she still couldn't bring herself to say the word.

"As a heifer," said Nurse Potter.

Five hours after Abigail Potter's conversation with Imogene O'Neal, every single woman at Jesters for Jesus knew about the pregnancy. One of the women, Miss Zinnia Wilson, the telephone operator and one of the few genuine misses in town—she was proud to say that she'd never kissed a man, never cared to—leaned over Harriet, who'd just arrived, and said, "Has Imogene told you?"

"Told me what?"

"Guess who's pregnant?" Zinnia's face swelled.

"You?" Harriet giggled.

"No, your neighbor's child."

"Which one?" Harriet's face turned ripe pink.

"Henry Nepper's girl."

Harriet's mouth fell open. She stood and pointed across the room, at Imogene. "I'm going to kill you for not telling me first!" she cried.

"You weren't here, or else I would've." Imogene said indignantly. "You were *supposed* to save me a seat."

"And you could have waited!" Harriet's eyes filled. She was so humiliated, she wanted to snatch Imogene bald-headed.

Miss Faye Hooper, Leonard's old mama, pinched her daughter-in-law's chubby arm and hissed, "What? What did she tell you?"

Zinnia Wilson left the meeting early, heading for Beaulieu Funeral Home to pay her respects to the Matheny family. Old Carl Matheny had fallen into the hog pen, leaving behind a bereaved widow, ten children, and thirty-six grandchildren. The Louisiana Room was packed with neighbors and friends. Carl's casket was closed, which, if the truth be told, disappointed Zinnia: She was an old maid, but she wasn't a shrinking violet; she liked blood and gore the same as any man. She made rounds in the viewing room, hopping from row to row, speaking to every mourner. She gave the undertaker, Cab Beaulieu, a wide berth. He made her flesh crawl, handling dead bodies and probably a good bit more. She talked to several Methodists and a whole slew of Baptists, going into detail about the poor little Nepper girl, adding—she couldn't help but embellish a good story—that Olive was carrying Siamese twins, thanks to the poison she swallowed. Zinnia had heard of a similar incident at the Jefferson Parish Fair in 1941.

"Joined at the hip," she said, clucking her tongue. "Or maybe the brain."

Mrs. Hattie Lou Whitlow, sister-in-law of the deceased, pulled herself away from the clutch of women. She didn't believe in Siamese twins. Zinnia Wilson didn't know the world was turning. Hattie Lou walked three blocks to Becky Trammel's house to buy a sack of pecans and have a cup of coffee. Hattie Lou baked cakes for everybody in town—birthdays, weddings, anniversaries, and seasonal—and when people called her the Cake Lady, she just chuckled. She was more than that, and she knew it. Without her cakes, no one in Limoges would have a decent birthday.

She had bought her pecans from Becky Trammel since 1923, when Coolidge was president. She accepted a slice of Becky's famous praline pie, but she couldn't get the Nepper girl out of her mind. During her visit with the Trammels, she drank two cups of coffee and told both Becky and Jimmy the wretched news. Then she held out her plate for another slice of pie.

The next morning, Jimmy Trammel stopped at Butter's Cafe to deliver a sack of pecans. Butter poured him a cup of coffee and plunked down his usual, a plate of bacon, grits, biscuits, hash browns, and two eggs sunny-side up. "What's the latest?" Butter asked, leaning across the red Formica counter, lighting a cigarette. She knew Becky Trammel had a long, sticky tongue, like flypaper; Butter could always count on Jimmy to keep her up-to-date on scandals, robberies, and beatings. In the course of the meal he told Butter, two waitresses, three mechanics in the corner booth, and the man who came in to deliver Moon Pies.

The Moon Pie man lived with his mother, Alice Womack, on Hayes Avenue, next door to Butter DeWitt and those loud-mouthed Robichauxes. Alice was recovering from the spring flu, thanks to her good neighbors who'd brought over bowls of chicken soup. The next morning she worked her way down Hayes Avenue, returning bowls, catching up on news, and exchanging gossip.

That spring, the influenza virus (not to mention measles, polio, and tuberculosis) was on everyone's mind. "The flu is a thief in the night," Alice told her neighbors. Everyone on Hayes Avenue agreed; they had come to dread the sight of Beaulieu's hearse, which doubled as an ambulance.

"Hope and pray it's not somebody with polio," they'd say, and run inside, slamming the doors, yanking down window shades. They feared germs the same way they feared the Red Chinese, who were slaughtering Americans this very minute over in Korea. The *Times-Picayune* explained that a virus was invisible to the naked eye, small enough to squeeze through a cell membrane and set up headquarters in the cell, replicating a malevolent version of itself. The virus streamed from the afflicted person's mouth and became airborne, like tiny paratroopers. The germs stuck to doorknobs, telephones, the handle of your refrigerator, spreading from person to person, hand to mouth, lip to ear, tongue to tongue. From house to house, neighbor to neighbor, lover to lover, husband to wife.

Gossip is clear as air, hissing through open windows like sound inside a conch shell. "I heard she was raped," someone said.

"A nigger broke through the window," said another.

"That baby'll be black as tar."

"The poison caused it to split into twins."

"One's white, one's colored."

"No wonder she drank poison."

"What a shame."

"What a sin."

"Let us pray."

"It's just not safe to go outdoors," Alice Womack told Butter, who was sitting on the front porch, braiding Billie Robichaux's hair. "You just never know what's lurking in the air."

"Anything could be." Butter looked down the length of Hayes Avenue, where her niece was walking home from work. DeeDee stopped and leaned over a forsythia, pushing her face into blooming yellow bells like she didn't have a care in the world. It broke Butter's heart when the girl quit the cafe and went to work at Nepper's Drugs last summer. When you have a family business, you like to keep it in the family.

Billie saw her mama and wriggled out of Butter's grasp. She ran down the sidewalk, calling out, "Mama, Mama!"

DeeDee Robichaux knelt and held out her arms, smiling her prettiest smile. Billie leaped into her arms, and they rocked backward. "Oh, my goodness!" cried DeeDee. "We're gonna topple right over!"

The Poor Side
of Limoges

❧

One day me and DeeDee were alone in the store. Against my better judgment, she coaxed me behind the soda counter, wrapped her arms around me, and kissed me full in the mouth until I got limp-kneed. I fell over backward—whether from fear of discovery or passion, I never knew. Turned out we weren't alone. A minute later I heard a voice say, "Mama? Why you laying on top of Mr. Nepper?" I opened my eyes and saw Billie Robichaux all balanced on the counter like a frog. DeeDee squeaked and rolled off me. I smiled up at the child and said, "I tripped on a banana peel. And then your mama tripped and fell over me." "I don't see no peel," Billie said. I laughed and said, "Done picked it up. But you're fixing to see a whole bunch of peels." I told DeeDee to fix Billie the biggest banana split she'd ever made. Inside, I cringed. Bananas were a whole twenty-nine cents for two pounds. Oh, God, I thought. This thing with DeeDee could bankrupt me.

—HENRY NEPPER, TALKING TO HIMSELF IN THE SHOWER

Billie Robichaux

Supper's been over a long time, and now it's getting dark. I look up at our house and wonder what my Daddy's doing. I can't go inside on account of him, not until Mama says it's safe. Ain't nothing good to do, like play kick the can or hide 'n' seek. So I take off running with the beagle puppies. I like to run 'cause the air cools my sweaty body, and I'm going too fast and I stop being me.

Like now. It's awful dark under the trees, and I trip on a rock. My foot mashes a puppy's tail. The poor little thing squeaks and rolls over on its back. The other pups stop running and bump into each other, twisting their heads, looking up at me. I scoop up the puppy and say, "Are you hurt?"

The puppy licks my face like it has forgive me. Then I lay down, letting all the pups crawl over me, their cold noses pushing under my shirt. I'm almost happy. The thing about happy is you can't enjoy it because you know it ain't going to last. Just like the evenings here in Limoges. Before you know it, everything is dark. Now the sky is full of purplish clouds. One in particular reminds me of a girl's face, kinda like a floating princess. My mama is pretty enough to be a queen, but this princess in the sky spreads her arms and waves. I think she looks just like Olive Nepper, who is laid out at Parish Hospital. "A coma of the brain," Mama calls it. This makes me think of a giant plastic comb dropping from the sky, parting the girl's hair.

Mama sits on the porch swing, painting her toenails. Her fingernails and lips are shiny red like those patent-leather purses at Hooper's. Earlier, she said we could take a walk, maybe stop by the hospital and visit the Neppers. "Don't you mean spy?" I said.

She laughed and yanked my pigtail. "You're nine years old going on twenty," she said. This is half-true. I know the moon is 240,000 miles away, I learned me that in school, but I don't see how they measured it. Unless scientists built a giant yardstick. I know how babies are made, from s-e-x, a word I am forbidden to say, even though I do. All the time. Mama used to cry because she said she couldn't get any. I pick up lots from her and Daddy's fights, and so does half of Hayes Avenue. She says I'm growing up too fast, to slow down and be her baby for a little while longer. One minute she's holding me in her lap, weaving pink ribbons through my hair, pulling my bangs so tight, my scalp stretches. The next she's bragging that I'm a genius. "Billie rolled over *all by herself* when she was two weeks old," she'll say. "Isn't that smart?" I can't even remember that far back.

Then, when we bathe Daddy, she tells me to get that dumb, bashful look off my face, because in a few years I'll be capable of bearing live young. She really said all that. She reads *National Geographic* at Mr. Henry's store, what he sells on the magazine rack, but she won't explain. I think of goldfish at the dime store— LIVE YOUNG MOLLIES, the sign says. Sometimes the babies get ate up. "Nature's wonderful," Mama says, but under my breath I say, "Nature's crap."

As long as I can remember we have lived with Aunt Butter on 102 Hayes Avenue, close to her cafe. It's the only house I've ever known. A long time ago Mama talked about leaving Limoges, but the Korean war broke out and a Chinaman shot my daddy with artillery shrapnel. Now he's all crippled. His name is Renny Robichaux, in case you don't know. It was in all the papers. We cut everything out and pasted it into a book. He gets around Aunt Butter's house in a wooden wheelchair that nobody will let me play in.

"Paralyzed from the waist down," Mama kept whispering those days and nights after he was wounded. We were in Aunt Butter's kitchen, the crumpled telegram sitting on the table, next to a sweaty pitcher of tea. There was a tin of buttermilk pie with one wedge missing.

"Pair-a-lies?" I said, trying to feature such a thing.

Mama nodded, her eyes filling, and said, "You can't possibly know what this means, baby."

"Crippled," said Aunt Butter.

"You mean, he won't be able to run?" I squinted.

"That's the least of it!"

Mama burst into tears, and Aunt Butter said, "What's wrong with you now? Always jibbering and jabbering, like the world's ending. So *what* if he can't run! You act like he's been killed. You ought to be thankful he's coming back."

"You're an old maid." Mama wiped her eyes. "What do you know?"

"More'n you might think," said Aunt Butter. "Anyhow, I don't crave men no more."

"No?" Mama looked up. "Then, what do you crave?"

"Oh, let me see," Aunt Butter said. "Corn bread and milk. Fried okra and squash. Sweet potato pie. Pralines. Divinity fudge."

I'll tell you what I myself crave: Peach Swirl. Peel one small peach. Then stick a fork into it a whole bunch of times. Put peach into a glass and pour in 7-Up. Mama uses wine, but you don't have to. In a little while, when enough bubbles gather under the peach, it'll flip over and begin to spin around and around. After an hour or so, take the peach out and eat it.

Now the puppies lick my face and neck. Night is starting, and the sky scoots down low. Aunt Butter's guineas are roosting in the dogwoods, flapping up into high branches. We are always finding eggs under crepe myrtles and forsythias. Last summer I even found some in the bush beans—real teeny-weeny. Most everybody in this part of Limoges, the west side, is getting ready for summer, tilling gardens and burning old crops. The warm weather has tempted old ladies from their houses up and down Hayes Avenue. They wobble down the front steps, wearing cotton dusters, and plant petunias in old tires. To me, summer means hot sidewalks that burn your feet. It means mosquitoes humming in your ear, and gardens with way too many vegetables. Two or three summers ago, Mama told our neighbor, Tamera Mashburn, that our cucumbers were big as dingdongs.

"Can I have some?" I asked. I was little, five or six, and I didn't know nothing. This was before Korea. I thought maybe she was talking about food—coconut-cream Twinkies, chocolate-covered DingDongs. My stomach started growling.

"Stop listening to us," she cried sharply, her cheeks turning red. A few days later, I heard her say that Daddy's dingdong was good-sized. She was laughing on the porch with Tamera again, and four of the Mashburn kids were digging up our whole front yard. I was squatting under the steps, and I crawled out, peeping up just in time to see Tamera swipe one hand between her legs.

"I've just about had it with Karl's. He makes me kiss it!" She stuck out her tongue and crossed her eyes. "Nasty old thing of his, always poking at me every time I turn around."

Mama snorted.

"What're you all talking about?" I said, popping up and staring, my hands on my hips.

"Lord, you get out of here!" Mama lunged like she was going to chase me, but I was too fast. Later, we went walking, and she didn't mention dongs. All she could talk about was how green and pretty the east side of Limoges was, full of big, old houses that was built before the Civil War. Mama said they had lawns, not grass, and their houses was mansions. Rich women lived there, sipping iced tea from crystal goblets, while maids polished silver. If you are rich, you buy vegetables at City Market and don't have to grow your own, squatting in a weedy row with chiggers itching you to pieces.

I have a strong memory of falling in Aunt Butter's garden and gashing open my knee on the tiller. I couldn't have been more than three. When I stood up, blood streamed down my leg. I screamed for Mama, but it was my daddy who came running into the backyard. The sun pushed hard against my head, yet when my daddy lifted me, his skin felt cool. I knew I was safe. We sifted through the corn, toward the house, and he said, "Daddy will always be here for you."

He lied. He's here, but he's not the same man. Now, from the house, I hear him yelling at Mama. The neighbors slam down their windows, snatch their paper shades. I imagine him pushing his wheelchair in circles, trying to tip himself over like he did a few weeks ago. Sometimes he curls back his lip and says we have him where we want him, all of us, even Aunt Butter, who is not his blood kin. She's ours. Those first weeks after he came home from the hospital, Mama and Aunt Butter propped him up on the living room couch to watch the World Series. He laid sprawled out, his feet frozen into place. I prayed and prayed for his big toe to move, but it never did.

Now my mama stands on the porch. She cranes her neck and hollers, "Billie? Bill-*lee*!"

I crouch down with the puppies. I know what she wants. It is time to go walking and spy on the Neppers, which is getting to be a regular thing with her.

"Billie! I mean it, come on! It's getting late!" Mama's voice sounds sharp. In a minute, she will traipse into the yard and give me a spanking. I lock the puppies in the shed. Then I turn up the path, following Mama's voice all the way to the house like she's reeling me in word by word. When I reach the porch, she's sitting in the glider again, painting her toenails, one leg bent at the knee, the other dangling. She glances up, taking care not to spill polish, because this is not her house. It is very much Aunt Butter's, who is down at First Baptist learning about missionary work, to make sure she gets a front-row seat in heaven. She said she got her start by taking in Mama and Dillon after their people died of TB.

"What took you so long?" Mama shouts, watching me climb on the railing. I hang upside down from my knees, feeling blood rush to my head.

"I was praying," I say. This shuts her up. All of us is Baptists, although Butter said we're backsliders. Last Sunday, Reverend Kirby put his hand on my head. "How's Billie Robichaux?" he asked. I giggled and he said, "You come see me sometimes, and we'll pray for your daddy." Two, three times I knocked on the rectory door, but he wasn't home. I just walked down to Butter's Cafe and fixed me a cheeseburger. Her place is on the corner of Hayes and Sparrow, with plants growing in the window. It has a long, red Formica counter and a row of silver stools. The rest of the space is took up by booths, and each one has a little jukebox. You can sit there with the air conditioner blowing in your face, watching Butter draw up milk from the silver machine. No milk ever tastes as good as Butter's. It goes down cold and thick, like a vanilla milk shake.

Mama used to be a waitress there, but she hated it. "We were meant for better," she said. "We are genteel." All of us were sitting on the front porch watching cars swish by. Mama lit a cigarette and threw the match into the dusty yard. I tried to figure what ginteal was, but I couldn't. All I could feature was ducks—green winged teals flying over Lake Limoges.

"Genteel?" Aunt Butter laughed. She was stringing beans into a folded newspaper that was wedged between her knees. "You come from Texas, same as me. We was churchmice. If you want to call that *ginteel*, then go right ahead."

"I know what *you* are. I'm talking about Mama. Her mama's family goes all the way back to kings and queens. We crossed the Atlantic on the *Mayflower!*"

"That's the biggest lie I ever heard in my life."

"It's not!"

"Look where you are now! With me on Hayes Avenue. The poorest of the poor." Aunt Butter laughed again. "The *Mayflower*, my foot. You didn't even have screens in your windows."

I never knew who to believe. And there was no one left to set things straight. Mama's baby brother, Dillon, went cuckoo in the spring of '43. He's still locked up. Daddy came along that same year. He and Mama met at a church picnic, and it was love at first sight. They headed to Florida for a honeymoon, took a wrong turn, and ended up in New Orleans. I was born nine months, two weeks, and four days later. Smack on Christmas Eve, which knocks me out of getting two separate presents. And all my birthday cakes say Happy Birthday JESUS and Billie.

When I was real little, Daddy sold Bibles. He drove our dusty black Nash all over northeast Louisiana—Lake Providence, Tallulah, Delhi, Monroe, Bastrop. Sometimes he'd let me go, and we'd just fly down dirt roads, the windshield all speckled with bugs. We stopped at every house that had a mailbox. Sometimes he got attacked by dogs and peacocks. He could write your name out in gold letters for $1.50 extra, but money was precious.

I heard the grown-ups talking about how fortunes was lost in the Depression. People hadn't got over World War II, even though we won. Daddy said folks was all upset by the notion of a cold war.

"Maybe they should get some flamethrowers and make it a hot one," I suggested, but he just laughed. He talked about Korea and said it was a shame seeing young men get drafted when rice and cotton fields at home needed work. Local pilots were needed to spray cotton and soybean fields. Daddy believed another, bigger war could break out any day. Bombs could fall on every major American city, even Limoges. It was not a safe world. Nobody wanted their money tied up in Bibles. They collected dust in Aunt Butter's sewing room. "I'm selling vacuum cleaners next," he told Mama.

"Amen," she said and rolled her brown eyes.

Not too long after that, he signed up to fight Koreans and got sent to the Chongjin Reservoir with the First Marines. I know because he drawed me a map. He said the weather turned bitter cold, and everything was froze solid, even the Yalu River. "The

Chinamens swarmed over the ice," he said. "And the marines retreated eighty miles, fighting the whole way back between two mountain ranges. We carried our dead and wounded, along with Korean civilians."

My daddy was one of those wounded. They fought all the way to the sea, where navy ships was waiting to save them. Daddy said it was like Dunkirk, when the English were drove to the sea by Germans, and the people came out in fishing boats and yachts, anything that would float, and saved the soldiers.

"And to think that President Truman wanted to get rid of the marines," said Daddy. "I would have froze stiff if they hadn't toted me."

Then he came home from Korea, paralyzed, his back full of metal shards. Me and Aunt Butter made him a little bed on the porch. We took turns holding his hand, smoothing his blankets, grateful that he was alive. We'd saw many veterans with missing arms and legs—whenever one would run for public office, he'd put an ad in the paper with a full-sized photograph. I figured that my daddy could run for mayor of Limoges—it seemed like a good desk job. Meanwhile, me and Aunt Butter kept him busy with gin rummy. No matter how much I pleaded, though, I could not make Mama play cards.

One night Aunt Butter opened the screen door and stuck her head inside the house. "DeeDee Robichaux," she hollered, her hands on her hips. "What's got into you? The poor man has just got back from war. Get your butt out here and play gin rummy."

"No," said Mama. She was sitting at the white enamel table, eating a wedge of lemon chess pie. She could eat all she wanted but never got fat, which irritated Aunt Butter.

"How can you be so cruel?" Aunt Butter's chin jutted out.

"Cruel? I've been waiting tables all day, and I'm tired!"

"It's all right, Butter," called out Daddy. "The three of us can play. If she comes out in a minute, we'll deal her in."

But she never did. Later, she turned on the record player, and Frank Sinatra started singing about broken dreams and this street where you can fix them all new.

"She thinks she's too cute," said Aunt Butter, reaching for the cards, peering through the screen. Inside, Mama was singing her fool head off. "That's her whole durn problem."

"Your brain'll bust if you keep hanging like that," Mama says.

I flip over, then lay flat on the porch, watching her dip the brush into the polish. I hope I'll be pretty like her. If I'm not, then at least I'll be older, with all of this behind me. They say my daddy was the finest soldier in Korea, but my mama has the best legs in all of Louisiana. She still does, in her opinion, and she shows them off every chance she gets. Like a fool. Like now, turning her foot this way and that, admiring her paint job. Nobody watching except me and the lightning bugs. She's got brown hair and eyes, just like Natalie Wood. I don't look a thing like her. I'm my daddy and Butter made over. I got her red hair and my daddy's green eyes. Butter's got pure yellow eyes.

Through the open windows, I hear Daddy rooting in the kitchen, cursing and throwing bowls of pinto beans. The broken china makes a high, singing sound. He's mad because Mama called him a suck egg dog. See, they're always yelling. Aunt Butter said he ain't got used to being crippled, but I don't see how he can. I'd miss my legs most, not being able to run with the puppies, or walk from one end of town to the other, seeing what I could see. All he's got left is his arms, which he keeps in shape by throwing food. Me, I stay out of throwing range. I hate to ignore him, but it is either that or get hit in the head with a bowl of sliced peaches. That hurts.

I lift my foot and drop it onto my mother's famous thigh. "Paint my nails," I say.

"Honey, don't jiggle." Mama slaps my ankle and squints at her little toe. Her hair is wove into a polished knot, but dark, damp strings have sprung loose, curling around her face. She paints toenails like her life depends on it, no smudges anywheres, stopping now and then to blow. Inside the house, Daddy is quiet, as if he, too, is watching. Then something crashes, followed by, "DeeDee? I need help in here, DeeDee!"

"Raised a princess," she said, rolling her eyes. "Married a frog. This is it, baby. We're leaving."

"But your toenails ain't dry," I say.

"I don't mean this instant." Mama smiles and wipes a smudge on her finger. Then she shakes the polish, the metal beads rattling. "I meant one of these days."

I hug my knees, trying to feature us sneaking away. Me, I'd like a trip, as long as we come back. Mama, she goes places alone, and I think it's our fault. We get on her nerves. One time I was playing hopscotch by Jefferson Avenue. I saw Mr. Henry's car slow down. A woman was sitting next to him. She kissed his lips, or maybe she just touched her head to his. I don't know. Then she got out of the car. It was my own mama. She started walking toward the corner of Pine and Jefferson, but I ran up to her. "Billie!" she cried and picked me up, glad to see me. But also surprised.

"Why did Mr. Henry drive you here?" I asked.

"He . . . well, he gave me a ride."

"But you kissed him."

"No!" She set me down and brushed off her skirt. "He just wanted me to smell his breath is all."

Durn if I'd work for a man who made me sniff inside his mouth, but I didn't say nothing. We needed the money. Now she looks up from painting and winks at me. "We're really leaving Limoges. I'm not kidding. One of these days you and me's going to light out of here."

"Yeah?" I say, but I don't really believe it. "Where we going?"

"Oh, I don't know. Got any ideas?"

I shrug and pick a scab with my thumbnail. She hates the weather in Louisiana, says the climate is against her. The Coca-Cola thermometer at City Market registered over 104 degrees last August, and it went all the way down to below zero in January in 1949. Mama says she's tired of suffering through droughts, burning summers, ice storms, and floods. It is almost as bad as living up north, only without the change of seasons and without snow, which I have an idea I might enjoy. Mama said she'd always counted on going back to Greenville, Texas, where she's from, but I don't know. My daddy says Texas has lots worse things than Limoges, like scorpions. He claims we'd have to set his wheelchair in pans of water to keep him from getting bit.

"No, we can't go there," he says, and Mama starts crying.

"One little grenade," she says, "and a spine full of shrapnel, and we're pinned to Limoges the rest of our damn lives."

"It wasn't no little grenade," Daddy says. "Those damn things expand."

Now, from the kitchen, another bowl crashes against the wall; Mama gets up from the swing and leans toward the window, peering through the screen. "He's gonna break everything in Butter's kitchen," she said.

"We ought to make him glue it back," I say, and Mama laughs. It is not a soft, motherly sound like you'd hear in the church nursery—more like a screech you'd hear in Africa.

"Should I go check on him?" I start to get up, but she waves her hand.

"No, let him stew," she says. "Anyhow, he can't get to us out here. That damn wheelchair can't squeeze through the door. Thank God."

"You bitch! Get in here and clean this up!" he screams from the kitchen. "DeeDee? I know you can hear me!"

"I can't take this anymore." She wrinkles her forehead. "Let's get dressed up and go walking, princess."

"Paint my nails first."

"You're too young."

"Oh, please! Just my toenails. Anyhow, I ain't so young. I know what sex is."

"Yeah? What is it?" She holds the brush like it's a cigarette.

"It's stupid. Only thing stupider is dying."

"I don't see how." She shivers and goes back to painting her nails.

"'Cause people worry about it all the time." I shrug. "Sex and dying. Stuff like that."

"Maybe they ought to." Mama grins. "Look at the black widow spider, what she does afterward."

"I don't care about no old spiders. Come paint my nails. I want to look like you."

"Well, I guess." She smiles and straightens out her leg. "Put your foot up here."

"DeeDee! Goddammit!" yells Daddy. "Ain't you listening? You don't got no business going out tonight. I know what you're up to! You're a bitch in heat. Don't think I can't smell it on you!"

"What's a bitch?" I ask. There's so much I don't know that my head will bust by the time I get growed. But I want so bad to learn it all so I can fix the wrong, broke things in our lives.

"It's nothing, just a word. Just like sex. But don't you go round saying either one."

"Why not?"

"Because some folks might take offense. Those words mean different things to different people."

"How?"

"People who raise dogs wouldn't think *bitch* is a bad word. They'd just think you were talking about a girl dog."

Inside, another bowl shatters, and I say, "Aunt Butter'll have a fit when she sees her kitchen, won't she?"

"Probably."

"Will she blame us?"

"Yeah, but I'll clean it up." She taps my ankle. "Point your toes down."

I arch my foot, dimpling my leg. While Daddy curses and screams my mama's name, I get my nails painted. Mama leans over each toe as if she is gluing doll dishes, teeny cups and saucers. When she finishes, she leans back in the glider and lights a cigarette. I hold up one foot, turning it this way and that. "How do I look, Mama?"

"You won't believe it." She grins and holds up two fingers, framing me between them. "No bigger than this."

102 Hayes Avenue

❧

On returning home from a Church of God picnic, Ricky Womack and his mother, Alice, found a huge, long-horned Hereford cow in their front yard. With the help of neighbors he succeeded in getting the much perturbed animal back onto Hayes Avenue. He called everyone owning such a cow and was told by each that their cow was safely at home. Meanwhile, each time Mr. Womack tried to put the animal back on the road, it would stubbornly return to the front yard. Mr. Womack and his mother were meanwhile looking for their own Hereford, fearing foul play by the long-horned visitor. They worried that lightning had possibly taken its toll. Two days passed, and finally the intruder proved to be Mr. Womack's own animal.

—FROM THE LIMOGES NEWS-LEADER, APRIL 1952

The houses on Hayes Avenue were built close together—white-shingled with deep porches and doors leading into long, narrow rooms. Shotguns, they called them in New Orleans, with deep backyards full of pecan trees, vegetable gardens, chicken coops, and rabbit hutches. More than a few owned cows, goats, and pigs. It was a noisy avenue, but of all the houses on Hayes, Butter DeWitt's was the loudest. Even before Renny Robichaux went to Korea, he and DeeDee used to stand in the front yard and fight. They'd scream over money, his gambling, even which doll to buy Billie. Once he chased DeeDee up the morning glory trellis.

"Why'd you fix me a white cake when you know chocolate's my favorite?" he yelled, kicking the trellis. "You'd better come down, girl, and bake me what I want, or I'll get me an axe and chop this down!"

"Chop it," DeeDee yelled, then spit right on top of his head. The neighbors watched, horrified but unwilling to help. They had their reasons. Sometimes DeeDee would sit in her bedroom window and stare down at the neighbors. She could name every family down Hayes Avenue, the rough, yellowed lawns and scorched petunias, houses so sad and crooked they reminded her of something a child would build. It was all so depressing.

There was Ricky Womack, of course, who let his cows run wild and terrorize the neighborhood. He would yell at DeeDee when she played records, but mostly he liked to hide in his darkened bedroom and watch her undress. There was Mrs. Narcissa Harkey, whose son Alwine had died in World War II, the Battle of the Bulge, and who sometimes forgot her boy was dead; you didn't dare mention that you'd been to the cemetery and laid gardenias on his grave. There was Mr. Johnny Lee Spruel, a bald, scrawny man with wide hips; he'd been a widower forty-odd years, and he spent all of his time in his yard spraying for bugs; he had a gray Amazon parrot who hung upside down in his cage and screamed, "Oh, my *God*!"

There was Rudy Jackson and his wife, Ida May, who thanked God every night that Rudy's drinking days were over; they had dozens of grandchildren and had weekly reunions, grilling hamburgers every Saturday afternoon, never failing to invite little Billie. There was Mrs. Pernella Shaw, a woman with thick ankles and a hearing aid, whose only daughter caught polio in 1949; the girl died before they could get her to Vicksburg (this was before Limoges received its iron lung).

There was Justina Wyatt, who smelled like she never bathed; she needed glasses, but all she could afford was a magnifying glass, which she wore on a filthy string around her neck. There was Santos Navarro, the butcher at City Market, and his wife, Juanita, who rarely came out of their house, and when she did, she wore dingy white gloves; the gossips said she had a tumor of the brain, but Ida May Jackson suspected the woman was a drinker. What Juanita did was beyond anyone's wildest dreams— she washed her hands, washed and rinsed and scrubbed until she'd stripped off her epidermis, which only made her feel dirtier.

At the end of the street was a genuine floozy, Louvenia LaCour, who had shoulder-length black hair and even blacker eyebrows, spread out like gull wings on her white forehead. She would prance down her porch steps to water her caladiums, wearing a man's shirt, and when she'd bend over, you could see she didn't have on panties. At the very end of the street were Karl and Tamera Mashburn, with their snot-nosed toddlers splashing in and out of inflated plastic pools, their diapers wet and baggy.

Hayes Avenue was like a little family—you could no more

choose your neighbors than you could blood kin. Spying was a favorite activity—standing at the window, peering through paper shades. The best scouts learned how to use peripheral vision to its fullest; Ida May Jackson was a champion at watering her holly-hocks, drenching the tall flowers while she watched front porches on either side, listening to three or four conversations at once.

"Pernella's got a growth in her womb. . . . And Santos's wife was screaming bloody murder last night. If you didn't hear it, you must be deaf. . . . Narcissa cooked a whole meal, then stood on the back porch yelling for little Alwine to come and get it, sup-per's ready." Somebody (who preferred to remain nameless) said Tamera Mashburn (who was pregnant with her fifth child) had gotten drunk on whiskey cake and jumped on Karl's back, her legs wrapped around his middle. Somebody else said they went into the bushes and didn't come out for a long, long time. Their babies wandered around the yard, whimpering. One fell asleep in the gutter. Thinking he was lost, the Mashburns called the police, fire department, and City Hall.

Everybody agreed that the old days with DeeDee and Renny were better than owning a TV set, which only a few families could afford. Butter DeWitt owned one, but the reception was awful—lots of snow and hissing. You could walk past Master's Appliance on Washington Avenue and see the sets all lined up in the window, each one tuned to the same station. (They had an antenna.) You couldn't help but stop and watch the boxes, with Desi Arnaz and Lucille Ball chasing each other around a black-and-white sofa.

Before Korea, all the old people had perched beside their win-dows or the edge of their porches, watching Renny chase DeeDee from one end of the yard to the other. She'd be cussing, throwing eggs and pecans, anything she could find. And poor little Billie crouched under the porch steps, hugging her knees, tears drip-ping down her dirty cheeks. This was where the neighbors drew the line—no need to curse and carry on in front of a little child. They could tolerate a lot, but not this trashy behavior. They'd pull down their shades and turn up the radio. Even Butter herself said it was awful. She let everybody know that Renny was from south Louisiana where men were wild and French, and DeeDee was a Texan, her dead brother's girl. One of these days, she told every-one, they'd be moving on.

"The sooner the better," the neighbors agreed, but privately they thought they might miss the little redheaded child. Billie was a charmer, with a smile that could break your heart. To entertain herself, she'd put on shows, singing everything from hymns to blues, dancing and turning cartwheels. It tickled the old people, who thought she was better than Shirley Temple.

Meanwhile, the Robichauxes argued. "You think you're a ring-tailed tooter, don't you?" DeeDee yelled on the front porch.

"What is that, DeeDee?" Renny hollered. "A cross between a raccoon and a fart?"

"Oh! You're so common!" she cried. "You're nothing but a trash mouth! I'm so ashamed!"

On Mother's Day, 1948, the year Billie turned five, Renny and DeeDee had a fight that ended up changing their lives. That morning Butter ran out to the mailbox and waved an envelope in DeeDee's face. "Your brother has sent me a card," Butter crowed. She had always been partial to Dillon, even though he was crazy, locked up in the state hospital.

"Look how pretty it is," Butter bragged. "He made it his own self."

"What a shame," DeeDee said through her teeth, "that he couldn't leave the asylum to buy you a real one."

Later, when DeeDee realized no one was going to acknowledge her on this special day—after all, she was the only bona fide mother on the premises—she went into the kitchen where they were eating watermelon, using newspaper for plates. DeeDee sat down and laid her head on the table.

"What's wrong?" asked Butter, spitting seeds.

"Nobody loves me!" DeeDee wailed.

"Oh, for heaven's sake." Butter rolled her eyes.

"This is the worst day of my life!"

"Shit." Renny wiped his mouth. "According to you they're *all* bad."

"That's not true!" DeeDee looked from Renny and Butter. They were laughing, pink juice leaking from their mouths. Even Billie laughed.

DeeDee pushed away from the table and stood up. "You make me sick!"

"Then vomit," said Renny, turning to Butter with a smile. DeeDee reached down, picked up a wedge of melon, and threw it at him, hard as she could. He ducked, and the green wedge sailed across the table, striking Billie square in the forehead. The blow knocked her over backward. Her chair hit the floor with a splat.

Later, Renny tried to take them downtown to buy DeeDee a card, but Billie threw herself on the floor. "I don't want to get her anything!" she cried. A red lump stood out on her forehead.

"I don't blame her," said Butter, causing Billie to wail louder.

"Come on, girls." Renny herded them down the porch steps.

DeeDee stuck her head out the front door and said, "Don't you forget my you-know-what."

"What, your *Kotex*?" Renny hollered, loud enough for all of Hayes Avenue to hear.

"Let her bleed," said Butter, who was mad because DeeDee hadn't gotten her anything, and because of the watermelon.

"Maybe I will." Renny laughed.

"You bastard!" DeeDee ran out of the house, trying to claw his face. Butter circled her arms around Billie and pulled her into the front yard.

"Go fuck yourself!" Renny's breath hit her in the face. His fingers squeezed her wrists. "You're acting like a madwoman. Now, calm down and tell me what you want me to bring you from the grocery."

"I just told you! Kotex!"

"I meant food, you little idiot." He threw down her hands. "What do you want me to bring so you can fix supper?"

"If I can fuck myself," DeeDee said, "then you can feed yourself."

He shook his head and walked away. Billie broke loose from Butter and ran over to him. DeeDee heard him say, "I'd just as soon fight chinks as look at her."

After the news spread about his injury, the neighbors brought platters of fried chicken and pecan pies, as if Butter didn't have a whole restaurant just around the corner. DeeDee was crying and carrying on, pacing the floor. Little Billie didn't seem to understand what was happening until they brought her daddy home, carried him through the front door on a long white cot. The neighbors took up a collection and bought him a wooden wheelchair. All of them, even Ricky Womack, got together and carried it over. When DeeDee came into the room, her face turned white. "Get it out of here!" She shook her head, her eyes closed. "Take it away."

"What's the matter with you!" Butter cried. "This is a gift for Renny, not you!"

"I'm sorry, I'm sorry." Tears streamed down DeeDee's face. "I'm just so sorry. I just now realized he'd never walk again."

"Hell, you don't have to remind me." Renny said. The neighbors stepped backward. It was one thing to witness a fight from next door, entirely another to be in the same room.

"I'm not, sweetie, I'm not."

"Can't you shut up?"

"I'm trying." DeeDee bit her finger. "Just one little thing worries me. What are we going to do with all those Bibles and vacuum cleaners in the back room? The ones you couldn't sell?"

"DeeDee! Stop it, I mean it!" Butter stood up. Alice Womack draped her arms around Ricky's neck, as if he were a toddler and not a full-grown man. Ricky made little whimpering noises, his eyes switching from DeeDee to Renny.

"Well, why don't you go get you one of them vacuum cleaners and clean this up." Renny picked up a vase filled with daisies and threw it across the room. It shattered, spraying glass into DeeDee's hair. "Then get you a Bible and pray that I don't kill you."

"Bastard!" DeeDee screamed. "Catch me first. How you going to do that, hmmm?"

Renny reached on the coffee table, picked up a candy dish, and threw it. DeeDee screamed and ducked a second before the dish thunked against the wall, leaving a chip in the plaster, then crashed to the floor. Chocolate-covered cherries rolled under the wheelchair. Ricky Womack squeaked, raising one arm over his eyes. Billie rolled into a ball and wailed. Her voice sounded like a newborn baby's. Butter tiptoed over the broken glass and drew the child into her arms.

"It's all right, sugar," she crooned. "Just cry it out, it's all right, just get it all out. You'll feel better in the morning."

But it wasn't all right. The next morning was more of the same—Renny shouting, DeeDee crying, both of them throwing things at each other. Come evening, when the neighbors went to pull their shades, they'd see Billie sitting outside with her dogs, her face buried in their fur. DeeDee opened the back door, dumping a dustpan full of broken glass into the trash, then stared off into the deep backyard. "Billie?" she'd say. "Bil-*lie*." She begged the child to come inside, but Billie acted like she couldn't hear. The neighbors didn't blame her. Who wouldn't be scared to have such flimsy parents, crippled in different ways?

Mr. Navarro offered to build a ramp for Renny's wheelchair, but DeeDee wasn't having any part of it. Renny was trapped inside the house—some of the door frames wouldn't accept his wheelchair. The last thing she wanted was Renny's freedom (she pictured him chasing her down the sidewalk all the way to town—how embarrassing).

"That's real nice of you, Mr. Navarro," she said, "but he can't push himself very far. His arms have gotten so weak." This wasn't a lie, exactly—the doctor had warned of a generalized upper-body deterioration, only it hadn't happened. He stayed in shape by throwing food and pottery, number-two cans of pears. His arms were stout, the muscles inflated. If he had a ramp, no one would be safe from his attacks, least of all DeeDee.

"Oh," said Mr. Navarro. "So that's why he's all the time lifting fruit-cocktail cans? He's trying to build up? I can get him some dumbbells. He can, how you say, *hoist* them."

"Dumb belles?" DeeDee blinked. She pictured Renny holding a giggling debutante above his head, the hoopskirt falling into his face.

"One for each hand."

She slapped Mr. Navarro's face, then ran into the house and locked the door, leaving him standing in the yard, shouting something in Spanish.

One of the neighbors, Rudy Jackson, said he was driving to Tallulah and thought he recognized Renny's old Nash on Highway 65. DeeDee was driving with all the windows rolled down, her dark hair streaming. The radio was turned up full blast, Rosemary Clooney, "Come on-a My House."

"That was DeeDee, all right," another neighbor said. "Rosemary Clooney is her favorite."

"What was she doing on Highway 65?" Ida May Jackson stared hard at her husband. "Speaking of which, what were *you* doing on that road? When did *you* go to Tallulah?"

"Just driving is all," Rudy said. His wife pressed her lips together, but she didn't ask another question. She'd never make a scene in public. After all, she wasn't a Robichaux. No, she'd get him alone and shut all the windows and then beat the hell out of him with a frying pan.

Rudy looked relieved when the subject turned back to DeeDee. "Did you pass her?" somebody asked. "Was it really her?"

"I passed her, all right." Rudy nodded.

"Was she alone? What was she doing?"

"Well, let me put it this way." Rudy scratched the back of his neck. "She wasn't selling vacuum cleaners."

Everyone laughed, even Ida May, but Rudy remembered how narrow the road seemed; on one side was the levee, the other was cotton. DeeDee was so pretty it brought tears to his eyes. When he finally got up the nerve to pass, he saw she was alone (although a man could've been hiding on the floorboard). Music blasted from her car, Rosemary Clooney singing like her heart was broken. Rudy accelerated, then shot out in front of her, praying she'd flag him down. Maybe they could stop for a cup of coffee. Or maybe they could just skip the coffee. Renny Robichaux was paralyzed, and Rudy knew what that meant. He kept staring into the rearview mirror, but she didn't recognize him. She did not look like a grieved woman. She looked like someone who relished the wind on her face, the smell of water, driving down a road divided by white dashes, all sucked under the car like something vacuumed—maybe bread crumbs, a trail she was following, laid out by God knows whose hands.

Why I'm Not a Homewrecker

~

*Some women you never forget. My wife, Corinne, is like Julius Cae-
sar—she came, she saw, she conquered. But DeeDee Robichaux was
like Cleopatra—she just came and came and came.*

—JACKSON BRUSSARD, DISCUSSING WOMEN WITH BOB
"MOBY" RIFFLE, MOBY'S CATFISH HOUSE AND MOTEL, HIGHWAY
65, APRIL 1952

DeeDee Robichaux

I was just dying to visit Limoges General, to pay my respects to
Henry and see Olive for my own self—I never saw a coma victim
before. I dressed me and Billie in black, due to the morbid nature
of the occasion, with gloves and matching pocketbooks. I had to
admit we looked stylish. The whole time we were getting ready,
Renny screamed out my name, "DeeDee! DeeDee!"

I pretended he was Mr. Spruel's parrot, a rare bird scattering
seed from his cage just to get my attention. Well, he wasn't getting it. I stepped outside and picked several daffodils, then
wrapped the stems in waxed paper. Renny's voice was creepy. I
imagined how loud he must've screamed when that grenade burst
over him.

"Goddammit, you answer me! You answer me now, right
now!"

I'd just as soon eat dirt. I found Billie on the corner and
grabbed her hand. We walked in silence down Hayes Avenue,
turning left on Delphinium. It was a cool, sweet evening; the air

smelled of honeysuckle. A good night to walk and not worry about perspiring, which was the main drawback of summer, if you asked me. If I was going to sweat, then I wanted something out of it, you know?

The streets were empty except for a few children riding bicycles. As we passed by store windows, I pointed at our reflections and said, "Who are those pretty girls?"

"Us?" Billie laughed and squeezed my hand. The hospital was straight ahead, and we turned left again, onto Jefferson, walking toward the main entrance. Here in Limoges the main avenues were named after presidents. You got Monroe, Hayes, Adams, Lincoln, Washington, Jefferson, and Madison. The streets either had bird names—Sparrow, Mockingbird, Finch, Cardinal—or else flowery ones—Geranium, Oak, Pine, Cypress, Delphinium, and Magnolia. I wished I lived on one of them.

Limoges was just a regular, squatty town, but it could twist your soul to live here. Cold in winter, hot as blazes in summer. The people were snotty, backward, or religious—sometimes all three. They pretended not to be ruled by gossip, but they'd die without it. Limoges thrived on illusion. Three years ago, a bunch of old biddies from the historical society got together and spruced things up downtown. The hysterical women, I called them; Henry's wife was one. They had a charity ball and earned enough money to paint the old brick buildings different colors, like flavors of sherbet. They fixed all the broken windows. They stuck up wrought-iron balconies and ceiling fans, planted geraniums in window boxes. It was cute and New Orleans-ish, but shrunk down, a trick of the eye. See, there was no Mardi Gras here, no fun at all. We were too far away from everything. You had the Mississippi River and levees on the east side, nothing but farms on the west. In between was the lake and the town. Below was nothing but bottomland, and above was Arkansas. Around here, all they cared about was crops, crops, crops. As if vegetables and cotton mattered.

I could be happy in New Orleans. Far as I remembered, it was humid as all getout, but it gets that way here, too. Only in the French Quarter the heavy, soggy air would be full of jazz weaving down the alleys. I'd been there once, on my honeymoon. We stayed at a place that rented rooms by the hour, The Hotel LeBlanc—all we could afford. That first night we ate supper from a vendor who pushed a hot dog–shaped cart. From our lacy balcony, I could see Bourbon Street. It was full of freshly shaved men walking around goggle-eyed. Renny said they were probably tourists, country boys who didn't know what to make of the whores and shouts, music and careening laughter. The loud-mouthed barkers stood on the curb and tried to lure them into the clubs.

Renny pulled me back inside. His breath smelled of gin and limes. Through the open French doors, saxophone music drifted by. A bottle smashed, and a woman screamed, "Fuck it!"

Next morning, I woke up early and walked out onto the balcony. The air smelled of melon rinds and coffee grounds. Bourbon Street was empty, the pavement strewn with paper cups, spilled popcorn, and cigarette stubs. Toilet paper rippled down from a balcony, waving in the air like crepe. Behind me Renny lay on his stomach, snoring. One hand lay palm up, the other clenched around the pillow. We left that afternoon. The farther I got away from New Orleans, the more I hungered for it. The city reminded me of an old-fashioned dish garden, where beads of water collect on the glass lid. I hated coming back to Limoges and Hayes Avenue.

I was a native of Greenville, Texas. Cotton from this rich black soil went to spinners in Manchester, England. Every day me and my brother Dillon walked down Washington to Boise d'Arc Street, then left for one block to Lee. We'd turn right, cross the railroad tracks, and stand out front of the Greenville Cotton Compress, waiting for Mama. In 1912 they processed 2,073 bales in a ten-hour day. That was eight years before I was born.

After Mama died, Aunt Butter came down for the funeral, saw that me and Dillon were all alone, and took us back to Limoges. She signed us up for school. Everyone stared at the sweetheart rose I wore in my hair, like it was nasty or an ugly color. I was fourteen years old, a country girl, but I was ashamed for people to know it. When the girls at Limoges High giggled at me, I patted my rose and said, "It's the latest style in Dallas."

"Well, it's not the style *here*," they informed me. They had their heads poked up in the air, these daughters of planters and merchants, and I knew they hated me for that rose. That I would not be invited to their parties. I went out of my way to be a Texan. It's all I talked about. In 1934, I won a red ribbon in the Blue Plate Mayonnaise Contest with my Eye of Texas Salad. Dissolve 2 packs of lime Jell-0 in 1 1/2 cups hot water. Then mix in 1/4 cup chopped celery, 1/2 cup mayonnaise, 1/4 cup vinegar, 1 cup crushed pineapple, 1/4 cup chopped cucumbers. Slice a big, green olive and put in bottom of individual molds. Pour salad mix into molds and congeal. Unmold, and the olive looks at you.

I was stuck in the one town on earth where I didn't belong, but if it was the last thing I did, I was getting back to Texas. Even my brother found a way to leave. He disappeared on his way home from prayer meeting in Shreveport. The authorities found him a month later in Hawaii, preaching on Waikiki Beach, offering to translate for those who spoke in tongues. He made enough money to rent a room at the Moana, with a view of Diamond Head. We still have a whole Roi-Tan box full of pictures he took. Me and Butter went to visit him in the state asylum. When she asked what had made him run off, he said, "Well, that's simple. I got a phone call from God."

Butter nodded, as if that explained everything, but I wasn't so easily fooled. "And what did He say?" I asked.

"I couldn't make out but one word," Dillon said. "Honolulu."

They let him out, of course, and he took a bus to New Orleans. In one day he rented a room on Bienville Street, got a job opening oysters at Acme, and adopted a three-legged Boston terrier (it followed him home from Acme). Six weeks passed, and his landlady noticed a smell coming from his room. No matter how long she'd stand and knock, Dillon never came to the door. When she used her pass key, she caught him on the floor with his naked butt stuck into the air; the little dog was just going to town licking Dillon's anus. To keep from fainting, she gripped the kitchen counter. Something tickled her hand— she looked down. The Formica was crawling with roaches, big granddaddy ones. The air swarmed with fruit flies. Butter had to sign him back into the hospital, of course, and this time they kept him.

It was hard to live with Butter, even though she was my daddy's sister. The only thing we had in common was our last name, DeWitt, and our Texas roots. On Wednesdays her cafe served only Texas food. She'd start the morning with peach coffee cake and huevos rancheros. When I got out of school, I helped serve chicken-fried steak with milk gravy, *sopa de fideo*, Bunuelo rosettes, salpicon, quesadillas, tortilla soup, all kinds of chili.

The newspaper came out and took a picture of me and Butter standing in front of the cafe. Butter was a full head shorter than me (I was tall for my age). She'd decorated the front windows with paper flowers and cowboy hats. One hat hung over my head like an empty caption in the comic strips. The girls at school started calling me "Little Orphan DeeDee." That's when I turned on both my heritage and Butter. When the teacher called out my name, everybody giggled; they said DeeDee DeWitt sounded like someone with a stutter. When Renny Robichaux stopped in the cafe to sell us a Bible, I knew he was mine. The best thing about him was his name, romantic and Frenchy, summoning up ladies in tapestry gowns, men in knickers and powdered wigs. He'd get me the hell out of Limoges.

"Butter may love Texas," I told my friend Tamera Mashburn, "but she sure won't move back there."

"Why not?" said Tamera.

"'Cause she knows I want it so bad."

"If you ask me," Tamera said, "it's got nothing to do with Texas. I think the woman's got a appetite for chili powder. I mean, since she can't get no man, she needs *something* to make her hot."

Me and Billie stopped at the corner of Jefferson and Delphinium. I glanced over at the hospital, and I almost lost my nerve. I didn't have no business here. Still, it couldn't hurt to peek inside and see what Henry was doing. "Come on, Billie." I took her hand and we walked up to the main entrance. Soon as we got inside, I started sweating under my armpits. I breathed deeply, smelling rubbing alcohol and soap. Down at the far end of a long, green-tiled hall, I saw two men talking to each other, the manager from Morgan & Lindsay dime store and the spidery man from Hooper's. Women were clustered around Vangie, but I didn't see Henry anywhere. For once, I was glad. I'd gotten hard in lots of ways, but it still hurt to see him living his other life.

We loved each other from afar, and close up, too, but we had to find a private place for that. Henry called his orgasms "little deaths." He told me the French name, but I forgot. I thought it was more like a little coma, the way he drooled and everything. After we did it, he turned back into Henry Nepper. He said poetry and foreign things to me. For a married man, Henry seemed so *sincere*.

See, before Henry there was this man from Tallulah. Renny had just come home all crippled up, and I thought my life was over. The man's name was Jackson Brussard, a curly-haired blond man. He had the longest fingers I ever saw, with an Ole Miss ring on one hand, wedding band on the other. He wasn't too much older than me, and he drove a brand new Cadillac. I was impressed. He traveled around buying and selling cowhides, then had them shipped to a factory. He started coming to Butter's Cafe after Labor Day 1950. Always ordered the same thing—tuna salad on toast, french fries, milk, and caramel cake or pie, depending on what was left.

"You go to college?" I asked, wiping the counter for the tenth time, all around his elbows, leaving beads of water on the red Formica.

"Yes, ma'am." He cut into the caramel cake. "I sure did. University of Mississippi."

"Then why you selling those cowhides?"

"Leather," he said, staring like I was stupid.

"Oh! Well, sure." I giggled, but I felt like a fool. Later, Butter came up behind me and said, "Oh! Well, sure!" Then she laughed. Made me so mad I picked up a whole caramel cake and smashed it against the counter. Then I yanked off my apron, threw it down, and stalked off.

But I had the last laugh. Next time Jackson Brussard came into the cafe, I'd done read up on the tanning process. Looked it up at the library. Next thing I knew I was taking down directions to Moby's Catfish House and Motel on Highway 65, north of Tallulah. This went on for a good, long while, maybe three months. He was real sweet and real, real tender. I fell in love, hard. When it hits you, it's like peeing all over yourself. You just can't hold it in.

He brought me daisies, chocolates, leather wallets, and pearl earbobs. He gave me gas money, too. Whole bunches of it, and I didn't even have to ask. "I'm crazy about you," he said. I believed him. I thought to myself, *DeeDee, you just got to have this man for your own.*

Two, three times a week I'd call his house in Tallulah just to stir things up. A colored woman always answered, probably the maid, but I never said anything. I generally called on our days at the motel. I'd get there before Jackson and look up names in the phone book—course his was right there in the *B*'s, Brussard, Jackson, 121 Bayou Drive. It sounded ritzy, but I didn't know. Soon as he opened that motel door, I threw down the book and ran into his arms.

"Do you think you'll ever leave your wife?" I asked him. It was maybe the third time we were together. I didn't want to rush him; I was just trying to feel him out, you know. To see if he was serious or just having a good time.

"You bet." He pinched my breast.

"When?"

"Soon, real soon. But now is not the time." He ran his hand down my thigh, then cupped my buttocks. "It's so small I can fit you in one hand. I just love shapely little women. I wish I could show you off. Every man in Tallulah would froth at the mouth."

He told me his wife, Corinne, was jealous, fat, and mean. Her daddy was known as the cowhide king in five states. Jackson said the old man carried his money around in wheelbarrows. He told me he'd leave Corinne in a second if it weren't for Little Jackson and Lilly. They all lived in mortal unhappiness in a house Corinne's daddy gave them. I drove by, of course, and it wasn't no little house. It was big as a funeral home. I parked my car and walked up, opening the little wrought-iron gate. The front door was all beveled glass. I saw a curved staircase, black-and-white checkerboard floor, and a chandelier full of beads and icicles, like something froze. I felt sick to my stomach. *He can't leave all this*, I thought. Not even for me. Through the glass I saw a colored woman walk by. She wore a gray uniform. When she saw me, she came to the door and opened it. "I didn't hear the bell ring," she said.

"Oh, I didn't ring it."

"Are you selling something, ma'am?" She looked down at my empty hands. I'd even left my pocketbook in the car.

"Bibles," I said. It just popped out. "Would you care to buy one?"

"No, ma'am. Don't think we'd be interested."

"Oh. That's all right." I shrugged, then turned to go.

"See, we've got Bibles."

"Yeah. Me too. It's hard to sell something when people's already got it."

I stared at her, and she stared at me. She started to speak, but a white woman came down the staircase, gripping the banister. "Who is it, Surphromia?" she asked. She had short black hair and a double chin, big fleshy arms. A teeny little mouth.

"Somebody selling Bibles, Miz Corinne."

"Tell her we don't want any."

"Yes, ma'am." At the top of the landing, a baby toddled out, her panties caught around her ankles. She had a head full of curly blond hair. "Mama?" the baby cried. "Sur'poma? I wee-weed *all* by myself!"

"Surphromia?" Corinne called. "You coming?"

"Yes, ma'am." She turned back to me, one hand resting against the door.

"Well, goodbye," I said. Then I leaned forward and touched her arm. "Give Jackson a big kiss for me."

She looked startled, then glanced back at Corinne.

"On second thought," I said. "You'd better not. Might cause Miss Corinne to twist her girdle. Could choke the life out of her. Then that poor little baby won't have no mama."

"You best go home, miss," Surphromia said, then shut the door in my face. The next time Jackson called, I half expected him to ask if I'd been to his house, but he never did. Right after Thanksgiving he brought a Purina sack full of quail to the cafe. I was so hot for him that we did it in the men's room, with me straddling the grimy sink. Then he helped me climb out the window, into the alley. I thought I was pretty smart.

That night I was sitting at my dresser, brushing my hair one hundred strokes. Butter came up behind me and said, "I know what you're doing."

"Brushing my hair?" I said, flipping my head over.

"No, you and that Brussard man. You're seeing him, ain't you?"

"No!"

"DeeDee, he's married."

"Well, so am I."

"He won't leave his wife. They never do. 'Course, there's exceptions, but he ain't one."

"You don't know what you're talking about!" I threw down the brush and knocked over a perfume bottle. The smell of White Mink made me cough.

"Honey, I'm just trying to help." She stroked the back of my head. "I know it's hard being married to a cripple, but this Brussard man ain't going to take you out of here."

"He might."

"I hate to see you get hurt. And you've got Billie to consider."

"I am considering her," I said.

"No, you're not. I see through you, DeeDee," she told me. "Straight through you."

The first Saturday in December, he didn't show up. I waited all day at the motel, working up all kinds of appetites, then I finally walked over to the Catfish House. I sat in a booth by the window. Just before they brought my meal, I saw Jackson's black Cadillac swerve into the gravel lot and park next to my shabby car. He got out, walked over to Room 6, where we always stayed, and rapped on the door. When no one let him in (how could I?), he peeked through the diamond-shaped window. Then he turned back, making sure my car was still there. He shook his head and started walking toward the restaurant. When he stepped inside Moby's, he spotted me right away. He walked over, stopping to shake hands with some fat man on a brown stool. When Jackson slid into my booth, his thigh pressed hard against mine. "I got tied up," he said. He reached down and rubbed my knee.

"How? Business or pleasure?"

"Neither. Corinne was carrying on. Made me take her over to her daddy's, then to her Aunt Elizabeth's to pick up a marble table. It's always something. But let's don't talk about her. It sure is good to see your pretty face. I knew you'd wait."

I held my breath. I had this temper, see, but I didn't care to make a scene, even in front of strangers. I had my pride. When the waitress brought my food, I just stared—a platter of fried blue catfish, hush puppies, slaw, okra, corn muffins.

"Is anything wrong?" the waitress asked, eyeing Jackson.

"It's just fine." He winked at her. She blushed, stared into his eyes, then twirled around and walked off, wiggling her hips. Jackson watched her turn around the counter. That wink got to me more than anything. I lifted the platter and dumped it over his head. Then I slid under the table and walked out, straight to my car.

I didn't expect to hear from him again, but the very next day he was back at Butter's Cafe, ordering tuna on toast, acting like nothing had happened. We did it in his car that time, parked in the Yellow Fever Cemetery, which was not as creepy as you might think.

I thought everything was fine. Then, about a week before Christmas, he called me up and said he couldn't see me anymore. That he'd bought me a gold locket with my name engraved and everything; like a fool he left the receipt in his billfold. Don't you know Corinne found it?

Well, I didn't know what to think. Maybe there wasn't any gold locket. Maybe his wife didn't know about me. My throat closed up, but I managed to say, "I'm sorry to hear it. I was looking forward to seeing you."

"Maybe I can get over to Limoges after the holidays." He sighed. "When everything calms down."

"What did she say, Jackson?" I was dying to know what *he'd* said, but I didn't want to push.

"Right now she's not saying much of nothing. She's at her daddy's."

"Then maybe we could get together—"

"No. At least, not right now. Let's wait till everything blows over."

"Sure."

"Talk to you later," he said, but he lied. I never saw him again.

Next I did it with a one-eyed jeweler, who did not give me so much as a bad diamond. And when his son came home from Korea, I did it with him, too. He didn't give me shit, either. When I told Tamera Mashburn, she said, "Gosh, girl. You've done slept with the father and son. All you need to find is the Holy Ghost."

I needed a change so I quit Butter's Cafe and started working at the drugstore, side-by-side with Henry Nepper. I didn't pick him out or nothing, and I sure didn't seduce him. I just had a feeling. I'd be working at the fountain, wiping down the ice-cold counters, and for no reason at all, I'd look up. He'd be huddled in his little glassed-in room, his white smock unsnapped at the neck, staring back at me.

Late one Saturday, I decided to test him. He was on his way to the Limoges Country Club, where I'd never set foot. I knew he was running late, knew that he was going to a glorified square dance with Vangie. So I conveniently sprained my ankle, and he had to help me into the employee lounge, to the red vinyl sofa. As he felt my bones, he kept saying, "I don't see any swelling. Are you sure you can't stand on it?"

"I'll try," I said. When I stood up, I fell against him, letting my hip bone stab against his male place. I clung to him. "Think I'm going to faint, Mr. Nepper," I said and went limp.

He lay me down on the sofa, and I raised my skirt above my knees. "It hurts all the way up my leg," I said, rubbing the skin. "It's a shooting pain. You know what kind I mean, don't you?"

"Yes, exactly." He leaned forward and put one hand on my leg. I knew then he was hooked, if not for life, then another hour. I was glad that I was wearing pretty underwear. I had a set that was embroidered with days of the week, and I was wearing *SAT-URDAY*, because that's what day it was. I couldn't be so forward as to push his hand up my dress, so I scooted down on the sofa, like I was shifting my position, and his hand skidded up to my panties.

Henry looked at me. I looked at Henry. We did it right there on the sofa, didn't even get all our clothes off. He was hard inside me. It was too long since I'd held a man, Lord help me for wanting it so bad. It was like swimming deep underwater, then back to the surface, toward the sun, your lungs bursting for air. After a while there was nothing but the feeling, all swelled up inside, and soon you learned to breathe underwater. As soon as he caught his breath, we did it again, and let me tell you, he was mighty late for that square dance.

The next day he called and talked about his land in north Epiphany Parish and how we could meet there. I had to pull the phone into the pantry so Aunt Butter couldn't hear. And when I came out she kept shooting me suspicious looks. "Ain't nobody interested in what you got to say," she told me, and I thought, *I'll bet.*

Sometimes he'd pick me up on the corner of Jefferson and Delphinium, close to City Market. Other times I'd drive out to his land on Highway 65. The gravel crunched beneath the Nash's tires, sending up a screen of gray dust. When I reached a grassy place, I cut the engine. Cypress and willows grew along a bayou. Mosquito hawks skimmed over a field. From somewhere far away, a dog barked.

I stepped out of the car and walked along the edge of the

field, picking goldenrod. The air was clear yet not empty, alive with dust, gnats, bird chatter. The wind blew my hair as I hunkered down to gather the flowers. I liked the silence. At home all Renny talked about was how Russia wouldn't stop at nothing to get the A-bomb. Maybe he was right. Maybe the world was getting more dangerous than ever—radiation, germs, wetness, kisses, sperm.

From the road, I saw dust moving toward me, and I knew he was coming. The blood started beating in my neck. Even before he could get out of the car, I threw myself against him, my arms circling his neck, kissing him slowly, our tongues joining, then flicking away. "I feel like taking off all my clothes right here," I said, dropping one hand between his legs. He was already erect. All around us crickets were char-charring. A wedge of sun blazed through the leaves. Henry opened both doors to his car and pulled me down on the front seat, his hand digging under my dress.

"Easy, now," I said.

"You don't have any panties on," he said in my ear.

"Can't stand them." I laughed. "I don't wear any half the time."

Which was not a bit true, I've got more panties than I need, but how would he know? He'd never visit me on Hayes Avenue and look inside my bureau drawers. I reached forward to unzip him, feeling his excitement. I love O how I love being able to do this to a man, getting a rise. He kicked off his trousers, then straddled me, his peter grazing my leg. When he entered me, he felt hot, like he had a fever.

We did it right there in the car, our feet dangling in midair, the seat cushion creaking beneath us. I thought of his wife, pudgy and round-faced, a long gray braid like a squaw. Maybe Henry would see that all this time he'd been casting his bait in the wrong pond.

For such a fast man, he lived his life real slow. Behind the scenes, I had my own ways of speeding things up. When I was on my way to meet him, I'd call up Vangie. When she'd answer I'd hang up. I thought maybe she'd get suspicious and follow him out to his land, but she never did. Then Henry told me she couldn't drive. I predicted he'd leave her before Christmas, but they went on a family vacation to New Orleans, taking that awful neighbor lady with them, Edith Galliard. I didn't get my Christmas present until after New Year's. First, he gave me a box of pralines, and I was so disappointed, I almost threw them in his face. Then he gave me my real present, a cameo choker. "This is real old," he told me, fastening the clasp around my neck. "I got it in an antique shop on Magazine Street. Oh, DeeDee baby, I just wish I could give you more."

Then do it, I thought, but I gave him a flirty smile and said, "All I want is your happiness, Henry." He never seemed to worry whether I was content. Any fool could see that I was still living on Hayes Avenue, poor and unloved. Sometimes I'd be reading the paper, skimming the society section, and I'd come across a tidbit that made me crazy. *Last Saturday evening, the Limoges Year-Round Garden Club hosted a party at the country club. The theme was Come in Your Gardening Clothes. The members and their spouses wore overalls, flowered aprons, canvas gloves, and straw hats. Canasta and rook were enjoyed at several tables. Delicious refreshments were served, consisting of punch, cookies, sand-wiches, and candy. The party was organized by Mrs. Zachary Gal-liard and Mrs. Henry Nepper.*

It just didn't seem fair.

Married men would be perfect if they weren't married. They have time that can't be accounted for, weeknights, Saturday nights, all day Sunday. You couldn't help but wonder what they did when they weren't with you. In fact, if they were so unhappy at home, why were they *there* all the time? The last thing you wanted to sound like was a wife, so you nearly killed yourself being kind. Acting like you'd be so understanding if they married you.

One day last January, I came to the drugstore and couldn't find Henry. I waited on a customer, then wiped down the pink marble counter. Two, three hours went by. I sneaked into the stockroom and dialed Henry's house. When Vangie answered, I hung up. Finally I asked Miss Byrd if something had happened to *Mr.* Henry. She said he was out golfing.

"What's that?"

"Why, it's the latest thing," she said, giving me a long, wither-ing look. "You never heard of it?"

"No. Is it like hunting?" I honestly didn't know what she was talking about, but it sounded illegal.

"No. It's what men in Limoges *do* on afternoons."

"Well, he's never done it before. This is the first I've heard of it."

"Why should he tell you his personal business?" She glared at me.

"I was just curious. He's always here filling prescriptions." I tossed my head, trying to be nonchalant. "So where does he golf?"

"What's it to you?"

"I don't know. I thought maybe I might take it up. Golfing, I mean."

"You can't. You have to be a member of the Limoges Country Club."

I went back to wiping the counter, and Miss Byrd said, "You're going to wear that marble down to the nub, girl. Give it a rest."

I walked back to the lounge and called Vangie again. "Hello?" she said. "Who *is* this? Why won't you say something?" I hung up, then stretched out on the red vinyl sofa. At least he wasn't with her. I didn't like him going to the country club, but of course I never said anything. I knew he and Vangie went to the club for parties. I wondered if they danced. A mistress is in no position to show her true feelings, much less ask questions, until she's been a wife for at least six months.

On my lunch break, I got into the Nash and drove around the lake to the club. I'd passed by it before but had never gone down the long, oak-lined road. Country Club Lane, it was called. I was not a trespasser. That day I not only drove down the lane, I parked my car next to Henry's turquoise wagon. I marched straight up the porch. It was an old mansion, white wood with twin balconies and big rocking chairs that overlooked miles of short green grass and clutches of pines. It was the biggest front yard I'd ever seen but not carefully mowed. In some places the grass was taller, like they'd run out of gas.

No one stopped me as I walked inside. The whole downstairs was one big room, paneled in knotty pine, with a gas furnace at one end and windows at the other. A bunch of wood tables and chairs in between. Off to the back was a kitchen that smelled of fried hamburgers. All this time I'd imagined Henry and Vangie dancing in a room that didn't exist, soft blue walls with a ceiling of stars, curved windows overlooking a pool, waiters in white jackets pouring champagne. The idea of champagne really got to me because I'd never tasted any.

Now I looked through the windows and saw pine trees, a concrete patio full of green metal chairs with shell backs. The pool was one-third full of blackish green water, a nasty gumbo piled with pine branches and trash. Beyond that I saw a red flag embroidered with a white 9.

One of the cooks stepped out of the kitchen and looked me up and down. "We're closing up, miss," she said. "What you need?"

"Nothing," I said and backed out of the room. I groped for the knob, pushed open the door, then stepped onto the porch. I took off running, my loafers slapping against the planks. When I reached the parking lot, I turned. Way out on the green lawn I saw men walking toward the red flag. They carried long leather bags and metal sticks that reflected the sun. There were white dots on the grass, too. One man walked up to the dot and hit it with a stick. The dot whooshed into the air, then bounced down on the smooth green circle. He turned back to his companions and grinned. None of the men was Henry Nepper. He was somewhere on that big green lawn chasing after white dots. For a wife, I suppose it's preferable to chasing women. For a mistress, it's just one more thing to take your man away. "So this is golf?" I said, shaking my head and laughing.

I drove back to the drugstore and walked straight up to the magazine rack. "Where you been?" screeched Miss Byrd. I ignored her and picked up a *National Geographic*. Maybe I was ignorant, but I wasn't stupid.

Billie and I walked around the hospital lobby, moving through clean air that reminds me of how a thermometer tastes. I was drunk with the memory of Henry, his hands cupping my breasts. Straight ahead, I watched his wife hold court, like this wasn't a deathbed but a cotillion, surrounded by her society friends. I couldn't stand that woman, and it wasn't because she was Henry's wife. She prissed in the store like she owned it, wearing linen suits and matching pumps, her stockings fashioned into jelly rolls, the dark seams straight as pipe cleaners. All the money in the world to spend, and she never worked a day in her life. She called herself Miss Vangie, pronouncing it Miz Vay-un-gee. "You're Henry's new counter girl!" she said to me last November, smiling like she was carried away with delight. And I thought to myself, *That's not all I am, sweetie. Wouldn't you like to know that your Henry gave me fifty dollars last week to buy myself a new dress?*

I couldn't put my finger on it, but she was what my mama would call hoity-toity. Always smiling like she was good to the poor or kind to orphans, but you knew it was an act. She wouldn't put herself out. Henry said as much. Anyhow, if she was so nice, then how come he was with me?

Now a lady kissed Vangie's cheek, then said something in her ear. They looked like long-lost gossips. The woman had wavy reddish brown hair, crimped to her shoulders, and she wore a navy blue suit and gloves. She was too old, if you asked me, to wear her hair that long. She patted Vangie's arm, then walked briskly toward me and Billie. Even from here I saw that she had high cheekbones and arched eyebrows, shaped into upside-down *U*'s. I squeezed the daffodils and stared down at the tiled floor, hoping if I didn't look at her, she wouldn't look at me. Instead, she stopped and gave me a look, raising one of those thin, misshapen brows.

"Excuse me? I'm Edith Galliard," she said in a high-class voice, extending one gloved hand. I already know who she was. I'd seen her picture in the society pages. She was Henry's weird sister-in-law, the New Yorker whose paintings hang on display in the lobby of the Limoges Hotel, where tourists and traveling salesmen could see how much class this town really had. I wouldn't hang one of her pictures in my house if she gave it to me. She painted gap-mouthed men that looked like somebody's nailed their fingers to their knees, or else she did these cubes. Sometimes, though, she does flowers.

I took the woman's hand and shook it, murmuring, "Nice to meet you. I'm DeeDee Robichaux."

She smiled and leaned toward Billie. *"You're* mighty cute," she said in a way that made me think I wasn't. "Do you have a name, sweetie?"

"Yes, ma'am." Billie tilted her head back and grinned up at the woman.

"Well? What is it?" Edith gave her a patient look, drawing her lips into a sour lemon curve.

"I'm Billie."

"Short for Wilhelmina, I suppose?" Edith glanced up at me. Her voice was scratchy from too many cigarettes, and foreign-sounding.

"Yes," I lied and Billie cut her eyes at me. I saw no need to tell Miss La-de-da herself that my mama's real name was Lady Willabell DeWitt, that we called her Lady. I smiled up at Edith, showing my naturally pretty teeth (I bleach them).

"Interesting." Edith sucked in her cheeks. "I like it. I'm truly tired of every other girl being named Cathy, Susie, Linda. I like ambiguous names for children. It lends an air of mystery."

A pregnant woman rushed in the front entrance, giving me a wide berth, don't think *I* didn't notice, either. She was Dr. Le-Gette's new wife, that beautician he married, although she's nothing special. She called out to Edith, "I've been trying to reach you all day."

"I've been here, with Vangie," said Edith, turning to the beautician. I strained to listen, but Edith's voice was too soft. I waited another decent interval, staring at the back of the beautician's long, bumpy curls. For a beauty operator, she didn't know shit about hair. Several grim-faced men walked in through the front door, lifting their hats to Edith and the blond woman. I nudged Billie and whispered, "Come on, let's go."

Edith was so deep into her conversation that she failed to notice me and Billie walk outside. Billie skipped down the sidewalk. Then I hung back, lingering on the front walkway, on the off chance that Henry might stroll by. The night air smelled of fresh-cut grass. Streetlights shined through lacy trees. Billie kept skipping down the sidewalk, glancing over her shoulder. "Let's go, Mama!"

I didn't know if Henry was coming or not, but I couldn't just stand there. I tossed the daffodils into the bushes and hurried over to my daughter. As we strolled to the corner, she tugged on my arm and said, "Mama, why didn't we go see Mr. Henry's girl?"

"Too many people."

"How'd she get so sick?"

"She drank poison, princess."

"Wouldn't it taste awful bad? I'd spit it out."

"Sure you would." I squeezed her hand. "I don't know why she didn't."

"Was it a accident?"

"Probably not. I heard she was pregnant by some boy."

"You mean, she went all the way?" Billie's eyes widened.

I stopped walking, then squatted and put my hands on Billie's shoulders. Sometimes I forgot she was just a child. "Never mind what I said, okay? It's just gossip."

"That she's pregnut?"

"Shhhh, don't say that!"

"You did."

"It wasn't nice of me. And don't you ever say it in front of people, like Mr. Henry or Aunt Butter. I mean, you can say it to *me*, when we're all alone, but not to anybody else."

She nodded solemnly. Then she dropped her head to one side and said, "How come so much happens that folks can't talk about? To each other, I mean?"

"Oh, Lord, Billie. I don't know." I stood up. "But it just does."

Billie's eyebrows slanted together. "It must be awful hard to be a grown-up."

"Yes, sometimes it is."

We walked in silence several blocks, then she pulled on my arm again. "Mama, what's a coma?"

"I think it's like being asleep. Why?" I grabbed her shoulders. "Did it scare you, baby? I mean, going to the hospital?"

"Shoot, I ain't scared. Not even of that durn flu. Didn't see nothing no way." Billie broke away from me and skipped down the sidewalk, hopping over cracks. Then she whirled around.

"Mama? If a person's in one of them comas, are they just sleeping, or are they all writhed up in pain?" She drew her fingers into claws.

"I haven't seen anybody having a coma, but I think they just lay there."

"Like Daddy?"

"Kind of. Only he can talk." I shook my head. Boy, could Renny talk. And scream and shout and throw. "We'd better hurry home, princess."

When we turned the corner, I saw shabby old Hayes Avenue and Aunt Butter's house, with the yellow porch light burning. It was the saddest thing I'd ever seen, except when Mama died. Butter was sitting on the porch, like everyone on Hayes, with her dress hiked up, fanning herself with a church bulletin. All the windows were pushed open, the air smelling of fried liver and onions, corn bread, and greasy cabbage. It just broke my heart to go inside. I'd give anything to be with Henry, even if we didn't do a thing but sit in his car, listening to early crickets. Sometimes we kissed in the stockroom, the shelves full of dusty Modess boxes, sun pouring through the high, cobwebbed windows. "I'm going to leave Vangie real soon," he told me. "When?" I said, my voice echoing inside his mouth. "Soon," he said. "Soon. I can't take much more." "I'll be so good to you, Henry. You deserve to be treated right."

Billie tugged my hand. "If I'm ever a real princess, I guess Daddy'll be king. Won't he, Mama?" She smiled, showing her two missing front teeth. She was late to lose her baby teeth, but I saved each one in a bottle. Just like I saved all of her baby hair.

"Sure," I said, swinging our hands toward the house, "but what'll we do with Aunt Butter?"

"Make her one of them duchesses?"

"How about if we just send her to another castle?" I said, but I'd just as soon send her to another planet. When we walked up, Butter circled one arm around the newel post and pulled herself up. "It's about time you came home," she said. "I been worried sick. You didn't leave no note or nothing."

"We been to the hospital," Billie told her.

"You're just a gadabout, DeeDee. Every time you run off, he pitches a fit. Have you seen my kitchen? This is the fourth time this month!"

It took both of us to carry Renny into the bedroom, with him screaming curses and insults, his face swollen and purple from rage. A stringy piece of onion had dried on top of his head. "I ain't ready to go to bed!" he yelled.

"Well, you're going," I said.

"You've got me by the balls." He slapped my face and shoulders. "Hell, men lead sorry lives. They weren't made to be ruled by women!"

We put him in the bed, then came downstairs to sweep up his mess. Fiesta dishes looked like crushed candy—bits of red, green, yellow, blue.

"DeeDee! Come to bed!" Renny croaked from upstairs, his voice slurred by whiskey. He used up his disability on Lucky Strikes and Wild Turkey, paid people to fetch it for him. "I got a surprise waiting for you, girl!"

I ignored him and swiped at the dried food, cupping it in a sponge. His voice flew through the open windows like broken glass.

"That fool's going to wake Billie," said Aunt Butter, reaching under the enamel table. She pulled back three-fourths of a glass bowl.

"I put the fan in her room," I said. "Maybe that'll drown out the noise."

"Doubt it."

"DeeDee!" he yelled. "I still got my lips and fingers! I can play your body like it's a piano. C'mere and see."

"Huh," I muttered, picking my way to the back door, through shattered Fiesta that Aunt Butter had bought one saucer at a time in Carnival Oats. I propped open the screen with a broom handle. Night air rustled through the trees.

"It's gonna rain all night," I said.

"Who cares?" Aunt Butter grunted. Behind her the kitchen walls were splotched with color, dented in places by thrown saucers. I bent over, scooping pinto beans into a dust pail. Aunt Butter gripped the counter and heaved herself up. She snapped on the radio, in the middle of Kay Starr and Tennessee Ernie Ford singing "I'll Never Be Free."

"To hell with you!" hollered Renny. "To hell with all women!"

"Maybe he'll hush now." Aunt Butter raked pottery shards into a dishpan.

I glanced out the door, half hoping I'd see Henry's Rambler. If I did, I'd run him down, climb into the front seat, and say, "Drive us to Canada." Way off in the distance I heard thunder, the low boil of it. Night washed down low, with black, soggy clouds. Through the screen, I saw Aunt Butter's chickens roosting in the trees. All the neighbors had pullets and laying hens, but we couldn't seem to keep ours in the pen. The backyard was full of feathers, too.

Sometimes, on my lunch break, I walked the four blocks to Lake Limoges. I always sat on the dock that faced Henry's house and threw stale bread to the ducks. Henry's yard looked like a postcard from Audubon Park, and I wished with all my strength that it was mine. If Butter knew that I coveted it, she'd say, "If wishes were horses, then we'd all ride."

Now Butter dumped pinto beans into the trash, and I thought, "You've been good to me, but I can't stay here." When I was thirteen Mama began sweating all night, coughing up her insides. In the morning her pillow was bloody. Her room stank. It was heavy air, pulled down by the scent of pee and sweat and blood. She was so skinny, it felt awful to touch her. I could feel bones through her skin. It was like deboning chicken to bathe her. I'd feel a handful of flesh move, like I was peeling it away from the muscles, exposing the pink sheen of her insides.

She was eat up with TB. Caught it from Daddy. I don't know why me or Dillon never got sick. Before Daddy came down with it, he worked as a foreman on the Wauford plantation.

We lived in a rundown house with all the paint peeled off. The kitchen floor slanted down so spilled water could run out into the yard. Mama was still young and pretty, and we'd sit on the steps and watch the planes fly low, crop dusting. The cotton surrounded us, with powder hanging in the air. Sometimes the fields seemed to spin around us, the dust rising in a wavy cloud.

"Let's pretend all that cotton is ours," Lady would say, flicking one hand toward the field. After she died, Butter paid cash for the funeral. Then she took us back to Limoges on the bus, holding Dillon's fat, sweaty hand. She didn't even try to hold mine. I thought Limoges would be a temporary stop for me, just like all the other little stops the bus made between Texas and the Mississippi River, dusty old markets that smelled of overripe bananas.

Butter was an old maid and ran a cafe. That seemed like a lot to me and Dillon. Even then she had the knack of seeing through me. I hated her for it, too. When I turned up pregnant not too many weeks after my honeymoon with Renny, Aunt Butter said, "You want a baby like you want a toaster for the kitchen. Like you want a puppy dog. Only you can't take care of nothing. You'd leave us all in a heartbeat if the right man came along."

Here I was all these years later, still on Hayes Avenue, scraping up thrown food and wiping a grown man's hind end. I became a wife and mother while I was still a child. Sometimes I wondered if my life had worn me out. Two things I knew for sure: I wanted to be taken care of by a sweet man, and my days with Renny Robichaux were numbered. If Henry didn't work out, I'd find somebody else. Sooner or later, I'd hit the jackpot—a man who'd risk everything for me. He'd leave his family, and I'd leave mine, except for Billie. I'd come back for her.

Now that I was in love with Henry, I knew Renny was a born failure. I married him to get away from Limoges, and he'd failed me. He couldn't sell Bibles to Jesus. No wonder he got bombed over in Korea. One day I'd have friends, not these old ladies on Hayes Avenue. I would mingle with club ladies who wore expensive clothes, good shoes, nylons without runs. I would rise above home permanents. I would have a beautiful house and drive a Cadillac or Oldsmobile Cruiser convertible. I would have a maid named Surphromia. Then people would know I was somebody. They would not call me "Butter's niece" or "that Robichaux woman."

Sometimes life was more than disappointing; it was downright painful.

Now Butter looked at me and said, "Renny Robichaux needs more help than I can give." She squeezed out her dishrag, then rubbed it over the floor. "He needs our prayers. He needs the Lord's wisdom. It's out of my hands. I'm turning it over to a higher power. And I advise you to do the same, DeeDee."

"That's just what I had in mind," I said, winking at Aunt Butter, but I knew the old woman didn't understand.

A Good Love
Is Hard to Find

❧

IN LOVING MEMORY OF MRS. OLIVIA NEPPER,
Who Passed Away One Year Ago, April 14, 1932.

There is someone who misses you sadly
We often sit and think of how you died.
Even though you sometimes acted badly,
At your funeral we all cried.
The blow was hard, the shock severe;
We never thought your death was near.
We know you are in Heaven,
Talking to Peter, Andrew, and Paul,
Counting backward in your serial 7s.
With love, from Henry and All.

—LIMOGES *NEWS-LEADER,* IN MEMORANDUM, ORIGINAL
VERSE BY HENRY NEPPER, [C] FEBRUARY 1933

Sophie Donnell shook out Bon Ami, the powder scattering into
the pink bathtub, then she dampened her sponge, squeezing out
excess water. From the bedroom, Miss Vangie was crying, her
sobs catching in her throat like hunks of wet cotton. Sophie
rocked on her heels, peering into the frilly bedroom. "Just tell me
what's wrong," Henry was saying, standing in front of his wife.
"Can't you tell me, honey?"

Vangie answered by crying harder. She shook her head back
and forth, slinging tears. The whole front of her dress was wet.
Sophie shook her own head and spit into the tub. She knelt over

the rim and began rubbing the gray, scummy ring, courtesy of Mr. Henry, who bathed more than any man in Limoges.

"Tell me, sweetheart," Henry coaxed, and Sophie spit again. Then she wiped the sponge under the faucet. She was always getting caught by squabbles, if not her own, then everyone else's. She turned on the cold tap, and water splashed down hard, filling the pink-and-black room with noise.

"Just tell me who you bought it for," Vangie said, her voice perfectly heartbroken. Then she blew her nose into a damp Kleenex. Weeks ago, for her fortieth birthday, Henry had given her a new Mixmaster and Triomphe perfume, the bottle a perfect replica of the Arc de Triomphe in Paris, France. After opening the presents, she kept smiling, fully expecting him to reach into his pocket and pull out the blue velvet case. "Your new watch," he'd say and fasten it around her wrist.

By the time she went to bed, her smile was a bit weaker. The next morning, she opened the sock drawer and stroked the box. She didn't understand why Henry was hoarding it. Every morning she slid open the drawer. It became a ritual—brush your teeth, check the box, make biscuits and coffee. This morning, when she opened the drawer, the box was missing.

"Who, Henry?" she asked again.

"Who, what?" He looked startled.

"I know all about that watch." Vangie pointed at the dresser. "When I was putting your socks away, I saw the box in your drawer."

"Watch?" he said, but his eyes darted to the dresser, then to the closet.

"The diamond one, with a sterling band. From Cox's Jewelry over in Vicksburg. When were you in Mississippi, Henry? And where is that watch?"

He sat down on the bed. "Well, you caught me," he said.

"I have?" Vangie blinked. She wasn't sure she wanted to hear another word. She wished with all her heart that she hadn't found that box. Henry rested his forearms on his knees, shaking his head. He got up, walked over to his closet, and opened the door. Reaching into the pocket of a wool overcoat, he pulled out the velvet box. "Leave it to you, Vangie, to ruin your own surprises."

"Surprise?"

"Here," he said, rattling the box, "Take it."

"No." She drew back.

"Might as well. It's yours." He shook the box again.

"I don't want it. Give it to whoever you really bought it for."

"There's no whoever." He sat down and pushed the box into

her hands. "I was saving this for Mother's Day. Take it. Enjoy it."

Vangie shut her eyes and rubbed her fingers over the soft nappy case. She threw her arms around Henry's neck and buried her face in the front of his white smock.

"I feel like an idiot!" she cried.

"That's 'cause you are, honey." He patted her shoulder. "You're the biggest idiot in the world."

When Sophie finished cleaning the bathroom, she found Vangie in the kitchen, happily making pimiento cheese. On her left wrist was the wristwatch. She did not say where it came from, and Sophie didn't ask. They moved around the kitchen, Vangie grating cheese into a bowl, Sophie peeling apples for fruit salad. Later, they walked to the hospital to sit with Olive. The girl was spread out on the narrow bed like a paper doll, thin and pliable. Vangie put the watch around her daughter's wrist, saying, "It's from Daddy. We'll just take turns wearing it, all right?"

Vangie sat down and read the newspaper aloud, her voice humming like a bumblebee. Sophie leaned against the window. These long, hard days were getting to her, settling in her lower back. She wondered if she'd cripple up like her mama. What in the world would Burr do to her then?

Around three o'clock they walked back home. They fried pork chops and baked cheese grits to go with the fruit salad. Mr. Henry came home, complaining about his day. He looked up at Sophie and said, "Well, I guess you're waiting to be paid." He opened his wallet and picked out two dollars.

It was always a shock, taking money from Mr. Henry. She wished he'd work late all the time. She stuffed her money into her purse, waved goodbye to Vangie, and left. She walked toward the corner of Cypress and Washington, past Miss Harriet's house, past Dr. LeGette's. Miss Waldene waved from the porch and called out, "See you tomorrow, Sophie."

"Yes, ma'am." Sophie raised her hand. Miss Waldene was wearing a green smock patterned with frogs. Her belly was slung low, like she was carrying a girl, but Sophie had guessed wrong before. She turned the corner, heading north toward the Yellow Fever Cemetery. Sometimes she stopped to pray over Fanny's mama. MISS MARGARET JANE LEGETTE, the stone said. BELOVED WIFE AND MOTHER, BORN SEPTEMBER 7, 1921—DIED JANUARY 10, 1951. Now that it was spring, Fanny kept it covered with wildflowers, but Dr. LeGette acted like this place didn't exist. Margaret Jane died with a baby inside her. She started bleeding, and nothing could stop it—prayers, God, not even Dr. LeGette himself.

Five months later, he married Miss Waldene. All she talked about was how Fanny needed a baby brother. How Dr. LeGette needed a son. "Don't you agree, Sophie?" she asked. Sophie kept drying dishes, stacking them in the cupboard. "I need to fill this house with babies," Waldene said. Fanny's eyes filled, but Miss Waldene kept on talking. Not too many weeks later, Sophie was cooking breakfast for Dr. LeGette and Fanny. They sat at the kitchen table, dipping toast into sunny-side-up eggs, and down the hall Miss Waldene was vomiting. *Serves you right*, Sophie thought. The next time she cleaned the Hoopers' house, Miss Harriet stared out the window, watching Dr. LeGette's bride shell butter beans, stopping every few minutes to gag. "I hope she vomits that baby right up," Harriet said.

Three miles from home, Sophie stopped at City Market and bought a tin of soda crackers for forty-nine cents and three cans of Royal Gem pork and beans at a dime each. She bought bananas, two pounds of ground beef, and still had change for Burr's Half and Half tobacco. Mrs. Hawley guarded the cash register because Mr. Hawley was sick with the flu. "A fever of a hundred and three," said his wife. "It's all over town. You take care of yourself, Sophie."

"Yes, ma'am," she called out.

She walked the three miles in cool, April air, keeping to the ditch alongside the road. The bottom of the grocery sack felt damp and cold, and she feared it might burst. When she reached the turn in the road, the sun was wedged between the trees. The air smelled of jonquils, which were blooming by her mailbox. She walked up the dusty road. Straight ahead was her gray wood house with its double porches and rusty tin roof. She went inside, set down her groceries, and tied on her apron. She started up the old wood stove, feeding corncobs into the grate. She chopped an onion and dumped the flecks into the iron skillet. While they sautéed, she set the kettle to boiling. She moved around the kitchen, cooking from instinct, the way she breathed.

She shook flour into her biscuit bowl, adding buttermilk and shortening, then she mixed everything into a firm ball. Picking up a fork with sticky fingers, she stirred the onions. When they were crystal clear, she crumbled in the beef, adding salt, pepper, Tabasco, and a lump of brown sugar. While it fried, she went back to kneading her biscuits.

The wood stove was salvaged from the LeGette house in 1939, when they modernized. It had reservoirs on each end that held hot water, a luxury in this house. Just off the kitchen was a rickety room with sausage crocks, shelves full of preserves and veg-

etables in Ball jars. Two hams dangled from the ceiling, swinging
on twine. The linoleum floor was buckled, and in one half of the
room the pattern didn't match. Sophie was tempted to kick off
her shoes and walk barefoot, but she knew she'd have to go outside to the wood pile for more kindling. This house had electricity
but no indoor plumbing; she knew folks without either luxury
who lived like kings. There was an old saying that Louisiana people ate better than anyone in the world. Her supper tonight wasn't
too grand—just some Red River Hash, what her sister Mary
Annie used to cook.

She rolled the biscuits, slapped them on a greased pan, and
set it near the stove. Then she opened the beans, dumping them
into the skillet. All the while she kept feeding corncobs into the
grate. The room filled with heat and the scent of fried food and
seasonings. When she leaned over to slide the biscuits into the
oven, Burr sneaked up behind her and grabbed her waist.

"You scared me!" she cried and jumped sideways, burning her
hand on the stove. The pan fell to the floor.

"You ain't hurt. Pick them biscuits up." Burr stepped back
and wiped his mouth. She smelled whiskey on his breath.

"You scared me." She knelt down, grasped the pan, shoved it
into the oven.

"You're skittish 'cause your people spoilt you." He reached
out and grabbed her again, fumbling under her dress. She felt his
hand against her bare leg.

"I got supper to fix," she said, squirming away.

"First you got to fix me." He reached up and jerked her
panties down to her ankles.

"You're too rough."

"You don't know what rough is." He raised his hand over her
head and laughed when she flinched. He shoved her back. Thinking he'd lost interest, she inched over to the stove to stir the
beans, but he yanked her back.

"Not so fast." He slid one hand up her dress, curving between
her legs.

"Don't." She shut her eyes. "The food'll burn."

He peeled down his overalls, the buckles jingling, and she saw
his poker sticking out. She started to run, then realized a second
too late that her ankles were hobbled by the panties. She stumbled, hitting the floor with her arms splayed out. She started to
get up, but he stepped over her, framing her between his legs.

"But my supper's burning!" She reached to pull up her
panties, but he lifted his foot and stamped her hand. Pain shot up
her arm, then he moved his foot. He reached down and raised her

dress, flipping it over her hips. His poker was sticking straight out from his underwear.

"Burr, please let me get the food off the stove."

"It won't burn, cause I ain't going to take that long." He dropped to his knees, then flopped on top of her, nudging her legs apart. He pushed himself high up inside her, mashing his shoulder into her face. He smelled like a goat, like something that should be tethered. When the teakettle started whistling, her legs automatically jerked, but she was pinned to the floor. He kept digging into her with that piece of bone, her dress bunched up around her waist.

Then he moaned, his legs jerked and stiffened. The kettle trembled, hissing steam. As soon as he rolled off, wiping a string of saliva from his mouth, she got up, pulled up her panties, and grabbed a dishrag. She slid the kettle to a cool burner, then bent over and checked her biscuits. They were browning nicely, but the beans were sticking.

He came up behind her, fumbling with the snaps on his overalls, and peered over her shoulder. "Hey, what's this?" he cried. "You call this food?"

"Didn't have time to catch me no hen," she said.

"You're too lazy is all. I ain't eating this shit." He picked up the hot skillet and carried it out to the porch. Sophie heard him whistling for the dogs.

"Burr, you bring it back! That food cost me good money."

He knocked open the door with his foot, and it banged against the wall. Glaring at her, he crossed the room in three steps. He was spoiling for a fight, and she was too tired to give him one. Too tired to stand up for herself. She turned back to the stove. Smoke curled up from the ham. When she reached for the fork, he slapped it from her hand.

"I said I ain't eating this shit. I been setting out trot lines, and what you been doin'? Lallygagging with rich ladies. Drinking tea and letting them pat you on the head. Give you ideas."

"I been working, Burr. Two dollars a day is good money."

"Yeah?" He spit on the floor. "That's how much I think of your two dollars."

"It bought them beans you throwed out."

"Then let me throw the bitch who bought them." He picked her up, high above his head, and held her there until a blue vein popped out on his forehead.

"Please, Burr." She groped for his shoulder. "Let me down. Please put me down."

"Yes, ma'am." He let go. She slammed against the floor, banging her head on a corner of the stove. Her good eye throbbed. The room was spinning. Burr leaned over her, staring her down.

"Please," she said. "My biscuits."

"My biscuits," he mimicked. His eyes were so close together, she wanted to mash them with her fingernails. "Try and get them, just you try." He raised his hand menacingly, and she rolled into a ball, covering her face with her hands. He reached down and grabbed her arm, yanking with his full weight. She heard the bone separate from the socket. At first there was no sensation, just an empty space, then pain slammed into her shoulder.

"Stop!" She tried to grab his overalls with her good hand, but he shifted out of her reach. He dragged her out of the kitchen, onto the porch, and dropped her on the edge, next to the steps. Then he swung back his leg and kicked her in the small of the back. She screamed, rolled off the porch, and landed with a hard smack in the dirt.

"He's unhinged my arm," she thought. It hurt to breathe. She heard the screen door slam, heard noises from the kitchen. A box of crickets sat on the porch. One time he grabbed her neck and shoved her head into a barrel full of hoppers. They flicked against her eyelids, crawled up her nose. The barrel held a stench like armpits. She couldn't breathe, couldn't scream, couldn't wrench free of his grasp. Now a burned, floury smell drifted onto the porch. From far away, she heard him holler, "So-fee! Git in here and clean up this mess."

Two, maybe three minutes passed. Or maybe a whole lifetime. She'd lost track. He banged pans, kicked a chair. It was full dark outside, and the air felt crisp, with a brittle edge. April was such an unreliable month. There was no moon, no stars. She ached to cry. From the woods, she heard two short notes of a bobwhite quail. Finally, Burr came onto the porch, clattering down the steps, and stood over her.

"Didn't you hear me? I said get in here. You ain't hurt."

She stared up at him with her good eye and spit blood into the dirt. It wouldn't do for Burr to know he'd hurt her. Pain thrilled him, as long as it wasn't his own, and he'd take her again, right here in the dirt.

"I think my arm's broke," she said, slowly pulling herself up. Her arm was curved around her side.

"Hell, you're just trying to get out of cooking." He stared, then climbed the steps, his boots dashing against the wood. He crossed the plank floor. "You cook everybody else's food in town. Why not mine? You tell me why, Sophie!"

"I need me a doctor." She cradled her injured arm.

"Well, you ain't getting one." He kicked open the screen door and stepped into the kitchen.

"Then you won't get no supper," she said, then flinched. Her mouth would get her killed one day. He turned, and even through the screen mesh, she saw his eyes bug out. She took off running, hugging her arm. She heard him scream her name and slap open the door, heard his shoes clap across the porch, down the steps. She ran toward the barn, glancing behind her. She leaped over a hoe, her hurt arm flopping against her side. Burr was just a few feet behind her. He stepped on the hoe, and the handle swung up and hit his face. He howled, but she kept running, past the barn, into the woods. She climbed over a fallen log, then splashed across a ditch, toward the bayou. She wanted to lie down between the crayfish traps, letting the current flow over her arm, but Burr would catch her for sure.

"Goddamn you bitch!" he hollered, but she couldn't see him. She waded into a fresh growth of plantain and timothy, then crawled into a cypress stump, folding herself into a tight ball. Behind her, in the clearing, she heard him step on fallen branches, splintering wood with his heavy boots.

"Sophie?" he yelled. An owl answered, and he jerked around. More branches snapped as he stomped down the path. She held her breath. Her arm felt severed, and her right eye was sore and puffy. Through the cypress cracks, she saw him veer off from the path, turning in a wide circle. Blood dripped down one side of his face, and he wiped his eye.

"Shit!" He kicked a tree. She watched him pick his way back to the path, then he turned and looked directly at her. She stopped breathing. His eyes swept past the stump, into the woods, where peepers were crying out.

"You got to come home sometime!" Then he spun around, kicking another skinny tree, and trudged toward the barn. She guessed the biscuits were burned, the kitchen full of smoke, maybe on fire. All her good Royal Gem beans getting lapped up by the skinny dogs.

She waited until she was sure he was gone. Then she crept out from the stump and stood up slowly. She swayed back and forth. If she fainted, he would find her and beat her senseless. Her body was a map of his anger, lines of old fractures. Muscles pulled from the bone. She saw a light inside the barn, and she knew he'd found a lantern. He'd come back and find her. Drag her back to the house, or maybe kill her right here. Bury her under the plantain. Who would ever know? It was no small wonder that his kids were gone, the boys working on the rigs in Morgan City, the girl gone back to Mississippi.

She had to keep walking, or else be found. She waded across the bayou. The water was cold and sluggish, rising to her waist. On the other side, she stepped through kudzu. The mud felt good against her bruises. Everything around her was black—the trees and air. She plodded forward, cradling her arm. Sticker bushes snagged her dress and scratched her legs. The Woodrow sisters owned land north of here, but she didn't know the way to their house from this direction. She'd only been from Highway 65. She wondered if she'd have to cross Bayou Maçon, which was deep from the spring rains. This time of year the woods weren't too snaky, but she had every reason to believe that rabid foxes were about. Late at night she heard them howling. Except for their lush tails, they reminded her of wormy dogs, with skinny haunches.

She had never ventured this far into the woods, and she feared making a giant circle, finding herself in front of her own house. Using her good hand for balance, she stepped forward. An owl hooted. Something scampered to her right. She saw a streak of brown—a buck arcing through thin pines. Beyond the trees was a clearing, and she walked toward it. A tar-paper house stood backlit against the dark sky. It reminded her of a Christmas-card house, smoke curling from the chimney. The windows were lined with jelly jars—red, purple, gold. She walked past a freshly tilled garden, a hen house with a piece of dirty cloth blocking the door, and stopped next to a cistern, where the ground was muddy. A dog crawled out from under the porch and barked. The sound held in the air. From the edge of the porch, a match flared, and someone held up a lantern. "Who's there?" a man called out.

"It's me," she hollered, stumbling forward. The air made her shiver, but it held a comforting aroma of hickory wood.

"Who's me?" The man stepped down the porch and walked toward her. When he held up the lantern, she saw the face of Israel Adams, the embalmer from Beaulieu's. "Sophie?" he said. "That you?"

She nodded.

"Lord have mercy." He looked down at her arm, her torn dress. "It *is* you. What happened to your face?"

"Got hit."

"Well, I can see that. Burr been drinking again?"

"He won't like me being here." She licked her bottom lip; it felt swollen. "If you could just point me toward the Woodrow sisters?"

"Your arm broke?" He swung the lantern.

"I don't know. I can't move it none."

"Here, let me help you inside—"

"No, the Woodrow sisters is fine. They can fix me."

"Burr might come hunting for you. At least let me drive you to Mr. Cab's. He's got a room where you can sleep the night. You'll be safe there."

She was too dizzy to argue. When he led her to his old black truck, she gripped his arm, shuffling like an old woman. He helped her inside, covering her with a scratchy blanket that smelled of mothballs. "I feel like I'm dying," she said and leaned her head back against the glass.

"No, you ain't. You just beat real bad. You going to be fine, just fine." Israel climbed into the front seat, making the truck sway, and started the engine.

Cab Beaulieu was sitting in his mother's old canning porch, smoking a cigarette. From the kitchen, the phone kept ringing, but he ignored it. He wasn't sure who was calling—maybe someone had died?—but he suspected it was that lady from Lake Providence who kept inviting him over for pecan pie and coffee. If she didn't have bug eyes and sour breath, he might have taken her up on it.

Headlights swept across the yard, shining into the azaleas. A door slammed, then another. He heard footsteps in the gravel, then he saw Israel coming up the walk with Sophie slumped against him. Cab stood up, ran outside, and threw down his cigarette.

"Burr been drinking again," Israel said.

"Ought to sew up his mouth," Cab muttered, helping them into the house. They led Sophie up the squeaky back staircase, guiding her into the guest bedroom. She seemed dazed. Cab guessed that her left shoulder was dislocated, but no bones seemed to be broken. Still, he was no doctor. He turned into the hall to ring up Phillip LeGette, thinking of Sophie's face. Her eyes were starting to swell, the flesh turning purple; her whole body was covered with cuts and gashes. He'd seen dead people who looked better.

When Phillip answered, Cab said, "I've got Sophie Donnell over here, and she's been beat up again."

"I'll be right over."

"Hurry." Cab hung up the phone, then turned to Israel. "I can't for the life of me understand why a man would do this to a woman."

"He ain't no man," said Israel.

"No, he's a son of a bitch."

They waited on the canning porch while Phillip LeGette walked over, crossing through a gap in the azaleas, butting the limbs apart with his black bag. When they started to follow him to Sophie's room, Phillip shook his head. "If I need you, I'll call. Last thing she needs is a room full of men."

Cab slapped his pocket, feeling for his cigarettes. He lit one, cupping his hand over the light. Then he braced one palm against the wall and blew smoke through the screen. Edith's house glowed cozily, and a porch lantern burned at the Hoopers'. In between, the Neppers' house was dark. They were probably at the hospital, watching Olive breathe. He'd heard that she was pregnant, but he was so tired of gossip. You couldn't believe half of what you heard. People always knew more about your life than you did. And the ones who were quickest to pass judgment had the smallest lives of all. Still, they caused trouble. Like all those nice merchants who formed the White Citizens Council, one step short of the Ku Klux Klan. Cab had refused to join, and it hadn't hurt his business. (It helped being the only funeral home in the parish.)

Well, hell. That was life. If you were different, people noticed. The gossips would have plenty to say about Sophie—blind in one eye and Lord knows what else. Half the gossips would condemn her for not leaving her husband, the other half would ask why she wasn't a better wife. If Cab were Sophie, he'd wait until Burr fell asleep, then he'd wrap him in a sheet, pinning his arms and legs in the fabric. Then he'd take a Coca-Cola bottle and beat the shit out of him.

"See how you like that," he'd say. Of course, if Sophie ever did that, Burr would kill her. In his years as an undertaker, Cab had observed the effects of violence on the human body. He had repaired the faces of young men who were beaten to death for nothing more than smiling at another man's girlfriend.

Cab himself was beaten by two huge football players when he was barely sixteen. The cocaptain of the Limoges Tigers was passing gum in geometry class, and Cab, thinking the gum was for him, folded the stick and bit down on it. On his way home from school, the football player and three buddies jumped him. They grabbed his shirt and ripped it to his waist.

"You stole my gum!" the guy yelled, his breath hot and sour.

"Gum?" Cab blinked. He honestly didn't remember any gum.

"In geometry, you asshole! I was passing it to Mary Kay Wallace, and you took it!"

"I thought it was for me." Cab shrugged. "I'm sorry. I won't do it again."

The guy made a fist and knocked Cab to the ground. Then he fell on him, punching his eyes and mouth. He tasted blood. Then one of the other boys lifted Cab's head by the hair and banged it against the sidewalk.

"That'll teach you to steal gum," he said, then he kicked Cab in the ribs. The boys took off running. Cab was sprawled on the sidewalk, his head resting in a chipped-out piece of concrete. Blood dripped from his nose, splattering on his arm. The last thing he thought before he passed out was that his daddy would have to saw a regular coffin in half because he was too large for a Babyline and too short for a regular-sized.

Cab and Israel chain-smoked until the canning porch was cloudy. Smoke sifted through the screen mesh, hanging in the black air. When Phillip LeGette walked out, he handed Cab a bottle of pills. "When she wakes up, give her two of these," Phillip said.

"She hurt bad?" Israel stepped forward.

"Yes, but she'll be all right," Phillip told him. "Maybe not the same, but she'll live."

The men walked out into the cool night air. A few early katydids clicked. Israel looked up at the second-story windows, all dark except for one. "Sleep, Miss Sophie," he said. "And let the devil take back his own."

The Long Egg

∾

THREE GENERATIONS
OF UNDERTAKERS AT BEAULIEU'S

Cabot Beaulieu has returned from the Ernest P. Swann School of Mortuary Science and Embalming in Alexandria. He graduated at the top of his class. Cabot's father, George Beaulieu, told this reporter that he's just as proud of his son's achievement as he is of his 40-odd-year subscription to the Times-Picayune. *Young Mr. Beaulieu will join his father and grandfather in funeral direction at 15 Oak Street.*
    —Limoges *News-Leader*, page 3, 1946

Cab Beaulieu

"He was my ninth-grade English teacher," I tell Twilly, looking down at the long, pale body of Mr. Jonathan Mires. We've just finished embalming him.

"Now he a corpse," Twilly says, pulling the sheet over Mr. Mires's head. I let this pass. You aren't supposed to call it corpse or dead body; they teach you in school to say deceased or Mr. or Mrs. Blank. Poor old Mr. Mires has been embalmed but not restored, which is a whole other procedure. The best time for it is eight to ten hours later, when the tissues get firm and dry.

I am a Doctor of Grief. In the 1800s, morticians were called the Dismal Traders. There is a living to be made—some say fortune—but I think funerals shouldn't cost a arm and a leg. It's not like folks can comparison-shop and get back to you.

Later, I walk to the kitchen. Israel is sitting at the table, drinking a cup of iced coffee and thumbing through a copy of *Embalmer's Monthly*. There is an empty cup next to his elbow and a crumpled napkin, and I know that Sophie has been there. She has also left a pot of chicken and dumplings on the stove, with a pan of rice. Cooked it all, I guess, with one arm. She is still living in my guest room, and at night she waxes the floors. I can't make her quit.

"You get Mr. Mires done?" Israel asks. Pinned to the wall behind him is a poster from Southern Bell Telephone & Telegraph. It features a smiling woman, saying, "I'll call you back. My party line neighbor needs to call the druggist!" Beneath the caption someone has written: *Telephone, Telegraph, Tell a woman.*

"Nearly done." I pour some coffee, then sit down at the table. A box of sugared doughnuts stands open, with a stack of cups and saucers where mourners can fix their own. Twilly sits down and pours coffee into the saucer. Then he blows on it. The liquid ruffles like small waves. He lifts the saucer and sips.

"My grandpa drank his coffee the same way," I tell him. "It burns my tongue when I try. What's the point?"

"It's a old custom." He smiles. "Way back when, cups didn't have no handles."

"Guess it's a dying custom, " I say. "Except for you, Israel."

"Ain't dead yet." He laughs. "No sir. Israel's here."

I stretch my legs under the table and look out the double windows into the shady backyard. The bushes and trees are green, and I can't see all of the Neppers' yard. A yellow Cadillac with a blue top is parked in the driveway, next to a black Pontiac. That is Mrs. Chenier from First Baptist, bringing supper to Vangie and Henry.

"I been thinking," Twilly says, pushing back his red-and-white checkered hat. "PURINA" is written at the top. "They's some advantage to being dead."

"What's that?" I laugh.

"Well, you don't get hot in the summer or have to fool with eating or shitting or sweating. You don't got bills. Alls you got to do is lay there and sleep."

"And let the worms eat on you," Israel says.

"They won't eat on me, no sir. I'll get me a airtight coffin."

"I bet you got one all picked out." I set down the saucer.

"As a matter of fact, I do." Behind Twilly the wall phone rings; he reaches back with one long arm and grabs the receiver. "Beaulieu Funeral Home," he says, his eyes darting back and forth. Then his face draws up, and I know it is a death. When this phone rings, it's generally one of two things, a widow wanting me to eat supper or somebody has died.

"All right. Yessir," Twilly says into the receiver, then hangs up. He looks at me. "You ain't gonna like it."

"What?"

"That was Sheriff Reems. They found a floater in Bayou Tenesas."

"Who drowned?"

"Amos Copeland."

"That old fool, " Israel says. "Fishing off that old bridge. Poor old thing."

"Doing more drinking than fishing, I'd say." Twilly shakes his head and sighs. "I been waiting for this. I just hope we got room in the freezer."

"We'll just have to make room," I say, but I dreaded it. I hate floaters worse than anything. "This is some bad day." Israel sighs. "First Mr. Mires, and now this drowning."

"They's all bad days, if you ask me," Twilly says, then throws his head back and laughs like crazy.

All night I sit on the porch, smoking and drinking Jack Daniel's, thinking about what I do for a living. It's a family tradition; my granddaddy started this place in 1901, and I didn't have a choice but to come back here and help out. The very word *undertaking* makes you think of taking somebody and putting them under. My job is this: selling funerals and comforting the grieved. Twilly says it rhymes with deceived, and when you get to doing that, you'd better look for another line of work. Israel says, "No, sir. Not me." He doesn't mind spending the better part of his time with dead folks. "I feel beholden to care for them who passed," he always tells me and Twilly. "They can't take care of their selves no more, and they counting on you to get them safe in the ground."

The Egyptians raised burial to a fine art. First, they removed the brain and entrails. Next, they scoured the body with palm wine and spices. They soaked it for seventy days in a saline solution, wrapping the corpse in linen strips. After being placed in a wooden case (human-shaped), the deceased was interred in a sepulchral chamber. When I told this to Israel, he laughed and said it sounded like a recipe for making pickles.

Now, sitting on the porch, enjoying being all alone, I hear the inside phone ring. Normally, I have a high tolerance for letting it ring, but tonight I rush to answer it, afraid the noise will wake Sophie. The least little thing wakes her up—last night some widow from Epps called, and Sophie started cleaning the oven, something she'd been threatening to do for weeks.

I grab the phone and say, "Beaulieu's." My daddy used to say "Funeral home" when he answered, but not me. I keep my distance every way I can.

"Well, it's about time," says a familiar voice. It belongs to a thirty-two-year-old widow from Lake Providence. I swear, I don't know what it is about me that attracts widows, but some nights I can't beat them off with a stick. "I guess it's too late for you to drive over, isn't it?" she says.

"Guess so."

Soon as I hang up, the phone rings again and a woman says, "Cab Beaulieu? I been trying to reach you all night." The voice belongs to a right cute girl, Cordy King, whose husband died a month or two ago in Korea. "I'm calling to invite you over for gumbo," she says, her voice thick as a roux. "I'm a real, real good cook."

"I bet you are," I say, but I think, "I swear! We just got her husband in the ground!"

I didn't start out being a loverboy. I am the only child of Emmaline and George Woodrow Beaulieu, three generations of undertakers. I led a sheltered life, even though my childhood, in retrospect, was morbid. I played hide-'n'-seek in the selection room, and every time a coffin was damaged, I got to add it to my collection; in the backyard I'd built a fort, turning the coffins sideways, the satin linings exposed and sagging, so mean kids from up the street couldn't see me. Mama used a mahogany coffin as a buffet in the dining room. She set it up on a little stand and decorated it with silver candelabras and the tea service. And when Daddy drove down to the L.S.U. ball games, he took the hearse.

You'd think a family this open-minded about death would not be closed about life, but I swear, I thought babies were ordered from Sears, Roebuck. Couldn't understand why Mother refused to place an order. I wanted a little brother real bad. "Ask the stork to bring you one," my daddy suggested. Every time I saw a crane or a stork wading in Lake Limoges, I'd holler out to it.

I grew up book-smart and people-dumb, especially ignorant about women. To this day I remember falling asleep on the davenport on the second floor of the funeral home. I dreamed about a pretty girl I'd seen in church. I'd just turned thirteen. When I woke up, I felt a straining in my groin. I looked down and saw a lump in my trousers. My privacy was sticking up. I wasn't for sure but what I'd messed my pants, or else laid an egg, a longish egg. I reached down between my thighs and grabbed it. A sensation shot through my insides, clear up my spine. I touched myself again.

My mother picked that moment to walk into the room. She was carrying folded sheets. When she saw what I was doing, she screamed and threw the linen into the air. All the color left her face. Never in her life had she taken the Lord's name in vain, but she said, "Good God almighty! What's gotten into you?"

I wondered, too, but it was more like *What had gotten out?* I was so embarrassed, I got up from the davenport and ran into the hall. Didn't stop running until I was in the backyard. Daddy was in the garage, taking spark plugs out of the hearse. Granddaddy was out in the yard, watering his tomatoes. I tried to explain what happened, but Daddy's face turned red, then purple blue. He laid down the spark plug, wiped his hand on a rag, and put one arm around me. A faint smell of engine oil drifted up. This comforted me. It was a normal scent for daddies, not like the sharp chemical cloud that waited for my own daddy in the embalming room.

"Son, has some girl been rubbing up on you?" Daddy looked grim.

"No, sir! I've never even touched a girl. Not even her arm."

"There's things you don't know about women." Daddy gripped my shoulder, squeezing to the bone. "Did you know it's wrong for your privacy to get hard with a woman?"

I shook my head. I couldn't imagine such a thing; I'd never thought about my privacy, to tell the truth, but exposing it to a woman sounded shameful and exciting.

"You can get a woman in real bad trouble, son." Daddy squeezed my arm. "And a whole lot more, too."

I couldn't imagine that, either, but I said, "Yes, sir."

"Don't you forget it, son."

"But what's it *for*, Daddy?" I stared down between my legs, then looked up.

"It's not for anything except peeing, plain old peeing! Don't you worry about it." He slammed down the hood and walked back to the house, looking old and stooped.

My eyes filled. Back then, I was tenderhearted. I wanted to be a perfect son for Mama and Daddy so they'd have another child. Still, I had me a feeling that I couldn't stop my thing from growing. So I decided to never touch it again, no matter how long it got, but deep inside, I was worried sick. The root of all evil didn't seem like money but what was stuck between my legs. I told myself that I couldn't help it, I was born that way just like some people had hair lips and hunchbacks.

Most terrible of all, I had an idea that I was changing from the inside out. My voice would get deep, then screak up like a girl's. Hairs were poking out of me. I felt like a molting chicken. Back in the Depression, we had Barred Rock hens in the backyard, and I'd been the one to gather the eggs and clean the coop. Daddy wouldn't set foot near the chickens. He said eggs were womanish. But Mama said an egg was anything. Inside the shell, the embryo could be a rooster or a hen.

Lord, I thought. What if it was catching and I was turning into an egg layer? I didn't know. Or what if I had an awful disease, where parts of my body swelled up double and burst?

In the back of my mind was the pastor saying that God does not smile on he who lusts after the flesh. I suspected that lust was a hard thing that came and went inside a man's trousers. It was the ache in my belly and what made me pee the bed at night. Mother warned me not to touch it, that it might snap off. I swear, I would've been happy to be smooth and clean down there.

When I was real little, I'd beg to visit Aunt Bell, Daddy's sister on Tater Peel Road. She had all kinds of animals running loose. It was impossible not to notice the animals climbing on top of each other. The goats climbed and the pigs climbed and even the durn chickens climbed. The old rooster sometimes bit the hen's neck. She would go right on pecking dirt, like nothing was happening, but it seemed like a powerful distraction to eat while all that commotion was going on behind you. When the dogs got hung up, Aunt Bell threw cold water on them, and they popped apart. Months later, puppies pushed out of the mama dog's tail. All of nature was the same way. Baby chicks pecked through their shells. Cows strained and mooed, and pushed out a calf.

I thought and thought about a woman's tail, and where my privacy fit into the scheme of things. Was I supposed to climb on her back and crow or what? By the time I enlisted in World War II, the youngest man in my company, I'd figured out a thing or two. I knew the general geography, just not the longitude and latitude. I knew where to visit, just not how long I ought to stay. I sure didn't want to wear out my welcome.

When the marines showed those films in basic training, I squeezed my eyes shut and hummed the "Star-Spangled Banner" until the man next to me socked my arm and said to shut the fuck up. I opened my eyes, and on the movie screen were nasty women and peckers with great oozing sores. I thought I might be sick. I did not want to know about those things. The man sitting next to me said not to get worked up, that it was a propaganda film, to ignore it. I was so grateful, I almost passed out.

* * *

They say you always remember the first woman you take to bed. I remember the first two because it took me twice to lose my virginity. Woman number one. After the war, I went to mortuary school in Alexandria. I got to seeing one Donna Clements, a widow I met at a First Baptist picnic. (Mama claimed you meet the best people in church.) Donna's husband had been killed on Guadalcanal, and she had two little girls. We dated six months, and at long last, she took me to her bed. My pecker got so hard, it lifted the sheet and made a tiny wet place on the linen. She was wearing a cotton nightgown that was printed with purple umbrellas. When I confessed that I was a virgin and she'd have to show me the way, Donna Sue turned her face into her pillow and said, "Please don't say any dirty words. I'll cry if you do."

"What'd I say?" I asked her.

"You know." Her lips screwed up and her face turned pink.

"No, I don't." I scratched my head and tried to think. "Virgin? Is that it?"

She rolled over and wailed into her pillow. It turned out that Donna was mortally ashamed of the naked body. I was shocked. She'd been married, and I figured she'd know what to do. After a few minutes she calmed down and wiped her eyes on the sheet. Then she nudged me with her elbow. "All right," she said. Then she squeezed her eyes shut and lay there. Her whole body seemed to blush. "I'm ready. I *guess*."

I leaned over to kiss her, but her lips were hard, all mashed together. When I put my hand on her waist, she whimpered.

"If you don't want to do this," I said, "then just say so."

"No." She grimaced. "I want to."

Well, she wouldn't let me do anything except hump against her leg like an old dog. She claimed I couldn't go further unless I married her, but meanwhile, I was welcome to rub myself between her knees.

"Okay," I said.

"You'll marry me?" Her eyes got big.

"No." I pointed between her legs.

She looked ready to cry again, but she lifted her gown and parted her legs. I rolled on top and adjusted myself. Then clamped down. Her knees were fleshy. I started moving my hips. It felt okay, I guess, nothing to write home about, but she made me stop after ten strokes. "Why only ten?" I wanted to know.

"Because," she wailed. "Just because!"

Woman number two. I was returning from an undertaker's convention in Kansas, and I stopped at the Broken Arrow Motel in Amarillo, Texas. That evening I walked to the cafe and slid into one of the brown booths. I ordered chicken-fried steak, mashed potatoes and gravy, fried okra, pinto beans, slaw, and corn bread. When the waitress found out I was staying at the motel, she kept coming back with fresh coffee, asking if I wanted dessert.

"I don't meant to stare," she said, "but I got me a weakness for green-eyed men. Can I get you some dessert, honeybunch?"

I ate a second piece of chocolate pie, and the waitress leaned over, as if to wipe a spot on the oilcloth, and said, "Hey, cowboy. You're a cowboy, ain't you?"

I nodded. It was not like me to lie, but I couldn't help myself. She was just so pretty. I wanted her to think good of me. Most women, when they learn I'm an undertaker, go, "Ewwww!"

"I thought so," she said, wiping under the counter, close to my legs. "You look cowboyish, you know? I get off in a few minutes. What do you think of that?"

"I guess you're glad," I said, feeling my face turn red. I hadn't been with a woman since Donna Sue, not that I'd *been* with her, exactly; I wondered if the waitress somehow knew I was a virgin, so to speak, and was cracking jokes at me.

"Yeah, I'm glad." She laughed. "But how 'bout if I get us some beer and drink it in your room? You *are* staying here, ain't you?"

"In my room?" I blinked, thinking something like that had to be against the motel's rules, having a woman in your room.

"Where else?" She grinned. "How 'bout it?"

"I guess." I was too afraid to refuse, and I figured if we got caught by the manager, then I could just drive to another motel.

"Good. My name's Loretta." She wrinkled her nose, and fifteen minutes later we were walking around the parking lot, looking at the different license plates. Most of the cars were from Oklahoma and Texas, but we saw tags from as far away as Arizona, Florida, Nebraska, and California. On one end of the gravel lot, a pink-and-red neon sign blinked on, pleading VACANCY.

Loretta pointed to a tag from Montana. "Boy, they're a long way from home."

"Yeah, Montana," I said, like I'd been there. I couldn't imagine such a distance, even though I'd fought in the South Pacific. I was very much a Limoges man.

"Where you from, cowboy?"

"Oh, here and there."

"You ever been throwed from a bull?"

"Sure."

"Get hurt? Got any scars?"

"I don't like to talk about my work."

"Yeah, me neither." She opened a paper sack and pulled out

two Lone Star beers. We sat on the pavement (I was ashamed to sit on the hearse, because then she'd know the truth) and watched traffic sweep down Route 65. I figured we'd talk until it got dark, but Loretta didn't seem to be in any hurry to leave. She lifted the brown bottle and took a ladylike sip. She was still wearing her pink uniform, with sweat stains under the armpits.

Once she stared hard at me when I swished beer in my mouth. "That sounds funny," she said.

"I know it." I wiped my lips. "I'm sorry."

"No, I like it. Do it again." She smiled and stared at the motel doors. "Which one is yours?"

"Right there." I pointed to number four. She kept staring, like the door led somewhere prettier than it did. Then she leaned forward and brushed her nose against my cheek. I felt a shiver shoot through me, and I was afraid to breathe. She brushed her lips over mine, then opened her mouth. Her tongue was cool, darting between my lips. With my free hand, I reached up to pull her close, but she leaned back and smiled. She took a sip of beer and said, "It's getting dark."

"You don't have to go, do you?" I tipped back my head and swallowed the rest of my beer.

"You crazy?" She held out her hand, wiggling her fingers at me. "Want to go inside?"

"Inside?" My heart started beating fast.

"Yeah, we'll draw attention if we stay out here. Come on." She took my hand, and we went into the room. Soon as she closed the door and lit a candle, we started kissing. She pulled my shirt from my trousers. We fell back on the bed, and she unbuttoned her dress, pulling it over her head. I shucked off my shirt, then kicked off my trousers, leaving on my underwear. My private was stretching against the fabric. I knew it went somewhere between her legs, of course, but after Donna Sue, I didn't know what to expect.

I didn't know how I'd squeeze it all in, or if I was even supposed to. I knew one thing for sure, if I rubbed it between her knees, we'd both end up chapped and raw. "Take it all off, honeybunch." She tugged at my underwear. "I want to look at you."

I wiggled out of my drawers and crawled over to her, thinking if I lived through this, I'd never pray for anything stupid again. Loretta shifted her legs, crinkling the sheets, and whispered, "I can't hardly wait no more."

She peeled off the sheet. In the mixed-up light of candle and pink neon, her breasts looked as if they could fit in my hand, and between my fingers and oh, mercy, into my mouth. She held my head between her hands. Her skin felt so warm and sweet that I knew she had to be the same inside, too. In her heart, where it counted. She pressed up against me, kissing me all over, her titties covering my face. "Just go slow," she said in my ear, stroking my hair. Her voice sounded old, like she knew how to talk to men. "Take it slow. That's right. Slow, slow."

She dropped her hands to my hips and touched my privacy, rolling it between her hands. I stared down at her pink hands in the neon glow, watching her stroke me. She rubbed her cheek against me, then touched it with her lips. My eyes fluttered in back of my head. I thought, "I must be dead, and she is an angel sent to welcome me, but no—this is not the way Jesus would break you into heaven."

Then I figured this was all a dream, that I'd wake up alone in the motel, the sheet spread damp and stuck to my skin. She reached for my hands and pulled me on top of her; I tried to fit it between her legs, but she kept moving. Her hand kneaded my butt. I copied everything she did. Whatever she poked, I poked back.

"Good, good," she murmured. "I *like* that."

Her legs were well muscled, and too thin for me to get a good grip, to work up any friction. And her knees looked bony. This could turn into something painful, I thought. One little nudge the wrong way, and I could end up with an injury.

She kept wiggling. I held my breath and felt my life curve over my head in little bubbles. I tilted my hips, swayed back, and slipped my privacy just above her knees. "What are you doing?" she said.

"I'm just—"

"Never mind." She grabbed my rear end and held on tight. She said things no nice girl ought to say, and I was so glad she was saying them, so glad I had stopped at this motel and that she'd waited on my table. We're getting into some serious digging here, I thought.

She rolled me over, straddling me, bending at the knee. She grabbed my privacy and aimed it between her legs. I felt something real smooth and tight. I squeezed my eyes shut. My whole heart was inside her, beating and beating. She started moving faster. My eyes tried to roll back into my brain. I wondered if my thing could snap off inside her like an icicle. I just knew I was too high up. She was so small, I was bound to spear her heart. I got ready to count to ten, thinking it was like a courtesy you did for women. A show of respect. I'd gleaned that from Donna Sue. I stretched things out, counting to myself. *One, two, three. Three and one-half. Four. Fo-fo-four and a quarter* and oh Lord why didn't anyone tell me that young men could have coronaries, I was having a fit, a seizure of the brain. I'd gone blind. When I reached ten, I lay there a second, then pushed her off, wishing I could have counted slower. "Did you already come?" she said.

"I don't think so."

"You *crazy*?" she cried, looking down at my erection. "Why'd you stop?"

"Ain't I supposed to?"

"What *for*?"

"I thought everybody did."

"Ain't you never done it before?"

"Done what?"

"Lord." She stared up at the ceiling. I ducked my head, afraid she'd see the truth in my face.

"You haven't, have you?"

"Sure I have." I shrugged. "All the time."

"Yeah? You ever had it like this?" She reached across my stomach and took my privacy in her hands, rubbing it back and forth. "Let's don't talk. Get over here, cowboy."

"Just let me get my breath," I said.

"Honey, you don't need to get it." She took me in her mouth and sucked. My hips lifted toward her face. She pulled away and wiped her mouth.

"You ready to try again?" She pulled me on top of her. "Don't stop this time, okay? No matter what happens, keep going."

"Okay." I closed my eyes, and her hand guided me to that same, tight place. She wiggled this way, that way, and I buried myself deep, keeping a secret count. I wanted to see how far I'd get. *One, two, three, four . . .*

I lost count after twenty-eight. I was out of my head, inside hers, *inside an actual woman*. I felt drugged by the salty dregs from her underarm, the scent of smoke and grease in her hair. I can't stand much more, or I'll bust wide open, I thought. And then I did: I busted. The sensation was so strong, a current drawing me into deep waters, that I thought I might pass out. When I could finally breathe again, I lay there in the dark watching the neon burn through the curtains, and I had an understanding in my heart for the caveman who'd discovered fire. Rubbing sticks together, waiting for the curling smoke, the sudden flame. She was smiling up at me. I let out a yell and beat my legs against the bed.

"Let's do it again!" I hollered.

"Whoa, cowboy. Give it a rest." She patted my belly. I reached up and touched her face. I loved the way she laughed, loved that wild jangle that rode up and down my backbone. Beneath us, the sheets were wet, and I wondered which one of us had sprung a leak. I was afraid I might have peed the bed during those spasms, so I scooted over and said, "I'll lay here. You get where it's dry."

"Nah. I like it wet." She grinned and raised her arms over her head like she was hugging herself. "You ain't never done it before, have you?"

I was too happy to lie. I shook my head, then grinned up at her.

"A big old cowboy like you. Well, I never." She pinched my leg. "Hell, I knew it! God, how old are you, anyway?"

"Old enough." I was ashamed to say I'd already been to war and mortuary school, that my job brought me into intimate contact with my fellow man, not that I would ever probe where I shouldn't.

"And you've never done it before, not ever?"

I started to tell her about Donna Sue, but I was ashamed. So I shook my head again.

"Why not?" Her forehead wrinkled.

I shrugged, thinking about how backward I was before I rolled into Texas. How I used to be. I was a whole new man.

"God," she said. "You ever seen men who walk slow and all stooped over?"

I nodded and thought about Daddy.

"That's what happens to men who stop doing it." She rested her face in her hands. "That's why I don't mind wet sheets. It's just sperms. That's what it's called, you know? It's good to get all of that out of you. You'll get clogged if you don't."

"Clogged?" I had a vision of my sperms backing up to my brain.

"Yeah. All that can lead to constipation and worse." She fanned the sheets.

"Don't look so worried. You walk just *fine*." She grinned, but I felt another blush starting. I swear, I hated the way I'd believe anything.

She scooted across the bed and pressed up against me. I put my arm around her. She closed her eyes and yawned. She breathed deeply, like she was humming. Beyond the gauzy curtains, the sky was pinker, as if the neon sign had leaked out. The clouds were mottled like tire tracks. Here we were, staring at each other in the dawn's early light, and I'd done fired all my ramparts. As I watched her sleep, she seemed like some kind of miracle. I was full of gratitude; it was backed up in me like years of sperm. Good, strong love like that wouldn't sour on your stomach or block your bowels.

She rolled over, out of my arms, taking the sheet with her, and mumbled something in her sleep. I watched her until the sky bleached out white behind holes in the curtains and someone shut off the pink neon sign. She awakened slowly, limb by limb. Her eyes blinked open. She arched her back, and her titties slid up on her chest like two pink yolks.

"Morning, cowboy," she said in a scratchy voice. I slid my arms around her. I pictured her years from now, in a white house with a wraparound porch—not the Beaulieu Funeral Home, either, but a regular home. There would be a wooden glider for her, where she'd do her sewing, and a rocker for me. She'd squat in the front yard planting tulip bulbs with a teaspoon, like my mother used to. I saw her clearly. Loretta would be wearing a pink dress, her hair braided over the top of her head like Miss Vangie's. Two babies in white gowns would crawl across the grass. One of the babies looked like me. They would hide in the hydrangeas and pinch off the petals. All over the yard, you would hear them laughing. Inside the house would be a table set with white china and silver, with a golden turkey I'd just carved. It would be such a pretty life, and I knew it was ours for the taking.

"I got something to say, Loretta." I cleared my throat.

She pulled back and stared up at me. "Yeah?"

"I will take you and dress you," I said.

"Huh?" She looked at me funny, raising her eyebrows. I turned my head and stared out the window. My voice wiggled in my throat like it was held together with Jell-O. She stared at me for the longest time. I tried to think of a better way to phrase it, but I was bashful all of a sudden. I wanted to tell her about that pretty white house and the turkey on the table and those babies in the hydrangeas. I wanted to tell her that I would give her anything, that all she had to do was ask.

"I want to take care of you and buy you things," I said. "I love you, Loretta."

"But you don't even know my last name."

"It don't matter."

"No?"

"Listen, I want you to bear my children. I want to give you a pretty house and a pretty life." I wasn't sure if I'd spoke or not, but her eyes were wide and gray, as if she'd seen all the way into the back of my brain.

"I'll do all this and more," I blurted out.

She pursed her lips. Her forehead wrinkled. "And what do I get in return?" she asked.

"Everything," I said.

"You sure do drive a hard bargain." She pinched my cheek. "Would I have to leave Texas?"

I nodded.

"Shoot." She socked her leg. "Guess I'll have to say thanks but no thanks. Sorry."

"Why?" My heart flapped beneath my ribs.

"'Cause I can't leave town just now."

"Why not?"

"Well, 'cause I'm married. I got kids. Stuff like that. Anyhow, this ain't love, this is lust. Like a appetite for buttermilk pie."

"Feels like love to me."

"Shit, you'll get over this. And you'll thank me a thousand times over that I turned you down." She laughed and dove under the covers. Her fingers walked up my leg, then circled my privacy, only it didn't feel like a private thing anymore. It felt like a penis bursting with sperms. I squeezed my eyes shut, and she pulled the covers over our heads.

I've bedded many women since, not that I've kept a close count (fifteen), but I've never met another woman like Loretta or Donna Sue Clements. I heard that Donna Sue got a job at the telephone company in Alexandria. Far as I know she never remarried. I have an idea that she mixed up sexual intercourse with the ten commandments—ten strikes and you're out, when all it really takes is one. As it happens, I'm just grateful that she didn't think we were playing baseball.

Lookout Mountain

❧

All my life I've had a weakness for Baptists and blue-eyed men. I know that's a lot of words starting with B, but it's true. I'm 5'3" with baby blue eyes of my own and real curly blond hair. I do not like to sew or garden. They say I'm real pretty, and next year I'll probably win the Miss Delta pageant, so if you are a blue-eyed Baptist boy, please write.

—OLIVE NEPPER, FROM *PEN PALS OF THE SOUTH*, JULY 1951, PAGE 5

Winters in Limoges were bare-branched and chilly. The air was hard, with sharp angles that scraped your fingers and toes. Way up in the sky, clouds peeled back to reveal blue. Blackbirds flew in ragged formation, over houses where women waited for spring. They curled up like hermit crabs stuck inside their shells. As Olive Nepper walked home from the rectory, she pulled her plaid coat around her thin shoulders and leaned into the icy wind. *All this cold,* she thought, *and it'll never snow here. Never.* When she cut through the scratchy azaleas, she saw Fanny LeGette crouched down behind a tree, her navy blue coat fanned out in the grass. "You spying on Cab Beaulieu again?" Olive called out.

"Shhhhh!" Fanny grabbed Olive's hand and pulled her into the bushes. Fanny was four years younger than Olive; they'd known each other since 1942, when Dr. LeGette bought the house next to the Hoopers. Miss Harriet predicted that Fanny would never amount to anything because Miss Margaret Jane let the child suck a pacifier until she was four and a half. Fanny called it her foo-foo and wore it around her neck on a grubby pink ribbon. "The child of a doctor!" chastised Miss Harriet.

"Let's find another spot," Olive said, kneeling. "These bushes are scrawny. He'll see us."

"No, he won't. He's got a woman over there!"

"Where?" Olive bent forward, sticking her hands into her pockets. An icy wind made her shiver. "I don't see anybody."

"Well, he did have one. That widow from Delphinium Street."

"The redhead with the pointy ninnies?"

"Uh-huh. They probably heard you and went inside." Fanny leaned back on the thick grass and grinned up at Olive. "Do you think Cab French-kisses his lady friends?"

"Ha! More than that!"

"Like what?"

"Oh, rub up against them. Feel their ninnies. And yeah, French-kiss."

"Pew, that causes babies. When I get big enough to date, I'm wearing a rubber girdle. Boys can rub till the cows come home, but they'll just bounce against the rubber."

"You're crazy." Olive laughed.

"I've got it all picked out at Hooper's. A creamy white girdle, a Maidenform."

"That won't work." Olive drew in a deep breath, and the air made her lungs ache. In the back of her mind was T. C. Kirby, washing a tea towel in the bathroom sink after he'd squeezed out his seeds.

"Why not?" said Fanny.

"It's too cold to talk. Come on." She grabbed Fanny's hand and pulled her out of the azaleas, across the grass, onto the Neppers' screened porch. She climbed into the wooden glider and made it sway. "Save your money, Fanny. Girdles are stupid."

"Why?" Fanny sucked the tip of her braid. "Looks to me like a Maidenform would keep anything out."

"You reach a point in life where the girdle comes off."

"Off?"

"Men and women take off all their clothes. They get naked together, Fanny. And the man's private thing grows real long and hard." Olive stretched her hands apart. "Then he sticks it inside you."

"It?" Fanny frowned. "What do you mean, it?"

"His . . . you know." Olive giggled. "His doohickey, his dinga-ling." She pointed between her legs. "It gets hard and he puts it right there."

"I don't believe it!" Fanny's mouth dropped open, then snapped shut. "That would *hurt* too bad! Wouldn't it?"

"Yeah, I'll bet it does." Olive grimaced. "They're *huge,* like those pickles at City Market, the ones in the gallon jugs. I don't want one inside of me. Especially if there's other ways to do it."

"Do what?"

"To get the baby stuff out, the seeds. That's the whole point."

"Of what?"

"Life. If it was up to me, though, I'd stick with straight old kissing."

"I don't understand."

"It's real simple. My daddy puts his pickle in Mama, and Dr. Phillip puts his in Miss Waldene."

"That's a lie! A dirty, rotten lie!" Fanny scrambled to her feet. "My daddy would do no such thing!"

"He would, too." Olive laughed again. "He *has*. You're living proof."

"Look, if my daddy had a giant pickle between his legs, don't you think I would've noticed by now?"

"They grow, silly."

"Shut up! My daddy saves people's lives! *And* he's a deacon. He would never do something that nasty. And neither would Waldene!"

"She would too. How do you think she got that baby inside her?"

"From kissing! You're just making this up, Olive Nepper!"

"I'm not." Olive smiled, showing small teeth. "Your daddy put seeds in your mama, and it grew into you."

"That's a lie!" She balled her hands into fists. "It wasn't seeds, it was saliva! Daddy told me!"

"Next you'll be saying the stork brought you." Olive slapped her leg and hooted. "One more time, Fanny. Dr. Phillip stuck his doohickey into Miss Waldene. And then he peed inside her, only it's not pee, it's white stuff that grows into a baby."

"How do *you* know, were *you* there?"

"I just know."

"There's no such thing as white stuff."

"Yes, there is. And now your stepmama's having a baby. Dr. Phillip's been peeing his brains out."

"Liar! My daddy would *never* pee in anything but a toilet."

"If he didn't, then somebody did. And you came out of her twussy. Right here." She pointed between her legs.

"I hate you!" Fanny grabbed the glider, flipping Olive onto the floor.

"It's true." Olive rolled over on her stomach and looked up at Fanny. "Go ask Miss Waldene. See what she says."

Even when Olive left for the Lookout Mountain choir trip, her dreams were stuck in Louisiana in the Baptist rectory, where it was always Saturday morning. While the others picnicked, Olive and the reverend kissed in a gully. "The Lord will guide us, Sister Nepper," he said, clasping his hands over hers. "For we know not what we do."

"We don't?" She raised her eyebrows and sat up straight. "But I thought you said—"

He leaned forward, crushed his lips against her mouth, and cupped one hand over her breast. Then he firmly pressed her to the ground. He pulled up her dress, then deftly peeled down her panties. She heard his zipper, saw him reach inside the dark trouser cloth and pull out his privates. The first time she'd seen it, back at the rectory, she'd gasped. It was slicker than she'd imagined, and a good bit larger. "You're not going to stick that in *me*, are you?" she'd said, pulling up on her elbows.

"It's the only way," he'd said. "It's the chosen path."

"It looks like a serpent." She drew back, eyeing it with considerable suspicion. He pulled her hand toward him and arranged her fingers. She thought, My gosh, it's like playing the clarinet.

"When the times comes," the reverend whispered, "I will fit it inside you. But don't you fret. I'll be gentle."

"Is it time now?"

"No."

Now, on the cold Tennessee mountain, he told her the time had come to join their bodies. "I don't think that's possible," she said, eyeing his crotch. Then she lay back down, feeling leaves crunch beneath her. "But you can sure try."

He moved on top of her, guiding himself between her legs. She couldn't help but wonder why he'd picked this place, out in the open, when he had a perfectly good bedroom in Limoges. "Why here?" she asked, her voice blunted by his shoulder. She dug her fingers into his red sweater. "What if somebody comes?"

"Somebody's fixing to," he muttered. His eyes held an unnatural glitter. He pulled back, licked his finger, and rubbed it between her legs.

"This was Adam's downfall," he whispered, "and mine, too."

I Spy

You can get to a man one of two ways—either through sex or his stomach. First time I saw Cab Beaulieu I guessed him to be a tallywacker type. We were walking around the display room, choosing a casket for my dead husband. I thought about climbing into one of the caskets, then pulling him inside, letting the lid bang shut. But I chickened out. I didn't want him to think I was strange or nothing. Instead, I asked if he cared to tie his handkerchief around my waist (this is usually a real good icebreaker). He declined, which shook me up a little, but I bounced right back. "So," I said. "Do you like lasagna?"

—CORDY KING, HAVING A MANICURE AT BEAUTY FOUNTAIN, APRIL 1952

Fanny LeGette

Waldene pushed open every single window in our house because she's scared of the flu. Said she's "airing" the house. Ha. Looked to me like she was drawing in every germ in town. I made me a banana-and-peanut-butter sandwich. Then I went into the backyard and climbed the oak tree, what Olive Nepper used to call Granddaddy Tree because it was low to the ground and crippled up. I looked down on my house and saw Waldene moving from window to window, wiping out the sills. She really got on my nerves.

Before she married Daddy, our drawers were crammed with empty sugar-ration books, old V-mail, and S&H green stamps that my mama never redeemed. Waldene got rid of all that. Here lately, she'd gotten worse, digging through our closets, calling the church to come pick up my mama's old clothes. She even gave away Daddy's intern suits that snap down the neck. Lord, I thought. She's not a beautician, she's a human vacuum cleaner. When she started on my closet, I ran down to my daddy's office. The waiting room was packed with people just a-sneezing and snorting. I marched right past them and found Daddy in the hallway, reading a chart. I burst into tears. He calmed me down and said to ignore Waldene, that she was nesting, a normal thing for expectant mothers. He knew everything; he was the best doctor in all of Limoges. Still, he wasn't perfect. My mother never nested in her life.

Here I was, twelve years old with a pregnant stepmother. As if people didn't know how it happened. I used to not, but Olive told me these awful lies and I had to go ask my daddy. He said storks brought babies. But I figured it out all by myself—if you wanted to have a baby, then kiss a man. Their saliva was like plant food. It caused the baby, which was like a tiny petunia seed in the woman's stomach, to grow. I was real careful to wash everything my daddy put his lips to—spoons, forks, cups. After what happened to Waldene, I wasn't taking chances.

I wanted to think my daddy was an exception, that he wouldn't put his tongue into Waldene, but she really was the type to egg him on. Always hugging on him, keeping the door to their bedroom locked, telling me to scoot. "We're having a talk," she'd say. "Go outside and ride your bike."

"Be careful!" Daddy would call out. Ha. Next to the black wall phone was a Coca-Cola notepad printed with SAFETY ABC's: Always Be Careful. It was too bad they hadn't followed their own advice, what with Waldene's stomach the size of a picnic ham. I didn't see how she slept. I got sick of her hollering for me to come feel the baby kick. I always ran and hid, but Daddy never tired of it. He'd slip on his stethoscope and press the bell to her belly.

"One hundred and fifty-eight beats a minute," he'd tell her. "That's for sure a boy. Their hearts always beat faster."

All over Limoges, women were getting fertilized by saliva. Just this morning, I saw that trashy Tamera Mashburn in City Market, her stomach bulging beneath a fabric that was patterned with sailboats. She thumped watermelons while three babies stood up in the cart, red-faced and screaming. I thought to myself, *Honey, it's not ripe yet, and neither are you*.

I leaned against the rough bark and propped my feet on a branch. Daddy told me not to climb trees, but you had to if you wanted to spy. I was an expert, and I thought I might grow up to be one, like the Rosenbergs. Only I did not want to get caught. The newsreels said if they're found guilty, they will get electrocuted next summer. When Waldene read in the paper that Mrs.

Rosenberg had little babies, we both cried. That was the only time I halfway liked her.

Olive and I used to climb the tree with bags of pecans and see who we could attack. We'd snoop on Miss Harriet and wait for her to sink into her hammock. Then we'd fire down pecans.

"Satan!" she'd yell up, spraying spit from her fat lips. "I'm telling your mamas!"

Our mamas didn't give a hoot if we tormented Miss Harriet, but they'd yell at us to show they had good manners. Sometimes Miss Harriet's awful niece would come over, Waynetta Dawn, a pudgy nine-year-old who enters the Little Miss Pecan Pageant every single year. I won it once, back in 1946, and all they give you is a fake crown, roses, and a sack of pecans. You get your picture in the *News-Leader*, and the next year you get to put the crown on the new Little Miss Pecan. But Waynetta Dawn won't win anything until she gives up eating pralines.

"That's why she and Harriet are fat hogs," Olive would say. We'd be high up in the tree. Looking down like God. "Just look at them waddling."

I tried to figure why Olive drank that poison, but I couldn't. The morning it happened, Waldene heard somebody scream polio. She went straight to the phone to call Daddy, but the line was busy. Turned out all the party lines in Limoges were snarled that day.

Later, Daddy and Waldene took me into the living room and sat me down on the green sofa. By then we knew it wasn't polio, that she'd swallowed Miss Vangie's rose poison.

"Fanny," Daddy said, "can you think of any reason Olive would do this? Did she say anything to you, just anything at all?"

"No." I shook my head. "She's not gonna die, is she?"

"I don't know, baby. She's in a coma, do you know what that is?"

"Like a deep, deep sleep, only you can't wake up?"

He nodded.

"But she will, won't she?"

"I hope so." He put one hand on my shoulder. "Think hard, Fanny. She's bound to have let something slip."

I couldn't think of anything. I hadn't seen her much since she went to Lookout Mountain. I'd go over to visit, and Miss Vangie would say, "Olive's taking a nap." She never used to take naps before Lookout Mountain. When she got back from that trip, she kind of looked down on me, treated me the same way I treated Waynetta Dawn. I didn't see how one little choir trip could make a person get too big for her britches, but it did. My worst fears came true. She wouldn't climb our tree, play I Spy, or watch "The

Pinky Lee Show." The last time we had a heart-to-heart was before her trip. I was spying on Cab, who was standing in the driveway talking to that widow lady from Lake Providence. Olive took me into her yard and told me how babies were made. I wanted to believe her because she was older and so pretty. I had a great fear that I would lose her if I wasn't careful. Deep down I knew we played together because it was handy. There weren't any big girls around for six blocks, and those were mean to Olive. "They're jealous of me," Olive confided, and I believed every word.

When she told me about the babies, my eyes blurred up. I worshipped Olive Nepper, but I worshipped my daddy more. He would never do dirty, peepee things like Olive was saying.

"Here lately, she's never had time to talk or anything," I told Daddy. "I guess she got tired of me."

"It just doesn't make sense," Waldene said. "Not a bit." She went back to knitting booties. She was thinking blue to help her get a boy. She said all men needed a son to take to football games. I hope she got one because I was sick of this baby, and it wasn't even here. Mostly I was scared that Daddy would love it more than he loved me.

Now I licked the edges of my sandwich, sealing it with peanut butter and spit. I loved this tree. Over the azaleas I had a good view of Beaulieu Funeral Home. Me and Olive loved to spy on Cab. He looked like Vic Damone. Olive and I fought over which one of us would marry him. Way down below, I saw a curvy brunette woman walk around Beaulieu's, heading for the back porch. She carried an aluminum pan with a blue plaid tea towel stretched over the top. When you saw people carrying bundles to Beaulieu's, it could be anything from a dead baby to a casserole. I sat up straighter. The woman's hair was all bushed out, like she'd been electrocuted. All she needed was a white streak, and she could be the bride of Frankenstein.

Even before she knocked, Cab came to the door and pushed it open. "Hi, Cordy!" he said, grinning. "Come on in, just come on in!"

She stepped inside. I bit into my sandwich, chewing furiously. I waited and waited, but this Cordy person never came out. By the time I finished my sandwich, my butt had gone to sleep and one leg was tingling.

I pictured his bedroom, the one with the carved walnut bed and windows that faced Oak Street. I just knew they were in that bed, sticking their tongues down each other's throats. The idea made me so mad, I climbed down the tree, walked over to the hedge, and squeezed through. Cab's backyard was sunny; he kept threatening to put in a garden, like his old granddaddy had. I didn't remember it, but they say his corn was taller than the azaleas, and Miss Harriet nearly went into heart failure. She believed the only thing that belonged in a yard were daylilies. Poor old Mr. Leonard agreed with everything she said. "Just like a good bird dog," my daddy observed.

I sneaked up to the back porch and pressed my forehead against the screen. It was an old canning porch with a beat-up white stove and a long counter with cracked green Formica. Wooden shelves were full of bluish jars, pressure cookers, aluminum pans, and food mills. Ladles and funnels hung from the rafters on rusted nails. Some shelves had dusty jars with food floating in pale yellow liquid. The labels were written in old Mrs. Beaulieu's spidery handwriting: *Beans, June 1946, Corn Relish, July 1948, Peaches, June 1936, Whole Peeled Tomatoes, August 1945*.

It had to be poisoned by now. No wonder Cab had let it rot. And no wonder women brought him food. I'd go hungry before I ate death in a jar.

I tiptoed into the kitchen. There on the counter was the lady's pan, one edge of the tea towel peeled back to show ruffled lasagna noodles spread with red sauce. Above me, a floorboard creaked. I held my breath, listening, but it didn't creak again. I just knew they were upstairs, so I headed toward the hall, hoping to catch them in the act. I had eavesdropped on Daddy and Waldene, pressing my ear to the wall when their mattress squeaked. "Mmmm," she'd say, and he'd answer her back, "Mmmm." Like they were eating strawberries, raving about the sweetness. Lately, though, their room had gotten quiet. I guessed they'd learned their lesson.

When I turned the corner, I saw Cab and the lady coming down the steps. "Fanny!" His eyes bugged, mashing his long lashes against his lids. The woman pushed her red lips to one side. She did not look happy to see me.

"Hi," I said, digging the toe of my red sneaker into the turquoise carpet.

"I didn't hear you knock," Cab said. "Is anything wrong?" The woman folded her arms and jutted out her left hip, so that it was almost touching his. I couldn't think of a reason for me to be standing in his hall, so I just said, "I thought I'd just come over and say hello." Then, to distract him, I pointed to the lady. "Who's she?"

"Why, this is Cordy King." He paused, exchanging glances with the woman. Then he turned back to me. "Did you want something in particular?"

"I thought you might have somebody laid out," I said.

"Laid out?" asked Cordy King. Her eyebrows were black commas against her white forehead. And her hair was way too dark, an unnatural ebony, like puppy fur. She looked at me and laughed. "I haven't heard *that* one before."

"A dead body," I said, trying to sound like a brat.

"You mean, deceased," Cab corrected, looking embarrassed. Then he fixed his green eyes on me.

"You are so smart," Cordy said, turning her face up to Cab. She drew her dark eyebrows together like she didn't know funeral parlor language and needed him to interpret. This made me mad, seeing her twist him around her little finger. I wanted her to know that I, child of a doctor, was not stupid. I spent my summers at the library reading up on things. I could tell her about weather, for instance. If you wanted to get simple, weather was decided by how much water was in the air. In every raindrop there was a tiny speck of dust. And lightning had to do with dust particles. Positive charges were tops of clouds, negative in the lower. When charges jumped from one area to the other, you got lightning. And it wasn't one bolt. It was negative charges going down, positive going up into the clouds. When you got right down to it, lightning was nothing but a giant spark of static electricity; one bolt could stretch a hundred miles long.

I knew lots about tornadoes, too, but somehow I didn't think this would impress Cordy King. Probably I could shock her about saliva. I'd tried to look this up at the library, but there were no medical books on the shelves; also, the librarian, Miss Nixon, wouldn't let me check out *You're a Young Lady Now*. "Not until Dr. LeGette says you can," she always snapped, snatching it from my hands. Which meant everybody in town knew I hadn't had my first period.

I was, however, full of other encyclopedic facts.

"The human body," I said, looking into Cordy King's tiny green eyes that weren't at all like Cab's, "is a source of wonderment, dead or alive. It never ceases to amaze me. Did you know that each pound of fat has a mile of blood vessels in it?" I'd heard my daddy say this a hundred times, and when I repeated it to adults, they called me a genius.

"Well, aren't you smart." She smiled, showing tiny white teeth, but her eyes were two frozen peas. "Maybe you'll be the first lady undertaker in Limoges."

I walked back home, lingering in the shady stretch of grass between my house and Miss Harriet's. Her windows were open, too, music oozing through the screens. Lord knew what else. I hated to think our two houses were exchanging germs. Daddy might catch being henpecked from Mr. Leonard, and Waldene might suddenly feel an urge to call people on the phone and gossip. And I could develop cravings for pralines. I held my breath and ran into our front yard. When I reached the porch, I flopped down on the wooden glider and gasped for air. I lay there breathing, listening to the rusty chain as the swing rocked back and forth. Our porch was real cool and shady. Waldene's red and white impatiens were planted next to the house, and come June she said they'd be thick cushions. I was so bored I could scream, but I didn't. That could draw either Waldene or Miss Harriet, the last two people I cared to see.

Without Olive, I didn't know what to do with myself. Every Saturday morning we tuned into the thirtieth century and watched "Space Patrol." I spent a whole week at her house after my mama died. Miss Vangie brought us breakfast in bed and let us blow bubbles inside the kitchen. Olive knew my thoughts, who I loved, who I hated. I could tell her anything. I didn't understand how she could keep secrets from me. How she could drink poison and not even drop a hint.

From the sidewalk, I heard footsteps, a man's heavy scrape-slap. I raised up and saw Reverend T. C. Kirby walking past our house. He was dressed regular, a plaid shirt with a blue sweater draped over his shoulders, and he was carrying a Bible. For a bachelor, he matched up his clothes right good.

"Hi!" I said, sitting all the way up, dragging one sneaker on the floor to stop the swing.

"Hi, yourself, Sister Fanny!" He waved the Bible.

"Where you off to?" I got up and leaned over the railing.

"The hospital," he said. "Some of the flock is sick." He stopped under the chinaberry tree and grinned at me. His eyes were bluer than Olive Nepper's. It was the first thing you noticed about him. Behind me, the front door opened and Waldene appeared, wearing a huge yellow smock that was printed with black bumblebees. "Well, hello!" she called out. "Do you have a minute to drink a cup of coffee?"

"We've got strawberry pie, too," I said.

"And chocolate chess," Waldene added.

"You ladies sure know how to tempt a man." The reverend smiled and spread his hands. "If it's no trouble."

"Not at all," Waldene said, standing back, opening the door wider for the reverend.

Revelations:

Reverend Kirby Tells All

❧

What goes on between a man and a woman should be private. If the door is shut, then who has the right to see through it? I'll tell you who—God. Here lately, I've been thinking about David and Bathsheba. David saw her on that rooftop, combing her hair, and he got all worked up, and next thing you know the Lord is pissed off. So what if Bathsheba was married? So what if David arranged to have her husband killed? A man's got to have a little joy in life, what with the Holy Ghost watching everything you do. Moving through doors and windows like Bela Lugosi. It's flat-out creepy.

—REVEREND T. C. KIRBY, TALKING TO A PROSTITUTE IN BOSSIER CITY, 1952

The First Baptist's steeple was the highest point in town, a landmark for local pilots, and a bird sanctuary. Four wooden arches opened to a platform where the bell rope hung down, the hemp worn smooth where preachers—or their youngsters, more likely—had tugged. Every decent church in Limoges had a bell. On Sunday mornings the town was filled with competing calls for worship.

"Like chattering magpies," Reverend Kirby thought, climbing the rickety stairs to the belfry, stuffing cotton in his ears. When he reached the landing, he peered over the edge and looked down on his town. All the little people scurrying about, plowing gardens and sweeping the sidewalk. In front of the church was a marquee with black plastic letters:

1 FREE TRIP TO HEAVEN
DETAILS INSIDE!

Last week it said, WHEN LOOKING FOR FAULTS/USE A
MIRROR NOT A TELESCOPE. That had gone over real big. It
was amazing how small things added up to a beloved preacher.
Already this morning he'd made his rounds at Parish Hospital, to
see whether Olive Nepper was still in a coma. One little mistake
(he had a weakness for blue-eyed blondes, Lord knew why), and
he could have lost this town, not to mention his parsonage, with
the nice cherry furniture and the free food, not to mention the
adoration of his fans. If Olive hadn't poisoned herself, he didn't
know what he would have done. Downstairs in the chapel, the
youth choir sang, *"Ho-ly, ho-ly, ho-ly, mer-ci-ful and might-y!/God
in three Per-sons, bless-ed Trin-i-ty!"*

"Hole-y," Reverend Kirby thought. That was a word his mama
could go to town with. She had a knack for twisting words to suit
her, but she hadn't bent him. "Everybody's got a hole in their
lives," he thought, then shut his eyes and tensed his stomach
muscles. His forehead wrinkled the way it always did when a sermon was coming on. (He felt the same way with bowel movements; sometimes it was hard to tell the difference.)

When he pulled the rope, four pigeons fluttered out of the
bell. The reverend cowered, throwing his hands in front of his
face. All around him gray feathers spiraled down. When he finally
looked up, he saw that the birds had made their nest on the crossbar above the clapper. What I need, he thought, is to rig me up
some screen mesh. Not the reverend personally, but one of the
flock, maybe a deacon who didn't mind heights, a gutter-man or
roofer. A good Baptist would sacrifice anything for his church.
He'd give up his weekends to paint the Sanctuary; he'd tithe and
let his children wear hand-me-downs. And the wives loved him,
too. When it came to Lottie Moon, they'd scrimp on meals—
canned tuna prepared one hundred ways. Why, he was a kept
preacher. Women brought him flowers, food, and their husbands'
old suits. If you stripped away the religion crap, it was a damn
good profession. All he had to do was visit the sick and troubled
and write three sermons a week. Like most successful preachers,
he was a born bullshitter.

So it shouldn't be hard to find someone to seal up the belfry.
At least it's not bats, he thought, shuddering. He closed his eyes
and imagined hundreds of stiff-winged creatures, like flying hamsters. He had never felt good about bats after seeing *Dracula*.
What a mistake! Every bat in that movie had a face like his
mama's. Even now, he still awakened in the night and imagined
her standing in the henhouse, chicken blood spilling down the
front of her apron. There were worse ways to die, he imagined,

but exsanguination and a snapped neck seemed especially gruesome. He tugged the rope, hoping to dislodge the pigeons' nest, but he managed only to set off a deafening series of chimes.

He climbed down the steps and walked into his paneled office. A fan whirred over his desk, vibrating an autographed photograph of the Reverend Billy Graham. In the outer office, he heard Miss Vidalia Rogers typing up Sunday's program. She was fifty-four years old going on one hundred. The perfect secretary for a man like Kirby, although he was irritated by her frequent hospitalizations. Vidalia suffered from tension headaches, cataracts, hemorrhoids, cystitis, and the heartbreak of psoriasis. Last year she became the town's most famous hypochondriac when apparently she dropped "dead" of a heat stroke. Dr. LeGette pronounced her DOA at Parish Hospital. Somebody called Beaulieu's, and Israel and Twilly showed up with a body bag. They zipped her up, transported her to the funeral home, and laid her out on the table. When Cab Beaulieu and Israel started to embalm her, they turned around, looking for something on a shelf. Behind them Vidalia slowly raised up. Her hand swept over a metal tray, knocking the trocar to the floor. Israel spun around and hollered, but Cab Beaulieu fainted.

Vidalia spent one month at Parish Hospital, courtesy of Beaulieu Funeral Home and Dr. LeGette. Five newspapers drove up to interview her, including the *Times-Picayune*, Memphis *Commercial-Appeal*, and Arkansas *Gazette*. The headline in the Lake Providence *Banner-Democrat* read, LIMOGES'S OWN LADY LAZARUS RISES FROM MORTUARY SLAB.

Kirby got up from his desk, walked across the room, and shut the door. Outside, the typing stopped, then abruptly started. Vidalia's absences, he noticed, seemed to coincide with his own moral weaknesses. When the secretary was away, the preacher would play. He sighed and sat down in the leather chair. Leaning back, he admired the framed diplomas on the wall—Lebanon High School, Earl Moleen Bible College, John the Baptist Home Study Course. During his singing days with the Crusade, Kirby learned what they didn't teach you at the seminary. He learned to drink black coffee on pastoral calls, so he wouldn't trouble the ladies (they tended to get all flustered while fetching cream and sugar). And no matter what dessert they served, no matter how sweet and slimy, you ate every last bite. He forced himself to alternately flirt and act holy with the blue-haired women. Old ladies generally sickened him, with their rumpled mouths, chewed-off lipstick, and faces like canaries. Yet they'd fill the offering plates with crisp dollar bills.

He'd been other places. One lady in Tampa, Florida, still wrote him long, passionate letters. And every Christmas, a woman in Phoenix sent him jars of jalapeño jelly. True, he'd loved and left those women, but he'd made them believe *they* were dumping *him*, breaking his heart. It wasn't foolproof. In Mims, Texas, he'd gotten a lawyer's wife pregnant, but she'd fallen down her cellar steps and snapped her neck. The lawyer came home and found her surrounded by broken mason jars and whole, peeled tomatoes. That was a close call.

By the time Kirby came to Limoges, he had learned to seek out prostitutes, even though his sermons warned against them. Just a few Sundays ago, after a wild night in Bossier City, he'd stood at the pulpit, smiling into the faces of Olive's parents, and quoted from Proverbs, "Do not lust in your heart after her beauty or let her captivate you with her eyes, for the prostitute reduces you to a loaf of bread." He paused, allowing this to sink in. "Brothers, this makes you worth about fourteen cents." His sermons were full of sayings like that, lifted straight from the Good Book itself and then twisted. He just loved to warp the Bible to where it made sense to common folk.

All those years ago when he'd headed south and took up preaching, he should have gone west, straight to Hollywood. Rather than preaching about heavenly stars, he would have been one, Lord almighty, sitting up in a mansion, a blue swimming pool with a fountain and palm trees, Mexican servants bringing him tequila on the rocks. Sitting in the cabana, wearing a silk paisley robe and sunglasses, talking to Louis B. Mayer on one phone, Ava Gardner on the other. A man could get depressed just thinking about what-all he'd missed in life; but when the Lord called, you didn't tell him He had the wrong number. You said, "Yes, sir. I'll be right there, sir. Just as I am without one plea/but that thy blood was shed for me/and that thou bidd'st me come to thee, O Lamb of God, I come! I come!"

About nine years ago he was a different man—literally. Before he was Reverend T. C. Kirby, his name was Vernon Ray Maggart. He grew up in Harrison, West Virginia, and the only way he could escape his crazy childhood was to grow up. His mama, Regina May Maggart, weighed over two hundred pounds. In spite of her bulk, she'd developed a reputation as an easy lay—the Maggarts owned a chicken farm. Sometimes men drove up at night, and Regina took them down to see the baby chicks. Vernon's grandmother, Mamaw, would drop to her knees and pray, begging Jesus to make Regina May stop sinning. Otherwise, Vernon Ray wouldn't have known Jesus from a June bug. The Maggarts rarely left the farm. The boy had no idea who his father was, but Mamaw hinted that it was a blind man from Peru, West Virginia.

Mamaw did not like routy little boys. She used to whip little Vernon with a hickory switch when he'd chase the baby chickens. Once, he tripped and fell, mashing dozens of hatchlings, and the old woman nearly beat him to death. He grew up hollering phrases: "Vernon Ray's a bad boy! Vernon Ray's a bastard. You little cocksucker, I'll kill you!"

On his tenth birthday, Regina May ate all the icing off his cake and then blamed it on Mamaw. The cake ended up on the kitchen floor, the two women rolling over it, trying to pull each other's hair out. When he was eleven, his mother got pregnant again, but she was so obese no one suspected, not even Mamaw. When the baby was born, Regina May carried it outside. Vernon Ray followed, darting into a lilac bush. He watched her go up to the well, set the baby in the bucket, and lower it into the water. The baby's cries echoed all the way down. There was a little splash, then Regina May leaned over the well. After a few minutes, she reeled in the bucket. Vernon jumped out of the forsythia bush, and cried, "What you doing to that baby?"

"Hush up!" Regina May hissed. Her eyes were flat, almost all pupil. "I ain't did nothing! And if you waken Mamaw, I'll sew your lips together."

"Why ain't the baby moving?" He pointed to the bucket.

"It was borned dead."

"But I heard it cry."

"You calling me a liar, boy?"

"No, but—"

"It was borned, and then it was dead." She lifted the bucket. Water streamed down. "See? Borned dead."

When he turned eighteen, Regina May tipped the scales at three hundred. She'd developed a hacking cough and wore a handkerchief tied around her face, bandit-style. World War II had just ended, and Vernon Ray, who'd been keeping up with the newsreels at the theater in Harrison, decided it was safe to join the army. He ended up at Fort Campbell, Kentucky. He was a shy boy with blue eyes that seemed eternally watchful. The kindest man on base was a chaplain named Thomas Covington Kirby, a Baptist minister who could repeat books of the Bible forward and backward. The chaplain was only a few years older than Vernon Ray, with thick eyeglasses and tiny gray eyes. He'd walk into the barracks and start talking about the Scriptures. When the men started rolling their eyes, Reverend Kirby said,

"Now, hold on. The Bible is one dirty book, don't kid yourself. It's just full of lust and perversions. I can cite chapter and verses."

Some of the men snickered, but Vernon Ray perked up. "Tell me more," he said. The reverend invited him to a tent revival just across the Tennessee state line.

"I'll buy your supper if you go," he said, and Vernon Ray smiled. They ate at a truck stop that specialized in deep-fried frog legs, then they drove to the revival down a cloudy dirt road. Vernon Ray had never set foot in a church, much less a tent.

In the tent he sat next to Reverend Kirby, fanning himself with a paper fan that said Anderson Funeral Home. Summer flu was going around, and all over the tent, people sneezed and coughed. They looked up at the preacher with feverish faces that had nothing to do with the sermon. Vernon Ray sat with his head cocked, listening to everything the preacher said. A couple of times Vernon's mouth sagged open. All this talk of Jesus got to him. Several men in the audience walked up to the podium and offered a prayer.

"Anyone else?" said the preacher, his eyes moving from person to person. Then he sneezed into a stained handkerchief. Vernon Ray swallowed hard, then stood up. He walked up to the pulpit and prayed. He didn't know where the words sprang from—it was as if he'd been born with them and they were just waiting to fly out of his mouth this very night. When he finished, there wasn't a dry eye in the tent. Even Reverend Kirby was sobbing, wiping snot on his sleeves. *Dang*, Vernon Ray thought. *I'm good!*

"You're a born preacher," he told Vernon. "You've found your calling."

"You think so?" Vernon Ray said, watching the collection plate with interest.

"The revival concludes tomorrow night," Reverend Kirby said. "Can you make it?"

"Yes, yes," Vernon Ray said, thinking he'd figure a way to tip over the collection plate and scoop up a few dollars. But the next afternoon, Vernon Ray was aching all over. One minute he was on fire, the next he'd start chilling. He lay in his bunk, drawn up in the fetal position, shaking so hard the cot rattled. The sergeant and another man carried Vernon Ray to the infirmary, where the chaplain was laid out in the next bed. "Hey, buddy," Reverend Kirby said to Vernon. "We'll get to that revival yet."

Thirty-six hours later the chaplain was dead. The doctor said it was encephalitis. "Is that like syphilis?" Vernon Ray asked, sitting up on his elbows.

"No," the doctor said. He spelled it. "It's a complication of the flu. An infection of the brain."

"Will I get it?" Vernon Ray started trembling.

"No, it's not contagious. Your temperature was ninety-eight point four today."

A few days later the sergeant put Vernon Ray in charge of gathering the chaplain's personal effects. "He hasn't got no family. No folks, no wife," the sergeant said. "I guess you can keep what you want and throw the rest out. It's worthless stuff, anyhow."

Vernon was still feeling weak, but he boxed up Reverend Kirby's suits, boxer shorts, assorted Bibles, and sermons. He sifted through medicine bottles, papers, diplomas, and photographs, putting together the chaplain's life. Kirby was born in Lebanon, Tennessee, on August 16, 1921. According to an old newspaper clipping in the *Lebanon Democrat,* he'd "surrendered to the call to preach and asked the church to license him."

"Who am I supposed to send all this shit *to*?" Vernon Ray said to himself. He couldn't just throw it away—somebody might steal the diplomas and try to pass himself off as a Baptist preacher. Vernon Ray blinked. "Now that's an idea," he muttered. "One I should've thought of myself."

He tried on the reverend's clothes—a little baggy in the waist and shoulders, but a few good meals would fix that. Then he boxed everything and hitched a ride to the Clarksville Motor Court, just over the state line. He rented a room, then dressed in a black suit with a clerical collar. He went outside and rocked on the long concrete porch, a Bible in his lap. Before too long he struck up a conversation with a couple from Saint Louis who were on their way to Gatlinburg. Parked in front of their room was a brand new yellow Buick sedan. It looked like a big crookneck squash, just soaking up sun.

Vernon Ray prayed for their safe journey into the mountains of east Tennessee. After the couple went to their room, Vernon Ray watched the woman pull the curtains, brown and yellow plaid. The light snapped out, and he lit a cigarette, trying to figure how many hours it would take him to reach Lebanon, Tennessee. He was AWOL, but he already had a plan. He threw out the cigarette, walked over to the Buick, and leaned inside. A box of yellow Kleenex on the dash, map folded up behind the visor, key in the ignition, hanging from a green rabbit's foot.

It didn't take long to pack. At four A.M. he put the Buick in reverse, rolled it out of the parking lot, then started the engine. He drove toward Lebanon, into the heart of middle Tennessee. He drove around the Square, parked in front of Khun's Five-and-

Dime, and waited for daybreak. When the dime store opened, he bought a doughnut and cup of coffee at the soda counter. Then he walked to the courthouse, where he asked a thin-faced clerk for a copy of his birth certificate.

"Name and date of birth, please," the woman said without looking up from her papers.

"Thomas C. Kirby." He spread his hands on the wooden counter. His fingers were shaking. "Born August 16, 1921."

"Martha Gaston?"

"Excuse me?" He felt perspiration popping out along his hairline, dripping down his sideburns. Maybe this was Kirby's mama, or it could even be an old girlfriend.

"Martha Gaston?" the woman repeated.

Vernon licked his lips. "Who, ma'am?"

"Martha Gaston is not a who." The clerk sniffed. "Don't you know which hospital you were born at?"

"I've been away a long time," he said. "A chaplain in the army."

"There's only two—McFarland or Martha Gaston. So which is it?"

"The latter, I guess."

The woman squinted, as if trying to place him. He half expected her to shout, "Why, you're not Thomas C. Kirby! I went to school with him. I even dated him!" But she only sighed and said, "One dollar, please. You can have a seat in the hall."

He went into the corridor and sat down on a bench. Above him ceiling fans circulated air that smelled of scorched coffee. A policeman walked by, and Vernon stiffened. He glanced over at a bulletin board, where a poster advertised the Billy Graham Crusade. It was an old poster, but it listed cities and dates of the circuit. Maybe he could drive down to Montgomery, Alabama, where the crusade would be next week. The policeman strutted past him, his heels clicking on the tile, and turned a corner.

"Mr. Kirby?" said the clerk.

Vernon Ray's legs jerked. He almost screamed. "Yes?" he said, leaning forward.

"Your copy is ready."

He drove west to Nashville, then south toward Birmingham. It occurred to him that he'd stumbled onto the perfect career. "Heal the sick," he said, laughing. "Raise the dead." And he could change his identity any time he pleased. He could be a doctor, even. All he needed was a real person, dead or alive, and a birthplace. You could fake everything else. Suddenly the world seemed good and wide and deep. A world full of college diplomas, licenses, references. Whole lives just for the taking. Like a lizard in a rock pile, he saw how he could disappear, not to mention shed his skin when he outgrew himself. He wanted plenty of distance between himself and Fort Campbell. He thanked God that Tennessee was a skinny state.

In Birmingham, Vernon Ray abandoned the Buick and stole a green Chevy. Then he stopped a man on the street and offered to trade for a battered black Pontiac. The man looked startled but handed over his keys. It's a more preacherly car, Vernon Ray thought. *And untraceable.* He headed south, with the reverend's belongings piled in the backseat. As the miles dropped off behind him, he discarded bits of himself. Gone was Vernon Ray Maggart, gone was his mama's god-awful chicken farm. He'd never set foot in Tennessee or West Virginia again. By the time he reached the outskirts of Montgomery, he scarcely remembered his past. He was miles away, years away.

He thought about driving until the road ended—Pensacola, Mobile, New Orleans—but he didn't like the idea of being hemmed in by the Gulf of Mexico. He imagined the police and MP's chasing him into the water. Lord almighty, he'd sink to the bottom, and a great big fish would bite him on the ass. Even if he could swim, the Gulf wouldn't hide him like piney woods and rough paved roads. Traveling from town to town would be best. It was too bad he didn't have the birth certificate of a circus man. He could run a kiddie booth, Toss the Loops or Pick Up Ducks.

In downtown Montgomery, he stopped at a red light and turned up the radio, wondering if a statewide search was in progress. Maybe the whole damn world was looking for him. A nasal-voiced man was reading the news—*Mrs. Edwin R. Lawler has been appointed chairman of the Mothers' March on Polio in Montgomery. . . . A twenty-inch TV set will be at the Montgomery Home Demonstration Club so that those attending the box supper can also watch the Charles-Walcott heavyweight fight at seven-thirty. . . . A University of Alabama home economist said that housekeeping would be easier for many American women if their training had begun fifteen or twenty years earlier. . . .*

The light was still red. He drummed his fingers on the dashboard. Maybe the police weren't looking for him. Maybe they didn't connect an AWOL private from Fort Campbell with a dead preacher or with stolen cars in Clarksville and Birmingham. He hadn't meant to go on a crime spree; he could see the headlines now. He thought about asking for directions to the police station. He pictured himself walking in, confessing his transgressions. Somehow that was not his style, telling his business to strangers.

A horn honked behind him, and he looked up. The light was green. He pressed his foot to the accelerator, drove one block, then turned right. Straight ahead was a police station, with black-and-white cars parked along the street. Above the station was a billboard painted with Billy Graham's face, big as God's. It was, in fact, like God was giving him a choice—turn yourself in or come with me. He remembered something the revival preacher said, "The Lord never closes one door without opening another."

"Damn, I'll take my chances with Billy," Vernon Ray told himself, his hands cupping the steering wheel with grace and mercy, steering him past the police station, around the corner, toward his new life.

From the chapel, the youth choir started singing Reverend Kirby's favorite hymn, "He Hideth My Soul." The children were practicing for Easter services. Kirby had a whole skit planned, too, right down to a fake earthquake. The sign out front would say HE IS RISEN. He just hoped nobody else did. Kirby bowed his head and prayed, "Lord? If you don't let Olive wake up, I'll turn over a new leaf. I won't shit where I eat, Lord. I'll drive to Bossier City, Shreveport, and New Orleans."

Kirby opened his desk and glanced at the list of deacons. Then he picked up the phone and dialed the first name on his list. "Brother Leonard?" he said. "So sorry to bother you while Sister Harriet is still under the weather, but I have a little problem. We've got pigeons nesting in the steeple. I'm just afraid it might be unhealthy. I know your Harriet wouldn't want to worry about mites."

"Maybe we can hire somebody to shoot the birds with air rifles?" suggested Leonard.

"Well, I don't know." Reverend Kirby thought it was a good idea, too. But he said, "Do you really think a Baptist belfry is the proper place to shoot a gun? I mean, it seems un-Christian to kill birds. You know what the Bible said, Leonard. He sees every sparrow. I sure don't want Him to think we're tampering with His pigeons."

"No, no. I guess not."

"Do you know anyone who could donate screen mesh? Then we'd need somebody, of course, to nail it up."

"Why, I've got some men working at my house right now. I'll bet they can help."

"God bless you, Brother Leonard," Reverend Kirby said. "And say hello to Sister Harriet for me. Tell her I'll be seeing her later, when I get to the hospital for my rounds."

Of all the places he'd been, he liked Limoges best. When he arrived, he had tried to be pure. He acted like one of the old ladies, eating pie, clucking about their grandbabies (like he gave a damn), taking prayer requests. He ignored the middle-aged women's glances and the way the teenage girls felt when he held them under water during baptisms. At night he'd look at pictures he'd bought in Nevada—women tied to bedposts, women with German shepherds and Great Danes, men and women together, piles of bodies, arms and legs writhing. Sometimes he'd take off on Saturday morning and drive one hundred miles. Just as every town had its churches, it had its whores, too. That, to the all-new Reverend T. C. Kirby, summed up the meaning of life.

Once, in New Orleans, he got drunk and paid for a virgin. A woman with blue eyelids and a hairy mole led him up a steep stairway that smelled of vomit. "Virgins is hard to come by," the woman said, rubbing one hand against his genitals. "See? You's already hard. That'll be one hundred dollars."

He handed over the money. She quickly counted it, then lifted her skirt and stuffed her money into her panties. She pushed Kirby into the room and shut the door. There on the bed lay a girl with a sheet drawn up to her chin. She raised up, and he saw long gold hair and blue eyes. She looked seventeen, maybe sixteen. Maybe a tad younger. With all that eye makeup it was hard to tell. She did things with her hands that made him squirm, and she spoke in an old, throaty voice, already ruined by cigarettes, urging him to be still.

She turned out to be no virgin (he knew chicken blood when he saw it), but he felt justified in spending the hundred dollars. It was good Baptist money, carefully filched from the collection plate, and he told himself that he was donating to poor little orphans. Maybe this money would help buy the girl a hot meal or two. That was the same summer he came to Limoges, during a week-long revival. The fifth day, the regular preacher was stricken with food poisoning and died the following night in Parish Hospital. Reverend Kirby preached the funeral, and everybody said it was the best eulogy they'd ever heard. The deacons approached the reverend, asking him if he would consider preaching until a replacement could be found. Meanwhile, would he care to move into the parsonage?

From the chapel, the children sang, *"He hid-eth my soul in the cleft of the rock/Where rivers of plea-sures I see . . . He hid-eth my life in the depths of his love/And cov-ers me there with his hand."*

Reverend Kirby rose from his desk and walked into the hall-way, following the voices. When he opened the chapel door, the children saw him. They swarmed out of the choir box, ignoring the protests of Mrs. Connelly, the bedraggled song leader, and crowded around the reverend.

"Tell us about the Easter egg hunt!" they said, jumping up and down.

"Well, it's going to be the finest one in Limoges. I'm going down to New Orleans next week, and I'm bringing back special Elmer's Gold Bricks." He laughed when they started cheering and clapping. "Are you kids thirsty? Why don't you kids meet me in Fellowship Hall, and maybe I can talk Mrs. Connelly into fixing us some Kool-Aid."

The children cheered again. They ran down the aisle, toward the side door. Mrs. Connelly was gathering sheet music from the podium. She was large-busted, and he could see the outline of her nipples against the cotton dress. Her waist was small, cinched in with a narrow green belt. He felt himself becoming aroused and folded his hands in front of his zipper, hiding his erection. Then she leaned over, showing a stretch of wrinkled thigh. His erection shriveled, and he moved his hand. *"If all my church ladies was this homely,"* he thought, *"then my job would be a whole lot holier."*

"I hope I didn't interrupt," he called out.

"Oh, well." She turned, brushing hair from her face. "We needed a break, I guess."

"You all sounded good. You've been working hard for Easter service."

"Thanks." She walked down the steps, then sidled up to him. "But you've been working overtime yourself. You're awful good to drive back and forth to New Orleans for our candy. Did you know Fanny Farmer pralines are my personal favorites?"

"Well, with parents like you donating money, I can't go wrong." He smiled and patted her shoulder, letting his hand linger. Up close she smelled like dog food, but she was a good tither. He let his hand fall to his side.

"No preacher's ever took an interest in Easter hunts, Brother Kirby."

"All the congregation must be tended, Mrs. Connelly. Little Baptists grow into big Baptists. If you lead a man down the right path, he will not stray."

"You're just too good to be true."

"Well, I try, Mrs. Connelly. I really try."

"You're wonderful." She looked up into his eyes, tilting back her head. From Fellowship Hall came a girl's scream, followed by a crash, but Mrs. Connelly didn't blink.

"You can call me Patsy," she said.

"All right." He leaned toward her. "Patsy." He thought about saying, *And you can call me Vernon Ray.* He even thought about taking her to the belfry. He'd lay her down and slowly unbutton her dress, telling her she was beautiful. The prettiest little thing he'd ever seen. People wanted to believe the best about themselves; it was pitiful how they'd suck up praise. She'd been a wife so long, she'd be grateful—not to mention flabby, but what the hell. She'd do whatever he asked. It would save him the trouble of having to drive hundreds of miles. Best of all, she probably owned a diaphragm. There were three little Connellys, but the youngest was ten.

Patsy lowered her eyes and hugged the sheet music to her chest. An uncomfortable silence sprang up between them. Kirby glanced up at the ceiling. Next year it would need painting, and Mrs. Connelly's brother-in-law owned Sherwin-Williams—not a Baptist, but still. Besides, she looked like the type who would not let you off easy after a sexual tryst. She'd follow you to the ends of the earth if you tried to leave her. He knew a woman like that in Houston, Texas. She left her husband and five children to follow the Crusade—specifically T. C. Kirby. If she hadn't had that nervous breakdown in Tulsa, he would have *never* gotten away.

"Shall we head on down to Fellowship Hall?" he said, touching her shoulder (just to egg her on. Probably a few more times like these, and she'd donate a whole stained glass window). "The children are waiting for their Kool-Aid."

"Kool-Aid?" She blinked.

"You know, like in raspberry? For your choir? Or should I say *our* choir?" He winked. "They're waiting for us."

"Oh! That's right, that's right!" She covered her mouth with sheet music and giggled.

"Ladies first." He stepped back, extending one arm.

"Why, you're such a gentleman," she said, then waddled up the aisle.

And you're just like a bride, Kirby thought. *A big fat bride. Thank God you're not mine.*

Day Work

❧

I'll tell you what's wrong with this part of the delta—there's one hun-dred and one Baptist churches, all shapes and sizes. Listen to the names they pick, like Girl Scout camps: True Vine, Seven Star Mis-sionary, New Light Jerusalem, Zebedee, and Zion Flower. First United Methodist sits between First Baptist and Plum Grove Missionary. Both are having Easter egg hunts next Sunday. All those little Bap-tists swarming like termites, chewing up candy, destroying private property. Why, it's sinful—and wasteful. Somebody ought to do some-thing.

——MAMIE MARSHALL, STUDYING THE PHONE BOOK WITH HER SISTER, MEREDITH, APRIL 1952

Billie Robichaux

I pulled my wagon down Hayes Avenue looking for empty Coca-Cola bottles. Mama said we lived on the wrong side of the tracks, but I didn't get it. The train depot was on the north side, miles from us. A long time ago Mama showed me how to tell the right and wrong side of Limoges. Stand on the courthouse square next to the statue of General Beauregard, and look east—you'll see nothing but shade trees and streetlights. Behind those trees are houses with columns, stained-glass cupolas, and wrought-iron fences. Face west, toward Hayes, you'll see cracked cement with weeds shooting up. You'll see a water tower, power lines, houses with tar-paper fronts, cotton gins, and the soybean warehouse. There's a feed mill, sawmill, cotton warehouse, and the Wells Lamant Glove Factory. A scattering of trees with dead limbs and squirrel nests.

Even in summer, with all the pretty petunias and marigolds, Hayes Avenue seems shabby. Dandelions grow through rusted wheelbarrows and wooden Coca-Cola crates. Busted cars sit on concrete blocks, the insides packed with thistle, grapevines, and honeysuckle, a sweet knot that is full of seed ticks, red bugs, and sometimes soda bottles.

I had already earned me $6.75, but it wasn't nearly enough. I needed so much money, the notion made me dizzy. I'd picked me out an Easter dress, blue dotted swiss with a sash and a stiff petticoat, for $3.98 at Hooper's. The saleslady wrote up the ticket and said if I put down one dollar a week, I would have the dress paid off by April 12, the day before Easter.

When she said that, I stared down at the dress. It was a Dan River, with puffed sleeves and big white buttons.

"That color will go good with your red hair," the woman said. "Do you need a handbag to go with it? We have a nice selection of children's purses." She pointed to a shelf of straw bags with plastic flowers glued to the sides. The one I liked best, a white purse with a heart-shaped lock, was $2.75.

"I'll take it," I said, but I had no idea where I would get the money in time to pay it off.

"How about a nice pair of nylon gloves?" the woman asked, going to another counter. "They're on sale for fifty-nine cents."

"I don't know." I shrugged. I needed shoes and socks, and I already had my eye on some at Bradford's, a pair of double-strap, white patent-leather sandals. They cost a whopping $3.98.

"Your ensemble won't be complete without gloves, young lady."

"It sure does cost money to dress up for church," I said, untying my daddy's dirty handkerchief. I counted out dollars in nickels and dimes.

The woman leaned over me and said, "Little girl, do you have a mother?"

"Yes, ma'am." I reached down and fingered the gloves. I heard this all the time from people, and it made me so mad, I could spit.

"Whose child are you, then?"

"Oh, you don't know us," I lied. "We're new in town."

"Then why isn't she with you?" The woman's eyes darted from side to side, like she was hunting for a grown-up lady who looked like me.

"She's got real bad polio and can't leave the house? And she sent me down here to get what I needed. She give me this money, see?" I held up the handkerchief, the coins jingling together.

"Yes." The woman took a step backward, bumping into a glass counter. "I wasn't aware of any recent polio cases here in Limoges."

"Well, she's got it." I paused and gave her my sweetest smile. "It's all right for me to be here, ain't it? I mean, is it legal for me to buy clothes without my mama?"

"My stars, yes." The woman's cheeks flushed. "Just sign your little name right here on the dotted line."

Now I hunted in a trash barrel, hoping to find a discarded soda bottle. I would never pay off my debts—there weren't enough soda bottles in all of Limoges. The old women on Hayes Avenue always left bottles on their back porch, but Aunt Butter said it would be stealing to take them. "You'd best stick to the gutters and people's trash," she'd said. I figured the ones in the alley were mine, though.

There were no bottles in Reverend Kirby's trash. I knocked on his door, but he wasn't home. A few Sundays ago, I heard him preach about the hereafter. You have two basic choices, heaven or hell, what he called the hot place. If you're real good, you get everlasting life in heaven, plus a mansion. Every day you see Jesus, God, and the angels. The streets are lined with gold, and there's air conditioning. You won't get thirsty or hungry. You won't have to go to the bathroom. Probably there's no birthdays, either. Reverend Kirby said this is divine satisfaction, but I don't know. It might be interesting the first week, then it would get boring. "Well, what're we going to do today? Sing 'Old Rugged Cross' for the 1,999,999th time?"

The other choice is to burn in hell forever. On the way home from church, my mama called Reverend Kirby a fool.

"He isn't!" Aunt Butter stopped walking and stared.

"Just think about it." Mama turned. "If you went to hell, you'd get third-degree burns, so all you'd have is three to five minutes of pain. Then your nerve fibers would get destroyed. At least that's what *National Geographic* said."

Aunt Butter narrowed her eyes and said, "Don't you *National Geographic* me!"

When my wagon was full, I stopped off at the bottling company on Ambrosia Street, collecting sixty-six cents. Then I pulled my empty wagon to the Square. I found trash in the alley but no bottles; I guessed I wasn't the only one in town who was low on money. I walked around the courthouse, past old men selling cane-bottomed chairs, my wagon bumping along behind me. Here on the Square, I had a good view of Lincoln Avenue. The trees were bright splashes of green, mingled with dogwoods and redbuds. I waited for the light to change, then crossed the street.

"Little girl!" hollered one of the old men.

I was in the middle of the street, but I turned. Aunt Butter trained me to be polite to geezers. The man looked to be a hundred, with sunken cheeks and silver hairs sticking from his ears like a kitten's.

"Yeah?" I called out, holding one hand over my eyes.

"Don't you go round stealing no pop bottles." The man shook his finger. "You hear?"

"*I* don't steal," I said and stuck out my tongue. Then I headed down Lincoln, toward the rich people. The lawns got bigger and bigger, dotted with flowers and fancy iron fences. One yard had so much iron furniture, it reminded me of the Yellow Fever Cemetery. Even the trees on this side of town seemed fuller, circled with lacy white benches, so's you could take a load off if you got winded.

I turned down Cypress because it was Mama's favorite. We'd been here lots of times after dark to look through people's windows, seeing what-all they had. It made me feel creepy, but Mama turned it into a game. "I spy a thick gold mirror over a carved walnut fireplace," she'd say, and then I'd have to see which house it was in.

I stopped at Mr. Henry's house, pulling my wagon up the brick walkway, past a black mailbox spelling out NEPPER. I opened the storm door, stood on my toes, banged the brass knocker three times. Then I stepped back and waited for somebody to come. I admired the tulips that were shooting up, their buds trying to open like puppy eyes. I even saw some irises, but it would be a while before they bloomed.

The door swung open, and I stared up at a round-faced woman with huge blue eyes, like glass eggs. Two braids hung down, making me think of Shirley Temple playing Heidi, but Mrs. Nepper was real old. I'd seen her at her husband's store. "You're Mrs. Nepper, ain't you?"

"Yes, sugar." She smiled down at me.

"You may not know me, but I'm Billie Robichaux? My mama works for Mr. Henry?"

"That's right. She does." She kept on smiling.

"Yes, ma'am. And see, I'm nine years old, and I was wondering if you needed any work done around here?" I put one hand on my hip, the way I'd seen Mama do, and I lifted my other hand, palm up, like I was carrying a tray.

"Well, hello, Billie Robichaux." The woman squatted down and took one of my hands. "Nice to meet you."

"Same here." I shook her hand then stepped back. "You need me to haul any trash or dead trees? I work real cheap."

"You do?" Mrs. Nepper pursed her lips. "May I ask why you're working?"

"See, I got these bills?" I shuffled my feet. I was starting to wonder if I'd made a mistake. A rich lady like her wouldn't understand why I needed money.

"Bills? What kind?"

"I've got me a Easter dress on layaway at Hooper's, and if I don't pay it off, another little girl will get it. Then I won't have nothing pretty to wear for church."

"Oh." Mrs. Nepper nodded, pushing her lips to one side. "Tell you what, I could use a strong girl to help me wash windows. Someone who could wipe out the sills. Think you can do that?"

"Oh, yes, ma'am!" I bounced up and down on the balls of my feet.

"I'll pay you a dollar a day, plus lunch. Does that suit you?"

I nodded. Then I frowned. "There's just one problem."

"What's that?"

"I wish you wouldn't tell Mr. Henry that I'm working here. He might let it slip to Mama, and see, I want this to be a surprise."

"Why, I understand perfectly." She patted my head. "It'll be our secret. Just park your little wagon over in the shade, and we'll get started."

Mrs. Nepper's living room was dark and cool, the windows blocked with bumpy, pale green drapes, like skin on an osage orange. Each lamp had crystal spears, long, pointy diamonds. When Mrs. Nepper stepped into the hall, I reached out and jingled them. I'd never seen such finery. There was a pink couch with green satin pillows. Tables were scattered about, and each one had slabs of marble, the wavy black veins curving like roads and highways. A colored lady stood in a sunny pink kitchen, standing in front of an ironing board. One of her arms was in a sling, and her face was bruised, like she'd fell down stairs or been in a war. With her good arm, she gripped the iron, the steam hissing each time she pushed it over a yellow dress. When she looked up, I saw that one of her eyes was nearly swollen shut, with a knob of purple tissue hanging down.

"Billie, this is Sophie," said Mrs. Nepper, pouring a cup of coffee, waving her other hand at the woman.

"Hi," I said, my eyes going back to the colored lady.

The woman smiled, and her eye floated behind the slit. "Hi yourself."

"Billie's going to do a little work for me," Mrs. Nepper said. "She's got an Easter dress on layaway at Hooper's, but it's a secret, so don't tell."

"I won't. You sure are smart, ain't you?" said Sophie. Then she stared at me, the pits of her eyes purple and black. "I seen you before," she said. "Your mama work for Mr. Henry?"

"Yeah," I said, bouncing against the counter. All the cabinets in this kitchen were pink, and you opened them with little crystal knobs. "You know my mama?"

"Seen her at the drugstore. She's pretty, your mama is."

"Yeah, she thinks so."

"I'll bet." Sophie smiled a little. If you looked past the beat places, you could see that she'd once been pretty herself. She had eyelashes that curved up like thick black feathers. "Ma'am, how'd you get hurt?"

"Got kicked by a old mule," Sophie said, pushing the iron over a buttonhole, steam drifting under her chin.

"You got a real live mule?" I stepped forward, expecting to see hoof prints.

"A mule named Burr," said Mrs. Nepper. "And she ought to either shoot it or sell it."

"Oh, that old mule always sweet as a puppy after he kicks me," Sophie said. She moved the dress and straightened a pleat.

"Must be a mean mule," I said. "To kick you like that. I'd tie it up, or at least hobble it."

"Maybe I will." Sophie grinned and cut her eyes at Mrs. Nepper.

"I sure hope you feel better," I said.

"Thanks." Sophie held up the yellow dress, then fit a hanger inside it. "Already do."

"If you get rid of that mule, maybe you want a dog? I got me some puppies." I held up six fingers. "But Aunt Butter, that's my aunt, she said they're digging up her whole yard."

"Puppies is bad to do that," Sophie said.

"You ought to trade one for your mule," Mrs. Nepper said, but Sophie just shook her head.

"Oh, you hush up," Sophie told her. "Just hush your talking."

I was squatting in the backyard, planting teeny-tiny petunia seeds where Mrs. Nepper told me. I'd cleaned all the windows, and then she asked me what I wanted for lunch. She said I could have anything I wanted, so I asked for a mayonnaise-and-cucumber sandwich. She said she loved anything with mayonnaise on it, but it went straight to her hips. Then she laughed and patted her own self. I thought she was right cute.

I worked a long time planting them seeds. Later, a tall woman came over. She had a narrow face and gray eyes. Her reddish hair was swept over to the side, held back with a beaded clip. She started talking to Mrs. Nepper. I kept glancing over, trying to see if I knew her, and when she laughed, it came to me, just like that. I'd heard that laugh before, kind of foreign-like. I'd seen her at the hospital visiting the Neppers, but I couldn't remember her name. Mama said she was mean and hoity-toity, not from around here.

"Who's your little helper?" she asked Mrs. Nepper. She leaned over the boxwood hedge. She was wearing green slacks and a matching short-sleeved blouse. Her arms stuck out like skinny vines, and she was holding a cigarette.

"Her name's Billie Robichaux. She knocked on my door this morning and asked if she could help out."

"Ah. Now I know who she is." The lady drew in a deep breath. I felt her watching as I shuffled down the row, dribbling the teeny seeds.

"She's got gumption," said Mrs. Nepper. "She's trying to earn money for an Easter outfit." Mrs. Nepper folded her arms and glanced down the length of her yard. I watched from the corner of my eye.

"She must be smart." said the tall lady. "And she's cute. I may hire her to plant nasturtiums."

"She'll do it," Mrs. Nepper said, "but I ought to warn you, I'm paying her a dollar a day."

"Goodness." The lady smiled.

"But she's worth it."

"Poor little thing." The lady leaned over the boxwoods. "Little girl?" she called out to me.

I looked up. "Yes, ma'am?"

"When you finish, I'd like to hire you to plant nasturtium seeds. You interested?"

"Yes, ma'am!"

Mrs. Nepper smiled, then bent her head toward the lady, making her braids swing. I couldn't hear what they said after that, so I concentrated on the seeds, making holes in the soil with the tip of a pencil, like Mrs. Nepper had showed me. Then I dropped in a seed, flicking dirt with the eraser. I pictured every-thing I would buy with my money: a four-ball croquet set; a straw hat for Daddy; Avon lipstick for Aunt Butter; a Dixie Lou frock for my mama, with a bolero jacket, piped in white pique for only $3.98. Or I could save my money and buy Daddy a summer suit, "cool and carefree linen," the ad promised, for $29. The sun beat down on the back of my head. The women laughed, but I didn't look up.

"Well, I know it," Mrs. Nepper was saying. "But I just couldn't place her. Guess I've had too much on my mind here lately. I've seen her before, though. Playing in front of the drugstore. I didn't know who she belonged to, but now I do. Her mama has worked for Henry since last September."

"Poor thing." The lady stared at me. "Could she be a feral child?"

"Oh, she's not." Mrs. Nepper chuckled.

I lowered my eyebrows, wondering what fear all was. It sounded bad, like I was a scaredy cat, and I ain't.

"What a cute little thing." Mrs. Nepper pressed her lips together. "I always wanted a little redheaded daughter, but daughters aren't easy to come by."

"You're telling me." The woman laughed and squeezed Mrs. Nepper's arm. "I don't even *have* a child. But we'll just borrow this one now and then."

"Maybe I will." Mrs. Nepper paused and ran her hands over the flat surface of the boxwoods. I sat down in the grass and looked up at the house. Sophie was sweeping the screened porch with one arm. I wondered why Mrs. Nepper let her work this hard, or if it was Sophie's way, to keep on moving no matter what. I thought of a mule named Burr kicking her face. I thought of my own daddy throwing bowls of food like they were hand grenades, the glass shattering against the wall, the food cold and muddy, oozing between my toes like land between the levee and Mississippi.

This probably went on all the time. Maybe that's why rich folks had maids and butlers and whatnot. To clean up after their temper tantrums. I thought of Mama getting dressed and perfumed, kissing me goodbye. "I'm going out for cigarettes," she'd say. "I'll be back in a while."

But she lied. I'd brush my teeth with baking soda, then go upstairs and lay on the bed, listening for her footsteps, listening to my daddy screech out her name, listening to the neighbors yelling for him to shut up. And Butter would be climbing the stairs, saying, "This house is cursed. Lord, how will I hold my head up?"

I pictured her head lolling on her shoulders, unhinged like a tore paper doll's. And us tying it to her wrists, using balls of twine like we was tying up tomatoes. Sometimes grown-ups didn't make a bit of sense to me.

Poison Pen

❧

It was Good Friday, just pouring rain, cold as my mother-in-law's gravy. I came out of City Market with my Easter groceries, dashing through the puddles, and I saw Henry Nepper's car cruise by. I tried to flag him down. He stopped at the corner of Jefferson and Geranium, and I took off running. Before I could cross the street, a little black-haired woman beat me to it. She opened the door, shook off her green umbrella, and scooted across the seat. As I live and breathe, I saw her reach up and kiss him, then lay her head on his shoulder. They drove down Geranium, turning right on Washington, toward Highway 65. I know it was Henry because no one else has a car like it—it's Galliard blue, the same color as his wife's eyes.

—Anonymous shopper, overheard on Gallery Street, April 11, 1952

The rain began on Good Friday, hovering over Limoges, glazing everything in fog, and by Saturday evening it was still falling. Old-timers argued among themselves. "Dogwood winter," said one. "Blackberry winter," said another. Everyone blamed it on leap year.

Vangie sat in her pink kitchen, sipping hot tea. Every few minutes she glanced out the double window. At the edge of Cypress Street, mist wafted from the lake, settling between houses and trees. The road was glossy black, and through gaps in the fog she saw lights shining on the opposite shore of Lake Limoges. Dr. Bryant lived over there, and Judge Green. Sometimes the judge's cattle grazed close to shore, wading down to the water to drink. Vangie had lived more years in this house than she'd lived on Galliard land, her birthplace. She pulled the green-and-pink afghan over her knees, tucking in the edges. The linoleum floor felt cold against her stockings. She drew her thumbnail down a crease in the tablecloth. It was old, bought on sale at Hooper's for ninety-nine cents, patterned with her trademark roses, all growing up a lattice fence, like the ones beside the patio. Roses she'd fed and fussed over. Roses that had indirectly put her daughter into a coma. That's what Harriet had hinted; last Wednesday she'd come to the hospital to settle her bills, and she saw Vangie in the waiting room. "All that time you spent in your garden," Harriet said, "and look where it got you."

Vangie drew back, too stunned to speak. Her eyes filmed over.

"You grew the roses that needed the poison that killed your daughter." Harriet shook her head. "It's the saddest thing in the world."

"How can you say this to me?" Vangie cried. "How can you *hurt* me?"

"I didn't mean to." Harriet lifted her chin. She was a whole head shorter than Vangie. "I didn't mean it in a cruel way. I just find it strange that Olive drank poison when she knew you loved your roses. It was like she was jealous. Or maybe trying to punish you."

"For what?" Vangie spoke barely above a whisper. She wanted to push Harriet against the wall and bang her head, but she'd never raised her voice in public, much less caused a scene.

"Do I have to spell it out?" Harriet grunted and shot a glance at Olive's door. "You picked the wrong hobby."

"You're such a comfort," Vangie said through her teeth.

"I do my best." Harriet smiled.

Vangie thought she might burst into tears, and she didn't want to give Harriet the satisfaction. She marched over to Olive's door, opened it, and stepped inside, shutting it before Harriet could see into the room. Then she slumped, feeling the cool wood against her face. Last summer she and Olive had bought the insecticide at Poteet's Hardware—three jars for a dollar. Mr. Poteet had explained the difference between insecticides and herbicides. They'd walked home, having a regular mother-daughter conversation, explaining about roses, which Olive would surely cultivate one day. As Vangie talked, she cradled the paper sack, the jars clinking together—the implement of her daughter's doom.

Now, sitting at the kitchen table, listening to rain blowing against the windows, she agreed with Harriet. She'd picked the wrong hobby. If she hadn't been preoccupied with gardening, then maybe her child wouldn't be in a coma. Olive might be bouncing around the house, singing to herself and playing Tony Bennett records. Knitting might have been a safe pastime—a child couldn't kill herself with yarn. The needles were sharp, but only an infant would be at risk. A grown girl would think twice before perforating herself, and yarn made an unreliable noose. Vangie hadn't knitted in years, not since Olive was a baby. Her fingers were adept with weeding and pruning. She pictured herself plowing through the yarn, holding it up now and then, stretching it into shape.

If only she had focused on the cooking end of home economics—perfecting recipes for watermelon pickles and caramel icing. But then Olive might have tried to eat herself to death. You just couldn't win. One thing was for certain: She was surrounded by roses. They grew on the bone china teacup, the silver spoons, and canisters. Even her salt-and-pepper shakers resembled two American beauties, with tiny black holes where the pistil and stamen would be—genitals of the plant, with ovaries and male parts.

Somebody at the garden club said that the rose was an ancient symbol of secrecy. When knights wanted to hold a secret meeting, they placed a rose on the ceiling of a room. Not that she held her roses responsible—no, she herself was to blame. That day in March, if she hadn't wasted time in the garden, she might have saved Olive. The mothering instinct should have been stronger than the urge to pull weeds. In her dreams, while Henry slept placidly beside her, she relentlessly revised the past. She saw herself walking into the kitchen. Olive was standing beside the sink, the Nehi bottle raised halfway to her lips. "No!" Vangie screamed. "Put that *down!*" She'd throw herself out of the dream, sitting bolt upright in bed, her gown sticking to her chest. Henry opened one eye, squinting, his forehead wrinkling. He said more with that one gesture than if he'd slapped her.

Now her eyes swept across the table. Next to the plastic napkin holder was a stack of unopened mail. The envelopes were damp and wrinkled as if they'd been held underwater. She'd fetched them earlier, but she hadn't noticed a leak in the mailbox. She reminded herself to tell Henry. Hours ago, before he left for his meeting—he was chairman of the barbecue booth at the annual Pecan Festival—he'd offered to turn on the furnace. "There's no use in freezing yourself," he said.

"You can do it tonight," she told him. "After you get back."

"It might be a while." He opened the back door and cool air blew in, smelling of the muddy delta. Rain hissed down behind the screen.

"I'll wait." She smiled. "Anyway, I hate to turn on the furnace when it's nearly Easter. It's just a dogwood winter."

"Whatever," Henry said. He dashed out into the night, and a

minute later the Rambler's engine sputtered. Headlights slashed down the length of the yard.

Now she gazed out the window, chin in hand, waiting for Henry. According to the clock radio on the pink counter, he'd been gone three hours and twenty-two minutes. It seemed whole days had passed, as if the sun and moon had sped across the sky without her notice. Rain can do this, she thought, pulling back the curtain, staring down at her drenched yard. Harriet's house was awash in yellow light, but all the curtains had been drawn. Dogwoods and quince sagged in the downpour, shedding limp, shiny blossoms. Water flowed past the azaleas, toward Cypress Street, where it fell over the sidewalk in a little ruffle.

She picked up her teacup, pressing her hands against the hot china. She couldn't remember the last time she'd gone to a garden meeting. According to the club bylaws, if you skipped three meetings without an excuse, your name was erased from the membership. And there was a long waiting list for every club in Limoges; when a daughter came of age and married, naturally she hoped to fill her days with meetings and worthy causes. Like new animals at a watering hole, they waited for a vacancy. Vangie's absences would surely be excused, but she'd just as soon give her spot to someone else. Her life had narrowed to Olive and church. Henry had made no adjustments. He was always dashing off to noon luncheons at Limoges Country Club. He served on committees, was the leader of this and that. Sometimes his meetings lasted way into the night, especially if the men started playing gin rummy.

Every time a car splashed down Cypress, she leaned toward the window, narrowing her eyes at the headlights, hoping to see Henry turning into the drive. Each car disappeared into the mist, leaving a wake on the street. She shivered, pulling the afghan around her, wishing she'd let him light the furnace. Now it was too late. Water under the bridge, her mama would've said. Vangie leaned forward and rubbed the windowpane, but it only distorted the view. She sipped tea, tasting sugar and lemon against the back of her throat. She had a strong feeling, almost like a premonition, that Henry wouldn't be back. He'd drive his car into a telephone pole. Sheriff Reems would knock at the door. "Mrs. Nepper?" he'd say, rain pattering all around him. "I'm afraid I have some bad news."

She set down the cup, clattering it against the saucer, and reached for the stack of mail. A bulletin from First Baptist. Burpee seed catalog. Five get well cards. She propped them on the table. One card, a Hallmark, showed a white hot water bottle tied up with a blue bow: *WARM WISHES FOR YOUR SPEEDY*

RECOVERY. Olive received plenty of mail, no fewer than two cards a day, but they never mentioned coma or poison; Vangie would be shocked if they did. Except for Harriet, her friends and neighbors acted as if a mysterious illness had befallen the girl, a condition too delicate for words. Her friends still brought chocolate pies and chicken casseroles. Her refrigerator was full of Jell-O salads, each bowl like a different stained-glass window.

The last envelope felt bulky, and her name was spelled out with a mishmash of letters, VANgie nEpPeR, in all sizes and colors, carefully trimmed from magazines, like what kidnappers send the victim's family. She slit open the envelope, and the smell of glue drifted up.

> dEAr VaNgie
> yOuR GArDeN iS fuLL oF MORE thaN wEedS. tHiNgS aRe gRowINg & tAkinG rOOt in tHe wRoNg bEds. ThaTs wHy YouR dAuGhtER dRanK thE pOiSon. Its whY HeNrY iS nEveR hOme. hE is hoEinG soMeone elses GaRdeN aNd mAyBe eveN plAnTinG sEeDs.
> OpEn yOuR eYes! doNt bE a foOL.
> A cOncErNeD FrIEND

Vangie's forehead wrinkled. She recognized the *M* in *soMeone* from the *M* in the April *McCall's*. She read the letter again, then looked up. "But Henry doesn't garden," she said, her voice echoing in the kitchen. She stared down at the note. Her eyes lingered on *A cOncErNeD FrIEND*. Yes, she thought. Leave off the r, and a fiend sent this letter.

It was true—she did have a weedy garden, but she couldn't be in two places at the same time. And Phillip LeGette said it was important to talk to Olive, to comb her hair and read. He said only the Lord knew what a coma victim could and could not hear. Her eyes swept past the spotless pink counters, the stack of freshly washed supper dishes and glass tumblers. The air still smelled of grilled cheese-and-bacon sandwiches and chicken noodle soup, rainy day comfort food. Now she tasted bile. She had eaten one sandwich in front of Henry, but as soon as he excused himself and went to take a shower, she'd stuffed his leftovers into her mouth without thinking. Then she fixed another, smearing huge globs of mayonnaise on the white bread.

She reached under the afghan and scratched her wide, dimpled thighs. *ITs whY HeNrY iS nEveR hOmE*, she thought. *ThiNgS aRe grOWinG iN tHe wRoNg bEdS*. A neglected yard was a signal of a troubled life, her mama used to say. Outer turmoil was reflective of inner chaos. But then, how did you explain Beaulieu Funeral Home, with its backyard full of abandoned coffins? Every year Cab threatened to grow vegetables, but he was bluffing. He was too busy with the ladies to fool with a garden. Yard work wasn't Cab's style. If Israel Adams didn't cut the grass, it would grow waist-high and mourners would gets chiggers and snakebites. You couldn't expect a bachelor to be his own wife any more than you could expect a wife to be her own husband.

Henry brought his own strengths to the marriage, and she brought hers. Well, she tried. Her mind was not mathematical, even though she couldn't be beat reducing recipes. That counted for something. When her high school home economics teacher came to Vangie's wedding, she bragged that Vangie was her prized student. "If only you'd go to college and get your home ec degree," she said. "Then if Henry ever dies, you can teach school."

Since the coma, Vangie had been cooking from cans; she'd let things slide. The letter was proof that someone, somewhere had noticed her pathetic yard, along with Starkist and Campbell's soup labels in the trash. Maybe other people could endure both a poisoned daughter and a tangled garden, but she could not. She scratched her head and blinked at the letter.

She tried to compile a list of suspects, quickly eliminating Edith and Waldene. Edith would never stoop to an anonymous letter—you never had to guess what she was thinking. And Waldene had babies on the brain. No one, not even Harriet, would have assembled that letter. Vangie had known these people her whole life—the Cheniers, Fondrens, Hobarts, Marshall sisters, even Leonard Hooper. These people were more than friends—they were bound by family and geography, deep roots that fed from the same spring. The day Olive took sick, even before Vangie herself made it to the hospital, Cypress Street was lined up with cars. They curved all the way up Lincoln Avenue.

"Who?" she said aloud, racking her brain for culprits. Who would take the time to cut and paste a whole letter? She closed her eyes and imagined each face at First Baptist, going from row to row, past little girls in taffeta and patent leather, past women with straw boaters and white gloves, their smiles sealed tightly by Max Factor lipstick.

She got up from the table and shuffled to the stove, pouring another cup of tea. She tilted the sugar bowl, and her hands shook, sprinkling grains all over her clean counter. "It's *not* my fault," she said, swiping the Formica with a sponge. Tears rolled down her fat cheeks. "I can't help it if my life's a mess!"

* * *

Shortly after eleven P.M. it stopped raining. Fog gathered on Lincoln Avenue toward Limoges proper, huddling between houses, trees, bushes, and telephone poles. The haze was thickest near the lake. Car lights gleamed through milky air, then swept into the Neppers' driveway. Vangie heard the engine cut off. A car door slammed; footsteps crunched in the oyster-shell driveway. When the kitchen door opened, Vangie was waiting with the letter. Henry poked his head inside. When he saw his wife, he drew back. "You still up?" he said, shaking off a green umbrella. He sold them by the dozens at the drugstore. Vangie stepped away from Henry, feeling cold droplets spray her legs.

"Henry, I've been worried sick," she said. Deep circles were carved beneath her eyes. "Where have you been?"

"At the meeting. We got to talking. That fog is thick as potato soup." He pointed out the door. "It took me forever to get home."

She watched him close the door. Then she held out the letter. "Here," she said. "Tell me what you think of this."

Henry frowned as he took the letter. His lips moved as he read. Twice he glanced up at Vangie. He turned the paper over and over, as if he'd see something new.

"Henry?" she said.

"Yes, dear."

"You'd never . . . I mean, you'd never lie to me, would you?"

"Lie about what, sugar?"

"Everything."

"I'm surprised at you. I'm *hurt*." He pursed his lips, then shook his head, holding his hands palm up. "Of *course* I'd never do any such thing. You know everything there is to know about me."

"But this letter—what does it mean?" She leaned forward and tapped the paper. "'Things are growing and taking root in the wrong beds'?"

He exhaled and sat down at the white table, running one hand through his wispy hair. The rumor had fallen into the wrong hands, someone who couldn't wait to tell Vangie. What if these notes continued—perhaps going on to name names? Then what would he do? *HenRY iS sCRewInG DEeDEE RoBIChauX*. He could add a line of his own: *sHeS gOt A pUsSy LiKE a sNaPPinG tURtle*.

"And why would that make Olive drink poison?" Vangie blurted out. "It says so right here. Do you think I'm being criticized for not keeping up my yard? Or because I was overly interested in my flowers?"

"Oh, no, darling. Not at all. That's an awful thing to say." Henry tilted back his head. He stared at his wife's braids hanging on either side of her puffy face. Her eyes were still blue and young, but sad and hooded. He'd always known she was a little slow, that her sheltered life on the Galliard place had made her naive. But until this moment he had not known that she was plain dumb. *It was that blow to the head*, he thought. When she fell off the wagon. Because how else could you explain the rest of the Galliards? Zachary made a judge, and the old man had been a shrewd cotton planter who spent whole months in Memphis, throwing money around the Peabody like duck food, yet his fortune seemed to multiply. Mrs. Galliard was a cultured if sharp-tongued woman. She worked like a man in her husband's fields. They had left Zachary and Vangie a fortune when they died—and all that land was still sitting there, with little volunteers of cotton shooting up in the flat, weedy fields.

Henry thought of all he stood to lose. He blinked at his wife and said, "This letter's a crying shame. It's a crime! Want me to call Sheriff Reems?"

She shook her head and sat down across from him, smoothing her hand on the pasted letters.

"Why not?"

"It's just a silly prank, that's all." She rubbed her nose and smelled Elmer's glue on her fingers.

"I'll hire someone to weed your flowers, Vangie." He patted her hand.

"Oh, it doesn't matter. I don't have time to look at it, anyway." She drew in a ragged sigh. "I'll never want a garden again."

"Sure, you will. You can have your cake and eat it, too."

"Is that so important?" She wiped her eyes.

"Of course it is. You'll come home from the hospital tomorrow, and everything'll be weeded. You won't have to lift your little finger." He flashed a patient smile, reserved for his most stubborn, suspicious customers, like Mrs. Eula Tatum, who thought her grandchildren had put both Henry and Dr. LeGette up to poisoning her heart pills—to steal her fifteen hundred acres of bottomland south of Limoges. She thought they wanted to chop down the trees, fill everything in with dirt, and plant soybeans—a ludicrous notion.

"You'll have your pretty roses, and at the same time you'll be with Olive."

"Oh, Henry." Tears dripped down her cheeks and pattered against the tablecloth; they gathered on the flat, oilcloth roses like dew. "You are so smart, honey."

"It's my job." He smiled and reached for the letter, tucking it into his pocket. "It's what I do best."

Turkey Dinner

❧

To dress a Turkey, you cut off the Head. Take out the innards, saving the Gizzard, liver, and Heart. Singe off the fuzz over an open Fire. Now cut off its Feet. Rub the outside with Lard. Sprinkle with salt and pepper all over, even up the Craw. Put in a pot and Boil 2–3 hours. Save stock for Dressing and gravy. Stuff Bird. Brown in hot oven till Done.

—Sophie Donnell, her mama's recipe for Easter turkey, 1901

Sophie Donnell

Easter falls on the thirteenth of April—a bad sign. That morning, while all of Limoges is at church, I run up and down Cypress Street, from Edith's to Vangie's to Harriet's to Waldene's. Back and forth, carrying Mr. Henry's umbrella. It's pouring rain. Above me the persimmons are soggy green, dripping water on the sidewalk. Already a inch of water has fell. Street lights blink on, gleaming down on the road, the pavement shiny as the lake. Me, I went to sunrise at New Bethel, but these folks on Cypress are late risers.

When I open Miss Waldene's kitchen door, I see Fanny lifting pot lids and wrinkling her nose. I set down the umbrella and wish her a Happy Easter. She's all dress up for church. "What the bunny bring you?" I ask.

"Basket." She lifts one shoulder. She has been tore up over Olive. They was close like sisters because they didn't have none of their own, you see.

"Pew," she says, drawing back. "What's this awful-looking stuff?"

"Turkey gizzards for Miss Waldene's dressing," I say. I got giz-

zards simmering in four houses, counting my own, if Burr don't
let them scorch. Before I left home, I told him to keep a eye on
the stove, and he said he'd try. I have me a nice twenty-pound
turkey heating in the oven, but I'm worried Burr won't watch it.

"Well, I don't eat gizzards."

"You have every year." I laugh and tilt the pan for her to see.

"Not this one." She draws back. "It's too slimy. It's *guts*."

"When I was little," I say, picking up a spoon, "my mama told
me that turkey gizzards was magical. Makes you pretty."

"I don't care about that." Fanny shrugs.

"Yes, but it makes your titties grow."

"Oh, Sophie! That's not true!" She laughs and spins around in
her yellow frock, twirling on white patent-leather shoes. Her long
brown hair is curled to her waist in ringlets.

"Look at mine," I say. "I've got a spacious chest."

We both laugh. This kitchen feels warm and sunny, even
though rain is streaming down the windows. Over by the sink, a
sweet potato grows in a glass jar, what Fanny did for science
class. Miss Waldene is in the dining room, setting out the silver
and china, clinking it against the mahogany table she bought at a
auction. She has a appetite for antiques, china, and colored jars
that she sets in all the windows. When the sun is shining, you
think you're in a church. I know for a fact that she is setting out
Miss Margaret Jane's Spode and two kinds of crystal, for water
and iced tea. She would never serve wine, even though Miss Edith
said it's the latest style in New York.

The holiday style in Natchitoches is to catch the turkey and
chop off its neck. Then my sisters and me would dress it. We'd
pull feathers and wash the bird inside and out. Our dressing was
made from corn bread, crumbled biscuits, giblets, broth, creamy
butter; we'd sauté onions, celery, bell peppers and mix it all
together with fresh oysters, spices, and a dash of sherry. In
Natchitoches, we know how to eat. Here in Limoges, they cook
plainer. No tamales wrapped in corn husks. No deep-fried meat
pies. One thing is the same in both towns—every Sunday peoples
eat chicken with rice and gravy.

The first meal I ever cooked Burr was barbecued quail. Soak
overnight 8 quail in 4 cups milk. Next morning fill each cavity
with 2 T. chop apple and 1/2 T. butter. Wrap with bacon. Cook 30
minutes on hot mesquite coals. The first meal Burr ever cook for
me was diamondback rattler. He rolled it in egg, cornmeal, and
flour, then deep-fried it. I should've known then something was
wrong with the man.

Now Miss Waldene strolls into the kitchen, humming "Shall
We Gather at the River," her big belly stretched out. She's in the

choir at First Baptist and prides herself on the way she carries a tune. "My, this looks good," she says, eyeing the pans on the electric stove. "Sophie, you've outdone yourself."

"Well, I try." I wipe my hands on my apron. "Now I got to run next door. Miss Vangie needs her turkey basted."

"Speaking of the Neppers," said Miss Waldene, leaning against the counter, "I really should've invited them for dinner, but it just slipped my mind. I ought to be ashamed of myself. I haven't been to the hospital in days. In my condition, I hate to expose myself to flu and all." She rubs her stomach. "If I didn't have Dr. Phillip telling me what's going on, I'd be ignorant." She calls her husband "Dr. Phillip" or "the Doctor."

"Miss Vangie lives at that hospital," I say.

"I know it. It just breaks my heart. Poor little Olive. You see Vangie more than me. How's she doing?"

"Same as always," I shrug. This is Miss Waldene's way, trying to get you to slip up and gossip. She knows how Miss Vangie is, she just hope I know more. But it is a different kind of picking from Harriet Hooper's. *She'll* just ask you straight-out. Miss Harriet's what my mama called a bone carrier. Miss Harriet, she don't mind saying the illest word about people, digging up what she ought not to. Miss Waldene is curious but in a more refined way. Like most women, she holds back. I busy myself with pot lids, checking giblets, sweet potatoes, green beans. I have eggs boiling in a pot, but they ain't quite ready.

"I feel so sorry for her," Miss Waldene says, "what with Henry carrying on with that Robichaux woman. In broad daylight, too. I don't think I could stand it the way Vangie has. And she's so kind to Billie Robichaux. Hiring her like she has. Does she know her mama is DeeDee?"

"You know Miss Vangie. She sees the best in people," I say, then clam up. This is where I draw the line, gossiping about Mr. Henry and that Robichaux woman, or trying to decide how much Miss Vangie knows. They's lots of mysteries in life, and in the mysteries is answers. Don't know why I think of this, maybe 'cause they ain't nothing left to ponder, but all the ladies on Cypress got a different color kitchen. Miss Edith's is got purple grapes and vines. Miss Vangie got rose pink. Miss Harriet got pond-scum green. Miss Waldene got yellow. And before she got hold of it, Miss Margaret Jane had it painted blue with forget-me-nots printed on the curtains. I think to myself, *Sophie? What do it all mean?*

"Don't let them eggs boil too long," I say. "I'll be back directly to fix your rice. And you're out of vanilla. I'll borrow some next door."

"Wish everybody Happy Easter for me," she says. I put on my sweater and go out into the damp air. My breath curves above my head. Water has puddled up on the sidewalk, and when I hurry next door, it splashes around my ankles. Big drops splat down from the chinaberry trees. Under the willows and persimmons, it falls harder. They's not a single cypress on this street. They's all on the lake. I think they should have call this road Persimmon. Where I live, Highway 65, could be name End of the Road. Ain't nothing above us but Arkansas. That's what Burr always said.

A few weeks ago, when I went back to him, he was sweet as sugarcane. He stared at my bandages and bruised face. His clothes all wrinkle like he hadn't washed since I left, and his cheeks was flushed red. He'd cleaned the house from top to bottom.

"Let me help you up the porch," he said. "Let me fix you some coffee."

Like nothing ever happened. Like I hadn't been gone seven days and nights and had my arm in a sling. Cab and Israel had begged me to stay at Beaulieu's and called me a foolish, stubborn woman when I refused. "Then pick out your coffin," said Mr. Cab. When I told Burr I was working Easter Sunday, I'd expected a fight. Instead he spread his hands and said, "I'll be waiting right here for you, watching them giblets."

I head toward the Neppers' house. I step up to the back door, stamp my feet on the mat, and then reach to open the screen. That's when I hear them fussing. "Well, I'll eat your G–D–ham," Mr. Henry cries, his forehead puckered.

I ain't never heard him cuss. I draw back, but they've done seen me. Mr. Henry blinks, runs his fingers through his hair, then leaves the room; Miss Vangie grabs my hands and pulls me inside. "Gracious, get out of that freezing rain before you die!"

Inside, the air smells clabbered. I set the umbrella on some spread-out newspaper that shows a picture of a mechanical heart, what they put inside a man in Pennsylvania, but he died anyway. I remember hearing about it on Miss Edith's TV. It sounded ghoulish to me. Pretty soon the world will be so modern, none of us can live in it. Next to the poor dead man is a picture of General Eisenhower. He wants to be president, but I can't see where he's got the experience. He's sure no FDR.

From the parlor, I hear Mr. Henry turn on a football game, static fizzing out of the box. Mr. Henry, he have a sneezing fit, then snort something out of his throat. Sound like an old hog. I step over to the oven, creak open the door, and start basting the ham. It's store-bought but smells good. The heat feels good on my face. Before daybreak, I'd killed my turkey and had her baking in the oven. I laid five slabs of bacon over the breast and ladled up juice. By the time I was dressed and ready for church, the whole house smelled good.

"What's going on over at Waldene's?" asks Miss Vangie. "Is she having all her people up from Tallulah?"

"I reckon. She put a extry leaf in her dining table." I keep basting. Miss Vangie has mixed up a potion of honey, brown sugar, and pineapple juice. Sometimes she uses Coca-Cola but not today.

"She's got a right big family," says Miss Vangie. "Her mama's still alive, and I think she's got, what, four brothers?"

"At least."

"What about Edith? What's she got planned?"

"I don't have no idea," I say, but of course I do. I walk over to the sink. Start peeling oranges. Besides the ham, we got English peas, carrots, potato salad, and something call minted fruit cup. Cloverleaf rolls are rising under a tea towel. Nothing fancy for dessert—just lemon icebox pie—on account of Miss Olive.

"What's Waldene having for dinner?" she asks.

"Same as you, except for a few dishes." They all the same, these women on Cypress Street. Not always eating the same foods, but asking the same questions. Picking here and there, like I can't see through them. Because Olive is so sick, and because Mr. Henry's in a yelling mood, I decide to make a exception. "She's got turkey and my oyster dressing. Some kind of yam casserole that's got orange juice and whiskey in it. You put corn flakes on top, with brown sugar and pecans."

"Wonder where she got the recipe?"

I shrug.

"Sounds tasty." She opens a cabinet and pulls out a tin of paprika. She takes a tiny spoon, fills it with crumbly red, and sprinkles it over the potato salad. The smell drifts over to me and my nose tickles.

After a minute she says, "And what's Edith fixing?"

"Whatever it is, it sure smell unusual." I laugh to myself, but Miss Vangie sees.

"Unusual? How?"

"Maybe that be the wrong word. It's colorful, that's right. Real colorful." I keep peeling oranges. I am real tempted to tell Miss Vangie the whole menu, right down to the things she had City Market special-order from New Orleans, but I bite down on my tongue. It's wiggling like a snake. If you talk about one lady, then pretty soon you be out of a job. It might take a year for the talk to creep back, but it always does. That's how domestic work is. So, I don't open my mouth. Just let little tidbits slip here, there. Nothing they can string me up by, you see.

"I'll bet she's fixed another one of her New England feasts." Vangie laughs. She wants me to talk, to say who-all Edith has invited, even though I know she knows. I peel oranges like I am unraveling a mystery, like they will show answers to every question.

"Who's she having for dinner?" says Miss Vangie. This is how she be, pushing and pushing until you spill all you know.

"She invited you." I give her a look. "You could've gone and seen for yourself."

"I know it, but I just wasn't up to being with a bunch of strange people."

"Ain't no strange about it. You should've gone."

"Well, I guess," she say. She looks so pale and sad-eyed that I break down.

"She got five places set on her table," I say, holding up one finger at a time. "She's having herself, Mr. Cab, the Marshall sisters, and Judge Harvey's widow. And, she fixing one of her New England dinners."

"Does that include turkey or a goose?"

"Neither. She got roast rack of lamb, mint pears, baby-doll carrots, salad that looks like cut-up plants, with almonds and oranges. And cream puffs with chocolate sauce for dessert."

"You're right. I should've gone." Miss Vangie clicks her tongue. She's all perked up by this news. Don't nothing she like better than food talk. Last Thanksgiving Miss Edith cooked her regular dinner—a goose in maple syrup, and she set it on a silver platter with crab apples. She had chowder that she made herself, but it didn't taste right on account of the oysters being canned. I told her she could get fresh, November being an *R* month, but she looked at me like I was crazy. She also fixed succotash. Said the Indians taught the pilgrims to make it, and I thought to myself, Well, hell. Ain't no pilgrim set foot in Louisiana. They can keep that succotash. Then she fixed Boston cream pie and something call ginger Indian pudding. And eggnog that would put hair on a monkey's behind.

"She serving clear, yellow wine," I say.

"My Lord, probably chablis. And the Marshall sisters are tee-totalers."

"Miss Edith, she don't care." I laugh.

"How true." Miss Vangie smiles. "What else is she fixing?"

"Some kind of rice, called a pilaf. And you should *see* how everything decorated. Got her pewter all laid out. Little china rabbits for salt-and-pepper shakers."

"Oh, I gave her those one Christmas. Does she have fresh flowers?"

"Tulips all over the house in milk-glass vases. A big bowl of them on the table, too. And a pitcher of forsythias in the living room."

"She does have a knack for decorating."

"Don't she?" If the truth be known, we all a little scared of Miss Edith, and also a little in love with her, too. When she first come to Limoges, everybody gossip. She'd walk her French poodle up and down the street. Nobody in town ever seen one. When I come to work for her, she had one party after the other. A Boston Tea Party was one, a buffet for twenty. She fixed a table with whiskey and wines, and everybody was scandalized.

"You can't serve that!" Harriet Hooper scolded.

"Why not?" Miss Edith poured herself a drink.

"Because it's a dry parish, and we're all Christians here, at least I hope we are! Didn't Zachary tell you what's what around here? Ladies are supposed to sip coffee in the living room, and the men, *if they must*, go into the bathroom and drink."

"That's ridiculous." Miss Edith laughed. She was very pretty spoken. She poured another drink and handed it to Miss Harriet. "Here," she said. "Have one on me."

People talked something awful, but they came to her parties because she sure knew how to throw one. And if she caught them trying to sneak a drink, she'd yell, "Not in *my* bathroom, you don't!" She'd grab the man's ear, pulling him into the open. (It was almost always a man, you see.) She didn't go to church regular except when she took a notion, but she had more goodness in her than all the Christians rolled up together. And that included Miss Harriet, who sat on the Amen row at First Baptist. If I had to take bets on who'd get to heaven first, I wouldn't put a dime on Miss Harriet. The woman got two ears and only one mouth.

It's three in the afternoon when I make it home. I am froze solid. The wind and rain cut through me. All this flu going around makes me worry. Miss Harriet herself catch the flu while she was in the hospital. She had to stay an extra week. Miss Edith, she come down with sniffles, but she ward it off with fresh orange juice. That woman *strong*. And today Mr. Henry sneezing and carrying on. They's so much to be scared of—all these things you can't see.

When I reach the house, Burr waiting on the porch. "Where the hell you been?" he yells.

"Working." I stop in the yard, feeling the rain beat around me. I see right then that he's been drinking heavy. Can smell the whiskey hanging in the cold air.

"You could've told me."

"I did. You said you'd watch my giblets and the turkey. Remember?"

"Then why's it done burned all to pieces?" He scrunches up his eyes.

I hold off from running past him, into the house to see for myself. Instead I lean to one side, trying to look through the screen door. My fingers and toes are so cold I can't feel them, and my breath is smoking.

"You been traipsing around town, ain't you? Yapping with them rich women you work for. Trying to fool yourself into thinking you's one."

"No, I been working. You know that." I reach into my bra, pulling out eleven dollar bills, holding them up for him to see. Today I got a bonus from everybody but the Hoopers.

"You mean to say you ruint my supper for *that*?" He starts down the porch steps, running straight toward me. I whirl around and take off running, throwing down the umbrella. I clutch the money to my chest.

"You git back here!" He grabs me from behind, yanks my collar and spins me around. I hold up the money, pushing it into his chest.

"See what I got? It's good money. Buy yourself something."

"I don't want money, I want me a wife! You been cooking everybody's food but mine." He flings my hand away, and the dollars scatter.

"But I did cook ours. Early this morning. I left it on the stove."

"Burnt it, you mean." He rears back and slaps me full in the face. To keep him from hitting me again, I fall into the froze dirt, skinning my knees.

"You was aiming to keep that money," he says. "I seen where you had it hid, in your titties. You can't fool me."

"I wasn't!" I start to get up, but he kicks my leg. Tears burn my eyes, but I don't move.

"Get your ass up, and go fix me a turkey dinner, like you's supposed to."

I try to shift my jaw, but it feels swollen and crumbly.

"Get!" He kicks me again, then grabs my arm and pulls me to my feet. I stand there all wobbly. Taste something salty. Blood. He shoves me forward, and I think I should go ahead and fight back. Let him kill me and get it over with. But I'm afraid he'll just half-kill me. I'm getting close to forty years old. Got a husband who beat me or else in jail for drinking. All the time. God, I think, where You be?

I walk up the slanted wood steps, into the house. He hovers right behind me. I wonder how to calm him down so I won't get hit, but all I can think is how bad he smells and how he's itching to hurt me. When I turn into the kitchen, the turkey sitting on the table, burnt to a crisp. The giblets be hard, welded together, stuck in the bottom of the pan. You can't trust a stove that ain't electric. You got to watch them every minute. What I should've done was cook it last night, leave it setting out, then reheat when I got home. We might have got poisoned but at least we'd be fed.

"Here's your pig slop." He goes over to the table and kicks it.

"I can fix you some smoked meat," I say.

"I don't want no old smoked meat. I want turkey, same as them rich folks you work for."

"But it's burnt. No time to cook another."

"Then go catch you a new one. And cook it right this time." He points at me, his eyes narrowing. He weaves back and forth. "And I don't care if it takes all night. Just don't make me wait too long, girl."

I pull on my heavy plaid jacket, what Miss Vangie give me last year, then step out the back door. The rain has slacked up some. I can feel him watching me through the screen, but I don't look back. I pull the axe from the stump, then pick up a can of grain and walk toward the barn. I look toward the woods, wishing I had me someplace to run. Someplace Burr can't find. Listen, I don't see how to rectify things.

I think about my only child drowned in the river. Thaddeus, name after one of the apostles. Burr's other boys name Peter and Thomas, a fisherman and the doubter, who didn't think Jesus had been raised until he put his fingers in the handprints. Simon Thaddeus was a zealot, you see, but my baby weren't nothing but a sweetheart—long eyelashes and a smile that could break your heart. I should have known my Jesus wouldn't let me keep him. The morning he died he said, Mama, I'm going with Thomas and Peter to help them tie trot lines. And I said, No. Said I'd beat him. Said I'd disown him. Didn't want him going off with those bad boys. Thaddeus, he sulk off. Burr was laying up sleeping, and I was late for my days work for Dr. LeGette. Fanny's mama was alive, Miss Margaret Jane. All day we took turns carrying Fanny in our arms, and all day that baby cried because she had roseola. We couldn't break her fever, you see, even with Dr. LeGette coming home at lunch to help us pack the backs of her little knees in ice.

The war was going on, we listened to the radio. *We interrupt our regularly scheduled program to bring you an update from the South Pacific.* Sometimes it was news from France or England. When I got home, the police was waiting. Burr stood on the porch, his eyes red from crying or whiskey, I could not tell. Police said, "There's been an accident."

Thaddeus had gone with Burr's boys to check on the trot lines, and somehow he got tangled up. I didn't see how, even when they tried to explain. Peter and Thomas look down at they feet. The police just stand there, red face. The girl, Rachel, she love Thaddeus like me. She roll up into a ball and howl. "Live by

the river," Sheriff Reems say, clapping Burr's shoulder, "die by the
river. Your boy was the same as you, Burr. Only you're luckier."

"Yessir, just like me," say Burr, grinning like a fool. Like his
baby ain't laying there dead, a quilt throwed over him.

"If you was home," Burr say to me, "this wouldn't of happen."

"If you was awake," I say, "it wouldn't of happen. No, you was
sleeping off whiskey."

He falls on me, and the police have to pull him off.

There are three turkeys and a slew of chickens in the pen,
their feathers slick and droopy from the rain. When the hens see
my axe, they scatter, but one of the turkeys looks at me and tilts
its head. "Gobble, gobble," I say, thanking Jesus that He made
turkeys dumb. They the easiest farm animals to catch. It waddles
over to me, and when I reach down to grab its neck, I think of
murder, of my hands squeezing Burr Donnell's neck, digging my
thumbs into his flesh until his eyes close. I imagine laying him
down in the deep, crumbly grave.

I think of the time he took me and his kids hunting. Burr shot a
rabbit, then cut off the strip of fur running down its belly. He slit
open the belly and scooped out the entrails. Then, with all of his
kids looking on, he skinned it, starting at the hind leg, pulling
toward the head. I was carrying Thaddeus inside me, and I vomited
into the dewberries. Burr just laughed and called me sissy. All his
kids joined in, too. When we got home, Burr showed me how to
soak the meat in salty water. It's how you drain the blood. Let it
soak about an hour; then you drain, wrap, and chill overnight. Next
day, it looks like a dead baby, one that's come too soon. Dredge the
meat in peppery flour and fry in hot oil. Add 1 cup cream, then simmer 1 hour. I call this dish smothered rabbit. Burr and his kids
reached for the platter, sucking on the little bones. Me, I couldn't eat
a bite. I was afraid it would mark my baby. Burr, he just laughed.
Said, You crazy woman. But you sure can cook.

Even when he was young, his heart was old and clenched,
the size of a fist, but mine is still sixteen year old, and it dances
inside my chest. When I hold my breath, I can almost feel the
cleft at the top, soft as a ripe peach. A fist would surely burst it. I
raise the axe, chop off the turkey's neck, then let the bird fall. It
flops in the dirt, hitting the hard ground, its pronged feet jerking.
I think to myself, You will get through this day, Sophie. You will
get through all his bad days and yours, too. Then I drag the
turkey into the barn to fix it for Easter supper.

Easter Blues

(On 102 Hayes Avenue)

&

It ain't the huge tragedies that break you. It's the endless disappointments, little daily heartbreaks that eat away at your spirit. As my brother Earl used to say, "One lone termite don't wreck your foundation. It's all of his kinfolk." In other words, life beats you down and then you die. Your house caves in, falls smack on top of your head.

—BUTTER DeWITT, SERVING PHILOSOPHY AND PECAN PIE, BUTTER'S CAFE, APRIL 1952

All morning DeeDee sat on the front porch, peeling apples into a paper sack, watching the rain blow sideways. She was making a high-class Easter salad, with coconut, oranges, cherries, and pecans. The door opened and a little girl walked out, wearing a gauzy blue dress. She wore new Buster Brown shoes with ruffled white socks, and she clutched a tiny pocketbook. Her hair was hidden under a straw boater, with baby blue ribbons trailing down one side. DeeDee pushed away the sack and stood up. "Billie?" she said.

"How do I look?" The child twirled around, her petticoat filling with air. Aunt Butter stepped out of the house and folded her hands under her bosom. She was wearing a faded pink dress with white shoes that had been polished so many times, tiny specks popped off each time she took a step.

"Why, I almost didn't recognize you!" DeeDee rubbed her hands down the front of her apron. "Just *look* at yourself."

Billie twirled around again, spinning on her toes. Renny

wheeled his chair to the front door and stuck his face up to the screen. "You look like a doll, precious," he said.

"A beautiful doll." DeeDee smiled, one finger pressed to her lips. "But you're not going to church in all this rain, are you?"

"We got umbrellas," said Billie, reaching down to wipe a smudge on her shoe.

"She wanted to surprise you," Aunt Butter said.

"Well, she certainly has. When did you get this outfit, princess? And who bought it for you?"

"Like it?" Billie held out the petticoat.

"I do. I *really* do."

"She's been doing work," said Aunt Butter. "Chores for rich folks."

"Who?" DeeDee stood up, her foot wrinkling the paper sack.

"Mrs. Nepper, Mrs. Galliard, Mrs.—"

"Wait a minute." DeeDee shook her head. "You worked for Vangie Nepper?"

Billie looked at her mother, then nodded. "Yeah, she's real—"

"*Vangie* Nepper? Henry's wife? On Cypress Street?"

"I hauled her dead roses." Billie held out her arms. "See these scratches? She paid me two whole dollars. And Mrs. Nepper said she had a whole slew of old pocketbooks and dresses that her daughter outgrowed. She said for me to come by next week and I can load up my wagon."

"Sure, sure." DeeDee's eyes filled. "We're paupers. We don't have *shit*."

"What's wrong, Mama?"

"The Robichauxes don't accept charity." DeeDee wiped her eyes.

"The Neppers is rich," said Renny. "Anyhow, it ain't charity. She earnt it fair and square."

"Fair and . . . " DeeDee whirled around. "You knew about this?"

"So what if I did?"

"You *did* know!" DeeDee held out her arms. "How could all of you know what my own child was doing, even the Neppers knew, for God's sake, and I'm in the dark? How come nobody had the decency to tell me? Or should I say nerve!"

"It was a surprise, Mama."

DeeDee leaned against the porch railing and wiped her eyes. Aunt Butter touched Billie's arm and said, "You'd better run on inside and fetch your Bible. We don't want to be late for the service."

Billie glanced at her mother, then she opened the door,

scooted around her father's chair, and ran into the front room, her new shoes scuffing on the linoleum.

"You're a mean woman," Renny said, staring at DeeDee through the screen.

"Me?" DeeDee wiped her face.

"I don't see no other mean women on the porch."

"I'm not mean, I'm *strong*." DeeDee beat her fist against her chest.

"Please," Aunt Butter begged, "don't ruin this for her."

"I can't have these rich women giving her handouts," DeeDee said. Billie walked to the door and stopped. Her daddy reached out and hugged her.

"My mother would roll over in her grave," DeeDee said.

"Your mama," said Aunt Butter, "was buried in a borrowed shroud. I know, because I helped dress her."

DeeDee started to say something, then she swallowed. Billie opened the door and looked from Aunt Butter to her mother.

"We'd better scoot, or we'll be late," Aunt Butter said. "Won't we, DeeDee?"

DeeDee lifted one shoulder. No one, not even Renny, could have called it a shrug. She looked ready to cry, but Aunt Butter knew she wouldn't. Her emotions ran fast and hot, like struck matches. Billie hopped down the steps, into the rain. She reached up, took Aunt Butter's hand, and then looked over her shoulder. "See you, Mama," she said. "See you, Daddy."

"See *you*, baby," Renny called out. "Keep that umbrella over you, now."

"I will, Daddy."

Renny pushed open the door with one edge of the wheelchair and stared at his wife.

"Ain't you ashamed?" he said.

"No. Why should I be?" DeeDee lifted her chin. She sat down, picked up the paper sack, and wedged it between her knees. She slipped the knife into the apple and peeled it back to white.

"I'm on to you," Renny said.

She turned her back to him, the peel making a red wreath around her wrist.

"You're diddling someone, ain't you?"

"Diddling? What's that? All I'm doing is peeling apples for salad. So why don't you leave me the hell alone?"

"Gladly." He jerked his chair away and pushed into the front room. The screen door hammered against the frame. It was only then, when she was certain he had gone, that she broke down. Tears fell against the backs of her hands. Nothing was turning out right. Yesterday, just before Henry closed the drugstore, he reached behind a counter and pulled out an Easter basket, all wrapped in pink cellophane. It was full of jelly beans, Elmer's Gold Bricks, foil-wrapped chocolate bunnies. In the center sat a pink jewelry box.

"For me?" DeeDee said.

"No." Henry's cheeks flushed. His eyes shifted back and forth. He held out the basket. "It's for your Billie."

"Henry, how sweet. You're so thoughtful." She took the basket, the cellophane crinkling in her hands.

"Actually, it was my . . . it was Vangie's idea." He glanced down at his feet.

DeeDee gripped the basket, digging her nails into the crinkly paper. What could be worse? The innocent wife bringing the whore's child a gift. Henry was bound to feel guilty. Or maybe Vangie wasn't so innocent. Maybe she knew about the affair and this was her way of killing it—with kindness and jelly beans, using Billie as bait. God, it was genius, a trick she'd have to remember. Her next words, she knew, were crucial.

"It's the prettiest basket I ever saw." She smiled up at him.

Henry put his arms around her, mashing wet lips against her forehead, then took her elbow, guiding her outside, to the alley. He was not especially circumspect in public—he had an air about him, a no-one-can-see-me air. An I'm-too-smart-for-them air. In some ways he seemed blunted, almost too wrapped up in himself. Every chance she got, DeeDee kissed and fondled him, hoping someone would see and tell Vangie. Henry seemed flattered by the affection.

As they stood in the parking lot, rain falling all around them, she rubbed her knee against his crotch. "When will I see you?" she asked.

"You're seeing me now." He pinched her arm. "I'll call. Have a happy Easter." Then he walked over to his Rambler and drove off, splashing her old car with muddy water. She thought about pitching the basket into a swamp, but it would be just like Henry to ask Billie if she'd enjoyed her basket. "What basket?" Billie would say. DeeDee didn't want the child to seem stupid or ungrateful. She wanted Billie to appear smart and well mannered, a stepchild Henry could be proud of. His own child was practically a goner.

DeeDee went home and gave the basket to Billie. "From the Neppers," she said. "Go ahead and open it."

Aunt Butter raised her eyebrows. She pursed her lips and leaned forward.

"I think I'll save it for tomorrow," Billie said.

"But the Easter Bunny'll bring you one," DeeDee told her.

"I know. I'll still save it."

"Well, all right, princess." DeeDee swallowed hard. Tomorrow's basket, like all the baskets before it, was wicker with a frayed handle and limp plastic straw, so old that the green tint had started to fade. At the dime store, DeeDee had bought marshmallow rabbits, tiny chocolate eggs in foil, and a pound of jelly beans. Butter had added her own touches—dyed hard-boiled eggs and a stuffed rabbit from Morgan & Lindsay. The basket looked pathetic in comparison to Vangie Nepper's.

She wondered where she'd gone wrong—her child was nine and kept secrets; her husband had withered from the waist down; she lived in a house that smelled of bacon grease and mothballs, where cobwebs collected in high corners and trailed sticky wands. Henry's days were built around church and Rotary, a life measured in covered-dish suppers and invitations to dances at the country club.

Oh, she knew all about the parties and clubs—Mrs. Henry Nepper hosted this, Edith Galliard hosted that. DeeDee read the paper, so she was all too aware of private Easter egg hunts, rich little children dressed in bow ties and organdy, searching tulip beds and birdbaths for the golden egg. She knew about the clubs—there was one for music, sewing, African violets, and cooking. The Limoges Year-Round Garden Club answered roll call with everything but their real names—their silver patterns and favorite flowers. The United Daughters of the Confederacy and Daughters of the American Revolution were full of hoity-toitys—women who lived in the past, measuring their social success by their forebears' rank, not to mention great big sections in the Yellow Fever Cemetery.

At this very moment, Vangie Nepper and Edith Galliard were probably holding court in church, telling all the Baptists how they saved the day for poor Billie Robichaux. They'd point at Butter and Billie. "Poor little thing," they'd say. "Her aunt has to bring the child to church. The mama is probably home asleep. Or painting her toenails." They'd laugh at DeeDee, saying they gave Billie a job so she could earn money for an Easter bonnet. Vangie would whisper how she'd donated a candy basket for the little ragamuffin.

"My life is none of your business," she said to herself, viciously cutting into an apple. But the real problem, she knew, was Henry. If she couldn't get him to make a move, soon, she would have to make one for him.

*   *   *

DeeDee washed the speckled tin dishes (unbreakable or your money back, said the man at Morgan & Lindsay) and set them in the plastic drainer. They'd eaten their big meal at four o'clock, nothing but chewing and swallowing, and the radio playing Bing Crosby in the living room. Her heart was not full of the holiday spirit. Last night Billie had displayed an unexpected talent by making origami rabbits and tulips. Probably that artsy Edith Galliard had taught her, but Billie denied it. She said she'd learned it at Sunday school. "Who was your teacher?" DeeDee asked. Billie shrugged. "Some lady with white gloves." DeeDee admitted the paper flowers gave the house a festive look. "Teach me how to do this," she told Billie, and they spent the evening folding and bending the thin strips of paper.

Neither Renny nor Butter had commented on the decorations, which was typical. They'd said grace, then eaten in silence, forks tapping against the plates. Now the food was set up on the table for leftovers—a whole turkey showing one wedge of white meat. Bowls of rice, gravy, fruit salad. Shelly beans they'd put up last summer. Desserts were lined up on the counter, pecan and lemon-chess pies, a coconut cake shaped like a rabbit, with long lacy ears. She couldn't get Henry out of her mind. Probably he was eating turkey on bone china, drinking from silver goblets, a rich man's Easter Sunday. Butter's table was draped with red oilcloth, the surface littered with mismatched spoons and knives, forks with bent tines.

DeeDee turned back to the dishes, swishing her hands in hot, greasy water. It struck her clearly that she would never steal Henry away from Vangie. The woman was attached like a seed tick, even though DeeDee was prettier and younger. Could give him more children, if he took a notion, not that she particularly did. Life on Hayes Avenue, with its snotty babies and hordes of visiting grandchildren, had permanently turned her against children. They'd stand at Butter's front door and knock, pressing their mouths to the glass. DeeDee ignored them, but they went on knocking, calling out for Billie, who wasn't even home. Their persistence amazed her.

DeeDee thought she'd developed an aversion to other people's children. To tell the truth, she didn't feel motherly toward her own daughter. Actually, she suspected she was a bad mother. Billie asked too many questions; she talked too much. Sometimes DeeDee had to clasp her hands to keep from smacking the child. She loved Billie, but DeeDee was a person too. A young, beautiful woman with needs, desires, and wants—all of them strong.

If Olive died, she suspected Henry would want another baby,

but a rich man's baby meant housekeepers to mop up pablum, sitters who could be persuaded to sleep in the infant's room and tend its every cry. The only bad part would be losing her figure, and she didn't think Henry would like that. "You're so tight," he'd say, and she'd wonder what he meant. That she was frugal? That her female parts weren't slack? His sexual appetite was strong and slightly embarrassing. She let him do it any way he wanted, and he wanted plenty. She wondered if this could be both the attraction and problem. Once she accused him of having his cake and eating it, and Henry laughed. "But sweetheart," he said. "If I have a cake, what else am I going to do but eat it? Put it in the freezer? Give it away?"

She finished rinsing the dishes, then wiped down the counters. They were scratchy yellow, snagging the tea towel. Through the window, she saw Billie chasing the dogs, running between the clothesline. She'd changed into denim overalls, a thick gray coat, and red rubber boots that were splattered with mud. Aunt Butter was in the front room, lying on the davenport, a newspaper over her face, and Renny was asleep in his bedroom.

DeeDee tiptoed over to the phone, lifted it from the cradle, and dialed Henry's number. Her heart thumped against the wall of her chest. He answered on the second ring, and she whispered, "Hey, it's me."

"DeeDee? You shouldn't call here, sweetheart. What if Vangie answered?"

"Say I had the wrong number and hang up." DeeDee leaned against the wall, digging her thumbnail into a dent in the plaster. "I just wanted to say Happy Easter."

"Well, you too." Henry paused. Static scratched on the line. He turned around, making sure Vangie wasn't listening. He saw a lamp burning in the living room window, the glass swathed in fussy, gauzy curtains, what she called her Priscillas—the latest style in draperies. Behind the curtains were venetian blinds turned at a forty-five-degree angle, showing Cypress Street, the damp sidewalk, and farther out, Lake Limoges. Lined up on the windowsilll were glass figurines—birds, deer, horses, angel fish. Vangie had made a cozy home, a nest for Henry and Olive. Ashamed, he shut his eyes. In his mind he saw Vangie arranging and rearranging the figurines, from tallest to shortest. "Does this look better, Henry?" she asked him.

From far away, he heard a tinny voice in his ear, almost like a mosquito. "Henry?" it said. "Henry, are you still there?"

"Yes." He cleared his throat. "But I can't talk now. I'll see you tomorrow, all right?"

"Henry?"

"What?"

"I love you." She squeezed the receiver, wishing he could feel the pressure on his end of the line. All she heard was a grunt, followed by a click. The dial tone shrilled in her ear.

Damn coward, she thought and banged down the receiver. Here she was, taking all the risks, sneaking out nights and on Sunday afternoons, lying to everybody. It was certainly no way to live. You just couldn't second-guess a married man; the rules kept changing. Probably he was feeling guilty. Probably Vangie cooked him a fancy meal, fancier than normal: shrimp cocktail served on crushed ice; Waldorf salad; crown roast of lamb with rice stuffing and paper frills; spinach from somebody's garden; king crab and mushroom casserole. Hot cross buns, champagne, praline ice cream cake.

Damn, she thought. *I can do this, too.* In a heartbeat. From the bedroom, Renny called out, "DeeDee?" His voice was high-pitched and cranky. "C'mere, baby!"

She walked into the hall and stood in the doorway. "What?" she said. He was sitting up in the wheelchair, a plaid blanket thrown over his knees.

"Was you talking to somebody just then?" he asked.

"No."

"But I heard you."

"Maybe it was from the radio."

"The hell it was." Renny frowned. "Shit, you think I'm both paralyzed *and* deaf?"

"Maybe I was talking to myself." She tossed back her head.

"You don't never do that. Anyways, I heard you dial. You're sneaking around with somebody, ain't you?"

"Keep your voice down." She stepped into the room and shut the door. Then she faced him. "I'm not letting you ruin Easter. You've ruined every other day, but not this one, do you hear me?"

"I hear you," he said, "but you haven't answered my question."

"Yes, I have."

Renny bent his head and cupped both hands over his eyes. His shoulders moved up and down, and tears streamed between his fingers.

"Renny, please. Don't."

"I'm sorry, baby." He shook his head. "I don't mean to accuse you of nothing, but you ain't been yourself. Look at that fit you pitched this morning. Look how you tried to spoil Billie's day."

"I've already apologized a hundred times."

"I know it." He held out his hand. "C'mere. Please? I'm begging you, DeeDee. Please come here and let me hold you."

She hesitated, afraid it was a trick, but he seemed shrunken and harmless. She walked over to him and put one hand on his shoulder, feeling the nubby flannel. It had been washed so much, she thought her fingers might tear through it. He reached up and grabbed her wrists. "Let go, Renny. I'm not in the mood to be touched." She tried to squirm free, but his grip was bone-tight.

"But I am." He slammed her into his lap, face down. Then he flipped her dress over her head, pinning her against him. Through the gap in his pajamas she saw his shriveled genitals. Is this origami? she thought. Or a penis?

She tried to roll off, but he clamped her arms behind her back. Then he bent over her, squeezing her chest. Her feet lifted from the floor. With one hand, he groped for her buttocks and jerked down her panties. She tried to pull her hands away, but he squeezed harder.

"Dammit," she cried. "Let me go!"

"Don't scream or I'll hurt you real bad." He slapped her bottom. Tears streaked down her cheeks. The skirt was tight over her face. She breathed in, smelling perspiration and urine. He probed between her legs, then jammed his finger into her, jerking it in and out. She screamed, and he pushed deeper. She kicked her right leg, but she was dangling in the air. He withdrew the finger and searched her backside, parting the cheeks. She felt a searing pain, and she turned her face toward his leg, biting into his wobbly, numb flesh. Too late, she remembered he felt nothing, neither pain nor pleasure. Dead from the waist down. She whipped her head from side to side, but he leaned his chest against her, grunting with the effort.

"Stop!" Her voice was muffled by the skirt. She kicked her legs again, but they wheeled in midair.

"Hush, or I'll ram my whole arm up you." His fingers stabbed in and out of her.

"Renny, please! It hurts!" She wrenched one arm free, then grabbed the wheelchair. She pulled herself forward, tilting the chair toward the left. As it started to flip over, he yanked out his hand to steady himself. DeeDee twisted away, rolling to the floor. She scrambled back against the bed. He gaped down at her with outstretched arms, his cheeks flushed.

"Bastard," she said and lurched to her feet. Then she stumbled to the door, into the hall, and turned into the kitchen. Behind her, his wheelchair rasped through the narrow door frame.

"What's a matter?" he said, drawing his mouth to one side. "You used to like it that way. What's changed you?"

"You! You've changed me!"

"I thought that's what you wanted!"

"Not like that. And not from you." She started clearing the table, snapping off sheets of waxed paper and crinkly foil. His wheelchair made a peeping noise as he rolled around the room, but she refused to acknowledge him. Here, of all places, in the kitchen's harsh fluorescent light, she felt vulnerable. There were knives in the drawers, glass platters he could shatter. "You don't have to be put out," he said, coming up behind her.

"I'm not." She smoothed tinfoil over a bowl of field peas.

"I can still do things for you, DeeDee. If you'd let me try." He grabbed the back of her dress. "Turn around and look at me."

"There's nothing you can do." She jerked away from his hand and crossed the room, setting the beans in the icebox.

"See, you're just mad, but if you get in bed with me tonight, I swear you won't regret it."

"No, thanks." She turned and stared down at the table, wishing he'd wheel himself into the front room, where the radio was playing "Easter Parade." She spread tinfoil over a pan of dressing.

"I said you won't regret it."

"You humiliated me, Renny." She narrowed her eyes. "Putting your finger in me like that."

"You was fighting me tooth and nail."

"You gouged me."

"I'm sorry, baby. Listen, I'll be real gentle next time."

"Sorry, there won't be one."

"Oh, come on." He circled toward her. "I know you got needs."

"I don't." She shook her head. "I don't." She glanced behind her. Through the window she caught a glimpse of Billie squatting down, petting the dogs. Her wool coat flared out like a bell, her legs two skinny clappers. Her pulse thumped in her neck. *Stay outside, baby*, she thought. *Just stay outside*.

"You gonna give me a chance to satisfy you?"

DeeDee looked at his hands, the way they gripped the rubber wheel, his long, tapered fingers, the nails hard as seashells. She pictured him grabbing her, flipping her over, and stuffing her with dressing. She glanced toward the door, wondering if she could run past him. He rolled toward her, and his wheelchair caught on the cabinet door. When he reached down to free himself, she stepped sideways until the table was between them.

"What's a matter?" His eyebrows slanted together. "You ain't *scared* of me, are you?"

"No."

"The hell you ain't." He laughed and scooted the wheelchair toward her. "I ain't gone hurt you, baby."

"You already have."

"Just come and sit on my lap."

She shook her head so hard, her hair came unpinned. When she reached up to fix it back, he lunged forward, missing her leg by inches. His hands knocked into the table, sending the turkey and fruit salad clattering to the floor. The salad bowl broke cleanly in half, sticky juice spilling out. "Now look what you've done." DeeDee grabbed a tea towel and squatted down to mop up the food.

"From the front room, Aunt Butter hollered, "What fell?"

"Renny's throwing things again," yelled DeeDee.

"Goddammit!" His fist slammed against the table. "I didn't go to. I bumped into it. I'm just trying to give you love, and by God, you won't take it from me!"

DeeDee leaned forward, using her hands to sweep up fruit and turkey. Aunt Butter came to the door, and said, "Not on Easter. Please, you two!"

"It was a accident." Renny jerked his chair around. "I swear, Butter."

"Don't you swear to me, Renny Robichaux," Butter said. "Anyhow, it don't matter. Pretty soon we'll be down to one dish, eating straight from the pan."

"That'll suit him fine," DeeDee said. "Like an old hound. He already smells like one."

"I can't help it!" Renny cried.

"Of course you can't," said Aunt Butter, glancing nervously at DeeDee. "Renny hon, why don't you come in here and keep me company? Something good's coming on the radio."

"I want to keep my wife company." He pointed at DeeDee.

"Oh never mind her." Butter grabbed the back of his chair, but he swatted her away. DeeDee bent under the table, grasped the turkey, but it slipped from her hands, thudding back to the floor.

"You don't have to get ill." Butter's bottom lip poked out.

"I ain't ill," he said. "Just crippled. And I can't fuck no more."

"Don't you *say* that!" Aunt Butter clapped her hands over her ears.

"So she's gone and found her somebody who can." Renny nodded at DeeDee. "Ain't you?"

DeeDee stood up, dumping the turkey on the table. "Yes. That's right, I found me a real man. And if he won't take me away from this shitty life, I'll find me somebody who will."

"Guess you'll have to fuck the whole town, then." Renny stared, then laughed. "If you ain't already."

"Thanks for the advice."

"Hush, both of you!" Aunt Butter stepped backward, one hand rising to her neck.

"Hell, I knew you had somebody," Renny growled. "Whoever he is, you can bet your ass he won't marry you."

"I'm already married." DeeDee jammed both hands into her hips, her greasy hands sliding against the cotton dress. "So he can do whatever he wants to my ass."

"I ought to kill you." His eyes narrowed.

"You'll have to catch me first, crippled boy." She turned and walked over to the window, watching Billie play with the dogs, trying to get them to stand on their hind legs. The rain had stopped, but it was foggy. DeeDee wanted to go outside, take her daughter's hand, and walk straight out of town. Or maybe she'd get a room at the Limoges Hotel and send the bill to Henry. Behind her Renny's wheelchair squeaked. Butter made a whimpering noise. "No," she said. "Please stop. Oh dear Lord, not on Easter."

"DeeDee?" said Renny. "Darlin'?"

"What?" She turned and saw that he was holding the turkey in a menacing way, high above his head. "I'd like to make a toast," he said. "To all the poor, suffering bastards in the world, and all the bitches. Because that's all you and me is." He threw the turkey hard as he could. DeeDee shrieked and ducked. The bird whooshed over her head and crashed through the window. It seemed to freeze against the purple sky, then it thudded against the ground. Aunt Butter screamed and dove under the enamel table.

DeeDee straightened up, careful not to step on glass shards. She looked at Renny. His eyes were squeezed shut, his mouth drawn down at the corners. Butter was crying, "Stop, please stop!"

"Oh, God." He clapped his hands over his face. "I didn't mean it, I didn't!"

Through the splintered pane, cold air blew into the room, moving the checked curtains. Billie and the dogs ran over to the turkey. She squatted, poked it with a stick, then looked up at DeeDee. "What happened to our turkey, Mama?" she cried.

DeeDee pressed one hand over her mouth and shook her head.

"Now see what you've done?" Butter peeped from under the table.

"She just made me so goddamn mad." He wiped his eyes. "If she's spreading her legs for some man, then you need to make her leave. She's a bad influence, Butter. A bad one for Billie."

"And what are you? You're not even related to Butter. This isn't your house!" DeeDee turned around. "I lived here before you! It's mine."

"It's *mine!*" squeaked Aunt Butter.

"You've ruined all our lives, Renny. Do you think we like wiping your ass a hundred times a day? You can't even feel it when you shit. You just squish it all over yourself like a baby. Only I'd rather clean up baby shit."

In one swift motion, he reached down, grabbed the sweet potatoes, and hurled them before she could dodge. The bowl struck her square in the chest, broke in half, and slid down her front. The bowl shattered against the linoleum. DeeDee sucked in air, too startled to scream, then reached down to touch her breasts, her fingers sinking into sticky yams. Her ribs felt shattered. Keeping her eyes on him, she backed up to the wall.

"I'm a person, DeeDee!" He beat his fists against the wheelchair. "I can't help being crippled. I married you for better or worse. Why can't you keep your end of the bargain?"

"Because I don't love you!" she screamed. Through the corner of her eye she saw Billie squatting in the mud, hugging her knees, tears streaking down her cheeks. Several feet away, the turkey lay on its back, drumsticks pointing up. One dog bit into the wing and dragged the whole bird across the grass. Billie stared up at the jagged hole in the window. DeeDee wished she'd stayed in the bedroom with Renny, let him stick his dirty fingers where he pleased. She could have bathed, soaked in lavender water, and none of this would have happened. Hindsight's twenty-twenty, she thought and ran out the back door, into the damp, foggy air. She put her arms around Billie.

"It's all right, princess." She pulled the child's head against her. Through the window she saw Aunt Butter rise to her feet. Renny sat motionless in his chair. DeeDee took Billie's face in both hands and wiped away tears with her thumbs.

"It's not supposed to be this way, baby. It's not."

Billie's lips trembled. Tears streamed down her cheeks. Over by the tire swing, the dogs snarled at each other. The mama dog, Mrs. Happy, bit into the drumstick and pulled the turkey toward the shed. Inside the house DeeDee heard Butter's tentative scrapes with the broom, followed by the dull plop of food being dumped into the trash. She sat in the mud, hugging her daughter, and wondered if she'd still be here next Easter. Maybe she was caught inside a wheel like those ridiculous hamsters at the dime store. The manager kept a rock on top of the cage. "Hamsters are escape artists," he explained to her and Billie. "Wherever they are, they want to be someplace else."

"Mama," Billie said, reaching up to touch her mother's face. "Don't cry, Mama."

"Can't help it." DeeDee wiped her face on her sleeve. "You're supposed to have silver on the table and music coming from a record player and a maid cleaning up after you. I'm a awful mother, a failure."

"No, you aren't!" Billie pressed her head against DeeDee's neck. "You're the best mother ever."

"Well, things are going to change around here. You give me time, just a little more time. And I'll give you a different life."

"I don't want one."

"Well, you're getting one anyway." DeeDee looked up at the sky, the cold etch of moon and stars. Her own poverty and weakness held her to Hayes Avenue, but she wasn't sure how to be strong. A woman needed a man, the same way little girls needed a daddy. She couldn't find a nice white house with pink shutters all by herself. Houses were bought by men. She closed her eyes and saw herself dressed in yellow gingham, standing in an immaculate kitchen, wrapping leftovers in tinfoil, while Billie stood on a stool, fitting china into a cupboard. Then they'd untie their aprons and carry a cut-glass pitcher of lemonade onto the screened porch. Henry would look up from the evening paper and say, "Here are my pretty girls, the loves of my life."

DeeDee would smile and think, Who says money can't buy you love?

Southern Living

❧

Men like variety, excitement, temptation. If Eve hadn't eaten the apple, don't you think Adam would have? After that first bite he probably had his eye on an orchard in another garden.

—DeeDee Robichaux, discussing men at the Beauty Fountain, April 1952

Edith Galliard

My first glimpse of Limoges was the cypress dripping into the lake, trees so alien and exotic I thought I'd moved to a tiny edge of Shangri-la. Mr. and Mrs. Galliard presented us with the deed to a gray, shingled house overlooking the lake. It was a wedding present—one I would have preferred to choose myself, if the truth be told, because I didn't like the idea of living behind a funeral home—or next door to my new sister-in-law. Although I was from New York, I was not without quirks. I liked my privacy. Zachary pointed out that we'd be sharing a rickety dock with the Neppers. "You can paint out there," he whispered in my ear.

It was September, and yellow leaves floated on the lake. Dragonflies mated in midair. I'd always thought of the South as where people came to swim every summer, the frothy beaches drawing them like a current. Now I wondered if it might be more. In the fertile delta, I was bound to grow a family and fill our house with paintings. There was so much land that it seemed primitive and mysterious, unexplored and dangerous. The first time I saw my father-in-law's cotton, I thought of the Original Sin, gardening being the root of the South's downfall.

The women in Limoges made me think of the Victorians— flowerlike ladies, fragrant and decorative; pleasing to the eye and senses, more ornamental than useful. I thought, too, of Charles

Curran's painting "Lotus Lilies," the bonnet-clad women sitting in the rowboat, organdy dresses hiding their ankles, tiny hands plucking water lilies. If you observe closely, you'll notice the incandescent green parasol stretched over the women, so much like the lilies themselves—lush, fragile, rooted. The boat's rower/owner is unseen, yet there's no doubt he's the one with the oars.

In some ways Limoges was wide-hipped and welcoming, like the *W* in *wife*. The day we moved in, Vangie came over with a wicker picnic basket and looked at my empty living room. I had no furniture, just my paints set up on the kitchen counter. "All we need is a bed," Zachary had told me, nudging my arm.

"Where're your boxes?" Vangie asked. She was walking through the house, opening doors, her footsteps echoing.

"Don't have any," I called out.

She appeared in the kitchen doorway. "But I came to help you unpack. Don't you have any doo-dads?"

"Doo-dads?" I had no image for this word, but I made a mental leap and decided she meant junk. I went over to the window and lit a cigarette. "I brought everything I needed in Zachary's car. My easel, paints, a few paintings. My clothes, of course."

"Oh." Vangie looked horrified. She shook her head as if to clear it and opened the basket, releasing a delicious aroma. "Mama sent over her barbecue, and I packed in some fried chicken, too. I just didn't know what you'd like." She removed foil-wrapped bundles as she talked. "Here's deviled eggs with bacon. Potato salad. Some sugared pecans—they're Zachary's favorite. Let's see, cheese biscuits to munch on. Oh, and a jug of Kool-Aid, cherry. Olive insisted. Hope it's okay."

From behind Vangie's broad hips peeped a skinny girl. My husband's niece, Olive. She was nine years old, tiny-boned and starved-looking, with those huge Galliard-blue eyes.

"I brought iced tea, too," Vangie said. "Like I said, I just didn't know what you were used to in New York."

Later, we walked into town and she coyly suggested we drop in at Bellar's Furniture. "Why?" I said.

"To open you an account."

"I just need a bed, you know?" I laughed and poked my elbow into Vangie's ribs, but she flushed red all the way down her neck. Once inside the store, I picked out a mattress and box spring.

"No headboard?" asked Vangie and Mr. Bellar. "No deluxe bedroom suite?"

It took me over an hour to convince them that I knew what I was doing, even if I *did* come from New York. Later I found out that Mr. Bellar had placed a sneaky call to Zachary, who laughed and said, "Give my wife what she wants."

That same fall, I shocked the town by walking to City Market and asking the clerk if they sold sour cream. "Yes, we have cream," the girl said, "but you'll have to sour it yourself."

In those days I walked my poodle, Fleur, up and down Cypress Street, all around the lake. I didn't wear a nice blouse-and-skirt ensemble, but trousers, with pleats down the front. And I smoked cigarettes while I walked, something no lady would do in the first place (and if she did, she would find a chair or bench to sit on, crossing her legs primly at the ankles). In Limoges, ladies did not even chew gum in public. So I smoked and walked Fleur, and the neighbors watched from their porches. "That," they said, pointing at me, "is what Zachary Galliard married."

My husband was a Baptist, but he went to church alone. I stayed home and drank coffee and painted. It seemed to me that religion controlled the town. Your social set was determined by your Sunday school class. There was mingling but no marrying outside their faith. Harriet Hooper informed me that I would never fit into Limoges. Not only was I from New York, but I didn't go to church—two things that would send me straight to hell.

We were standing in the Neppers' yard, at the exact junction where Vangie's rose hedge stopped and Harriet's spotless green lawn began. "Hell?" I said, lighting a cigarette, throwing the match onto her grass. "I take it you're not invited?"

We never got along after that. You'd be surprised how you can avoid disgusting people, even in a small town. It was like learning to live with cockroaches and mosquitoes. I'd run into Harriet at country club gatherings—she'd be sitting at a table, sipping ginger ale, and I'd be dancing barefoot, drinking scotch on the rocks—or I'd see her in the backyard, or sometimes shopping with Leonard. We ignored each other. If others were around, she would speak to me in a frosty tone, technically polite, of course.

"Why, Miss Harriet," I'd say, mimicking her voice. "How you *do* run on."

At first I thought, God, she's obnoxious! What made her this way, what had twisted her? I wondered if she'd grown up poor, scarred by the Depression, and if all her wants had turned her mean and small and greedy. I wondered whether her father had been eaten by hogs or a train had rolled over her mother. I wondered whether someone had regularly beat the shit out of her, whether she'd been raped, tortured, or sodomized. I asked Vangie, Mrs. Emmaline Beaulieu, and the late Margaret Jane LeGette, hoping they'd have answers. They said Harriet had always been this way, even as a child.

She was an artificial Baptist, the kind who thought she'd found the Way by regular church attendance, taking food to the sick, and having other little old Baptists over for cake, coffee, and Bible study. If you weren't a tithing church member, forget it. They'd let you starve. People like Harriet turned me against religion. I didn't see the point of rubbing elbows with someone shallow and intolerant. She, if anyone, was on a hell-bound train. I mean, if you're masquerading as a do-gooder, why not go *all* the way?

The Galliards were so Baptist they'd donated four stained-glass windows and two pews. Their home sat in the middle of twenty-five hundred acres of cotton. It was a three-story white clapboard, with dark green shutters you could close and porches on all sides ("Verandas," Zachary explained). The attic was tucked away on the third floor, with arched windows, each pane a different color, like in a church. It seemed shameful to waste such beauty on an attic, but the Galliards didn't seem to notice.

I coveted the furnishings—great curled sideboards, cherry beds with four posts, canopies of hand-tatted lace. The floors were slick, hardwood, covered with ancient oriental rugs. The ceilings were at least fifteen feet high, with egg-and-dart molding. In the dining room, huge silver platters and bowls were crammed into corner cupboards. A butler's panty held shelves of flowered china and etched crystal. Oil paintings were hung over every mantle, except in the living room where a huge mirror slanted at an odd angle, reflecting the whirring ceiling fans. Sheer lace panels blocked every window. I had a sense of old money without frivolity. I was awed by it. And also by my new family.

"You talk so *fast*," said Mrs. Galliard. "Slow *down*, darlin'. I can't under*stand* that New Yoke *twang*."

"New Yoke?" I said, blinking.

"Isn't *that* where you're *from*?" she said.

Any normal woman would have been insulted, but I wanted the Galliards to like me. All my family were dead from consumption, and I hoped Zachary's mother would consider me a second daughter. She was not the soft Louisiana woman I'd envisioned. She called me Eat-us. "Eat*us*?" she'd say. "Pass the gr*a*vy, pl*ease* ma'*am*." Sometimes I'd glance up and catch her watching me. She'd look away and sigh. Or run her hands through the wispy white hair. I told myself she had too many burdens, because even then Mr. Galliard was losing his mind; his blue eyes made no sense of the world around him, and he grew childlike and rude.

The burden of the farm fell on my mother-in-law. She walked the cotton rows, hired and fired gangs of pickers. Like most of the planters, she hired Mexican workers after World War II because they were cheaper. They arrived on flat-bed trucks in the spring to

chop weeds out of the cotton. The fields were full of people heaving hoes. Mrs. Galliard hauled sacks of flour, meal, and beans to the
work shed, where two Negro women cooked huge lunches for
the workers. They set everything out on wooden picnic tables in the
boiling sun. Gallons of barbecue, slaw, and iced tea. Bushels of
pears and apples were set about, depending on what was in season,
along with sandwiches and hunks of store-bought angel food cake.
She'd get the cooks to make huge pots of poke salad, red beans and
rice, chicken gumbo. Then she'd serve it with slices of white bread.
At night she spent hours on the adding machine, her fingers whisking over the keys, the white paper curling around her ankles.

After I had collected a smattering of furniture, I wanted to
make an impression on my new family, so I invited them to
Cypress Street for Thanksgiving. We'd been married three months.
Zachary said, "The sky's the limit, baby. Put on a show. Give my
hick family a New England dinner they won't ever forget."

At first, Mrs. Galliard balked. "We've al*ways* had Thanksgiving at *my* house," she complained. "It's a tradi*t*ion."

Somehow Zachary convinced her; he never said how. I was too
busy to wonder why. I rushed down to City Market, insisting they
order special foods from New Orleans and Memphis. A friend from
Murray Hill sent a box of required items. I cooked for five solid
days. Vangie came over to help, but she only complicated matters.

"But where's your good china? Your crystal and silver?" she
asked, opening cupboards.

"I don't have any." I looked down at my dime-store dishes—
thick white plates with black rims. I'd planned to spruce them up
with orange-and-brown plaid napkins.

"No china?" Vangie drew back, one hand on her chest. "Well,
that won't do. We've got to get you downtown this instant!"

"Why?"

"To buy you some dishes, and a lace tablecloth. And I can
loan you my silver. Buttercup's my pattern."

"Vangie, I don't have time for this. And it's not necessary." I
was getting angry. My chestnuts were simmering in a bouillon
stockpot, and I had to peel them while they were still hot.

"Honey, it's the most necessary thing in your life. You've *got* to
have dishes, Edith." She wrung her hands. "Pretty bone china,
with cabbage roses or birds. Or whatever you like."

"It's a waste." I shrugged. "The food will cover up the pattern."

"Then will you at least borrow mine? Olive and I can bring
them over later. They're so precious. Little cornucopias and
turkeys, even on the teacups. And I've got matching amber gob-

lets in all sizes. But don't you worry—Mama won't know they're mine. She's never eaten a single meal at my house."

I stared at her. Now she'd captured my attention. "Why?"

"Well, Mama likes the family to come to her house. Her mama was the same way. That's one reason I was surprised that she agreed to come here."

"I don't understand." I sat down at my shiny new dining room table, admiring the Windsor chairs, like I'd seen one time in Westport at an old boyfriend's farmhouse. The boyfriend went back to his wife, but his lovely chairs stayed in my mind.

"That's just how Mama is. She likes to fill her house with food and family. Going to my house would break her heart."

"Will it break coming to mine?"

"Oh, probably." Vangie laughed.

"That's sad."

"No, what's sad is my brother." Vangie tapped the dime-store dishes. "Having to eat his meals on these sorry things."

"He's never mentioned it."

"Then you must be an awful good cook." She winked.

"Awful good?" I grimaced. What a peculiar expression, awful good. I didn't see how I'd ever understand what these people really meant.

That morning I walked around my yard, snipping holly. The air was washed and yellow, moving through pecan trees. This same exact air might have been in California yesterday, the South Pacific the day before. I reluctantly went inside and made a centerpiece of gourds and orange candles, surrounding it with leaves and holly berries. Instead of place cards, I drew individual scrolls, writing out the menu in tiny, elaborate black-ink script:

Wellfleet Oyster Chowder
Maple-Glazed Turkey with Roast Apples and Pears
Applejack Gravy Apple-Chestnut Stuffing
Skillet Squash with Red Onions
Oven-Stewed Succotash
Steamed Red Cabbage Wedges with Horseradish Butter
Brandied Mincemeat Pie
Pumpkin Black Walnut Pie
Gingered Indian Pudding with Iced Sweet Cream
Cloverleaf Rolls
Coffee Hard Cider Eggnog Sauvignon Blanc

It was not the success I had envisioned. They arrived together, the Galliards and the Neppers, a full hour before the appointed time. My quiet and serene kitchen grew as noisy as the emergency room at Bellevue. Zachary's father, whom everyone called the Major, sat by the new Addison radio, switching the dial. When Olive walked up to him, he scowled and said, "Who are you?" "Your granddaughter," Olive said, putting one arm around him. "Why, law," he said, "I thought you looked familiar."

In the dining room, Henry was walking around the table, reading a scroll. "What's hard cider?" he asked me, laughing. "Don't you have any soft?"

"How about a sample?" I smiled and pressed my teeth together.

"Me? No, I'm not much of an apple eater." He waved the scroll. "Guess I'll just fill up on rolls. Unless you put real clover in them."

I fled into the kitchen, fished out one of Vangie's crystal cups, and dipped up eggnog. The smell of cognac and whiskey tickled my nose. Mrs. Galliard and Vangie came into the room. "My, my that smells . . . strong." Mrs. Galliard pinched her nose. I could see that she was just Baptist enough to disapprove of the alcohol content.

"It's an old recipe." I took a long, dreamy sip.

"Family recipe?" asked Vangie.

"No." I wiped my lips. "Actually, it's from a Russian artist I used to know. Sasha Vasilevich. He lived in Greenwich Village." I could see him in my old red-and-yellow kitchen, his hand a blur on the rotary beater.

"A Russian?" Mrs. Galliard released her nose and breathed deeply. "Was he Communist?"

"No." I drank the rest of my eggnog, then dipped up another cup, ignoring my mother-in-law's disapproving eyes.

"Hmmmm, Greenwich. What a nice name for a village," said Vangie. "Whereabouts in Russia is it?"

We ate buffet-style, apparently a novelty in this part of the country. One by one, they sat down. I stepped around the table, lighting candles. I'd arranged them down the center, an unconscious attempt to divide Neppers and Galliards. After a protracted grace, courtesy of Henry, everyone picked up forks and began examining the food.

"'Ever since Eve ate the apples, much depends on dinner,'" said Henry.

"How true! Did you think up that all by yourself?" said Mrs. Galliard.

"Yes, ma'am."

I nearly choked on a roll, but Henry refused to look up. Across the table, Mr. Galliard tasted his soup, then spit it back into his spoon.

"Major!" scolded Mrs. Galliard. "How uncouth!"

"I can't help it, Lallie. It tastes spoilt."

"It's not," she said, holding up a spoonful and eyeing it. "It's bound to be delicious."

"Tastes fishy." He laid down his spoon and glanced down the length of the table. "Where's the dressing? Pass me it."

"Thanksgiving's not Thanksgiving without my oyster dressing." My mother-in-law sighed, passing the apple-chestnut stuffing.

"Thanksgiving's not Thanksgiving without dressing, period," said Henry. "I hate fruit in mine."

"We should all try new things," clucked Vangie.

"Like brandied green-tomato mincemeat pie?" Henry laughed, shoving in a mouthful of skillet squash.

Mrs. Galliard gave Olive a sympathetic smile. "Why, sugar. You haven't eat a bite. Here, fill up on rolls, and your mama can fix you a nice turkey sandwich later."

"No, it's good," Olive said, reaching for her fork. "I'm just a slow eater."

The orange candles threw shadows on the walls. All around me was the sound of fork tines scraping on bone china. Except for Zachary, they weren't really eating—they were rearranging food. As they picked, sniffed, and prodded, it occurred to me that this was more like sheep-herding than eating.

"Excuse me while I check on something," I said, pushing back my chair and rising.

"Baby? You okay?" Zachary looked alarmed.

"Fine." I squeezed his hand.

"Need any help?" asked the ever-cheerful Vangie.

"No, thank you." I stepped into the kitchen and slurped down three cups of eggnog. It got me through the second most difficult night of my life. The first was when Mother died at Bellevue, on the indigent ward, wearing a gray-and-green striped gown that the nurses handed out to both men and women. I drank another glass of eggnog, then weaved back into the dining room, where I smiled a smeary, drunken smile through all of their insults. I looked straight at Henry and said, "'Let us have wine, women, mirth, and laughter/Sermons and soda water the day after.'"

"That's so . . . nice," said Vangie, drawing her eyebrows together.

"Except the part about the wine," Mrs. Galliard said. "You're good with words, just like Henry."

"Oh, it's not original. Lord Byron wrote it about a hundred years ago," I said, smiling at Henry. As his face reddened, I closed my eyes, picturing my hands on Sasha's round face. For your own wretched nights, here's the recipe, courtesy of Sasha Vasilevich, wherever he is:

HOLIDAY EGGNOG

All you need is an electric mixer. Separate 12 eggs—yolks in one bowl, whites in another. Add 1 cup sugar to the yolks, and beat with the mixer. Slowly add 1 cup cognac and 1 cup bourbon. Chill. Beat egg whites with 1/2 t. salt until they make stiff peaks. Now whip 3 pints heavy cream. Blend whipped cream and egg whites into yolk mixture. Chill for 2 hours. Sprinkle with nutmeg.

I've entertained for so many years that my food no longer bothers the locals. My Easter dinner was complimented and consumed. Now all my guests were gone except for Cab Beaulieu. We sat on the screened porch, in the new lounge chairs, green metal—"Bell-pepper green," I joked, but he said, "Why, they sure are that color." The cool backyard drifted around us, streaming through the mesh.

"This is a set-in rain," Cab said. "It's gone pour all night."

I nodded and took a sip of coffee that I'd laced with cognac. Above us wind chimes clinked, the glass panes identical to microscope slides but painted with Chinese letters. I'd brought them from my third-story walk-up in Murray Hill. I'd traveled a long way from those cramped rooms, where every square inch of space was ingeniously shaped into shelves, drawers, and cabinets. I'd hung belts, scarves, and pocketbooks from the bedroom ceiling. The walls of that room were goldenrod, serving as a backdrop for my angular paintings. I owned an iron bed, glossy black with polished brass posts. It had a deep feather mattress that I bought one summer in Maine. Even on the coldest nights I slept with the windows open, while sirens and horns pierced the dirty, steamy night, and the radiators clicked like huge crickets. On one memorable occasion, Zachary made love to me four times. "I know this is putting the cart before the horse," he drawled, "but now that I've taken you for a test drive, I don't think I can live without you."

You might say I married well, even if the geography was not of my choosing, but I loved Zachary Galliard. And I missed him dreadfully. He had always awakened me with his annoying little whistling—the same tune, "Alice Blue Gown." I missed his sarcastic insights about assorted friends, Galliards, and neighbors, and the way he threw his head back when he laughed. I knew, of course, what local gossips claimed, that he'd suffered a stroke during the act of love, but the truth was, he had died exactly three minutes postcoitus, not *during*.

"Think I blew a fuse," he said, sitting up, squeezing his temples. "My head's killing me."

"Sweetie, should I call Phillip?" I asked, but he'd already slumped over. I scrambled across the bed and put my ear to his chest. I heard no heartbeat, felt no breath from his lungs, and I knew he was dead. So I did what any good wife would do. I pulled up his pajamas and *then* called Phillip LeGette. "Get your ass over here, Phillip," I said. It was after ten o'clock, but by eleven, half of Cypress Street had squeezed into the bedroom. That's how fast news travels in Limoges. Instead of beating drums and smoke signals, you've got the telephone.

Now I lit two candles and set them on the table between us. Cab sipped his coffee, then excused himself and went to the bathroom. I wondered if he wanted to leave and didn't know how. Southern men seemed especially prone to politeness, even at their own expense. I found it baffling, irritating, and mildly amusing. Earlier, the Marshall sisters had apologized for eating and running, something Limogeans looked down upon, but their age excused them. Mamie had to be close to eighty-eight, and Meredith was older. Their daddy had served in the Civil War. Cab probably thought I was another lonely widow. He knew so many, an occupational hazard. My house seemed widowish and introverted—paints scattered about, canvases leaning against the walls, the oil still gummy. Even the screened porch seemed feminine and introspective, with packets of petunias, nasturtiums, and four o'clocks strewn about on the little white shelf, next to peat pots, garden gloves, and a trowel. A wooden easel stood in the corner, holding a freshly gessoed canvas.

Living in Limoges taught me the art of trompe l'oeil. In the study was a white, Louis XIV desk, the surface painted with three-cent stamps, a stack of airmail letters, and a crystal inkwell holding a tiny peacock feather. On the far wall of the kitchen stood a hutch that showed white rabbits huddled behind chicken wire; in the bedroom was a walnut armoire, the doors painted with double wedding-ring quilts and china-faced dolls. What you see is not always what you get. I sighed and peered into the dark, clammy yard. From a distance, I suspected the candles resembled tiny yellow specks, like caught fireflies. That's how I'd paint it.

The door to the kitchen stood open, showing a chrome table and a wall of white cabinets stenciled with grapevines. When Olive was ten years old, she came over every morning to watch me work, squatting next to my elbow. All the windows were pushed open, and the air felt cool on my bare arms. The smell of turpentine hung in the air between streams of exhaled cigarette smoke.

"I want to be a painter someday," said Olive.

"Artist, you mean." I touched my brush to the tip of her nose, leaving a tiny smudge of green. "It sounds more glamorous, don't you think?"

"That's what you are, Aunt Edith." Her irises were the color of hydrangeas, the same shade as Zachary's. She clasped her hands around her knees and watched me dab purple onto a cluster of concord grapes. After a minute I put the brush in her hand and showed her the motion, using her wrist as a point of flexion. That whole afternoon, she painted grapes and I drew vines. By dusk, our paths had grown together in a tangle of color.

I stared at the Neppers' backyard, the damp Saint Augustine grass that Henry had trimmed yesterday morning. The square white house was illuminated from within by harsh, fluorescent bulbs. Vangie's face appeared in the kitchen window. She was washing dishes, and she wasn't smiling. There was no sign of Henry, which did not surprise me.

Everyone was buzzing behind their backs, talking about Olive drinking the poison and Henry drinking the Robichaux woman's nectar. To me, gossip is like pollen—invisible to the naked eye, irritating to some, necessary to others. You simply can't do anything about it. Because I'm a New Yorker, my "behavior" is excused. I get away with plenty; I'm given much more leeway than Vangie, a native Limogean, would ever be allowed. If she crossed the boundaries of good taste, she would be ostracized. The women instinctively know better than to spike the Sunday school punch or to sit in the bank president's lap (or to call him "the Prez").

When I tell people that I once spent the Fourth of July in Central Park at a picnic with a thousand other people, they act as if I've gone to the moon. "Why would you do *that*?" asked Harriet. "Why would you want to be with strangers?" As if people born above the Mason-Dixon lack the capacity for grace, love of family, hospitality, kindness, and an eye for genuine antiques. I've been called hard, color-blind, rebellious, flashy, cheap, and razor-tongued. I cultivated my accent, protecting it like an heirloom (although it's really no accent at all). I refused to split words down the middle—Limogeans talk the same way they snap beans—you end up with a huge pile of husks and strings, and a smaller, edible pile of vegetables.

And it's more than how people talk—it's what they say. I've heard Harriet bitterly complain about Henry's dogs. "I'm going to tell him off!" she'd cry. "They bark and stink up the neighborhood. I'm sick of it!" And the next time she saw Henry hosing out the kennel, she'd holler, "I've been saving dog food coupons for you! Do you want me to run inside and get them?"

I've heard Waldene accuse Vangie of being forgetful. "I told her five times that we needed forty dozen cupcakes for the bazaar, and she said she forgot. You just can't depend on her." But to Vangie's face, she was all smiles. No one ever tells you the truth. They just tell everyone else.

They say I'm aloof and private, lonely and alone. Not the same things, you know. They join clubs and I paint. People draw conclusions, and I draw mine. The truth is, most artists work in silence but not a vacuum. It's hard to explain your passions, but sometimes it is harder to live them. If I'd moved into Limoges without Zachary, I would have been an outcast, an oddity who paints. Parties would have flowed around me like an inland tide, and I would have been a stationary rock. But if I hadn't met Zachary, I would have stayed in Murray Hill. It makes me shudder to think I might have missed knowing him. Zachary adored me, petted me openly, even in church, and people began to think, "What is it about her? What's her secret?" They thought I'd cast some New York spell on him, as if I made love in a whole different way and he couldn't get enough. Maybe it was true. I'll never tell.

From within the house, the toilet flushed. A minute later Cab's footsteps clapped down the hall. He pushed open the screen door and eased back into the green chair. He lit a cigarette, his palm briefly turning orange behind the flame. I thought that, too, would make an interesting painting.

"I should have insisted they have dinner with us," I said.

"Who?" Cab exhaled smoke.

"Henry and Vangie." I watched him over the rim of my cup. The cup was blue-sprigged Limoges, bequeathed to us by Mrs. Galliard. She bought two sets in 1923, when she went abroad. (Vangie inherited the pink set.) Half of Mrs. Galliard's antiques and collectibles came to me, a relative by marriage, as family fortunes so often do. After I die, it's anyone's guess who will inherit the silver, etched crystal, bone china egg cups, and all the money sitting in Hibernia Bank, compounding interest. I'd planned to leave it all to Olive.

"I should have forced them to join us," I said, sipping coffee, drawing in a mouthful of sugar. I glanced back at Vangie's house. She was gone from the window, but the light was still burning.

"It's hard to force them two to do anything." Cab laughed. He had lovely eyes, blue Sèvres.

"When I invited them, Vangie said she had a perfectly good Christmas ham in the freezer, and she hated to let it go to waste."

"That sounds like Miss Vangie." He smiled. "At least you didn't invite Miss Harriet."

"Huh, I wouldn't dare." I rubbed my finger around the rim. "Did I tell you that Henry's paramour's child is working for me?"

"No." He laughed.

"I'm serious. I've hired Billie Robichaux. She's even working for Vangie. She hauled away three wagon loads of rose clippings for her."

"Yes, I've seen her around the yards. She's a cutie-pie."

"The child is endearing, even if her mother isn't."

"Depends on your viewpoint." He raised his eyebrows, and I looked over at Vangie's house. Through the kitchen window I saw her briefly appear, crossing back and forth, from the counter to the icebox. Out in the yard rain had started up again, pattering against the pavement, and I heard thunder, like marbles thrown over a tin roof.

"I don't believe he's ever done this before," I said. "Been unfaithful to Vangie, I mean."

"Could be right, I've never heard a breath of gossip, and I hear plenty. That Robichaux woman is married to a paralyzed veteran. And she's got the little girl. What's she going to do—dump them for Henry? I can't see him leaving Miss Vangie."

"It happens. Men leaving."

"Not in Limoges. In fact, I don't think it's *ever* happened."

"The town's changing, Cab."

"Maybe. Looks to me like that Robichaux woman would be ashamed."

"I don't think she *has* any shame. And I don't see how her daughter stands a chance."

"Well, from what I've seen she's pretty sturdy. And smart."

"Smart can't overcome a mama like DeeDee Robichaux."

"You don't like her a bit, do you?" Cab grinned, drawing his lips to one side.

"Vangie is my family. Naturally, I'm biased. What do I know?

Perhaps they're *all* lovely people." I stood up. "Listen, I'm going to have some wine. Would you care for a glass?"

"Oh, no, ma'am. I've stayed too long as it is." He set his cup on the table, rattling the spoon. "I need to get on back."

"I'm not a ma'am." I reached down and swatted his leg. "Shame on you. Anyway, it's started raining again. You'll get soaked. Come on and have a glass with me." I glanced at my watch. "It's not even ten o'clock."

"Well." He scratched his head. "I guess I could. If it's no trouble."

"If it were trouble, I wouldn't have offered." I smiled down into his startled face, then opened the screen door and stepped into the bright kitchen. From the counter, the radio was playing an old Tommy Dorsey hit, "I'm Getting Sentimental Over You." As I gathered tulip-shaped goblets, I thought back to the night Zachary and I went dancing at the Stork Club, and the band was playing this same song. The floor was packed with enlisted men and their overdressed dates. Zachary, a naval lieutenant, wore his white summer uniform; he hugged me close, drawling his own version of the song, "Things you say and do/Make my balls turn plumb blue /I'm goin' mental over you."

As I filled the wine glasses with chablis, my hands shook. To steady my nerves, I took a swig from the bottle. Then I set the glasses on a silver tray and walked over to the screen door, pushing it open with my hip. Cab leaped to his feet. "Here, let me help you, Edith."

I balanced the tray and handed him a glass. "I heard some disturbing news at canasta the other day," I said.

"Women are always hearing things at canasta." He grinned, took a sip of wine, and sat back down. "What'd you hear?"

"That Olive is pregnant. How can people say ridiculous things?"

"I don't know, but I heard it too. Way back in March."

"I wonder if Vangie knows?"

"About the gossip?"

"She hasn't said anything to me."

"Could just be talk. There's so much of it. And not just about Olive."

"True." I rubbed one finger around the rim of my glass and looked thoughtfully toward the Neppers'. The kitchen was dark, and rain washed over the house. "But it all fits, don't you see? Maybe she *was* pregnant and tried to kill herself?"

"I wasn't aware that Miss Vangie let the girl date."

"You don't need to date to get pregnant, Cab."

"Guess not." He tilted back his head and drank the last of his wine. "Anyhow, if it's gossip, it'll die down, like everything else."

"For Vangie's sake, I hope you're right." I stared into my glass, then took a long swallow. "This calls for another drink." I got up and went back into the house, returning with the bottle.

"You'll get me drunk, Edith," he said, holding up his glass.

"Not a new condition, I hope." I poured myself a glass, then dipped one finger in the wine, rubbing it over my lips and behind my ears, for luck.

"Not hardly." Cab shifted in his chair. I briefly closed my eyes. The alcohol had set off a faint buzzing in my extremities. When I looked again, Cab was tilting back his glass, draining his wine. He set the goblet on the metal table and stood up, wobbling a little. "I really should be going."

"Nonsense." I waved one hand. "We've just gotten started."

"Started what?" He sat back down.

"Being neighborly. We've never really had a conversation before. Not alone, I mean." My voice sounded slurry. The wine had shifted in my blood, enveloping me in a rosy sheen from my forehead to my toes.

"Do tell," he said, grinning rakishly. "Do tell."

After we polished off the second bottle of wine, we moved up to Drambuie. We ended up in my gold-and-violet bedroom with the fleur-de-lis border that I'd painted one stir-crazy summer. Between the long windows, Cab kept trying to stand on his head. "One more time," he'd say, his feet thumping against the wall, shaking my painting "Still Life with Gladioli."

He was buck naked.

"Almost got it," he said, pushing his head into a pillow; then he lifted his legs, swinging them toward the wall. His arms shook, and his face turned scarlet, but he managed to balance himself.

"Bravo!" I clapped, managing to spill Drambuie between my breasts. I giggled, pointing to his private parts, which were dangling in the wrong direction. His legs flipped down, one at time, then he sat on the floor, grinning up at me.

"God, you're cute." I hiccuped, walking on my knees to the edge of the bed. He reached up and pulled me down, into his arms.

Red Beans and Rice

❧

I spent Easter by myself reading the Bible. Reverend Kirby gave me a list of the dirty parts: Solomon and his seven hundred wives, three hundred concubines; Judah and Tamar; Amnon and Tamar, Dinah and Shechem, and all the wicked cities. My favorite is Genesis 39. Joseph and the Potiphar's wife. The woman sneaked up behind Joseph and grabbed his coat. He took off running, leaving the coat in her hands. She waited till the Potiphar got home, and she showed him the "proof" that Joseph had tried to seduce her. The Potiphar threw Joseph in jail, and even though God let him prosper in prison, the truth never came out. Shoot, I'd never do that to a man. There's more ways to get a man's coat off than to sneak up behind him.

—CORDY KING, READING THE BIBLE AND DRINKING MOGEN DAVID, EASTER SUNDAY 1952

All over Limoges women were faced with leftover Easter food. The turkey people made salads and casseroles, but the ham people were lucky—they cooked red beans and rice. It was hearty, filling, and even beguiling. Also it froze well. It was standard Louisiana fare. Ask anyone, and they'll tell you why ham bones were invented.

Some leftovers live in the blood. Wine, for example, floats in the blood for hours, flotsam and jetsam, then it's metabolized in the liver, through thin layers of vascular tissue. It's more fragile than a heart. Cab Beaulieu opened his eyes, blinking at the ceiling fan as it turned backward circles against mottled, funeral-home plaster. His skull felt elongated, and his mouth was so dry that his teeth stuck to his lips. He thought he might have died of thirst, but surely not. He remembered drinking all the Drambuie, then opening a bottle of Wild Turkey. Outside, rain trickled down the windows. The sky was grayish blue, and he didn't know if it was dusk or dawn. He sure hoped nobody had died during the night, because he was in no shape to dispense comfort to the bereaved.

Soon as the rain stopped, he thought he'd walk over to Edith's and see if she had a hangover too. Maybe they could drink coffee together or whatnot. Last night felt like last year; he had a dim recollection of walking home, but all that he remembered was getting stuck in the azaleas. Rain whipped against his shoulders, and he felt water rising above his ankles. Somewhere between his yard and Edith's, he'd lost a pair of wing tips, brand new Easter shoes. He just hoped they didn't wash down to Harriet Hooper's yard.

His stomach burned, and he wondered if a doughnut might settle it. So he threw back the covers, climbed out of bed, and lurched to the kitchen. Israel was sitting at the table, sipping coffee from his saucer. "Morning, boss," he said.

"You mean moaning." Cab sat down at the table and held his head between his hands.

Israel laughed. The radio on the counter blared out the morning farm report. Through the double windows he watched water gather into a fast stream between the dip in his yard and the azaleas. At the end of the street the stream poured into a drain that disappeared under Lincoln Avenue. Between Edith's and Vangie's houses, Lake Limoges spread out like flood water. Ducks drifted on the ruffled surface, weaving between the cypresses. Edith's roof was shiny black, her kitchen window a blurry green square.

For the first time since Amarillo, Texas, Cab thought he was on the verge of love. All these years he'd lived behind Edith, and she'd seemed so proper, so different. Now just the thought of her thick, nasal voice excited him. He saw her crossing her legs, looking up at him with those heavy-lidded, gray eyes. She always had a cigarette caught in the *V* of her fingers, smoke escaping from her smeary mouth. She looked like Lauren Bacall on Harry Truman's piano. Maybe a little older than Bacall, but then, Cab was no Bogie.

There was a leak in the canning porch's roof, and water pattered down one drop at a time, into a pan on the old stove. Israel slurped from his saucer, a deafening sound, watching Cab with eyes the color of unshelled pecans. "Feeling better?" He smiled.

"My brain's pickled." Cab put his hands on his temples and squeezed, making his forehead pucker.

"What'd you get into last night?" Israel asked. "You spend Easter with Mr. Jack?"

"Jack who?"

"Daniel's."

Cab shook his head, setting off new waves of pain. "Can you fix me some coffee, Israel?"

He pushed away from the table and walked to the stove. Then he picked up the tin pot and poured. Coffee splashed into the curved china bowl, making a roaring sound. Cab curled his fingers around his ears and shut his eyes. From the porch, water pinged into the pan, a double drip, *E-dith, E-dith*.

Israel fixed his famous blood neutralizer, made with 6 oz. tomato juice, 6 oz. beer, 1 t. lemon juice, 1 t. Worcestershire, and a shot of Tabasco. He served it in a tall glass with chunks of ice. Then he suggested Cab return to bed.

"Sleep it off," he said. "That's all you can do when you make a fool of yourself."

When Cab awakened, the rain had stopped. Steam rose from the pavement. Fog skimmed over the lake, drifting toward Cypress Street. The other side of the lake had vanished behind thick, gray air. Cab pulled on a plaid shirt and trousers, dabbed Old Spice behind his ears, then walked into the backyard. Even though the rain had stopped, muddy water rushed along the azaleas. To reach Edith, he'd have to walk the long way, on the sidewalk.

As he turned back, toward Lincoln Avenue, he stopped to pick five yellow irises that Mrs. Beaulieu had planted the November Teddy Roosevelt was voted president. Water dripped onto the back of his hand, sliding around his wrist. The stems collapsed like paper straws beneath his fingers. On her deathbed, Mrs. Beaulieu had fretted about those irises, making Cab promise he'd divide them. He'd gotten Miss Vangie to show him how, and every few years she'd come over with her trowel and dig everything up. It seemed almost surgical, as if cutting through those roots would kill the plants, but it made them flourish. Just the opposite of his profession—the division of parts, the emptying of vital fluids. It was enough to break his heart.

He walked to the corner, turning right on Lincoln. This road terminated at Cypress, because of the lake. Even from here he saw mama ducks waddling to shore, trailed by scruffy babies. As he neared Edith's house, he slowed, blinking at the green-and-white striped awnings, dented in the centers where rain had collected. She needed a man—him—to go from window to window, pushing a broom into each sagging canvas. Her house was gray-shingled, trimmed in crisp white. "The colors of Long Island," she used to say, and he acted like he knew.

He looked forward to summer when she'd haul out her redwood lounger—he'd help—and lie in the sun, the straps of her swimsuit pulled off her shoulders. She'd done this every summer Cab could remember. He'd always managed a few sneaky glances (she had the longest legs), but he'd never put her into the category with other widows. She was the Judge's wife, even though he was dead. She was a cultural oddity. After his funeral, everyone thought she'd return to New York. Cab imagined the high-rises in Manhattan were shingled, too, big old apartment houses beached on the cement.

He cut around the boxwoods and veered toward her back porch, his shoes squeaking in the grass. The screen door was locked, so he rapped hard on the strip of wood. Edith's house needed a man's touch—not that he was a carpenter. He could learn; he'd ask Israel and Twilly for advice. Straight overhead, one of her gutters had come unhinged, the long white nails sticking out. Algae grew in a fuzzy sheath along her bottom steps, making him think of burials. In mortuary school they'd exhumed a body. It had long whiskers of penicillin, like dust from inside a vacuum cleaner. In Cab's opinion, the phrase "a-moldering in the grave" really summed up death.

Edith appeared in the doorway, between the kitchen and porch, wiping her hands on a green dishrag. She looked at Cab briefly, then stepped forward. She flicked the lock with her thumb and pushed open the screen door. She looked haggard, with deep purple lines carved beneath each eye. Her hair was pulled back by a wide barrette, setting off her angular cheekbones. She lifted her eyebrows, wrinkled her forehead, and said, "Yes?"

Cab cleared his throat. He thought she could pack more into that one word, *yes?*, than Reverend Kirby could squeeze into a whole sermon. He felt demoted, as if he were a delivery boy, someone collecting dimes for polio. He held out the irises, which suddenly seemed all wrong, skimpy and rushed, obviously picked at the last minute.

"Did you want something?" She took the irises, not looking at him, and stepped back inside. She laid the flowers on a green metal chair. As she walked back to the door, it bounced shut, but she made no move to open it.

"How you doing this morning?" Cab leaned against the door, staring at her through the mesh. He smiled, but the corners of his mouth shook. "Boy, I have me a headache you won't believe."

She raised her eyebrows.

"Do you have one?" he asked. "A headache, I mean."

"No."

"You're lucky, then." He knew he sounded dumb, but maybe

he was. The hangover wasn't helping. His head felt as thick as watermelon rind, the insides pale pink and watery, filled with seeds.

He leaned toward the door, but she pressed her hip against it, as if blocking him.

"I was painting," she said.

"Painting what?"

"A still life."

"What's that?"

"Just a picture," she said irritably. "I need to get back, if you don't mind."

"Can I see it?"

"I'd rather you didn't. I prefer painting alone."

"I didn't ask to watch. I just wanted to see the picture."

"Well, you can't." Her eyebrows slanted together. She looked grainy behind the mesh. "I hate to be rude, but I must go now."

"Well, you *are* being rude."

"Sorry."

"No, you're not."

She shrugged.

"What about last night?"

"What about it?"

"I don't understand." Cab scraped his thumbnail along the screen. He wasn't accustomed to outspoken women. All the ladies he'd ever known were the most dishonest creatures on earth—they'd lie and cheat before they'd hurt a man's feelings. Any other woman in Limoges would cut her eyes at him and say she had a headache, an awful terrible headache, could he come back later? They talked in euphemisms, and it was up to the man to translate. Most men wouldn't look beyond the "headache." They'd accept it as gospel and try again later.

"Can't we at least talk?" he asked her.

"Sorry, I'm all talked out."

"Why? What have I done?"

"It's not what you did, it's what *I* did. And it's what I am."

"What's that?"

"It was all my fault, getting drunk like we did. It shouldn't have happened."

"Well, I had fun."

"I'll bet."

"You acted like you did, too."

"Did I?" She lifted one shoulder. "Do you realize I was seven years old when you were born?"

"So?"

"Do I have to say it?" She sucked in her cheeks. "I guess I do. I'm too old for you."

"That's not old! You're just embarrassed about what-all we did."

"Me?" She rolled her eyes. "Don't make me laugh."

"Can I come inside?"

"You already did. A number of times." Her eyes blinked open wide. There was no hint of amusement on her face. "As a rule, I don't sleep with my neighbors. I'd like to forget it happened. If you're smart, you'll do the same thing."

"That's not smart. That's being a turtle, hiding in your shell."

"I am *not* a turtle. I'm too old for you, all right? It won't work."

"How do you know?"

"Because I've *lived* longer than you, that's how." She turned and walked into her house, shutting the kitchen door, leaving the irises on the metal chair.

"Hey, don't run off!" Cab called out, but she was gone. "You could at least hear my side. Last night was special to me, Edith!"

The door stayed closed. In less than a day, he'd gone from making love on the floor to getting his heart broken. Not that a heart could really break. In his opinion it was a misunderstood organ. He'd often wondered why it was connected with love. Probably because it sounded better—he couldn't imagine people saying, "I'm liver-broken. Zing went the strings of my liver. Don't break my liver."

I love you from the bottom of my liver.

It just wasn't romantic. Although you could say, You make my liver quiver. Cab thought of all this as he stared at the door, hoping she'd come back, even if it was to order him off her property. He laid his palms against the screen and stared at the burned-out candles on the metal table. It started raining again, cold drops that stung his neck and forearms. He ducked his head and trudged into her backyard, stopping abruptly when he saw the gully wash. Orange water had seeped past the azaleas. It looked shallow, but Cab didn't feel like ruining his shoes (his last good pair!). Anyway, Edith could be watching from behind a pinched-open curtain.

He ran back to Lincoln Avenue, his hands stuck in his pockets. Once, he turned back to stare at her house, but he saw no sign of her. Go on, he thought. Stay inside. Count your gray hairs, and I'll count mine. Emory Brown, a fellow Rotarian, said he wouldn't date a woman he couldn't get a menstrual history on, somebody he could have babies with. Cab didn't care about that, but the last thing he needed was some Yankee lady who could make him stand on his head. She was dangerous. Maybe he ought to stay away. "Next thing you know," he thought, "they'll be carrying me out of her house like they did Zachary."

Edith saw his face in the upstairs windows at Beaulieu's, moving from pane to pane, not even bothering to hide himself. She knelt in her flowers, pinching and thinning her scarlet impatiens, a task she loathed, but the flowers would otherwise grow leggy. Vangie called it suffering to be beautiful. Edith tolerated gardening—she would rather be inside, working on a sketch of red bell peppers. "Life is passing you by," Mrs. Galliard used to say. "How can you paint when the sun is shining and birds are singing?"

"Time spent preparing a drawing is never wasted," she said, and Mrs. Galliard laughed.

"You don't know the world's turning," she scolded, "and Vangie's just as bad. Look how she coddles her roses and tomatoes. If you girls want to be smart, plant cotton!"

Now Edith looked up from her flowers and glanced over at Vangie's house. The flower beds were full of dandelions. Since Easter the Neppers had been ill with flu. Edith made chicken soup (the secret is adding chicken feet to the stock—it lends a rich, deep flavor). Waldene, who was scared of catching the virus, sent Fanny over with a jug of cherry Kool-Aid and a pan of Jell-O (Dr. LeGette believed in fluids during an illness—any solid that became a liquid at room temperature was his standard prescription).

Later that afternoon, while Edith was resting in the hammock, she heard a noise behind the azaleas. A motor whined, followed by a thump-thump, then a man shouted, "Stop! Stop!"

Edith rose from the hammock, shielding her eyes with one hand. The azalea hedge was a green blur, moving back and forth in the wind. She swung her legs around and stood up, the hammock banging into her legs. Almost without thinking, she walked to the hedge, drawn by the sound of the motor. Through the gap, she saw figures moving back and forth.

"No, that's not right!" Cab shouted to Israel, who was pushing a tiller through the grass. The tendons stood out on the old man's arms. He shoved the tiller, and the motor sputtered and died. Edith started to retreat; she wasn't ready to face him. In her mind, he would always be naked and grinning. Their friendship, or whatever it was, had risen up into the air like noise from the tiller—loud and instantly gone. She thought some noises were like odors—strong at first, then you either grew accustomed to them or they dissipated, borne upward by the wind. But other sounds were relentless. An outboard motor, a screaming infant, a barking dog at three A.M. The soothing burr of the Electrolux, as if you are sucking up more than dirt. The grinding dentist's drill, the cold metal tasting of pepsin, boring straight to your brain. It seemed to her that love was like noise—loud soft harsh faint grating. Comforting. Maddening.

"Hell, I knew it." Cab flipped one hand at the tiller. "I just knew it. Anyway, it's too far over." He looked up at the sky, then down at the wedge of freshly turned soil. "There's not enough sun here. Corn needs lots of sun." He started to turn, and he saw Edith's face in the green branches. His eyes blinked open wide.

"I thought you said for me to use my own common sense," said Israel. He looked at Cab, saw him staring at the azaleas, and he turned. When he spotted Edith, he stepped backward. "Why, Miss Edith! What you doing there?"

"Sorry I startled you." She hesitated, then gracefully stepped through the gap in the bushes. To make them stop staring, she pointed at the tiller. "Are you putting in a flower bed?"

"Vegetables," Cab said.

"He's got him a wild hair," said Israel.

"Since when is Silver Queen a wild hair?" Cab reached in his pocket and pulled out a handkerchief, rubbing it over his forehead. He wouldn't look at Edith.

"It's just about too late to plant," Israel said. "But we had all that rain."

Edith stared down the length of the yard, resting one finger against her cheek. Almost all of the grass was gone, replaced by a rectangular strip of crops. Popsicle sticks held up empty seed packets—spinach, radishes, parsley. She saw three rows of scraggly tomatoes, four bell-pepper plants, six cabbages. The Galliards always had a large vegetable garden, but she'd never set foot in it. She preferred to learn about nature from afar. Mrs. Galliard used to say there was nothing any sweeter than Silver Queen pulled off the stalk, but it tended to lose its flavor in fewer than four hours. "Store-bought corn can't hold a candle to fresh," she'd say.

"What's all *this*?" She waved one hand at the plants. "Your own personal victory garden?"

"Why not?" Cab stuffed the handkerchief into his pocket. "They had cabbages on Canal Street this big." He made a circle with his arms.

"World War II is over," Edith said. "Isn't it a little late to plow up your whole backyard?"

"Not the *whole* yard," Cab said, irritated. He glanced at her, and their eyes briefly met. Then he looked away, gesturing at his raggedy land. "I just need room for the Silver Queen."

"Ain't nothing like fresh corn." Israel shook his head.

"That's what Zachary's mother used to say." Edith smiled.

"It's the truest thing. But Mr. Cab ought to save him the trouble and let me bring him in a bushel every week."

"Then it won't be fresh." Cab lifted his eyebrows.

"Fresh enough. And mine's already planted. I got me fifty acres, nothing *but* corn."

"Why so much, Israel?" asked Edith. She tried to imagine corn towering over the azaleas. Then she looked up at the sky. An airplane circled, emitting a stream of crop dust.

"Eat what I want, put by as much as I can," Israel said. "Grind up the rest for my cows."

"He's more farmer than mortician." Cab laughed and clapped the old man on the shoulder. "He's one to talk about wild hairs, with his nanny goats. Beehives, chickens. Geese. Pigs. And he cans, makes his own jelly, and even sews quilts."

"Shoot, you quit teasing." Israel's face turned the color of an eggplant. He glanced down at the tiller.

"I'm not teasing." Cab's hand dropped. "I admire you."

"I do too," Edith said. "More men need to be like you, Israel."

"Don't you do no admiring, either," Israel said, but he looked pleased.

"But how do you keep it all hoed?" Edith asked Israel. "Looked like you'd have weeds tall as the corn!"

"Some places I do, I sure do." He laughed. "Can't keep it all weeded. It don't bother me none."

"You must have a high tolerance for disarray."

"Disarray?" Cab snorted "Now what the hell is *that*?"

"Why don't you look it up?"

"Maybe I will."

Edith's heart thumped inside her chest like a tiny tiller. She looked up into his eyes. From the canning porch, Twilly opened the screen door and hollered, "Mr. Cab? Telephone!"

Cab turned and hollered, "Who is it?"

"Miz King. She's wanting to know what time you be coming round tonight."

Cab glanced at Edith, then turned back to Twilly. "I can't come inside cause I'm all muddy. Just tell her I'll be there around five-thirty."

Edith folded her hands, forming a cradle with her fingers. Her right thumb twitched. Her worst suspicions were confirmed—once a ladies' man, always a ladies' man.

"We've got to hurry and get this done," Cab said to Israel. "I've got to be somewhere."

"With one of your merry widows?" Edith's voice was cold and flat.

"So what if it is?" Cab said, then shrugged. "She invited me."

"I always thought you were the sort of man who couldn't turn down an invitation," she said. "In a few months you can supply *all* of your widows with corn and okra. Who knows what you'll progress to? Your own restaurant, The Widow's Inn? Or should I say Widows' End?"

"You're a widow."

"Yes, but not a merry one." She pushed back her shoulders and lifted her chin. At five feet eight, she'd towered over Zachary, but the top of her head came up to Cab's chin. She tried to see herself through his eyes. She was just another widow; Zachary had left her behind like something in a refrigerator.

"Vegetables in the back of a funeral parlor," Edith said, laughing. "Next, you'll have a little produce stand up by the cemetery." She narrowed her eyes and sucked in her cheeks.

"There's nothing wrong with growing vegetables here." Cab tapped his foot on a clod of dirt. "My yard's no different from anybody else's."

"No?" She tossed her head and laughed again. "I should think this ground would be . . . moister than most. Almost like grave-yard soil."

"You're crazy, Edith. You know that?" Cab turned to Israel. "Know how to make pepper jelly, Israel?"

"Why, sure." Israel looked surprised. "Hot or sweet?"

"Both. Might have to ask for your recipe. This lady I'm see-ing? Well, she said she likes it both ways."

"I'll bet she likes *lots* of things both ways," Edith snapped.

Cab ignored her and said, "She said she'd come over to help me make it. I told her I'd ask you for the recipe."

"If your widow likes pepper jam so much," said Edith, "then I'm sure she has her own recipes."

Cab hunkered down beside the tiller. He looked up at Israel, acting like Edith wasn't standing there. "I may buy me a freezer, too. They're on sale down at Master's Appliance. Maybe I'll take Miss King and ask her opinion."

"Well, don't count your chickens before they hatch," said Israel. "Your peppers just started blooming."

"I got them in the ground late 'cause of all the rain. Couldn't plant in mud."

"Have fun with your wild hairs," Edith called out, starting for the hedge.

"Don't you worry," Cab said. "I will."

* * *

When you are outdoors, the angle of light changes impercep-
tibly until suddenly it's dark; birds hunker down in their nests,
the sun shrinks to an orange spark in the pines. You've got miles
of empty earth stretching out around you, and crinkled sacks full
of seeds—pinkish Kentucky wonders. It was late afternoon when
they finished planting corn. Cab was amazed that he'd lost track
of time. When they began, the sun was straight overhead. Now it
was dusk. Israel had taught Cab to plant two rows at a time, three
weeks apart. This way he'd have corn and beans all summer. The
work left Cab tired but satisfied, a clear feeling, his thoughts
translucent as the strained apple jelly his mama used to make.

He stamped his feet on the back porch, then went inside to
wash up. He had a hot date tonight with Cordy King, a big-
bosomed widow with a small waist—she claimed it was eighteen
inches. "The same as Scarlett O'Hara's," she'd bragged when they
met. She'd come to look at caskets when her husband was killed
in Korea. Cab raised his eyebrows, trying to look suitably
impressed. He found her behavior a trifle odd, but lots of women
acted strange when they were planning funerals. He'd had women
pitch fits, fainting and frothing at the mouth; others laughed and
carried on like they were at a reception. It seemed as if so many
women in Limoges had lives with perforated tabs, like season
tickets. Married at seventeen, first baby at nineteen, second at
twenty, grandmother at forty, widow at sixty-two.

Cordy King, a twenty-year-old widow, had stood in his selection room and asked him if he cared to tie his handkerchief
around her middle. "Whatever for?" he'd asked, trying to be polite
and assuming she was touched in the head by her grief.

"I'm the only girl in Epiphany Parish who can tie a handkerchief around her waist."

Cab declined. Later, after Edith turned him away, he
thought about Cordy's figure and decided he'd been a fool. Why,
she'd practically rubbed herself in his face. He called her up,
inviting her to see *A Place in the Sun* at the Majestic. She
accepted eagerly, and all evening she rubbed her titties against
his arm. The next afternoon, they picnicked at the lake, and he
hoped Edith saw the spread Cordy had fixed—fried chicken,
pickled eggs, beaten biscuits, strawberries, and slaw that gave
him diarrhea.

Tonight she had invited him for supper, and he wanted to
look snazzy, like Cary Grant in *The Philadelphia Story*. He chose a
wheat-colored linen suit, burgundy bow tie, and a crisp white

shirt with his initials on the collar. He slapped Old Spice on his cheeks. Then he drove the hearse five blocks north to her house on Pine Street, a peach-colored shotgun with white shutters propped open with sticks. Her front yard was deeply shaded by pecans and live oaks, and the ground stayed littered with nuts. Cordy was waiting on the front porch, barefoot. When he walked toward the wooden steps, she ran down and grabbed his hand.

"What took you so long? I've been waiting and waiting."

"Didn't Twilly tell you I said five-thirty?" he said, starting to look at his watch, but she pulled him up the steps, into the house. Cordy was pretty, with dimples and dark, shoulder-length hair. Her lips always looked blurry, like she'd been kissing somebody too hard.

"Come on in," she said. "Keep me company while I finish cooking." As she bustled around the narrow kitchen, slicing tomatoes, she kept talking. "I've lived in nearly every state in the union," she said. "Go ahead, name a place."

"Texas?"

"Houston, third grade." She fanned the tomatoes on a white plate. "Name someplace else."

"Tennessee?"

"Johnson City, 1942. I spent one whole summer there. Go on, keep guessing."

"I believe you." He held up both hands. "I give up."

"I've lived in northern California, Texas, Montana, Wisconsin, Mississippi, Florida, Arizona, New Mexico, and Virginia."

"Because your husband was in the military?" Cab asked, trying to keep up with her. She talked fast, ending her sentences in questions, and she moved her hands the whole time, cutting her eyes, smiling up at him provocatively, which, he had to admit, was as sexy as Rita Hayworth's hoochie-coochie looks.

"Lord, no," she said, waving one hand. "My husband didn't have a thing to do with it. See, my daddy died young? And he left my mama with too much money? You know? So we just traveled. When I was real, real little we lived in Napa Valley—you know where that is?—and Mama would say, 'Children, go pick some grapes, and Mother will make us some wine.'" She held her hand five feet from the ground. "The grapes grew *this* big, just wild along the road. Oh, how we loved Napa. There was five of us kids, but I was the only girl. The baby of the family. They spoiled me rotten."

Cab nodded. He had never been to California, except for basic training, and that hardly counted. He eyed the woman and took a sip of Mogen David, which she had thoughtfully poured into a jelly glass. He had a dreadful feeling that he'd stepped into a rabbit hole, but it was a cute hole, just the same, and supper smelled so nice.

"Yeah, Daddy just left Mama a fortune." Cordy shook her head and picked up another tomato, peeling back the skin. "'Course I didn't get a drop. She drank it all up? Mama was an alcoholic, and you know how they go through money? I'd wake up in the morning, and there she'd be, sprawled out in the front yard? I'd have to go bring her inside."

"Passed out?" Cab, overwhelmed by pity, stepped toward the girl. He pictured her, all innocent and pig-tailed, dragging her mama inside, folding a damp washcloth over the woman's eyes. Bringing trays of dry toast and chicken soup. Sitting by the window, watching children walking to school, laughing and acting normal.

"Yeah. Drunk as a skunk. I always thought she was kind of jealous of me. 'Cause I was such a beautiful child? Actually, I was an *exotic* child? All my life men couldn't resist me. Even Mama's own boyfriends. Or should I say especially?"

Cab tilted the jelly glass, holding it up to the light, wishing she'd hush, but Cordy was still talking. "And *then*, when I was thirteen? One of Mama's boyfriends attacked me? I wasn't a virgin or anything, and it wasn't exactly an attack, but I still got pregnant. Mama got so mad, she kicked me out of the house. My brother took me in. He lived in Jacksonville, Florida?" While she talked, she peeled tomatoes, leaving red chunks in the bottom of the sink. "That's when I met Julian. We had us a fine old time until he got sent to Korea."

"What happened to the, you know, baby?" Cab drank the rest of his wine, then wiped his mouth with his fingers. The rabbit hole was getting darker.

"Enough about me," she said, turning around with a smile. "Tell me all about you."

He shrugged, looking into his glass. He had no desire to exchange biographies with this worldly woman. If he left now, he supposed it would seem rude. But as soon as they ate, as soon as he helped her clear the table, he would make his excuses. One way or another he would get the hell away from Pine Street. She lifted a pot lid, and he saw a thick, rose-colored sauce, with a ham bone jutting up.

"Your red beans sure smell good," he said.

"Learned how to make them in New Orleans, where I was a beauty operator? The secret's adding wine." She smiled, then picked up a pan and dumped rice into an orange Fiesta bowl. "I sure do miss it. Not the wine, I mean, but New Orleans." She pronounced it like a native—newORleeuns.

"Do you like pralines?" she asked suddenly. "I can make some that beat the pants off Fanny Farmer's. I sure hated to leave New Orleans, but this man fell in love with me? Lord, *I* don't know why. I didn't encourage him or nothing. I guess my beauty just bowled him over. He'd leave flowers on my front porch? A couple of times he stood in the street and shouted my name. Like to drove Julian crazy. That's one reason he enlisted, to get us out of New Orleans—"

"Wait a minute," Cab interrupted. "I'm confused. How'd you get to New Orleans? I thought you were in Jacksonville, Florida, with your brother."

"No, I *met* Julian in Florida. He was a drinking buddy of my brother's? But a man fell in love with me there, too, so we moved to New Orleans. *Then* Julian went in the army."

"Why enlist?" Cab looked over her shoulder, through the open screen door, staring longingly through it. "I mean, wouldn't it have been simpler to just move again?"

"Well, you know. Moving costs money, and Julian didn't have a job, exactly. One time we talked about me going into the movies. Like I told Julian, I was meant for greatness." She slit open a loaf of French bread. Then she rubbed her hands together and flashed a huge, dimpled smile. "Well, I guess we're ready to eat."

"Hey," he said gently. "Are you making this up?"

"No." She pointed to the food. "It's ready. It's cooked through and through."

"Actually, I meant all those stories. Were you telling the truth?"

"What do you think?" She grinned, wrinkling her nose, and stepped forward. "To be perfectly honest, I wish I *was* making it up. You know what else? You have the prettiest eyes."

"I do?" He walked backward until he banged against the counter.

"Want to make love to me right now?" She started unbuttoning her blouse.

"Maybe we ought to eat first?" He pointed over his shoulder to the counter—the red beans, plate of sliced tomatoes and deviled eggs.

"I been waiting and waiting for the right time. Don't you think this is it?" She pulled off her blouse, then unzipped her skirt and stepped out of it. She was wearing a lacy white slip, and her breasts were puffed up, like something slightly inflated. She took his hand and led him to the bedroom. When she sat down on the bed, she kissed his hand and said, "I been dying to see how you look naked."

She dropped his hand, then unbuckled his belt. He shucked off his trousers, loose change jingling in his pockets, and kicked them to the floor. She stood up on her knees and helped him peel off his jacket, then she unbuttoned his shirt, kissing his chest as she moved down the row. There was a moment when he feared he might not be aroused, and he thought, If I get out of this alive, I'll never ask for another blessed thing. Lord, I promise I'll settle down.

His penis curved up between his legs like a peeled cucumber. She slipped it inside her mouth, pushed back the foreskin, and sucked. Her cheeks dented, her teeth gently scraping the rim. He closed his eyes and sagged down on the bed. "Maybe I won't settle down, exactly," he thought. "Maybe I'll just float."

"I can taste you," she murmured, and pushed her lips down the shaft, the suction a bit stronger, which made him groan. He grasped her head, guiding it up and down. The back of her throat opened. He shut his eyes.

"Now put it inside me," she said.

Cab glanced behind him, trying to see where his clothes had fallen should he need to grab them and run. She pulled him toward her. They stretched out on the bed, looping their arms around each other. She made weak, cooing sounds. He felt her smooth shoulders, the rise of her buttocks. She was rounder, wider than Edith, yet shorter and firmer. But no, don't think of Edith now, think of Cordy, think of her dark, sweet hair, and her deep mouth. Think of her hands touching you there, kneading and pulling, the rhythm faster and faster.

Once, she banged her hip bone into his erection. "Oops," she said, reaching between his legs, cradling his testicles. "Did I hurt your gentiles?"

"You mean genitals, don't you?" he automatically corrected.

"What ever *this* is," she said, grabbing it. He drew in air, then slowly released it. *Genitals, Gentiles,* he thought. Whatever. He rolled on top of her, spreading apart her legs with his knees, and rubbed against her. She reached down, circled him with two fingers, and fit him inside her. She sighed and tightened her hands around his neck.

"There's just one little thing," she said into his ear.

"Mmmm?"

"You can't come inside me. Not even a drop."

"I've got safes." He drew back, staring down at her.

"It's not that." She averted her eyes. "I want you to come *on* me."

"What?"

"See, Julian used to pull out at the last minute and come on my stomach? Then he'd make me rub it, all over me, like this. Sometimes he'd massage it in, too." She demonstrated, rubbing her hands over her erect nipples, then dipping low, over her pubic mound, where they were still joined.

"He got to where he couldn't come any other way. He'd shoot it all over me, on my breasts and my neck, just all over me." She closed her eyes and arched her back. "Makes me go crazy just thinking about it."

Cab flopped back on the bed, his penis shrinking back into himself.

"What's the matter?" She sat up, pulling the covers around her. "What'd I say?"

"I just—"

"What? Tell me." She pinned him down, her hair swishing into his face.

"It's . . . I wish you hadn't brung up your husband."

"Why not?"

"Just wish you hadn't of." He patted her arm, remembering the pitiful funeral. They'd lowered his cheap veneer casket into the ground with just a handful of mourners, three beauticians and the Baptist minister, Reverend Kirby. "Why don't we get dressed and eat that fine supper you cooked, and then we'll just see what happens."

"No." Her lower lip jutted out. "I want something to happen now."

"I don't think it can." He glanced at his penis, which had all but disappeared. He didn't know it could *get* this small.

"I know what." She threw back the covers, walked naked to her bureau drawer, and pulled out a box. She flipped off the lid, lifted a handful of red fabric, then she crawled back in the bed. "Now close your eyes," she said.

"Okay." Cab leaned against the headboard. This was embarrassing. He felt her groping, her hands moving deftly over the floppy skin.

"You can look," she said. He opened his eyes. On his penis was a tiny suit of clothes, mouse-sized, a red shawl with a black sombrero.

"What's *this*?" he cried.

"Ain't it *cute*? I sew these for Christmas presents. In fact, one of these days I'll have my own store."

"Clothes for genitals?" Cab stared at his penis, horrified.

"Them too. See, I used to sew doll clothes for a living? And then I got this idea?" She snapped her fingers. "It came to me, just like that. I've got a whole drawerful of costumes. Doctor, lawyer, Indian chief, preacher. I may start sewing Bible clothes—a tiny Coat of Many Colors, a Pharaoh's suit. I even thought about doing Jesus. Last week I sewed a pirate. I fixed the outfit so it's one-eyed. Want to see?"

Cab shook his head. His eyes swept past her to the door. She laughed and flicked off the hat, squeezing his penis, causing the urethra to open. "Olé, baby!" she said. Then she threw back her head and laughed again. "Oh, that's so funny! You've got a Span- ish cock!"

"And what're you supposed to be?" He glared at her.

"A red-hot mama?" She giggled again, holding her hands over her mouth, causing her breasts to jiggle.

"Guess I am, I really am. Cause one time a man was two-tim- ing me? And you know what I did?"

"There's no telling."

"I waited till he fell asleep? Then I took his doohickey and opened up the pee hole. And then I dropped in a sewing needle." She flopped backward on the mattress, smiling. Cab reached between his legs and plucked off the sombrero and cape. His daddy always said that two things cannot occupy the same space at the same time. If your glass is filled with mop water, you must empty it before it can be filled with champagne. For a brief span of time, the glass is empty—seconds to hours.

Cab climbed out of the bed and gathered his clothes. *It's time for me to go thirsty,* he thought. *It's time to give up the widows.*

"What's wrong now?" she cried, scrambling to her knees. "I thought you'd get a kick out of it. I wouldn't drop nothing like that down you."

"You're too peculiar, Cordy," he said.

"I am not!" She jammed her hands on her hips. "You're just mad 'cause you can't get it up."

"I can't get it up because you kept talking about another man doing things with you!"

"You're jealous."

"No, but it's distracting. What if I talked about another woman?"

"Why don't you try? I'd probably like it."

"It's time for me to go."

"You're impotent!" she yelled, pronouncing it "em-PO-tent."

"The word is *im*potent," he said. He tucked in his shirt, buck- led his belt, and picked up his jacket, folding it over his arm.

"Well, whatever it is, that's what you are. You probably can't do it with a live woman," she said. "They probably got to be cold and blue. Laid out on a slab."

"Good night, Cordy." He turned into the hall, past the living room, which suddenly seemed overdone, crammed with paper roses, china figurines, and a Singer sewing machine with a basket of scraps. He opened the screen door and darted onto the porch. He heard her scurrying behind him. She came to the door, dragging the sheet, holding the pot of beans by the metal handle.

"You forgot your supper!" She heaved the pot. It crashed next to his heels, splattering beans like grenade fragments. They smattered against his suit, down the backside of his trousers, but he kept running. When he reached the hearse, he turned back.

"What's a matter?" she yelled from the edge of the porch. She was wild-eyed, the sheet draped around her waist, fixed as a Greek statue. "Don't tell me you want my recipe?"

"No, ma'am," Cab said, opening the hearse's door. "I don't want nothing from you."

"Impotent!" she hollered, waving her fists. Next door, the porch light switched on, and a face appeared behind the paper shade. "You ain't nothing but a impotent old scaredy cat!"

Cab slid into the car, switched on the engine, and backed out of the driveway, knocking over her metal trash cans. "This is it. I'm through with women," he said, turning the wheel, slinging the hearse onto Lincoln Avenue. "Through with the whole damn breed. They're all deranged."

Red Beans & Rice

From the kitchen of Cordy King, an old family recipe
- 2 cups red beans, washed and soaked overnight.

Next morning, drain beans. Chop 2 cups onions, 1 cup celery, 5 green onions (tops and bottoms), 1/2 cup chopped green pepper, 2 T minced garlic (1 jalapeño, seeded and chopped—optional), 3 T. minced, fresh parsley. Fry bacon in 2 T. olive oil. Remove bacon and add above ingredients. Sauté till done (onions will be clear). Add 1 T. flour while you are sautéeing for a little roux. When it's good and brown, add 2 qts. water, 1 cup red wine, and 1 large ham bone with meat on it. Salt and pepper to taste (I use 1 T. salt and 1/2 t. black pepper). Add 2 whole bay leaves, 1/8 t. cayenne, 1/2 t. sweet basil, 1/4 t. thyme. Cook 4 to 5 hours, stirring frequently (or beans will stick to bottom of pot). After three hours or so, add another cup of water (if beans have cooked down).

Serve over long-grain rice, with French bread and spinach salad. Rub salad bowl with garlic first.

What Men Really Want (I Think)

❧

A lady I know, Cordy King, said the way to a man's heart is through his stomach, but I don't think she understands anatomy. Just in case she's right, I've been bringing cakes to the drugstore. Henry's favorite is Florida Cake, a recipe from Cordy. All you do is beat together 1 box of yellow cake mix, 1 small box orange Jell-O, 4 eggs, 2/3 cup oil, and 2/3 cup water. Pour into a tube pan. Bake 1 hour at 350. Ice while warm with orange juice icing. Mix 2 cup sugar with 2 cup orange juice. Cook in pan 5 minutes. Pour over warm cake. Using a straw, punch holes in cake to let sauce go down. And then do the same to him.

—DeeDee Robichaux, talking to Tamera Mashburn in City Market, May 1, 1952

DeeDee Robichaux

Seems like I wasted every summer picking and canning. It was early for bush beans, but my aunt has a way with vegetables. She set them out early. When the temperature dropped, she made me and Billie put mason jars over each little plant. Also, the April rains helped. Me and Billie hunkered in the garden, squatting in the first row, spreading the stiff leaves and snapping off bean pods. The secret to good beans is picking them when they're tiny—that way you don't have to fool with strings. Aunt Butter crouched in the row, grunting to herself. The vines were full, like long green fingers. We would never get them all picked, much less canned. Weeds brushed against my knees, nettles and purple clover. Aunt Butter kept a messy garden, wouldn't take time to hoe, and I didn't have an instant to spare.

Billie's small hands fit deep within the bush. She was a fast picker. Our corn had tasseled but not silked, and it stood tall enough to cast shade. Kentucky wonders grew in a spiral vine around each stalk, and already they were packed with beans. The tomatoes were still knobby green—those we got in the ground too late. This whole garden was just now starting to come alive. A green bottle fly dove between us, and Billie caught it in midair. "Bugger!" she said and mashed it under her shoe.

"You're good at catching flies." I smiled.

"Yeah." She grinned. "Butter said it runs in the family."

"Well, she's wrong. I only caught June bugs." I scooted toward the next bush. Sometimes I felt like a June bug on a string, Henry's string, flying in circles.

We canned the beans in the pressure cooker, and the whole time Butter griped. "I don't see why we just can't water-bath them," she said, eyeing the rattling metal weight on the cooker. She was scared to death of steam, because she'd been burned too many times at her cafe. I'd bought the canner last week after Henry warned me about food poisoning. "Henry Nepper said this is safer," I told her. "He's a druggist, so he understands these things."

"I know what he is." Butter walked over to the sink to wash another set of quart jars. "And he ain't no county agent. Them's the ones who knows about canning."

"Do you want botulism?"

"I ain't never poisoned myself with anything I canned. Long as the lid's sucked down, the food's good."

"That's not what Henry Nepper said."

"Don't you Henry Nepper *me*! I been canning since before you was born."

"Beans don't have enough acid," I say patiently.

"Huh, you're just trying to be modern."

"Then you finish canning. I'm going to bed."

"No, you ain't!" She whirled around, her hands dripping suds on the linoleum, and gave me a pleading look. "Don't you leave me alone with this pressure cooker! It could blow up!"

"Then be nice to me." I sat down at the table and started writing out labels: *Beans—July 1952*. I add my initials, DDR. Any jar with Butter's handwriting on it I wouldn't touch. I didn't want to die young.

                              *   *   *

While the house slept around me, I made myself beautiful. I
washed my hair in lavender-scented water, then rolled it in old
socks. Henry said that lavender was nearly an antibiotic, good for
cuts and burns. It was also a soother for jangled nerves, but I'd be
scared to drink it. I touched up my nails with red polish, using
wads of cotton between each toe. While they dried, I hobbled into
the kitchen and ironed a pink-and-white striped dress, the one
with a huge white sailor collar that I got on sale at Hooper's. A
woman couldn't pamper herself too much. If you didn't, you'd
turn into Vangie Nepper.

The next morning, I splashed White Mink perfume on my
wrists, throat, and between my breasts. When I walked into the
drugstore, I made sure Henry saw me. There were no customers yet,
so I strolled past him, moving in a sweet cloud of scent, causing
Miss Byrd to wrinkle her nose and exclaim, "What's that odor?"

"It's not an odor, Miss Byrd," I said, rolling my eyes. "It's perfume."

"Whatever it is, smells like somebody got locked up in a New
Orleans whorehouse."

"That's right," I said. "Didn't you used to work in one?"

"Well, I never." Her cheeks reddened. "You know I've lived in
Limoges all my life."

"That doesn't mean you've never been to New Orleans. Anyway, how do you know what a whorehouse smells like?"

"I got a brain. I got imagination."

"Are you sure?" I smiled and lifted my newly plucked eyebrows. "Because if you had a brain, you'd take it out and play
with it."

Miss Byrd's mouth sagged open. I knew she hated my guts,
but I didn't care. I was used to women hating me. Miss Byrd was
nothing but a dried-up virgin. She was so far gone that even a
good screw wouldn't save her. I knew Henry was watching, so I
curtsied behind the counter, striking a sexy pose as I fit my purse
under the cash register. I leaned over in such a way that my hair
rippled down my back, tickling my shoulders. This I've practiced
in the mirror. Attracting a man is one thing; keeping his attention
is another. When I looked up, Henry was smiling. I thought to
myself, DeeDee Robichaux, today is your lucky day.

I just had a feeling, you know?

When Miss Byrd hurried off to the rest room (she always
waited till the last minute; one day she would burst), I darted over

to the cash register, opened my purse, and pulled out the bottle of White Mink. Then I turned over her stool and sprayed it good, misting the register, the floor, and even her balled-up handkerchief. A couple of customers started coughing and swiveled around on their stools to watch. When I finished, I slipped back to the soda counter, innocent as you please, and started slicing lemons.

Miss Byrd pushed open the stockroom door and marched down the aisle. She paused once, sniffing, and said, "Hmmmph!" When she got to the register, she positioned herself on the stool and frowned. Her nostrils twitched. She started to rise but was seized by a coughing fit. She reached for the hankie, clapping it over her mouth, and made a dry, gagging sound.

"Pew, White Mink! You did this, DeeDee Robichaux! I know you did!" Tears poured from her eyes.

"Excuse me?" I said. The customers turned around and gaped, startled at her outburst. Normally she sat on her stool like a parakeet, snapping up money like it was birdseed. Now she flew down the aisle and hopped up the rickety steps into Henry's perch. She whispered furiously, pointing at me. Henry talked in soothing tones, gesturing with his right hand, but I was too far away to hear. When Miss Byrd came out, she gave me the evil eye, clasping Henry's hankie over her nose and mouth.

That whole morning, I went out of my way to brush close to Henry, leaning forward so that my cleavage showed. I stared at Henry like I wanted to say something, but I let my eyes speak for me. Twice he spilled a bottle of tablets, the pills pattering to the tile floor, rolling under the high wooden shelves. He only did that when he was real nervous.

By midafternoon, after the lunch crowd had peaked, he cornered me in the stockroom. "You look so pretty today," he said, pulling up my dress, sending up waves of White Mink. He touched my crotch, feeling the rim of my panties. I sighed and groped him, feeling him stiffen. That condition, male rigidity, never failed to arouse me. All I had to do was see one poking up, and I was ready to sit on it. I was a virgin when Renny married me, and he had to use Vaseline on me and him both. It hurt so bad, I walked gap-legged for a month. When he'd do it to me, I'd grit my teeth and squeeze the pillowcase to keep from screaming. After I got pregnant with Billie, my body softened up. I found myself enjoying the feel of Renny inside me, the whole smooth length of him plunging and plunging. I would lift my buttocks, and he'd fit his hands beneath me, pulling me tight against him. "What's got into you?" he said in my ear. "Besides a baby, I mean."

"You," I told him. "You, Renny." He laughed and said, "You've turned into a fiend, woman." And it was true. I lived for nights. He showed me a ticklish place between my legs called a button, and he rubbed his mouth over it. Then he gently sucked. I nearly sprang off the bed. My back arched. I grabbed his head and pushed it against me. "Oh," I said. "Oh!"

Now that was gone forever. We couldn't even dry-hump. You can't do much of anything when you're paralyzed from the waist down. Sometimes I thought I was seeing Henry just for the sake of my little button, and other times I thought it was love. He looked so handsome in his white smock, almost like a doctor. My mama would've been proud.

Now I squirmed away. "I don't know about this." I pushed the heel of my hand against him. "What if somebody walks in?"

"I'll lock the door." He disappeared around a corner, and I heard the bolt slide. He'd installed it right after his daughter went into a coma. I closed my eyes, took three deep breaths. I was just too easy for him, no challenge at all. If he ever got tired of me, I'd be out of both a lover and a job. When he returned, he lifted my dress and peeled down my panties. His hands moved over my bare hips.

"It won't take long," he said into my hair. "I'll be quick."

I'll bet, I thought, but I pulled away, drawing up my panties. Henry was not the world's best lover. He shot off like a rabbit. (But he could hop many times in a single night. Everything in life was a trade-off, one way or another.) No matter how passionate he'd been, after the moment of orgasm, he'd get real disinterested in me. It was almost like he suffered from split personality. I touched my lips to his ear and whispered, "Not here. My dress'll get dirty."

"I'll buy you a new one, baby. Or we can do it standing up."

"Let me kiss you a minute. Oh, I've missed you so much, Henry."

"You were just with me last night." He chuckled and pulled me against him. I ran my tongue over his lips, then fastened my mouth over his, tasting tobacco and the faint sweetness of root beer. I wrapped my arms around his neck and kissed him deeply, the way Renny used to like it, rubbing my breasts against his chest, grinding my hips into his groin. I caressed, mashed, and teased until every cell in my body drummed electricity. His peter poked into my stomach. I pictured it straining against layers of cloth. I wasn't a bit surprised when he reached to unbuckle his belt.

"No." I pushed his hand away from his zipper. "Not here."

"You let me before. And I'm about to go in my pants."

"Then go, darling." I raised his smock and slid my fingers over his stomach, down to his half-open zipper. His underwear was visible, red plaid, and through the slit in the fabric, his peter poked out, surrounded by a nest of curly hair. I pressed my hand against him, moving back and forth. A tiny spot of moisture bloomed on the red plaid. I moved my hand faster, my palm scraping against the material. His hips rotated, dipping toward me.

"Just let me—"

"Not *here*."

"Then where?"

"A bed, Henry. A real bed. Do you know we've never done it in one?"

"What about the Bayou Motor Court?"

"Oh, that wasn't a real bed."

"I'll buy you a whole furniture store if you let me do it now."

I shook my head.

"What, are you having your monthly?"

"No. It just makes me feel, well . . . dirty."

"Darlin', it *is* dirty." He stuck his hand inside my panties. "That's why it's fun."

"Stop, I mean it."

"You're being a cocktease." He put his hands under my armpits, then picked me up and held me against the wall. He rotated his pelvis against me, bruising my hip bone. A line of perspiration trickled along his neck, curving behind his smock. He breathed hard into my ear, dampening my hair. Almost without thinking, I tilted my hips forward, jerked back, then dipped forward again. I felt powerful—as if I could make him leap through fire hoops.

"I want to feel you inside me, Henry. So bad. It's just . . . we can't do it here. But when we do, I'll show you things that you can't imagine."

"What things?" His eyes were pinched shut, the lids thick and freckled.

"Just your basic . . . " I pressed my lips into his ear and whispered a bad word.

"What?" Henry said. One eye peeped open.

"You heard me."

"I can't believe you said that." He blinked. "But say it again. In my ear. Come on, say it again."

Well, I did. The word hissed between my teeth. I was close to giving in, letting him take me on the dusty floor. That was the story of my life: I made these traps and then got caught myself. His hips battered against me. Above my head, the windowpanes rattled. Just as I started to feel a tingle, he groaned. His eyelids fluttered. Then he slouched against me, his chin resting on my shoulder, then he slid down my front, dropping to his knees.

"Are you all right, Henry?" I reached down and shook his shoulder.

"Whew!" He gasped for air. After a moment, he said, "I swear . . . I haven't done . . . this in . . . years."

He laid one hand over his heart, and the other dropped to his crotch, lifting his smock. A puddle of sticky ooze had leaked through his trousers. "I creamed . . . my . . . pants," he wheezed.

"You certainly *did.*" Even though I was repulsed, I was also a little tempted to push my panties aside and sit on him, wiggling until I got my own release, but I knew I had to stay in control. I slapped my dress, brushing lint and dust from the hem, then walked over to the far shelf, cool as you please, and picked out a tube of Cara Nome lipstick. "Can I borrow this?" I asked him. "Just to freshen up?"

"Honey, you can have the whole damn store." He waved one hand. "You can have anything you want, baby."

"Then take me someplace romantic, Henry. Like New Orleans or Florida. Just the two of us."

He gave me a blank stare. He looked like a man sitting on a low toilet, with his trousers heaped around his hips, part of his round, hairy stomach showing. This startled me. In my mind, even when he was naked, he always wore a starched white smock with silver snaps down the neck. You might say he was a vision in white, somebody I couldn't help but look up to. Now, with his pants in a wad, I wondered how I'd ever put him on a pedestal. I wanted him to pull up his trousers and turn back into Henry, a registered druggist.

"The two of us?" he said.

"Who else? Listen, I'll even go to Shreveport."

"Sure, baby." Henry smiled, his lips barely curving.

"I mean it. Let's go somewhere, you and me. You can tell your wife that you're going on a hunting trip. She'll believe you."

"Far as I know, no hunting season's open. And I can't possibly get away just now."

"Why not?"

"Well, for one thing, my daughter's in a coma. And another, I've got a store to run." He got up from the floor and stared down at his trousers, pulling the damp spot away from his skin. "I can't just take off. I *am* a married man. And you've got a family, too."

"Not much of one."

"You've got little Billie."

I frowned, feeling my forehead crease, but I quickly smoothed it out. I had no intention of letting myself get premature wrinkles. And I wouldn't let him hold my family over my head. I knew we were married to other people. I didn't need *National Geographic* for that. A sucking silence filled the stockroom. My eyes smarted. Now that he'd put himself back together, he was turning into the old Henry, the one who called the shots. The one who gave me sulfur when my pee started to burn. "Too much loving," he would say. "You don't need to see Dr. LeGette. Hell, I *know* what the matter is. Honey, I've rubbed you raw."

After a minute, I saw that he wasn't going to take me on any trip. He wasn't even going to try and sweet-talk me.

"Now I've got to run home and change pants," he said. "I'll just sneak out the back door. You'll cover for me, won't you?"

"By all means, Henry." My voice was cold. "Keep using back doors and backseats, sneaking through life."

"Oh, sugar. Come on. I can't help this." He pointed to his damp spot. "It looks like I've peed in my pants."

"Maybe you did!" I stomped over to the bathroom and flung open the door.

"Oh, don't be silly. You saw how bad I wanted you. And I want you all the time."

"How, Henry? Sunny-side up or over easy? In your station wagon? Under the lunch counter? We haven't tried that yet."

"We can do that tonight." He grinned. "Want to?"

"Find yourself another girl. This one's tired of being used."

"Used?" He laughed a choppy laugh. "Hell, baby, I want you."

"You've got you now. You don't need me."

"Baby, you're just upset."

"Upset?" I rolled my eyes. "Look, either you take me someplace fancy, a motel with a bed, or I'm quitting both you and the store."

"Don't say that. Don't even think it."

"I might have been silly to suggest someplace far away, like Florida, but I wouldn't sneeze at Vicksburg. I'd go there. I'd go to Tallulah if you were with me. Can't you take off one little day and night, Henry? Can't you? Will the world end if you do?"

He just stared like the thought had never entered his mind. Probably it hadn't.

"Do you realize we've never spent one whole night together? Surely you can think up something. If *I* can get away, it should be easy as pie for you. And Henry, I'll do things to you that'll make you think you've died and gone to heaven."

"But I can't leave." He swallowed, and his eyes switched back and forth. I stepped inside the bathroom and slammed the door.

"DeeDee?" he called out. "What things would you do?"

I smiled to myself but didn't answer. After a minute, I heard him mutter, "Women." Then his footsteps creaked over the wooden floor. The back door squeaked open, and I imagined the flash of hot sun. The door clicked shut and his wing tip shoes scuffed down the concrete steps. A few seconds later his engine sputtered, and his car rumbled out of the alley.

I stood on my tiptoes and looked into the mirror, smearing lipstick over my cheeks and mouth. Now it was time to scare him, to drop out of sight. If I knew Henry Nepper, he'd seek me out, promise me the moon, and talk me into having regular sexual intercourse with him. Another stolen evening in the locked stockroom, on the hard, dusty floor. Somehow I was the only one who got screwed. I supposed it was better than driving to Tallulah, waiting for some other married man. I stepped out of the bathroom and walked into the outer store, ignoring the customers at the lunch counter. I yanked my purse from beneath the cash register and tucked it under my arm.

"I'm feeling sick, Miss Byrd," I said. "I'm going home."

"You don't look it." She wiped her nose with the hankie.

"Well, I am."

"Does Mr. Henry know?" She pushed up her glasses, then leaned back to stare.

"No, but I'm sure you'll tell him."

"He'll be riled." She pointed to the lunch counter, where several children were twirling on their stools. "Who'll cook?"

"I guess you will."

"That's not my job," she snapped. "It's yours."

"Then close it down. I can't help being sick." I turned and walked back to the stockroom. When I stepped outside, the air revived me. It smelled of popcorn from the Majestic. My old Nash looked like a rolled-up doodlebug; one day I'd have a Cadillac. The key to a man was making him crave you. If Henry called, I would let him sleep with me, but I would dole myself out like candy, one piece at a time.

Scenes from a Belfry:

The Bell Tolls for Olive Nepper

❧

I like to see how far I can go. The innocence (and ignorance) of my fellow Limogeans never ceases to amaze me. They're all too ready to gossip, these good Christians, but sinners are too busy having fun to meddle in others' lives. Which makes me wonder if the Bible is mostly wishful thinking written by people who were trying to pass off their failings as virtues. Maybe the poor in spirit will stay poor. Maybe the meek won't inherit shit.

—Reverend T. C. Kirby, private counseling session with Cordy King, May 1952

Wednesday morning, and the sky was dark and grainy, with a strong southern wind. The radio said a low-pressure system was hovering over the Gulf of Mexico, sweeping moist air into the delta. Shortly after breakfast it started raining. All over town, people were caught in the downpour. The Marshall sisters were in the cemetery setting out white irises. Vangie Nepper was in her garden, dusting her cabbages. Harriet Hooper was swinging in her hammock, spying on Vangie. Dr. LeGette got soaked while running across Delphinium Street, hurrying to deliver Tamera Mashburn's latest baby.

All day the rain beat against the flat hospital roof, gathering in clear circles. It was an old roof, but everything in Limoges was old. By noon the largest puddle broke through, splattering through the ceiling just outside Olive Nepper's room. Nurse Abigail Potter strutted down the hall, her arms loaded with soiled linen. As she turned a corner, her shoes skidded over the wet tile.

Still clutching the linen, she fell with a sickening thud on her elbow. She heard her collarbone snap out of the socket. For a second she seemed to taste the pain—a kind of sweet metallic flavor. She had no time for dislocations.

"Shit!" she cried, then looked furtively around to see if anyone had heard. The hall was clear in both directions. She was a nurse, an example to the community. Hoisting herself to her feet, she lurched down the corridor, cradling her injured arm. She collapsed in a swivel chair and told Nurse Clayton to page Dr. LeGette.

"Who needs him?" Nurse Clayton asked, reaching for the phone.

"Christ, I'll do it myself." With her good arm, she shoved Nurse Clayton out of the way. She paged the doctor; then she sent housekeeping with a mop and bucket. "Outside Olive Nepper's room," she said. "We've got trouble."

By late afternoon the rain washed down hard, splattering against the sidewalk; it collected on the roof and sifted through the ceiling. Each drop rang down into the enamel pail. Nurse Potter and Nurse Clayton trudged down the hall, circled the pail, and opened the door to the Nepper girl's room. Nurse Potter wore a sling; she'd refused to clock out. "A wounded nurse is still a nurse," she'd told Dr. LeGette. "My mind's still good. I can take orders."

Now she prepared to take vital signs. She wrapped the blood-pressure cuff around Olive's arm and inflated the rubber bulb. "Christ," she thought. "I wish *I* had these skinny bird arms." Then she looked down at the girl's protruding abdomen. To Nurse Potter, pregnancy was no different from being eaten alive by parasites. The fetus was a blood-sucking leech. She wouldn't get pregnant if you paid her a million dollars. She remembered her days on the maternity ward at Baptist Hospital in New Orleans, watching women grunt out slick, wet screaming creatures. Why, getting born was not much different from pulling your upper lip over your head. No, you couldn't *pay* her.

From her hospital bed, Olive Nepper watched full-grown pigeons fly around the room. They were all white, with tiny human faces. Sometimes they swooped low, their wings rolling her sideways. She felt ice-cold claws probing private places. She wished they'd fly out the door, into the green-tiled hall, where they perched with other birds along a low counter. Today, though, they were arguing, which amazed Olive; she had no idea she could understand bird language.

"She's wasting away."

"Skin and bones."

"Except for that belly."

"I'll bet some hot-rod teenage boy did it."

"In Limoges? You can count them on one hand. And they're all Methodists."

"It could've been an out-of-towner."

"She'll never tell. She's in this coma forever."

"When I was a student, I had a man-patient in a coma."

"So did I."

"Did his tallywacker stay hard?"

"I don't remember."

"Well, I do. That poor man just kept an erection."

"Bet you fanned the sheets constantly."

"I did not."

"Bet you sat on it."

"I'd never!"

"Well, *I* would have."

While they endlessly speculated, Olive's little finger twitched. She opened her eyes, saw potted tulips and hyacinths in front of wet, blue windowpanes. "Mama?" she said, but the birds were already walking into the green hall, their voices hanging in the air.

Around three o'clock the rain stopped suddenly. Two pigeons flew toward the First Baptist steeple, fluttering against the screen mesh, confused by the new barrier. One arch was only partially sealed—nailed at the top, with the bottom half lifting in the wind. A strong gust blew the screen above the arch, where it briefly hung. The pigeons flapped inside, hovering around the bell, rain spraying from their feathers. They drifted to the crossbar, then twisted their heads, working their beaks through the feathers. Outside, the rain began falling again. A car swept down the street, tires splashing, and turned right on Washington Avenue.

At the bottom of the long, twisty staircase, a door creaked open, flooding the lower steps with yellow light. A hooded figure climbed the stairs, each riser creaking. Behind him a woman with bushy black hair looked up at him. "Brother Kirby?" she called up. "I locked all the doors, like you said, but—"

"Then join me," said Reverend Kirby. He stood on the wooden platform and looked down the stairwell—a sinister figure in his black rain slicker. He raised his arms like a giant bat, the black plastic fanned out. Above him the pigeons danced on the crossbar, excited by the voices.

"*Please* don't make me come up there!"

"But Sister Cordy, you must face up to your fears."

"Can't I face up to them when it's not raining?"

"It won't count."

"Who cares?" She put her foot on the first step, testing it.

"Look, I thought you wanted to come up here," he yelled.

"I didn't mean literally." She took another step. "And don't you have to preach tonight?"

"I've got the Wednesday supper to lord over, too." He threw his head back and laughed. "The worst damn food in town! Stringy roast beef, frozen peas, gummy rice, grocery-store rolls."

"Hey, I cooked them roasts. They're *not* stringy."

"They're tough as Satan's ass. Now get yours up here. We're running out of time."

"Not unless you take it back about my roasts."

"I was just kidding, darlin'. You know I was." He held out both arms and smiled. She was the only woman in Limoges, perhaps even all of Louisiana, who understood him. If they weren't so much alike, he might have considered marriage. Below, her footsteps were light, like mouse scratchings; she paused at the landing. Then she walked up to him, pressing her blue dress against the black slicker. She tasted of fruit punch and cigarettes. The first time they were together (in the biblical sense), he'd sucked hard on her neck, feeling the thin tissue swell between his teeth. She had lifted his shirt and raked her fingernails across his back. They were in a frenzy; he couldn't distinguish pain from pleasure. When he pulled away, he had been surprised at the marks they'd inflicted on each other. It struck him that love and violence were not so different.

Now she gave him a skeptical look. "What's so special about the belfry?" she asked.

"It's the best view in town. It just gets my pulse going. You know, doing it up here, above the whole town. It reminds me of Moses going up the mountain and coming back with them tablets? Only God knows what he really did up there."

"Probably he was mopping up bird shit." She pointed to the floor.

"No, I'll bet he had a party with them Sodom and Gommorhians."

"Moses?" Cordy shook her head. "He don't seem the type. I mean, he looks so *old* in that Charleston Heston movie. Anyway, didn't Moses live about six hundred years before Sodom and Gomorrah was even a city?"

"Where'd you hear that?"

"Right here." She pointed to the floor. "In Sunday school. Dr. LeGette was teaching."

"Time is timeless in the Bible, Sister Cordy. It's not chronolog-ical. It all runs together."

"I just think you like taking risks." She licked his neck. He tilted his head so she could reach a crevice. "You know what I like about you? You're not some holier-than-thou man. You're real."

"I'm also a gentleman." He pulled off the slicker and wrapped it around her. "So you won't catch your death of cold. When you get naked, that is."

"Well, now that I'm here, I might as well." She unwrapped the slicker and handed it to him. He spread it on the platform, blot-ting out feathers and bird droppings. Then he undressed and lay down on the cold black plastic. Wind rushed into the bell tower, flowing over his erection, making it bob slightly. He seemed to lie there forever, waiting for her to unfasten her brassiere, then step out of her panties. She stood above him, naked except for white shoes with big blue buckles.

"Want me to get on bottom?" she suggested.

"No, that's all right. I will." He glanced up at the pigeons, remembering his ruined wool sweater, cherry red, a personal favorite. He'd never laid a hand on Olive Nepper except her sex parts (did breasts count? he wondered). He'd meant her no harm. Even if she hadn't met him, hadn't swallowed the poison, she would still be in trouble. The girl was traveling down a one-way road, Unwed Mother's Lane. If it hadn't been him, it would've been someone else. Therefore, it was not his fault.

"Can we play choo-choo?" Cordy said.

"Climb aboard," he said, but she was looking up into the tower. She grabbed the rope and pulled hard. The bell swung 180 degrees, hung upside down, then started falling. The pigeons flew straight up, beating against the slanted ceiling.

"Don't!" he shouted, but she was already swept into the air, yanked upward by the rope. She wiggled like a minnow. Her mouth dropped open, but he couldn't hear her scream over the bell. Feathers drifted down. Kirby wondered if insanity was like this—no room for thoughts, just noise. A pigeon flew over Cordy's head, a blur of brown feathers. She let go of the rope and fell, crashing to the landing. For a second she didn't move, then she sat up and looked at Kirby. "I'm getting the hell out of here!" she cried, then snatched her dress and ran down the stairs.

Kirby glanced up. Something splattered into his face. *If thy right eye offends thee, pluck it out.* "Damn vultures!" Shaking his fist at the birds, he walked over to the archway, lifting one edge of the mesh. Down the street at First Methodist, cars were gathering, their windshield wipers snapping back and forth. "Leave it to the Methodists to be punctual," Reverend Kirby thought. "But when they get old, they become obsessed with bowel movements."

He glanced up, and another splat hit the side of his face, spreading into his sideburn. Above his head the bell kept pealing, *Come all, Come wor-ship.* It rang out two flat notes, over and over, joined by gongs from other churches. The noise swept all the way to the end of Geranium Street, leaping over houses to Delphinium.

In Parish Hospital Olive heard the bell and dreamed she was walking to church. In her mind's eye the rain had stopped, replaced by glaring sunshine. The church's roof was black and slick. Water dripped from the eaves, onto dogwood trees and crepe myrtle. In the tower, Reverend Kirby was backlit by sun and pigeons. The birds flew out of the belfry, fluttering down to the lawn. As Olive walked toward them, they lifted into the sky. She hurried down the wet sidewalk, walking toward Reverend Kirby, her feet skimming over the pavement as if she were walking on water.

Naked Truths

❧

If I had a man like Henry, I'd drain him on a regular basis. If he told me he had a Chamber of Commerce meeting at seven P.M. on a Sunday night, you know what I'd do? I'd corner him in the bedroom at six. If he was meeting a lady, he'd be a little mellow. The edge would be gone. That's the secret of faithful love—you just fuck the hell out of him. If he still fools around, then at least you've had first servings.

—DeeDee Robichaux, visiting Tamera Mashburn and her infant son, Parish Hospital, May 15, 1952

Vangie Nepper

Right after Easter, Henry got the flu. He stayed home one solid weekend. Then I came down with it. Spent four days flat on my back, too weak to lift my head. I worried and worried about Olive, but Edith took my place. She also brought soup and tried to spoon it down my throat. Then I slept, having one feverish dream after the other. Time slipped from my hands like shelled peas, skipping on the rag rug, vanishing into crevices.

On the fifth day I was well enough to watch TV in the living room. I kept glancing out the double windows, watching a young squirrel climb up and down a bird feeder in the front yard. The lawn stopped at Cypress Street, and beyond the lake was ringed in cypress, the water shimmering. An aluminum boat sputtered across the lake, flashing sun. A mallard and her babies floated as if stuck to the water. It was hard to believe they were alive. They looked plastic.

Piled up around me were gardening books, and I didn't even remember pulling them from the shelves. All I could think of was death, planting people in the ground like tulip bulbs. Just last night I dreamed about my mother's funeral, and I woke up crying my eyes out. "Henry," I said, shaking his arm. "Henry, tell me it's not true."

"What's not true?" He opened one eye and stared.

"Mother," I stammered. "I dreamed she died, but I know she's still alive. Isn't she?"

"Oh, for heaven's sake." He scooted toward the edge of the mattress, saying, "She's been gone five years, Vangie. What's the matter with you? Go back to sleep. I've got to get up early in the morning."

I lay there viewing baby pictures in my mind. Giving Olive a bath, how slick and cold she felt when I'd lift her from the pink tub. I remembered going to the lake with Henry, where I sat pregnant, brownish green water lapping against my knees, while the baby rolled inside me. From the banks, cicadas buzzed like carbonation. We were so young and so full of hope for our baby. We'd always planned to have another, but Henry caught mumps from Olive when she was two. His scrotum swelled up like two pink grapefruits. I had to gently prop them up on feather pillows. He would never admit that his sperm was cooked—he always kindly acted like it was my fault.

Olive was a blond, big-eyed baby. She'd run around the house without a diaper. "Where's Olive?" I'd say, clapping my hands, and she'd race down the hall, laughing and squealing. I'd pick her up, wrapping a towel around her, and she'd rub her face on my collar. It seemed as if I'd spent years raising and lowering that child, only to have it come to this: coma, oxygen, a cold green room. If only I hadn't bought that rose poison. If only I had baked cookies that day—I would have been right there when she walked into the kitchen.

If only I hadn't planted hybrids back in 1937. I used to be an expert. People used to call me before they called the agricultural agent. I could tell you the best way to prepare the soil, with rotted manure and a splash of lime and ashes. And I told many a person that the best roses for cemeteries were *R. hugonis*, Gruss an Teplitz, hybrid perpetuals, and polyanthas—they more or less take care of themselves.

I'd noticed how Henry left early for his store and came home after dark; his store closes at five o'clock, and it didn't get dark here till seven-thirty or so. Before the flu I'd always left a plate of food, sealed in tinfoil, on the table, framed by flatware. Then I'd walk to the hospital. My whole married life I'd had supper on the table at five-thirty, but Henry hadn't eaten with me in weeks. Once a week I fell asleep on the sofa watching Milton Berle, and he was my favorite. I knew this wasn't natural. And I knew Henry was somehow at the root of my fatigue. I'd worn myself out missing him.

"Where do you go, Henry?" I asked him. "Why aren't you ever home?"

"Playing golf," he explained. "Just driving around the parish."

"Maybe I could use a drive, too," I said, but Henry just laughed. Opened the newspaper and held it in front of his face.

"You hate the country, and you know it."

"That's not *true*. Why are you always saying I hate things when I don't?" I shook my head. "Don't you forget I grew up on a cotton farm."

"Vangie, that's not something you'll ever let me forget."

Some things I myself can't forget—like that poison pen letter. Henry called it a pack of lies. "Somebody is just trying to get your goat," he told me. "They're just pointing out how you've let things go."

"Have I?" My forehead wrinkled. I stuck my fingers through my braids.

"Yes, you have," Henry said. "But that's all right. I can tolerate anything as long as it's temporary. I'm a very understanding man."

Marriages aren't too different from gardens. They fall into ruts. You must endure dry spells. And under certain conditions, they run amok. Your tractor might get a flat tire. You have to tie up your tomatoes. My mother always used old stockings, but I suppose anything will do. Gardening, cooking, love—it's all the same. Ignore your squash, and they'll rot on the vine. Leave out the egg whites, and your soufflé won't rise. Plant the same old crops, and some woman will show your husband her cantaloupes.

My own mama stood back and shut her eyes all those years ago when Daddy was running with women. Those nights he was gone, Mama acted like he wasn't doing anything more than playing poker. "A man's got to have his diversions," she'd say. The glow of my own marriage was awful dim, but Henry took good care of me. I really couldn't complain. He was just distracted by Olive's coma—grieving in his own manly way.

I rested my chin on my fists and glanced at the clock. In this house time got lost quicker than I could say Jack Sprat. It seemed to me that all days were alike: The sun came up pink, fell down in flames, and in between I waited for the people I loved. I waited for Olive to wake up, for Henry to come home. Meanwhile, I looked at seed catalogues and planned gardens of the future. It kept my mind from wandering, which was a family trait.

I lifted one foot and jiggled the pink terrycloth slipper, then I looked down at my dress, a yellow-sprigged housecoat that fell below my knees, a gift from Henry and Olive last Mother's Day. Olive picked it out herself at Hooper's. Wouldn't let Henry go shopping with her. "All your clothes are so stiff and formal, Mama," she said. "You need something loose and casual."

"But I *like* stiff and formal," I told her. (I didn't really. I preferred ruffles like General Eisenhower's wife.) Olive and Henry laughed, but I swallowed hard, struggling not to cry over something this silly.

"It flatters you, Mama," Olive said sweetly. "You look ten pounds lighter."

"Take it back and swap it," said Henry, lighting a cigarette. "No need to get all emotional."

"No, I'll . . . keep it," I said. I was so disappointed; it looked like something an old woman would wear. Now I wore the dress at night; the fabric was a comfort against my skin, soft and airy, and I was sorry I had made such a fuss. I glanced back at the lake, watching the mama duck rise from the water, shaking her feathers, then folding each wing back in place. Each baby copied her, and one turned itself completely over in the water. It was so cute I could cry.

I had a queer, itchy feeling at the base of my neck, the sensation that someone was watching me. I glanced up, and sure enough, it was Henry, standing in the doorway, pressing one hand against the frame. He was frowning, his forehead puckered, and his smock was draped in front of him.

"Goodness, you startled me!" I said.

"I'm sorry, Vangie. You busy? I thought you could fix me a bite to eat." He grinned, spreading his hands. "If you're well enough that is."

"Is it dinnertime already?"

"Well, I thought we'd eat together because I won't be home for supper tonight."

"Oh, Henry. Not again." I gripped the sides of the couch and stood up. "Where're you going? You haven't sat a single evening with Olive."

"I have too."

"When?"

"It's not my fault that I've got a store to run. That I've got inventory to count. Have you any idea how tedious this is for a druggist? Counting millions of pills?"

"Inventory? But I thought you did that once a year, like in January."

"I like to keep on top of things."

"Do you need me to help?"

"No, that's all right." He scratched his scalp, then examined his fingernails. "Don't wait up on me, now. You go on to bed. I'm apt to be late."

After he walked away, I remembered when he was a handsome pharmacy student, and how much I loved him. I am not bragging to say that I never worked a day in my life except to can fruits and vegetables, sew a suit of clothes, diaper my baby, knit afghans, raise prize-winning roses, and give garden talks at the home demonstration club. Now, you can call that what you want, but that's work.

"Vangie?" hollered Henry. "Were you going to fix me a bite?"

By the next week I felt strong enough to work in my garden. In another week, especially if it rained, the dandelions would take over. Sometimes I wished I had a yard like Harriet's—nothing but bushes and grass, a clean-swept patio with metal loveseats. I walked into the hall, past my daughter's blue room, where Sophie was pushing open the windows. The flesh on her arms was firm and smooth, as if packed tightly into the skin. The gauzy white curtains rippled against the screens. On the dresser was Olive's Bible, Girl Scout badges, and an empty milk-glass vase. A basket of marbles, a bone-china cat (because she's allergic to real ones), and the broken snow dome. I couldn't throw it away even though the water had leaked out. Before she went on that youth trip to Lookout Mountain, she practiced her solo, "Softly and Tenderly." Seemed like I could almost hear her sweet little voice.

As I walked down the hall, the hymn welled up in my throat. I headed into the backyard and arranged myself in front of the rose beds. The floribundas seemed saddest, full of leaf hoppers and dandelions. I yanked up a weed, soil clinging to the roots like coffee grounds. The curtains in Olive's window waved back and forth, and beyond them Sophie stripped the bed, fresh linen billowing over the mattress. She was singing my and Olive's hymn, like it was catching. Her voice was sweet and young-sounding. "*Softly and tenderly Jesus is calling/Calling for you and for me.*" I hummed along with her, working my way down the row, the sun beating into my back. We sang together, "*Shadows are gathering/Death beds are coming/Coming for you and for me.*"

I concentrated on one weed at a time. My mama used to say the best way to teach a child about life is to let her have a garden. Let her plant seeds and wait for them to sprout—a teepee of bean vines, pumpkins to sell at Halloween. Squash, tomatoes, corn, peppers. Some seeds are sterile or just too weak and get squeezed out by bigger leaves. Some plants take sick and die on you; others live to be ripe and old. And the child learns what needs coddling and what can thrive on neglect. I tried to do that with my Olive, but it's hard to say whether the lesson took. From the looks of things, I'd have to say no.

* * *

The sun worked its way across the sky. I was barely over the flu, and sweat dripped into my eyes. Still, I felt strong. I scooted down the row, leaving clumps of pulled dandelions, the roots dangling like white thread. By the time Sophie came out of the house, her pocketbook slung over her arm, it was almost evening.

"I ain't near finished in her room," she said. "I got to cleaning her closet, and I just piled everything to one side. I'll have to do it next time."

I stood up, reached in my pocket and fished out a handful of dollars.

"Oh, I can't take that." She pushed my hand away. "This is my gift to Olive."

"Don't be silly. Here." I held out the money. "Your time isn't free."

"But my gift is. And you got to let me give it."

She was a proud woman, kind and strong, and I saw that she would be hurt if I made her take the money. "Thank you, Sophie," I said and stuffed the bills into my pocket.

"See you, Miss Vangie." She waved and turned toward the street. She had a prematurely aged walk, swaying from side to side. I glanced back at my flower beds. Another day of weeding, and I'd be done. I walked to the house, stripping off my canvas gloves. The afternoon light turned my kitchen deep pink. Even the air had a rosy tinge. The stainless steel toaster gleamed. Sophie had gone over everything, leaving the room spotless. There was even a fresh three-layer hot-milk cake on the counter, with coconut icing.

I stepped into the bathroom, pushing back the plastic curtain that was decorated with pink and black seashells, and drew up hot, sudsy water. Steam rose toward the frosted-glass window. I stripped off my dusty clothes, then eased down into the tub, grimacing at the heat. My legs blushed scarlet. On the opposite wall Henry's toiletries were arranged on the glass shelf—razor, shaving mug, hair tonic, Old Spice. A green stick of Mennen deodorant. Another shelf was decorated with lipsticks, dozens of gold and silver tubes. Steam wafted up, fogging the mirror. An idea gradually came to me, a notion to fix my face, dab perfume behind my ears, and walk over to Henry's store. I'd help him count penicillin tablets, working side-by-side with Miss Byrd and DeeDee Robichaux. I thought of Billie—not too long ago I thought I saw her and her mother at the hospital, but they darted around a corner before I could speak.

Tonight, if I saw DeeDee, I would ask about the child. She had worked so hard for her Easter money, then she never came back. I'd tell her that it sure would be nice to have a little girl again, to fix her hair and let her play with my costume jewelry, even if she wasn't mine.

I buttoned up a blue linen dress with cap sleeves and a white belt that cinched in my waist. My hips swelled out, but maybe Henry wouldn't notice. Last but not least, I brushed out my braids and twisted my hair into a skin-tight knot. Then I hurried into the kitchen and found our old picnic basket. I made roast-beef sandwiches, Henry's favorite, and celery stuffed with my famous pimiento cheese. I gathered paper napkins, an ice-cold jar of sweet tea, two slices of Sophie's milk cake.

His store was only three blocks away. Dusk was falling, and street lights blinked on, shining on the cracked sidewalk. I strolled to the corner of Lincoln and Gallery, turning left onto the Square; I walked past Ed's Shoes, Bellar's Furniture, and Hooper's, with its waxy mannequins dressed in the latest styles. According to the clock on Hibernia Bank, it was twelve minutes after eight o'clock. When I crossed Gallery I saw that Nepper's Drugs wasn't open. The SORRY, WE'RE CLOSED sign hung crookedly in the door. Next door the Majestic Theater was all lit up, its red neon glowing against the evening sky. Mrs. Quarles, the owner's wife, sat in the glass case, reading *Photoplay*. I walked up to the front of Henry's store and peered through the window. All the aisles were empty. The lunch counter was a gleaming sheet of pink marble. A sickening feeling swept over me—what if Henry had lied? What if he wasn't at his store at all?

I walked around to the alley, where the air smelled of burnt popcorn. Straight ahead was Henry's turquoise wagon, parked next to a dusty old Nash with a rusted fender. The back door to Nepper's Drugs was bolted with the folding iron gate, and a faint light glowed from the dusty stockroom windows. I walked up the crumbly steps and pressed my face against the grille. It was dark inside the store, but I saw the chipped wooden counter where Miss Byrd wrapped packages at Christmas. Over to the right were tall wooden shelves crammed with vaporizers, toys, enema bags, cologne. On the farthest wall was a peeling door leading to a bathroom that always smelled of pine soap.

A flash of white moved down the medicine aisle, and I leaned closer. Henry appeared behind the counter, peering down at a wooden clipboard. The counter came up to his waist. He plucked a pencil from the pocket of his white smock and wrote something down. Flooded with relief, I started to rap on the window, but before I could extract my hand from the wicker basket, the bathroom door swung open, and a long-legged, naked woman stepped out. It was the Robichaux woman, Billie's mother, Henry's counter girl. For just a second I didn't understand. She wore black high heels and carried a bottle of champagne, which was illegal, Epiphany being a dry parish. Her breasts bobbed as she walked toward Henry, and I understood everything.

I thought I'd faint same as I did when Olive went into her coma. I saw myself rolling down the concrete steps, cracking my head wide open. When those sweethearts came out, they'd see me lying there like a bird that's flown into a window, attracted by a false blue sky in the glass. They'd know I'd been spying and God had struck me down.

But I did not faint. I gripped the basket as if for balance and watched Henry step around the counter. He was naked from the waist down. I clapped my hand over my mouth, banging the basket against my ribs. His personal parts stood at attention, jutting into the air. He pulled off his white smock, then held out his arms to DeeDee Robichaux. I breathed in and out; I knew I should do one of two things—leave or knock on the glass—but I could not tear my eyes away from this spectacle.

He shook out a quilt and spread it on the dusty floor. I recognized it as one of my best, a Bible verse quilt. My grandmother won it in a church raffle in 1902, and I had no idea how he'd smuggled it out of the house. He took the champagne, planting a kiss on DeeDee's painted lips. She stretched out down on the quilt, her body blocking out all the middle verses, cutting them off midsentence. Outlined around her was *Thou Shall Not Commit, Jesus Wept,* and *The Truth Shall Make You Free.*

Henry took a long swig of champagne, then wiped his mouth with the back of his hand like my alcoholic Uncle Bun used to. I'd never seen Henry do this. No, he was always Mr. Perfect. Mr. Religious. Mr. Nice Manners. Now he was drinking straight from the bottle. I briefly closed my eyes and struggled to compose myself. Please do not collapse, I thought. "Please do not vomit."

When I looked again, Henry was lowering himself onto the girl, his privates bobbing. I gritted my teeth, but I was glued to the window. I had never before seen the intimate act, not even when I was a participant (I kept the bedroom dark, my eyes closed, the way Henry always said it should be). He fit himself into the girl as if threading a needle. His head dropped to her breasts, sucking the pink nipples, which he'd never done to me. He had never touched me but one place and not with his hands. Sometimes I felt like a piece of cloth, with him stitching into me hard, a sewing machine on high speed.

Now I watched him kiss her ear. She looped her arms around his neck and turned her mouth toward his tongue. If they saw me, then I'd gather my dignity and act like a lady, I'd even admit to spying, but something told me not to worry. They wouldn't look up unless the building caved in. I wished to the Lord that it would. Henry's broad buttocks dimpled, inflated, as he pushed into her. I gripped the iron grille, bending my fingers around the **V**. Above his head was Genesis 37:19, *Behold, this dreamer cometh*, and I thought to myself, Well, it won't be long.

The back door to the Majestic Theater slammed shut, and I whirled around. Mr. Quarles was carrying a box of trash to the Dumpster, whistling "Hey, Good-Lookin'." He stopped walking when he saw me, the tune trailing off.

"Mrs. Nepper?" He set down the box. His gray hair reflected red neon from the tall, blinking sign. "That you?"

I nodded, then climbed down the steps, bracing my hand on the cement wall.

"Can I help you, Mrs. Nepper?" he said. "You locked out or something?"

I shook my head. I walked over and handed him the wicker basket. "A little snack for you and Mrs. Quarles."

"Us? Well, gosh." He looked down at the basket. "That's awful generous. Thanks, Mrs. Nepper."

"Don't mention it."

I walked out of the alley, my head held high. The whole way home, I recited Bible verses, imagining the quilt square by square. *"Love never faileth,"* I whispered. *"Love suffereth long. Let not your heart be troubled."* I didn't see how I could ever put that quilt on my bed, much less read Bible verses to soothe my nerves. As I walked home, I started humming "The Battle Hymn of the Republic"—*My eyes have seen the glory of the coming of the*—I broke off, covering my eyes with my hands. Oh, Lord, I thought. Now they'd even ruined hymns for me! Well, I didn't know whether to laugh, cry, or go back and shoot the both of them. Maybe aim at a place that might be embarrassing to explain.

On Lincoln Avenue someone called out, "Vangie! Vangie Nepper!" I didn't answer. I kept on walking. I couldn't have said a word. My tongue had shriveled to the size of a raisin, the same exact size of my brain. The *idea* of Henry seeing another woman was bad enough, but my head was crammed with moving pictures that wouldn't stop playing. Things I saw for real. Things that made me crazy. The poison pen letter had taken on a deep meaning. Everybody in town must know. "There goes Vangie," they were probably saying. "Her husband is seeing DeeDee Robichaux."

Before I knew it I was back home, praise the Lord, standing in the bedroom I'd aired, vacuumed, and polished for the last twenty-four years. The sheets Sophie and I changed on Tuesdays and Saturdays at Henry's request. This whole house was geared to his comfort and upkeep. King for a day, for the rest of his life, and I supposed that included a harem. I piled all my clothes on the bed. Then I packed everything in suitcases and paper sacks. Anything I could get my hands on. I threw in body lotion, my rag curlers, and a photo album. In the back of my mind was Edith's spare bedroom, the one with sour yellow walls and sunflower bedspread that she said reminded her of somebody named Van Go, probably a painter she knew in New York. She had always been partial to Russians. I thought I could ease into her house in nothing flat. Let Henry see how long he lasted without somebody cooking, washing, and ironing for him. Buying food. Matching up his socks, rolling them into fuzzy eggs. DeeDee Robichaux would be champing at the bit to do all of this, but I couldn't think about that now.

I sat down at his desk and wrote him a note.

> Dear Henry—
> The one thing I can't stand is a liar and that's what you are. Now I know the truth about you and Mrs. Robichaux, and I am leaving you. So you go on and do what you want. You broke your vows to me and now you are free as a bird. One thing— Louisiana's got Napoleonic Law, but don't expect to get an inch of Galliard land. In case you need me, that's where I'll be— squatter's rights. If you cause trouble, I'll take my half of your drugstore. We can split it down the middle.
> —Vangie

Now that I'd caught him in a lie, I couldn't think of anything else. I imagined all those meetings Henry had missed and how I'd believed. I pictured them on the quilt, Henry on his hands and knees. I thought of all those Baptist women who sewed the Bible verses, working night after night, their heads bent over the squares, talking about men, babies, and recipes. Why, some of those women had been dead over forty years. My head tingled and my stomach heaved. I barely made it to the bathroom. "Oh, Vangie!" I said, my voice echoing in the toilet bowl. "You've been deceived!"

Then I lay down on the cold tile floor, staring at tiny squares of pink mingled with black. There was one black tile, surrounded by five pinks. No rhyme or reason, yet when you leaned back, the pattern came together.

As soon as I told Edith I was leaving, she said, "You have every right, God knows you do, but Vangie . . . " She broke off and lit a cigarette, narrowing her eyes at the smoke. "Is this the only time he's been unfaithful?"

"*Only?*" We were in the kitchen, where I'd dragged all my belongings. The door stood open, and the night sky showed the Big Dipper. I did not drive, and that in itself presented a problem. Even if I knew how, I didn't have a car—Henry had it. And I wouldn't know how to buy a new one. Henry had always tended to everything. I had money from Mama and Daddy, a teeny bit more than half because they hadn't liked Edith all that much. The money was in my and Henry's name down at Hibernia bank, a joint account.

"I shouldn't try to influence you, Vangie." She held up both hands and shook her head. "But honestly, if this is the first time he's had an affair, then you ought to reconsider. I'll help you unpack. But if you think he's done this before, then leave."

"But I didn't suspect *this* time!"

"True."

We fell silent. Then I said, "He might've been chasing counter girls for years."

"I don't know." Edith inhaled smoke, then rubbed her temple. "Sooner or later one would have called you, or come over to your house."

"My house? Why?"

"Lots of reasons. To let you know she existed. To let you know your husband was a liar—and not just any liar, but a *fucking* liar. They're the worst."

"Edith!"

"It's true."

"I don't believe it. Why, if a woman came over and told me she'd been seeing Henry, she'd be a fool. That wouldn't be a way to win Henry Nepper, making trouble for him."

"Sweetie, the whole idea is to make trouble for *you*. So you'll kick him out. And she'll be right there to tell him it's all right, that he can stay with her. That he's smart and handsome and strong and wonderful."

"Well, DeeDee Robichaux." I paused, wiping my lips as if the woman's name tasted bitter. "*She* never called me up."

"That you know of." Edith took a long, luxurious drag from the cigarette, then tapped it against the ashtray. "What about all those calls you were getting?"

"I didn't think, I mean, I never guessed it was a woman." I rubbed my hands over my face. My skin felt like old tomatoes left to shrivel in the refrigerator, cool and mushy. About to burst. "I'm just stupid."

"No, just trusting. And innocent."

"And you're not?"

"No."

"Well, I'm surprised at you, Edith. How do you know so much about affairs?"

"Sweetie, I'm not from around here. That's why." Edith ground out her cigarette. "And I had a life before I married your brother."

"Your life has always seemed bigger than mine."

"Different, maybe." She lit another cigarette, then shook out the match. "So, are you going to talk to Henry?"

"About what? No, I'm leaving."

"Why should you give up your house? Why leave it to *him*?"

"Don't want it."

"If Zachary were here, he'd tell you to call the Foutch brothers to change your locks. Let Henry find a place to stay. I'm sure that Robichaux woman will accommodate him."

"Oh, Lord. I wish this hadn't happened." I clasped my hands behind my neck, keeping my eyes on Edith. I hoped she'd say, *Come stay with me, sweetie.* I pictured us turning into the Galliard sisters, Edith driving us to the Yellow Fever Cemetery to set out flowers on Zachary. I would sit in the passenger seat, my knees gripping wet vases of gladioli. "Are we there yet?" I'd say.

"I can't stay here," I said.

"Why not?"

"The house is too full of Henry—his suits and his dirty socks, even down to his smell. I'll go crazy here. Can you drive me over to the Limoges Hotel?" I stared down at all of my paper sacks. Then it hit me—I couldn't go anywhere. I had exactly ten dollars in my purse. "Forget the hotel," I said. "Can you carry me to the homeplace?"

"Not the Galliards' farm?" She lifted her eyebrows. "Tonight?"

"I don't mean the Neppers'. Besides, they were town people."

"But why?"

"I'm going to live there. For a while, anyway."

"Sweetie, this won't work. You've never lived by yourself. And that farm is so isolated."

"I was born there."

"But it's been shut up for five years, ever since your mother died."

"There's noplace in the world where I feel safer."

She tried to talk me out of it, but like Henry always said, I could be stubborn. While she carried on, I propped my goodbye note against the toaster. Then I loaded Edith's car. By the time we drove the eleven miles to LaGuardo, crossing Bayou Maçon, she had taken to scaring me.

"Look how *dark* it is out here." She gripped the steering wheel. "What if a hobo breaks in? Strangles you? And you won't have a phone. You don't even have the electricity turned on."

"If I'm strangled, then I won't need a phone, now, will I?"

"Even I'd be scared out here." She stared out the window. There were no lights for miles in any direction, except the way we came. "Scared to death."

"I don't care." My voice was flat. "I'm too stupid to live anyhow."

"Don't say that!"

"It's the truth."

"I'm going to turn around and take you home with me." She stepped on the brake.

"That won't solve anything. And I couldn't stand living next door to Henry."

"But I don't want to live beside him either." She reached across the seat and squeezed my wrist. "I'll miss you, Vangie. And I'll worry."

"I'll get me a dog," I said. "A great big one."

"You ought to bring Checkers and Dot. They'd love it out here."

"Why, if I took Henry's precious dogs, he'd die."

"Yeah." She laughed. "He's a fool about those damn dogs."

We fell silent. The car seemed to float in the warm, black air, lifting us over fences and cotton rows. "Edith," I said. "I don't understand men. Do you?"

"No." She shook her head. "I don't even *try*."

"If he wanted to see other women, then why didn't he have the gumption to leave me?"

"He's selfish, that's why. The sorry bastard wants too much." She turned down the gravel road, where a tuft of grass grew down the center, brushing underneath the car. Then I saw the house, the roof's sharp upside-down *V*, the peeling veranda, white paint hanging in strips. Henry wouldn't let me spend a dime to keep it up. He figured I'd give up and sell, but he just didn't know me. "I know you're stubborn," he'd say. "You dig in your heels and hold on tight."

From the front veranda, the screen door gaped open, scraping on its hinges, as if the house knew I was coming. Edith helped me haul in the suitcases and sacks. We fumbled in the dark rooms. "I can't leave you here," she said. "I'll stay with you. Come on, let's find some candles. I've got matches in my purse." I heard a zipper, then a scratchy flash. She held up the match while I opened drawers in the dining room. I found two candelabras in a cabinet that smelled of silver polish.

"Here, let me help." I felt her cool hand on my arm, and it reminded me so much of Mama's I wanted to cry. Once we lit the candles, we looked all around the room. The rugs were rolled up, and sheets were draped on the sofa and chairs. We found beeswax candles in the dining room. Hurricane lamps were anchored with mantel dust. I walked in a daze, yanking off sheets, sending up layers of gray fuzz that made us sneeze. The kitchen counters were dotted with hard black specks, mouse droppings. The house had a closed-up, sickly smell. Cobwebs trailed from the egg-and-dart molding. A whirring noise drifted down from the attic.

"This is insanity," Edith kept saying, rubbing her nose. "Sheer insanity. Have you figured out how you'll get back and forth to Limoges? To see Olive?"

"I'll hire somebody to drive me."

"With what? Henry's got all your money."

"He'll give it back."

"Vangie!" She slapped a sheet. "Don't be so trusting!"

"I can't help it. It's my nature."

"That's no excuse."

"Oh, Edith. Let me be. I've got other worries." I dusted off the ancient black telephone. "Like how to get this thing hooked up."

"That's the easiest part of all. Don't you see?"

I shook my head.

"Never mind. I'm taking you to Hibernia Bank tomorrow. Henry Nepper can't steal your money and give it to that woman."

"He wouldn't dare."

"Oh yes, he would." She threw down the sheet. "Never trust a man in lust. They do outrageous things."

"What kind of things?"

"A hard dick has no conscience."

I started laughing, but my face twisted, and I realized I was crying. A frayed sob escaped from my throat. Edith put her arms around me. "You don't need the bastard, Vangie," she said. "You're just too good for him. I mean, really *good*."

I didn't know what to think. I couldn't sort things out. It was all mixed up like a casserole—rice, cheese, broccoli, chicken. Love him hate him want to stay want to go.

The next morning we were on the veranda, busy sweeping cobwebs from the railing. I couldn't help but admire the intricate spider webs. Each one had a fancy zigzag design. Edith said they're supposed to lure insects. I stopped sweeping and leaned against the railing. I had to admire the sky, too. I never knew there was so much deepness to it—it just looked flat, but I heard on the radio that it was really packed with years of sound that went all the way back to creation.

Edith shook my arm and pointed to a cloud of dust moving up the road. "My God," she said. "It's Henry."

Sure enough, his turquoise Rambler wagon shot out of the cloud. He parked it under a pecan tree, got out, and walked over to the edge of the veranda. He put his hands on his hips, nodded at Edith. She briefly glared at him, then she went into the house, watching from behind the screen.

"I came to bring you home, Vangie," he said.

"I am home." I squeezed the broom handle.

"You can't stay here all by yourself." He shook his head. "You'll be too scared."

"Better scared than living with a liar."

"Now listen, Vangie. I read your letter, and quite frankly, I don't what you're talking about." He lifted his leg and set it on the step. "I don't know where you got the idea about me and Mrs. Robichaux, but it's wrong. Whoever told you that is a trouble-maker."

"Nobody told me a thing," I said. "I saw you with my own eyes. At your store on my Bible-verse quilt. You were drinking champagne."

"Why . . . that's just . . ." Henry's face turned so red his ears seemed to swell.

"You told me you were doing inventory," I said.

Behind me, Edith shouted, "That's right, Henry. What were you counting, pubic hairs?"

"You stay out of this, Edith," he cried. Then he looked at me. "You don't know what you saw."

"So now she's blind?" Edith said.

"Can't we talk alone?" He frowned at Edith, then took the broom from my hands and laid it against the house. He grabbed my elbow and guided me across the veranda. For a moment he didn't speak, just rubbed his fingers back and forth across his mouth. He watched me with hooded eyes. "Vangie," he finally said, "you are right about one thing. I did have an infatuation with that woman. But that's all it was."

"Infatuation?"

"It doesn't matter. It's over."

"Since when?" I jerked my arm away. It was all I could do not to slap him.

"It's true! I just had a moral weakness. She was so pretty, I just couldn't resist." He started crying. Mama always said that the man who cried the hardest at his wife's funeral was the first to get married. Henry reached in his back pocket and pulled out a hand-kerchief. "We've been through too much for you to act like this."

"What about you!"

"I was wrong, but I believe in the institution of marriage."

"But not the vows?"

"It's not what you think! I swear it's not!"

"How do you know what I think?"

"Because I've lived with you for twenty-four years, that's how." He combed his fingers through his hair. I gave him a look, then walked over to the broom and snatched it up. I started sweeping. Dust billowed around my ankles, making Henry step backward.

"I'm not coming with you, Henry. So just go on, leave."

"You can't stay here." His eyes filled again, but I saw that he was not crying for me. He was used to getting his own way, feeling sorry for himself when he didn't. Except for holding firm to this land, not letting him sell it, I had never denied him anything I was capable of giving.

"I'm going to try."

"You don't mean it." He wiped his eyes. "You don't mean a word. Edith's put this in your head."

"No, you did. You and DeeDee Robichaux."

He started to say something, then sighed. He walked to his car, stoop-shouldered and old-looking. As I watched him drive off, Edith came out and put her arm around me.

"You did well, Vangie." She squeezed me. "I'm proud of you. A little surprised, but proud."

"I was good, wasn't I?"

"Damn good."

We watched his car chug down the road, stirring up dust. I was plenty upset, but I'd faced worse. So far my life had been one big circle—I was back where I'd started, my childhood home, miles from anywhere with nothing but a crooked road leading to the blacktop highway.

"Let's finish with these cobwebs," I said, reaching high with the tip of my broom. "I'm cleaning this house from top to bottom."

"It needs it," Edith said, leaning on her broom, smiling at me.

"I'll get used to it. I'll get to where I like it," I told her, but inside I just had to wonder.

She Flew the Coop

She was standing on the back steps with this little picnic basket, and when Elmer saw her she got all flustered and told him she'd fixed us this food. Then she practically ran out of the alley. It was real mysterious, what with Henry's car parked in plain sight. We thought they'd had a spat. About two hours later, the back door to Nepper's Drugs opened. The Robichaux woman stepped out, followed by Henry. They got into their cars and drove off in different directions. I have one question: What did Vangie see?

—MRS. YVONNE QUARLES, COLLECTING DIMES FOR POLIO (DOOR-TO-DOOR), MAY 18, 1952

A plume of dust moved down the long driveway, reminding Vangie of a tiny cyclone. When the Galliard children were little their mother, Lallie, read stories about the Old West. Zachary loved Indians and would crouch on the chifforobe, clapping one hand over his mouth, emitting a monotone *wa-wa-wa-wa!* But Vangie loved hearing about the emigrants. She couldn't imagine striking out across the wilderness. As her mother read about the prairies, Vangie imagined green, windswept fields full of gophers and rabbits. Her mother's voice droned on, talking about the dangers of living in the open. Every night before the settlers went to bed, they scanned the horizon for sparks—signs of grass fires, disasters equal to hail and grasshoppers. Imagine being able to see danger approaching from such a distance and being so helpless to avert it.

Vangie watched a rusty pickup emerge from the dust cloud. The door creaked open, and Emmett Welch hopped out, holding a cardboard box. He walked up to the veranda, cradling the box, and said, "Morning, Miss Vangie. Got you a little something."

"Me? That's thoughtful, Emmett." She watched him set down

the box and open the lid. Instead of a chicken dinner, out popped a dog with short black fur and a tan chest. It licked Vangie's hand. "My goodness," she said.

"Thought you might could use some company. I heard you was staying here by yourself."

"Where'd you hear that?"

"News travels. You know how it is."

"I'm afraid I do." Vangie waved one hand at the wicker chair. "I just made a pound cake. Would you like a piece?"

"Oh, yes, ma'am. That'd be real nice."

She brought out a tray holding four hunks of the cake and two iced-tea glasses. For fifteen solid minutes, Emmett ate and drank tea, scraping his fork along her mother's china. Vangie fed bits of cake to the dog. "What's her name?" she asked, glancing up at Emmett.

"It's a him. I been calling it Dog." He scratched his sideburn with the fork. "He's half Chihuahua."

"Whatever he is, he's sure got a sweet tooth." The dog stood on his hind legs, begging for another piece of cake. Vangie set her dish on the floor, watching the animal gobble the cake in three swallows, his whole body shaking with the effort. Then he methodically licked the china, causing the plate to scoot across the porch.

"He likes frog legs, too," Emmett said, "but you got to take the bones out first."

"I prefer my frogs alive."

"You eat them live?" Emmett's eyes widened.

"No, no." She laughed. "To look at. To hear them croaking at night."

"Oh. Well, me too." Emmett looked down at his plate. As he set it on the porch floor, he looked up shyly at Vangie. "I should've known you wouldn't hurt a fly, much less a frog. You always was the sweetest little old girl." His face instantly filled with color.

"Sweet but dumb," Vangie said. "That's me."

"Oh, you wasn't! You could do anything—ride in planes, climb trees. Shoot, you wasn't scared of nothing!"

"That girl is gone, Emmett."

"Where to?" He looked frightened.

"I don't know."

"Oh, you just pulling my leg, Miss Vangie. You're right here. And you're still the prettiest little lady I ever saw."

"You're a nice man," Vangie said, hastily adding, "and a good crop duster. I need a friend who's a crop duster. I mean, if I'm going to plant cotton next year."

"You are? Well, I can sure do that for you, Miss Vangie." He smiled with his whole face. "Whatever you need, just say the word. Old Emmett'll be right here."

"You wouldn't be interested in teaching me how to drive, would you?"

"Why, sure. I can do that, too."

"Daddy's old Buick is just sitting out back. I doubt it'll even start."

"I'm real good with engines." He scratched his sideburn again, then scraped his hand into his hair, making the grizzled tufts stand up. "But I can carry you where you want. When I'm not dusting fields, that is."

"See, my daughter is ill, and I can't depend on people to drive me. It's time I learned." She stuck two long fingers into her glass, raked out an ice cube, and threw it to the dog.

"When you want to start?"

"Today?"

That afternoon, Henry called his attorney. "I've had an affair, and now Vangie's left me," he told Lewis B. Atchley.

"It's the shock," Atchley said. "It's entirely normal. Do you love your wife?"

"Yes?"

"If that's a question, I can't answer it for you, Henry."

"I know it, I know it. I'm just so confused."

"Well, call back when you're not."

Henry hung up the phone, then briefly considered overdosing himself on phenobarbital. He'd had the best of both worlds—Vangie running his house, cooking his meals, seeing to the laundry. Then he'd have wild interludes with DeeDee. He was wringing out the best from both women, but maybe it was the other way around.

He drove out to north Epiphany Parish, down the rough-paved highway, keeping his eyes on the old Galliard house. A black dot bounced on the horizon. It took him a minute to recognize it—the Major's old Buick. It careened across the field, mowing down dried cotton stalks. Dust lifted into the sky. A little bow-legged man stood in the turn row, waving his arms. The car was aimed straight toward him. Henry thought he saw a long braid flapping out of the window.

"Vangie?" he said, leaning forward. Just before the car almost plowed over the little man, he dove into a dirt pile. He came up, shaking his head. Inside the car a woman sat hunched behind the wheel. The car shot off behind the house, the little man in pursuit.

"My God, it *is* Vangie," he said, slapping the dashboard. He waited for the car to return, but it never did. All the way back to Limoges, Henry grinned and talked to himself. "She'll be back," he said. "Hell, yes. She'll cry and carry on, she'll make me give up DeeDee, but she'll be back. And old Henry Nepper will be back in the driver's seat."

Learning to drive was not easy. In fact, Vangie would rather cook a pig. It took fifteen to twenty hours to cook a 120-pound pig, give or take a few pounds. This did not including preparation time—like building a pit, trimming off the inner fat, salting the cavity, and splitting the breastbone. When Vangie married Henry, she had weighed 110 pounds. He kept her well fed and gave her free run of the pink house on Cypress Street. On their first anniversary, the Major invited everybody in town to a July Fourth barbecue. The pit was four feet long, four feet wide, and three feet deep, with a hole at one end large enough to stick a shovel through. It was just big enough for a 138-pound pig.

The best pits are lined with a sheet of stainless steel, forming a giant rack; add seasoned pecan and mesquite and light the fire. Preheating a pit is no different from preheating an oven or a man. Once you get them started, you're ready to cook. After the first ten hours, turn the pig. From then on you can't turn your back for an instant. Like a man you can't trust, the fat is highly flammable. The heat is so intense it can singe your eyebrows. Cook until the meat falls off the bone. Yield: 120 servings.

Vangie wondered how something as big as a marriage could just end. One day she was serving Henry crawfish étouffée, stinking up the house, and the next she was living in a totally different kitchen, eating corn bread and milk, using a single glass and spoon. Whole mornings passed and she didn't make it to the hospital, didn't see a soul, just the land spreading out like a bolt of green calico. And above her was a million miles of sky. She thought of her daddy, how they'd sit on the porch and watch the night like people nowadays watched TV, waves of wind in the cotton, stars thrown across the sky like seeds. There would be no other sound except the crickets and the chain clinking against the flagpole.

It was early evening, a night so warm you could go barefoot. From the second floor of the old house, Vangie heard the chain singing in the wind. Through her old bedroom window, the moon drifted low in the sky, a hunched backbone that seemed to rock back and forth. She was working on her recipes, trying to figure how to shrink her jambalaya down to two servings—an impossible task, but it was better than driving. Last week she'd mixed up the pedals and drove her daddy's car into the ditch. Emmett had to call a service station. And just the other day she decided to take the car for a little spin all by herself, something she'd promised Emmett she'd never do. On her way to Parish Hospital Sheriff Reems pulled up behind her, his siren blaring. "You just ran the last seven stop signs," he shouted, sticking his thumbs into his belt.

"Oh," she said. "I didn't think they were for *me!*"

"Do you have a license?" He leaned into the old car. When he saw Vangie's stricken face, he said, "Hell, move over. I'll drive you home. But next time, you're getting a ticket."

Dog was curled up beside her. From downstairs, she heard a scraping sound, then a thump like a screen door banging. Dog lifted his head. His ears swiveled, scrunching up his forehead. She was always hearing things at night—noises in the wind, voices, nothing she could make out, just a hum like crossed telephone wires. Sometimes it sounded like women praying or singing, sometimes screaming.

She tried to concentrate on a recipe for red beans and rice—how in the world to reduce it? The wind howled over the fields. She thought she heard the faint crunch of gravel, a car driving up. She set down the index cards, climbed out of bed, and looked out the window; she couldn't see anything. Just wind in the squatty mimosa. A crumpled paper sack wheeling across the yard. A skinny, bent moon hanging by a thread, like something caught by a spider. She didn't like how Dog's ears were perked up. Then, from the veranda, she heard the screen door squeak open, the one on the front porch with the torn mesh. She had meant to call a carpenter, but the telephone company still hadn't hooked up the phone. The noise could be anything—mice darting across the floor, birds nesting in the attic. The house was falling apart. All of the faucets dripped, leaving an orange stain in the porcelain sinks, and all night long the pipes rattled behind the walls.

"It's the wind," she said. Dog glanced back at her, then stood up on the bed. His fur spiked up along his back. Above the wind came a rattling noise, then the high, sharp sound of glass breaking. Vangie jumped. Dog coughed out a bark, then glanced back at Vangie. Her heart was wound tightly, ticking so fast she couldn't tell one beat from another. Downstairs, she heard the whomp of a kitchen chair falling over backward. Dog growled and showed his teeth.

Vangie tiptoed to the door, turned the key in the lock. *That's no good*, she thought. *If it's a prowler, he knows I'm here.* She looked around for a weapon, but the room had only a Bible, recipe cards, an alarm clock, and a plastic bottle of Jergen's. She heard another crash—her mama's crystal? She reached down and picked up Dog, who dug his claws into her forearm.

If she could just get into the hall; the farthest door led to the attic. She twisted the doorknob, then hesitated. What if the man was standing on the other side? *It won't take much to silence me,* she thought. A blow to the head. A big hand snapping her neck like a chicken bone. Something shattered in the kitchen, followed by the chinking of spoons and forks. Knives. She turned the key, waited the space of five heartbeats. Then she opened the door. Nothing but darkness. Nothing but cool, deep air. She leaned into the hall and saw a spill of orange light at the foot of the staircase—she'd left it on to frighten prowlers, and instead it had drawn them. Dog wiggled against her, growling.

"Shhh," Vangie whispered, then she took a step toward the attic. The floorboard screeched, and she thought, *I should have bought rugs.* Thick rugs that would hide an old lady's footsteps. She hurried up the attic stairs, her bare feet shuffling on the dusty treads. She counted sixteen steps, each one creaking a different note, like keys on an organ. She imagined the prowler listening, slouching toward the staircase in the front hall.

When she reached the landing, she stepped into warm air that smelled of pine resin. She held out one arm, groping past her mama's old clothes that were hanging from the rafters. She bumped into an Addison radio with a cracked dial. Three paths led to the dormer windows, a fourth to a pine chifforobe. Cobwebs stretched from floor to ceiling. The dormer windows showed chips of black sky. She heard a flutter and almost cried out. In the dim light she saw swallows huddled along the eaves. She crept to the chifforobe, squeezing the dog to her chest, and opened the door. It made a splintering sound. With her free hand, she pushed back old coats and crawled inside. Easing down, she grasped the latch, pulled the door to, and held it shut. The latch was old metal, and she wondered if it might snap off, causing the door to swing open. Or maybe it would break off, leaving her and the little dog to suffocate. Her mama always said if you shut yourself in a wardrobe, you'd never find your way out, but that was not her worry just yet. She just hoped no one found a way inside.

To distract herself, she thought about the Bible quilt—how was she supposed to sleep *under* it when Henry and that Robichaux woman had done their business *on* it? It was unforgivable of him to bring her quilt into his affair. She shut her eyes, then opened them. It was all the same, all black. The dog was a warm lump against her stomach. He licked her hand, as if to comfort her. Outside, the wind roared against the house, rushing up against the eaves, making a low moan. She patted Dog. "Good boy," she whispered. "You tried to warn me. You did."

Inside, the wardrobe was steaming up; it reeked of dog breath and sweaty flannel. Vangie's hair had come loose and was sticking to her neck. She could suffocate and no one would ever find her or the dog. They'd say, *She flew the coop. She just disappeared.*

While she sat there curved into a *C*, she remembered a woman in Lake Providence who'd killed herself after her husband died. She'd been scared most all her life. She lived out in the country too, and she said she couldn't sleep. Said someone was bound to get her now that her husband was gone. Two months after his funeral, she went to the beauty shop and kissed her beautician and gave her a hundred-dollar tip. Then she drove home and shot herself in the heart. Everybody said she was too scared to live by herself, but Vangie wondered if she was too scared to live.

She awakened with a start, nearly throwing the dog out of her lap. Light splintered through cracks in the wardrobe. Still, she was frightened to open the door. She pictured herself climbing out of the chifforobe, finding the man next to the stairs, waiting with a rope. Dog's tail thumped against the side of the wardrobe. Vangie patted him and thought, "Well, I'm going to live alone, then I'll just need more dogs—big ones that can roam the porch." She'd heard that peacocks were even better than watchdogs, but she didn't know if she could stand their squawking.

She reached up, turned the latch, and pushed open the door. Light streamed through holes in the east dormer. Bits of colored glass glinted on the floor. Dog leaped out and stretched his short legs. "Go downstairs, Dog," Vangie said, feeling braver. "Run! Sic 'em!"

The dog's nails ticked over the wood floor and down the steps. The swallows exploded from the rafters, swarming through the broken window. As soon as the phone was hooked up, she'd call someone to fix the panes. Only to be cautious, she'd hire Poteet's Hardware to install sturdy locks—not that she planned to turn the place into Fort Vangie. In daylight, the attic looked benign, a place to store things, not to hide.

Downstairs, Dog was barking. She crept down the staircase, pausing now and then to peep through the railing. It sounded as if Dog had cornered someone in the kitchen. She hurried into the foyer, then raced down the hall. When she turned into the kitchen, Dog was yelping on his hind legs. Two raccoons scurried across the counter. The floor was full of broken dishes, coffee cups, orange rinds, pork-chop bones. One raccoon stood on its hind legs and sniffed the air.

"Varmints!" Vangie reached for the broom. Dog barked, then ran in circles, chasing his tail. She swept the raccoons off the counter, herding them out through the torn screen. They flopped onto the veranda and scampered away. Vangie sat down, the broken crockery cracking beneath her hips, and she watched the little dog snarl at his tail.

"Poor old Dog," she said, "I know just how you feel."

Emmett forced her to drive the car into town, coaching from the passenger seat. When she passed City Market, she slammed on the brakes, sending Emmett into the dashboard. "Whoa," he said. "Just tap the brake, Miss Vangie."

"I have to stop." She pointed at the market. "I need eggs."

"I don't know about this." Emmett scratched his head, staring at the curb. "I don't think you're ready to parallel-park."

"Sounds awful." Vangie shuddered.

"Just pull into the lot."

Vangie shook her head. Her hands slid down the steering wheel. "I don't think I can!"

"Turn like this." Emmett reached across the seat and pulled the wheel. The tire bumped over the curb, then crashed down. She cruised up the side of the store, parking at a funny angle.

"How's this?" She grinned, shifting to park.

"It'll do for now." He pointed behind the car. "How you going to get out, though?"

"You'll just have to be a gentleman and do it for me." She gathered her purse and climbed out of the car. She walked into the market, nodding to Mr. Hawley, and turned up the first aisle. Straight ahead was a woman in a pink dress with glass buttons. Her waist was cinched in with a white patent-leather belt, showing off her figure. Her hair rippled down her back, so dark it seemed blue under the fluorescent lighting. When the woman turned to pick up a jar of mayonnaise, Vangie recognized her— DeeDee Robichaux. Vangie just stood there, watching the woman lean over and fit the jar into her cart. Then she placidly drifted down the aisle, her hips swaying. Vangie was drawn to her smell, a clean, rain-washed scent. DeeDee turned down another aisle, and Vangie thought she might have to sit on the mayonnaise jars and put her head between her knees. It was hard to believe that little Billie had a mother like that, a callous creature who just took what she wanted, like something on a grocery shelf.

But Henry isn't a mayonnaise jar, Vangie thought. He didn't have to go along with her.

She backed out of the market, not answering Mr. Hawley when he asked if everything was all right. Then she hurried to the Buick. "Where's your eggs?" Emmett asked.

"They were out." She started the car, threw the gearshift into reverse, and backed out of the lot without rolling over the curb. Emmett watched, agape, as she flipped on her blinker and turned onto Delphinium Street. When she reached the corner of Washington and Geranium, she started trembling. "Look at me," she said. "I'm driving. I'm really and truly driving."

"Yes, ma'am," Emmett said. "Like you been doing it all your life."

Vangie stood at the kitchen counter making a vanilla-wafer cake when her phone rang for the very first time. She'd forgotten she paid to have it hooked up.

"Hello?" she said cautiously. In the back of her mind was the telephone pervert.

"You poor thing!" crooned Harriet Hooper. "We all knew he was slipping around with that Robichaux woman. He's been seeing her since September—did you know that? None of us had the heart to tell you, least of all *me*."

"That's never stopped you before," Vangie said.

"You don't have to take my head off." Harriet breathed into the receiver. "I'm not the one who had a sweetie on the side. And it's not my fault that you'll be kicked out of the country club. Leonard's on the board, and *he* said you'll be kicked out. No single woman can be a member, you see. The club bylaws clearly state that membership is only available for members and their *spouses*."

"Yes, I know." Vangie twisted the cord around her wrist. "Then I'll just have to hurry and get a new spouse. I may even get a job. Why don't you ask Leonard if he needs a secretary?"

"Leo*nard*?" Her voice screaked up at the edges.

"Well, he's not my first choice, but you know us single women—any port in a storm will do."

"He doesn't need any help," Harriet said. "It was nice talking to you, but I've *just* got to run."

A few days later Waldene and Edith ganged up on Vangie, begging her to let Waldene cut her hair. "You need a new look," Edith said. "To go with your new life."

"I don't want a new one," Vangie said, eyeing Waldene's bottles.

Waldene laughed and said, "You will when I get through with you."

The women washed Vangie's hair in the kitchen sink. They rubbed something into her scalp that made her eyes burn. "This isn't shampoo!" Vangie sputtered.

"Watch it!" Waldene pushed Vangie's head down. "You're splattering this everywhere."

"You tricked me! This is hair dye!"

"It's Midnight Blond by Helena Rubenstein," Waldene confessed. "When a woman goes gray, she needs to go lighter, not darker."

"I don't want either one! Henry hates artificial color on a woman."

"Henry doesn't live here," said Edith.

"But *I* hate artificial."

"Vangie, hush."

They weeded her eyebrows and painted her nails a color called Hibiscus Petal. Waldene handed her a mirror, saying, "There! Don't you look pretty?"

"Well, not pretty, but different." Vangie had to admit that she looked better; in fact, she didn't look like herself. The frizzy braid was gone, replaced by a blond, swingy pageboy—but not *obviously* blond, with brown and gold streaks. Not garish in the least.

"You have to fix up to keep a man," Waldene said.

"Depends on the man, wouldn't you say?" Edith lit a cigarette.

"I don't know about men," Vangie said, laughing, "but if I can knock off thirty pounds, I can advertise for Betty Crocker."

"Oh, you'd be a natural," Waldene said, bringing her hands together under her chin. "Don't you feel better?"

"No, I'm afraid to move." Vangie held her head stiff, shifting her eyes to see the women. "What if something cracks?"

"It won't." Waldene began sweeping up chunks of hair. "Honey, you can dance all night and you'll hold up."

"My feet won't." Vangie peered into the mirror and sighed. "All dressed up and noplace to go."

"Oh, we've got someplace to go, all right," said Edith. "We're going shopping."

Henry spotted the women on Gallery Street, their arms loaded with paper sacks, and he thought, *Vangie?* She had a new hairdo, a bouncy pageboy, and she looked as if she'd lost weight. An ugly little part of him hated to think she was having fun when he was so miserable. Bachelorhood, under the scrutiny of assorted gossips, was less enjoyable than he'd imagined. Everything seemed so unsatisfying. Last night, while talking on the phone to DeeDee, he heard water running down the sink and assumed it was flowing down the drain. He had no recollection of plugging it with the rubber stopper. When he finally hung up, he was astonished to see an inch of water on the floor. He waded toward the sink and shut off the tap. He didn't know where Vangie kept the mop; perhaps she'd taken it with her. It occurred to him to just sweep it out, but he couldn't find the broom either. Finally, he brought out towels and sheets, scooting on his hands and knees, blotting up the flood. He wasn't sure, but he suspected that all of this was DeeDee's fault—if she hadn't called and distracted him, none of this would have happened.

Not that she wasn't trying to save him. This morning, he'd slipped his laundry sack to DeeDee—same as every other day. He did it furtively, as if he were handing over something illegal. She said she'd take it home and smuggle it into her own dirty clothes. He knew it would reappear a few days later under his desk, smelling of 20 Mule Team Borax. It seemed to him that a man ought to be allowed to bring his laundry into the open. His empty clothesline inflamed the gossips. "It sure is funny," Harriet said the other day, "but I never see your towels on the line. Is your washer broken?"

"No," Henry said.

"Then you have a laundress?"

"No."

"How are you staying clean?"

"I have my ways." He gave her a thin-lipped smile, then laughed when she fled into her house.

Now Henry stood in the window, watching Vangie disappear into Mary Lou's Fashions. His mouth drew into an *O*. DeeDee looked up from filing her nails and said, "What are you staring at?"

"Just daydreaming."

"About me, I hope."

On the other side of the store, Miss Byrd hopped off her stool and stalked down the aisle. She narrowed her eyes at DeeDee and Henry.

"What's the matter with *you*?" DeeDee said.

"I quit, that's what."

"Why, Miss Byrd!" Henry said. He started to run after her, but DeeDee grabbed his smock.

"Goodbye and good riddance," she called after the woman.

"Stop it, DeeDee!" Henry wrenched free, but it was too late. The back door slammed, and Miss Byrd was gone. She walked over to the Majestic Theater and told Mrs. Quarles that Henry Nepper had suffered a nervous breakdown.

"What kind?" asked Mrs. Quarles.

"Pussyitis."

"Miss Byrd!"

"It's true. One minute he's mooning over Vangie, and the next he's sniffing after that awful DeeDee. It's just a matter of time before he gets to me. It's disgusting, a man his age."

"You poor thing."

"For as long as I can remember, I've been a loyal employee. Polite, helpful, punctual. Honest as the day is long," said Miss Byrd. "But I can't work for a man who lies to his wife. Next thing you know he'll be cheating me out of vacation time. He'll cheat on his customers, filling their bottles with salt tablets."

"Does he do that?"

"No, but he'll probably start."

Mrs. Quarles heartily agreed and offered her a job on the spot.

Henry stood on the veranda, knocking on the front door. A little black dog charged up the steps, snarling, and bit into his trousers. "Vangie!" he hollered. "Help, I'm being attacked!"

Vangie came into the hall and opened the door. Her hands were sticky with biscuit dough, and she wiped them on a towel. She snapped her fingers at the dog. "You go on now," she said. The animal gave the trousers one last shake, then scooted under a wicker chair, keeping his eyes on Henry.

"Thank God!" Henry cried. He slumped into the glider, the wood creaking beneath him. He narrowed his eyes at the dog. "What sort of creature *is* that? It looks rabid."

"Did you want something, Henry?" Vangie propped open the door with her elbow. She was determined not to invite him inside, even though she wanted to show off how clean it was.

"I just . . . " He covered his eyes with one hand. When he looked up, tears streamed down his face. "You look so pretty, like a whole new woman. I just want to stare at you."

"It's a little late for that, isn't it?" She wiped her forehead with the back of her wrist.

"No, it's not. Look, Vangie. I need to explain something. I know what you're thinking, that I was involved in some, I don't know, *romance*. But it's not that way at all."

She just stared.

"It was one time, Vangie. One weak moment."

"That's not what I hear." She held her breath, realizing how much she wanted to believe him. Wanted to believe that he'd been led astray by a conniving woman. Wanted to believe she could return to Cypress Street and put the infidelity behind them. If she knew Henry, though, he would misunderstand. He would think he could do anything to her, and she would always take him back.

"Honey, you know how gossip is in this town," Henry said, slapping a mosquito between his hands.

"They say you've been seeing that woman since September."

"Since . . . who told you that?" His face turned pink. "Was it Edith?"

"No, somebody else."

"Well, they'd better get their facts straight. That's how long the woman has been working for me." He rubbed his forehead, then slid his hand down to his bald spot. "And I've only been with her a couple of times. Maybe six in all."

"Six!"

"Well, it could've been seven. Hell, I didn't keep count."

"Can't you just tell the truth? First, you say it was an infatuation. Then you say you were with her once. Now it's up to seven. My mama used to say when you ask an alcoholic how many beers he's drunk, you multiply whatever he said by four. So maybe I should do this with you."

"The number of times doesn't matter."

"It doesn't?"

"No, because I meant I was unfaithful this *one* time, with this *one* woman." He drew in a ragged breath, then exhaled slowly. "Vangie, we got married so young. And this woman just rubbed it in my face. I swear it'll never happen again. Can't you forgive me? Can I please come inside and talk to you?"

"Long as you keep lying, there's nothing to discuss."

"I'm not lying." Puffy blue circles made his eyes seem small. He looked—she hated to say it—seedy. It would be so easy to climb into his Rambler and let him drive her back to Cypress Street. If she kept standing here, watching him cry, she'd invite him inside and cut him a big piece of cake. She pictured undressing him with sticky fingers, pulling down his trousers that the dog chewed, then lifting her dress.

"Come on, Vangie. Let's talk this thing out. Pretty please?" He smiled, showing crooked teeth. That smile, more than anything, made her think he was enjoying this. She stepped backward, her elbow jutting into the screen mesh, and tossed her head, feeling her pageboy bounce. "Sorry, I'm just too busy. I've got company coming."

"Who?"

"None of your business."

"See? I care about you, or I wouldn't be interested in what you're doing."

"I really have to go."

"You're just trying to punish me." Henry stood up, wiping his face. "But that's all right. I need punishing. I did have relations with DeeDee, and now you're making me pay."

Vangie, hearing the woman's name, let the screen door slap between them.

"I'll just be honest," he said, coming over to the door. "I was

attracted to DeeDee, but that's no reason for you to end our marriage. I thought you were stronger than this. In case you haven't
noticed, our baby is lying at Parish Hospital. She needs her family around her."

"We're around her."

"But not at the same time. Anyhow, since you moved out
here, the nurses said you're not visiting her as much. They think
it's shameful."

"Well, I'm sorry to disappoint the nurses."

"See? When I'm honest, you just get mad. So what's the use?"

"I'm not mad."

"Then why're you acting like it? I never deserted you. I never
once told that woman I'd divorce you and marry her."

"And that makes it all right?" Vangie's eyes burned. She ached
to cry, but anger made her strong. Henry seemed puffed up,
almost proud of himself in a way she didn't understand. Having
an affair didn't mean he was a loverboy. It just meant he was a
liar, someone capable of betrayal.

"I still love you, Vangie. I never stopped. Even when I was
with her, I was with you in my heart."

"Shut up."

"It's the truth. Hell, that woman didn't mean anything to me.
Being with her wasn't any different from peeing into a urinal."

"*Just shut up!*" Tears streamed down the sides of her face. She
kicked the door, causing Dog to scoot out from under the wicker
chair, all of his hair bristling.

"How could somebody so nice turn so mean?" Henry said.
"You've always had your moods, but this isn't my Vangie talking.
It's Edith who's done this. You've gone as mean and crazy as her."

"You're the one who's crazy. Just like your mama." She
inhaled so sharply that she made a little sound. Henry rocked on
his heels. He opened his mouth, and she saw a gold tooth. She
remembered how he'd suffered before he went to the dentist—
she'd bathed his jaw in warm water, then packed it in ice. Now
she covered her mouth with one floury hand, smelling yeast and
buttermilk. In all the years they'd been together, she'd never belit-
tled his family (not that she hadn't thought of it). Not even the
time his mother locked herself in their house and ripped through
the cedar chest, all the closets and drawers, claiming Vangie had
stolen her silver iced-tea spoons.

"Henry," she said, her voice patient. "Do you remember when
I spent one summer canning beans?"

"No! I don't care about beans!"

"Well, listen. I canned those beans, and they looked so pretty
on the shelf. When I went to open a jar for Christmas dinner, the

liquid spewed up. Do you remember that, Henry? It didn't smell bad, like you'd think, but the beans were spoiled just the same."

"Get to the point."

"That is the point. Beans can spoil, Henry. They can turn right before your eyes, and you don't even know it."

"Hell, I'm not a vegetable. I'm a man, Vangie. A flesh-and-blood man. I'm not a bean. And I'm not a saint."

"Well, whatever you are, leave. I've heard just about enough."

"You don't have to be so ugly." He jammed his hand in his pocket, jingling his keys. "All I'm trying to do is get you back."

"You're going about it all wrong."

"Then tell me what to do!" When she didn't answer, he said, "I know you still love me. I know you do!"

"I don't respect you."

"You don't have to."

"But I should at least like you."

"You're just in shock."

"You're right. I'm so shocked I'm liable to shoot you."

"No, you won't." He shook his finger at the screen. Dog walked up to him, sniffed his trousers, and then lifted his leg. Vangie looked down. A yellow puddle was gathering on the plank floor.

"Goddamn dog!" Henry held out his leg, shaking off the urine. Dog crept backward, snarling.

"You'd better leave, Henry." Vangie opened the screen door and handed him the tea towel. "I don't think he likes you."

"I'll be back." He jerked the towel out of Vangie's hands and dabbed at the wet spot. Then he walked toward the steps, giving Dog a wide berth. Before he got into his station wagon, he turned back and hollered, "You haven't heard the last from me, Vangie Nepper! I'll be back, sooner than you think."

Dressing up, Vangie thought, was the most bothersome task in her life. Waldene stood behind her, rolling chunks of wet hair. "You'll get you another man," she said around a bobby pin. "Just you wait."

"I don't want one!" Vangie snorted.

"Oh, don't be silly." Waldene laughed and combed out another section of hair. "You don't want to be like Edith, do you?"

Edith looked up from painting her nails. "And how is that, Waldene?"

"You don't fool with men." Waldene reached for a curler.

"And what do I fool *with*?" Edith lifted one eyebrow.

"Nobody, that's my whole point. You're loyal to the memory of your husband."

"Yes, we can't *all* be loyal," Edith said. "Phillip sure wasn't *loyal* to the memory of Margaret Jane, was he?"

Waldene bit her lip. She wound Vangie's hair around the curler and stabbed it with the bobby pin, causing Vangie to yelp and slap her hand.

"Oh, I'm sorry, hon!" Waldene picked up another curler.

"No, she's *not*," snapped Edith. "Because if she dies tomorrow, she knows Phillip will remarry within six months. Just like he did after Margaret Jane. Men *don't* change."

Waldene pressed her lips together. She threw down the curler and ran out of the room.

"Edith, you don't have to be cruel," Vangie said. "She didn't mean any harm."

"I know." Edith rubbed her neck. "I shouldn't have said it."

"Don't tell me. Tell her." Vangie squeezed water from her hair, and it dribbled down the plastic apron. "Make it right, honey. You all are neighbors."

Edith sighed and walked out to the veranda. Vangie rose from her chair and followed, one half of her head rolled, the other half still dripping water. Dog skittered ahead, running past Waldene, who was all hunched on the steps. Her big belly seemed to float on her long thighbones. As Edith sat down, she said, "I didn't mean to hurt your feelings."

"Did too. You're just rude is all. You hate me!"

"No, I like you, Waldene. But you hit a nerve."

"Where?" Waldene's eyes moved in circles.

"Inside me. I'm tired of being a good widow. It makes me cross."

"Maybe a hobby would help." Waldene's brow puckered. "Do you like to sew?"

"No, I need sex." Edith pounded one fist against her knee. "I'm too young to give it up."

Waldene's lower lip trembled. "I know *just* what you mean."

"But you're expecting a baby," Edith said.

"That's the whole problem." Waldene wailed.

Vangie, who'd been hanging back, walked over to Waldene and crouched behind her. She patted her shoulder. Waldene was saying, "After what happened to Margaret Jane, I reckon he's scared."

"Right. The hemorrhage," said Edith.

"In her ninth month." Waldene's eyes filled again. "He swears he caused it accidentally."

"Surely not," Vangie said, then leaned forward. "How?"

"Screwed her to death," Waldene said.

"A doctor wouldn't do that!"

"I don't know. He says they got carried away, then fell asleep. All night long she bled to death." Waldene placed both hands on her stomach, then looked down. "It was a tragic thing that happened to Margaret Jane, a pitiful thing, but I'm not *her*."

"He knows it. He loves you," Vangie crooned. She glanced over at Edith, who stared back, one eyebrow raised.

"Ha." Waldene blew her nose on her smock, then leaned back against Vangie's knees.

"No man for twenty miles," Edith said, lighting a cigarette, exhaling smoke, "and here we sit, three horny women."

"I'm not," Vangie said.

"Give it time, sweetie." Edith winked. Then she draped one arm around Vangie, the other around Waldene. Beyond the veranda, on the grass, Dog chased his tail, biting the tip.

"I'll bet you money that dog's a male," said Waldene.

That afternoon a station wagon with wooden sides clattered down the long drive. Mr. Flavious Pippin parked under the mimosa tree, then reached into the backseat. He got out carrying a huge vase of red roses. He walked up to Vangie and said, "Somebody must love you an awful lot!"

"It's awful, all right," Vangie said.

"Is something wrong with the roses?" Flavious blinked.

"They're lovely." She accepted the vase and waved goodbye to Flavious. As soon as he drove off, Dog dashed down the steps and chased his car. Flavious shot forward, leaving the little dog running in a furious circle. Vangie ripped open the envelope and pulled out the card. I LOVE YOU WITH ALL MY HEART, HENRY.

"Must be a damn small heart," she muttered. Dog climbed onto the veranda, his tail wagging. "I don't mean *you*," she said. Probably Edith would have thrown the roses into the trash pit, but Vangie carried them into the living room and set them on her mama's piano.

Through the French windows she saw Emmett's plane, a tiny red dot on the horizon. Floating above the plane was a powdery mark. Nowadays his marks seemed different, more like *V*'s than checkmarks, as if he were leaving messages in the sky. Or maybe they hadn't changed at all, and it had taken her all this time to notice.

Birds and Bees, Baptist-Style

ॐ

TEMPERATURES AROUND LIMOGES

Courthouse   85
Inside Nepper's Drugs   92
Limoges *News-Leader* 100
Hooper's 100
Beauty Fountain   104
First Baptist Church   106

The last two were affected by the sun's rays on the thermometers themselves.
—LIMOGES *NEWS-LEADER*, MAY 1952, PAGE 2

Fanny LeGette

When Sophie got to work this morning, she slumped into a kitchen chair. Sweat was beaded on her forehead. "Mind fetching me some water, Fanny baby," she said, wiggling her hand at the sink. "It's crazy hot out there. And it ain't even June."

I fixed her some water with chunks of ice. She drank it in five swallows, her brown throat moving up and down like an elevator. She patted my head and said, "You a good girl, Fanny. Kind and sweet and pretty like your mama was."

Later, Waldene made me carry a vase of coral roses over to the parsonage. Normally Miss Vangie supplied the church, but now we're doing it. Miss Vangie moved away and left Mr. Henry, and nobody would tell me why. I took my time walking to the church. A heat wave was passing through Limoges, and I felt about an inch tall, squashed down by the sun. I felt sorry for Waldene. We didn't have air conditioning, and she was swelled up like a tick from the baby. Even her fingers were puffy. She couldn't pull off her wedding rings. I pictured my daddy sticking his tongue down her throat, planting the baby.

I walked to the parsonage on Geranium Street, thrilled to deliver the roses by myself because I had a crush on Reverend T. C. Kirby. It didn't start for real until Olive got sick. Now, *she* had a crush the size of New York City. Somehow loving the reverend made me feel closer to her. It was my way, I guess, of keeping her alive, because my daddy said she's wasting away to nothing. But I wasn't supposed to go around telling this.

When I walked up to the church, the reverend was pushing his new gas mower—the Ladies' Auxiliary had bought it on his birthday, his twenty-seventh. A little redheaded girl sat on his porch. She belonged to that Robichaux woman who works for Mr. Henry. I'd heard Waldene and Miss Edith whispering about it, but they clammed up whenever I walked into the room. I wondered what the little girl was doing here because the Robichauxes sure didn't come to church regular. I heard that she rents herself out for yard work, so maybe Reverend Kirby hired her. She wore a dirty yellow-checked playsuit and scuffed Buster Browns without socks. There were scabs on her ankles like she'd been bit by fire ants. Reverend Kirby shut off the motor. As he walked over to me, he glanced up at the Robichaux girl. He looked from me to her, like he was confused.

I held up the vase, which was heavy Austrian crystal, an inheritance from Granny LeGette. I made up my mind to act Olive-ish, grown-up and sophisticated. "Hello, Reverend!" I tossed my head. My ponytail was too long and heavy to move, and I wished I'd worn it lose, streaming over my shoulders like Lady Godiva.

"Hi, Fanny!" He turned to the Robichaux child, who was now squatting on the steps, watching ants carry off a huge chunk of bread, something I myself liked to study.

"Billie?" the reverend called out. "You go on home. We'll talk later, all right?"

"But you said for me to come today." She stood up.

"Tell you what. You stop by Monday morning. Think you can remember that?"

"Yes, sir." She sounded disappointed. Then she took off skipping down the sidewalk.

"Did you hire her?" I asked.

"Hire?" He turned and watched her skip down Geranium Street. "Why, no. She just has some, ah, personal problems."

I was dying to ask what kind of problems, but I knew it was rude. Preachers are like doctors; they can't tell secrets. Now my daddy will let things slip—I've heard him—but you could trust Reverend Kirby. He was too close to God to be a tattletale. That was one reason I loved him. Last Sunday his devotional subject was "Gossip Will Be Our Downfall."

"These roses are for tomorrow's service," I told him. "But Waldene wants her vase back." Then I felt like a pure fool. My face got hot. Of course he knew we wanted the vase back; I just didn't know what else to say. "Shall I run them over to the chapel?" I asked, walking toward it.

"Sure. Let me go with you." He reached into his pocket, pulling out a blue plaid handkerchief. He wiped the back of his neck. "Sure is hot."

"It'll get hotter." I looked up at the sun. It shined through cottonwoods that grew along Bayou Maçon, which ran down the backside of the Yellow Fever Cemetery, just catty-corner from here.

"Let's put these roses up and then go over to the rectory," he said. "I could sure use a glass of water. How about you, Fanny? You thirsty?"

"I guess." We walked in the freshly clipped grass toward the church. I kept stealing glances at him. Waldene once said the reverend needed a wife, someone who could help carry the load, cook three square meals a day, and keep his dress socks mended. Every Sunday young women paraded to the church, wearing straw hats and white gloves, dresses colorful as Easter eggs scattered in the heart-of-pine pews—all hoping Reverend Kirby would pick them. Olive was the worst of all, the way she'd make sweet eyes and sidle up to him. Once she pledged forty days of continual prayer and didn't have time for doodly squat. It galled me, but I guess I was jealous, afraid I'd lose her to him.

I stepped inside the church and breathed in hot, stale air. After I set the roses on the altar, Reverend Kirby stepped back to admire them.

"Pretty as a picture," he said and let one hand rest against my shoulder. "The prettiest roses in all of Limoges."

"They're Miss Vangie's, not ours."

"Yes, I know. But you were mighty sweet to bring them." He smiled, showing crooked lower teeth. His eyes reminded me of blue rock candy at City Market. Freckles were scattered across the bridge of his nose, and his cheeks were red-tinged from the sun.

"Now let's go next door for our water." He dropped his hand to my elbow, touching the knob of bone. Then he led me outside, down a concrete walkway, to the rear of the parsonage. We climbed two steps into the kitchen, where an empty cereal bowl sat on the counter. Several Post Toasties floated in an inch of milk—a bachelor's breakfast. He didn't have anybody to fix him ham and eggs, biscuits, and cheese grits. I'd been collecting recipes for my hope chest since I was old enough to write my name. Waldene said I had the right idea; she'd heard at the Beauty Fountain that the way to a man's heart was through his stomach.

"A knife is much quicker," said Daddy, and Waldene stomped off. Before she got pregnant, they kissed all the time. Used to worry me to death. I just knew we'd have a whole slew of babies.

Reverend Kirby took two dented aluminum cups from the shelf and turned on the tap, filling them with water. I accepted one and made a silent vow to save my allowance and buy him a matched set of glasses from Morgan & Lindsay. I'd seen some cute ones all decorated with strawberries, or wedges of lemons and limes. The parsonage needed a woman's touch—frilly curtains, a lazy Susan on the kitchen table, wind chimes like I'd seen on Miss Edith's screened porch. Through the narrow door, I saw into his bedroom, the saggy mattress and plaid spread. It was just pitiful. He lived like a pauper. On the pine table was a wagon-wheel lamp, Bible, and Big Chief notepad. I watched him tilt back the cup and drink, his Adam's apple lifting, falling.

"You been working on the sermon?" I asked him, peering into the room. It was real hot in here. A black fan sat on the counter, sweeping back and forth. I took a sip of water, feeling my teeth click against the aluminum rim.

"I sure have." He set down the cup and walked into the bedroom. "Want to see it?"

Even though I knew better than to enter a man's private bedroom, a thrill shot through me. I felt special, chosen above all the other girls in Limoges. I scooted after him, hugging the tin cup to my chest. He sat down on the bed and opened the notepad, peeling back the top page.

"Now, let me see. Last night, I got all tangled up in Revelation." He sighed and shook his head. He lifted the paper with two fingers. "I sometimes wonder if John was mad when he wrote it."

"John? Mad at who?" I wrinkled my nose. "The Lord?"

"No, I meant *mad*, as in *insane*. They burned his eyes out when he was on Crete."

"Oh." I nodded, but I'd never heard that before. I had an idea that the Reverend was talking blasphemy, or else he was a genius, bound for glory like Peter Marshall. Maybe he saw things in the Bible that the rest of us couldn't.

"You're a pretty little person." He nudged me with his elbow. He had a way of staring like he could see to the back of your brain. If he'd been Catholic, there'd be no need for confession because he'd know your every thought.

"In fact, you are a little beauty."

"Me?" I set the cup on his night table and looked up into his eyes. All my life I've been called "cute as a button," which is impossible if you think about it. I've secretly held a grudge against all those powdery old ladies who'd grab me in church and say, "Oh, look here! It's Doc LeGette's child! Cute as a button!"

Well, they were cute as frogs, but I had too much pride to get down on their level. I wasn't naturally gorgeous like Olive. I was round-faced and glum. "You never smile," Waldene complained, but my mind was teeming with important thoughts. I wanted to be the first female doctor in Limoges, in the event that I didn't marry a minister. I saw me working alongside my daddy. "Scalpel," he'd say, and a nurse would lay it in his hand. "Sponge," I'd say, and the nurse would hand it over. Me and Daddy would take a boat over to Africa and do missionary medical work. We would leave Waldene and the new baby at home, of course.

"Just as sweet-smelling as those roses you brought." The reverend grinned down at me. "But a thousand times prettier."

I glanced up, suspicious. Probably he was trying to build my Christian courage. Next, he'd say I was beautiful in God's eyes. If you can't be pretty here on earth, what's the point of being gorgeous in heaven? Everybody else will be, too, so you'll all be the same. Waldene said that's why ugly Catholics become nuns, because no one else will have them. They become brides of God, wearing a wedding dress down the aisle; then they take their vows and wear black forever.

"You have nice wrists," Reverend Kirby said.

I folded my hands and stared at my stubby fingers. He lifted my chin with one finger, tilting my face up to his, and planted a kiss on my lips. I was too shocked to move. I never thought a kiss would feel so wet and soft. A tickle started way down deep in my stomach like a scratch I couldn't itch. In the back of my mind was the seed on his tongue, waiting to slip inside my mouth, and I got scared. If we grew a baby, Waldene would have to buy another crib—if she didn't slap me into a Florence Crittendon Home. I squirmed away, rubbing my mouth with the heel of my hand, wiping away all traces of saliva.

"What's the matter? Was I too rough?" The reverend kneaded my arms with his fingers.

"No." I blinked. I wanted him to kiss me again, but I wasn't sure how to make him do it without the tongue.

"Relax."

"I can't. A baby may get inside of me." I rolled my eyes, then reached up and scratched my neck. I wondered if I looked silly. It was a nervous habit. When I did it at home, Waldene said I looked like a monkey. Daddy took up for me, though. He said, "Scratching and picking fleas is a communal activity among baboons."

"But I don't understand," Reverend Kirby said. "How?"

"From your saliva," I whispered. My cheeks were burning hot. If anyone took my temperature, it would've registered 104. "It leaks into me when we kiss."

"What?" He smiled and shook his head, taking my hands. His fingers felt smooth and warm. "That's not true. You can kiss me all you like, and you'll never get pregnant."

"I can?"

"Yes, indeed."

"Then my daddy was right?"

"I guess he was."

"Storks really *do* bring babies, then?"

"No!" He threw back his head and laughed. "Nonono*no*! What have they been telling you, child? Just *think* about it. You're a smart girl. If babies were brought by storks, don't you think somebody would've *seen* one flying by now? Flapping across the sky, a little pink or blue bundle hanging down?"

"Maybe." I scratched the nape of my neck, digging my nails into my scalp.

"And every year there'd be babies who'd wiggle out of the blankets and fall. Why, there'd be squashed newborns all over the world. Wouldn't there?"

I nodded.

"I've never heard of any fallen babies. Have you?"

"No."

"And if babies are made from kissing, then Limoges would have over nine million people instead of 905. Or is it 906? I can never keep track." He shook his head. "Why, it wouldn't be safe to eat at restaurants. Family reunions would be dangerous."

I felt a brand new itch on my chin, but the reverend was staring. "I'll tell you what," he said. "Let me kiss you, and if you turn up in the family way, we'll drive to New Orleans and get married. I know a justice of the peace who owes me a favor." He picked up the Bible and laid his big hand over it. "I swear, so help me God."

I was so relieved I threw my arms around him, knocking him over. We bounced on the bed, but my lips stayed fastened to his. I rubbed my hands over his chest, down his sides and belly, like I'd seen Dorothy Lamour do in the movies. He pulled his lips away, breaking the suction with a smack, and shook his head. "We'd better stop right here, Fanny. Your daddy is a deacon, but he's also my doctor."

"He won't find out." I reached for his face, drawing him toward me, but he laid one finger across my lips.

"I'm a man of patience." He squeezed the baby fat on my arm. "I can wait for the fruit to ripen."

"It *is* ripe!" I said.

"You're just a young girl." He ran his finger along my face. It tickled.

"I'm not, either."

"You don't know the first thing about a man's needs."

"I do too. Olive told me all about it before she, well, before she—"

"Olive? What did she say?" His eyes went flat, making me think that he'd touched her, too. But I would've known something like that. If she'd kissed any boy, she not only would've told me, she would have bragged and exaggerated.

"Well," I said. "She told me that a man puts his *you-know-what* into a woman's china."

"China?" He looked confused.

"Yeah, right here." I pointed between my legs.

"Oh," he said, nodding.

"But I didn't believe her. I mean, it's just not possible. My daddy said she was lying."

"Well, he lied about storks, didn't he? I hate to tell you this, but Olive was right."

"Right?" I started to stand up, but he pulled me down.

"Please don't tell your daddy I told you. He wouldn't like it any." He licked his lips, put one hand on either side of my face, and said, "Don't be shocked, Little Sister. Your daddy was just trying to protect you. Keep you innocent as long as he could."

"That figures."

"He just loves you." He paused. "But you can kiss me all you like, and you won't have a thing to worry about. See, there's this little place inside you called your cherry. And I have something between my legs that breaks it open."

I knew men had the dangly things. I'd helped change many a diaper in the church nursery. But I'd never seen how they looked on a grown man.

"I fit part of myself into you, and we become one. Married in God's eyes. It's how the Lord intended."

"It is?" It sounded nasty to me, but what did I know. Plus, I'd lay down and die if I thought Waldene and my daddy did it.

"It hurts the woman the first time. Getting her cherry busted and all."

"It does sound painful." I tilted my head. "Why do they call it cherry?"

"Well, because it's red, but it doesn't have a seed. And it helps me love you in the strongest way a man can love a woman." His hands fell away from my face, bumping against my chest. "How old are you? Fourteen? Fifteen?"

"Sixteen," I lied.

"I've been watching you for the longest time, you know."

"You have?" My eyes widened, and I couldn't stop the smile from creasing my face. I scooted across the bed, close to him, feeling the heat from his skin. "Me?"

"Yes. I see you at church, and you always look so pretty and smell so sweet. I can hardly keep my mind on the sermon. My heart beats so fast, like it's doing now. Feel." He picked up my hand and slapped it against his shirt. "Do you feel that, Fanny?"

"No." I shook my head.

"Then I've gone past repair." He shut his eyes but kept my hand pressed to his chest. "My heart's just beating a mile a minute. I could go into a heart attack, right on the spot. Maybe I should lie down?"

"Should I call my daddy?" I was scared.

"No, no! It'll pass." He rolled over on his back, taking my hand with him, and squeezed his eyes shut. "I can feel it passing. It's almost passing."

"Can I do anything? Get you some more water?"

"Just lie here with me. Till the pain's gone." He opened one eye. "And please, don't mention a word of this to your daddy. I'll be transferred out of Limoges as fast as you can say John three-sixteen."

"Why?"

"They don't want sick preachers administering to the congregation. They need strong, healthy men."

"You're strong."

"Not really. I mean, if I was," he said, giving me a searching look, "then I could resist kissing you."

"Don't resist," I said, licking my lips. There was a big bulge in his trousers, his manly parts, and all at once I knew he'd been telling me the truth. I felt just like Susan Hayward in *I Want to Live*.

It took me over an hour to walk home, even though the parsonage was barely five blocks from Cypress Street, because I was forced to take baby steps. Two washcloths were folded between my legs, but it did little to stop the blood. Reverend Kirby said this was normal, to think of it as cherry juice. As I inched down the sidewalk, walking hunched over, red dots formed a crooked trail behind me. When I looked back and saw, I figured I didn't have long to live. It seemed like a whole lot of blood. The reverend had torn something inside of me, and it sure wasn't any cherry.

It took forever to walk down Geranium, then Lincoln. Luckily, I didn't see anybody I knew. Nobody called me down and asked why I was walking so peculiar. That in itself was a miracle. When I turned down Cypress Street, the sun shimmered on the lake, as if fireflies were breeding in the water. I thought about walking straight to the dock and jumping in. I figured I could swim to my house, if I didn't pass out and drown. I started to cross the street, but Miss Edith saw me. She was standing in her front yard, trimming her boxwood hedge. The clippers gnashed together, bits of green dropping from the bush.

"Hello, Fanny," Miss Edith called out. I drew my lips together in what I hoped was a smile. Then I lifted my hand and waved, keeping my elbows close to my side. I glanced behind and saw more splotches of blood, the size of quarters. My insides were throbbing.

"Are you all right?" Miss Edith bent over the bushes. "You're horribly pale."

"I'm fine." I forced my eyes to open wide. Then I swung out my right foot, hoping a giant step would get me home in a hurry, away from Miss Edith and all the other nosy neighbors. Way up ahead, I saw Miss Harriet sweeping her front walk, her upper arms just a-jiggling. I would never make it past that woman, but I had no choice. I took another huge step, and the cloths plopped onto the sidewalk. Pink spots danced before my eyes.

"Fanny?" Miss Edith's face loomed close, huge and distorted, like the magnification side of a mirror.

"I'm just . . ." I wobbled back and forth. The oak trees swirled. My addled brain told me to walk straight home, counting clotheslines until I found my house. It seemed to me that I was miles away. My house could be anywhere.

"Fanny, you're scaring me." Miss Edith set down her clippers and started to walk around the hedge. I tried to run and fell flat on my face, skinning my forehead.

"Dear God, you're bleeding!" Miss Edith cried, lifting my dress. She picked me up and started running toward Waldene's house. Miss Harriet threw down her broom, wrinkled her pug nose, and said, "What's the matter? Did she have another bicycle wreck?"

"I don't know," Miss Edith hollered over her shoulder. She ducked under a low chinaberry branch.

"What? What'd you say?" Miss Harriet puffed up the shady sidewalk, trying to catch us, but Miss Edith's legs were longer.

"Run faster, Miss Edith," I said into her neck.

"What happened to you?" She glanced down, and her nostrils looked like fuzzy portholes.

"I got my cherry busted," I said, gulping air.

"Your *what*?" Miss Edith stumbled.

"That's what he called it."

"Who?"

"Keep running." I pinched her arm. "Whatever you do, don't let Miss Harriet get me!"

Saturday Afternoon
in Limoges

❧

The Good Book is full of affairs and rapes. Like when Amnon tricked Tamar, his brother's wife, into baking him some bread, and when she brought it to him, he raped her. Seems like food and passion go hand in hand in the Old Testament, like one big appetite. The heathens were always sacrificing something, but God stayed in a bad mood all the way through Genesis. He shut down Eden. He liked Abel's lamb, then got pissed off when Cain tried to give Him vegetables. And He tortured Job. Sometimes I think I'm in the wrong profession.

—REVEREND T. C. KIRBY, PACKING HIS EARTHLY BELONGINGS, MAY 1952

Come Sunday, the Lord's Day, everyone in Limoges celebrates. All the stores are closed, and a stillness hangs in the air until the church bells begin to chime and the choirs begin to sing "Holy, Holy, Holy." Women dress up in hats and gloves, and the men look slick and uncomfortable, wearing tight shoes that squeak. Sundays are little family reunions, with people gathering on front porches, swollen from fried chicken, rice and gravy, biscuits, lemon pie with six inches of meringue. The men sit on one end of the porch, arguing the finer points of the war, praising Nathan Bedford Forrest, condemning Braxton Bragg. "We'd win a battle and have the Yankees on the run, and Bragg would retreat," the men would say, as if they'd been right there.

"Didn't even steal their supplies or take no prisoners," says another.

"Bragg acted like he'd lost instead of won."

"If only he could've been a Yankee."

On the other side of the porch, old ladies sit in rocking chairs, waving cardboard fans that say "COURTESY OF BEAULIEU FUNERAL HOME." The younger women comb one another's hair, speaking in hushed tones about tumors, comas, and other scandals. "Aunt Lizzy has a growth in her womb the size of a five-month baby."

"Speaking of growths, have you seen the Nepper girl?"

"How can Vangie not notice?"

"Well, she must've noticed something. She's left Henry."

"Because Henry has a sweetie."

"And the sweetie has a crippled husband."

Out in the front yard, children play in their dress clothes. Little boys squat in the dirt shooting marbles; their sisters and girl cousins dress kittens in doll clothes. Whole families line up in the front yard to have their picture taken by one of the heavy-set aunts (who does not care to go down in family history as Big Bessie Lou).

Before you reach Sunday, though, you have to get through Saturday, and Saturdays aren't holy in the least. Women spend the whole day polishing, vacuuming, scrubbing. Even the children pick vegetables, chop onions, gather eggs, polish silver. All over Limoges, up and down streets named after flowers and presidents, women are getting ready for the Sabbath. They iron dresses and trousers. They polish shoes, gather Bibles, slide quarters into small white envelopes. While they sift flour for Red Velvet Cake, a family-reunion standard, they call out to their children to study their memory verses. They send the oldest boys down to City Market to pick up food coloring; some recipes for the cake call for a whole bottle.

RED VELVET CAKE
1/2 cup vegetable shortening
1 1/2 cups sugar
2 eggs
2 T. cocoa
2 oz. red food coloring
2 1/2 cups sifted cake flour
1 t. salt
1 t. baking powder
1 cup buttermilk
1 t. vanilla
1 T. vinegar
1 t. soda

Cream together the vegetable shortening and sugar. Add the eggs. In a separate bowl, make a paste of the cocoa and red food coloring. Add to creamed mixture. Now mix sifted cake flour, salt, baking powder, buttermilk, and vanilla. Add creamed mixture to flour mixture. Fold in vinegar and soda. DO NOT BEAT after adding vinegar and soda. Bake at 350 degrees in two 9" pans or three 8" pans.

ICING
4 T. regular flour
1 cup milk
1 cup sugar
1 cup butter
1 t. vanilla extract

Mix regular flour with milk. Cook until smooth, then cool. Cream together sugar and butter. Add to cooked mixture and beat until creamy. Add vanilla extract. Beat until mixture resembles whipped cream. Ice cake.

This recipe is reputed to be very soothing to bake on Saturday afternoons when your husband is fishing or otherwise absent.

As the children pass by First Baptist on their bicycles, change jingling in their pockets, they wave to Reverend Kirby, who is loading boxes into his car. "Need any help, Brother Kirby?" they holler.

"No, thank you, boys!" Kirby waits until the children pedal to the end of Geranium Street, then he shoves the box into his trunk. Do unto others as you would have them do unto you, Reverend Kirby thinks. He isn't sure he wants anyone doing anything unto him, although a seduction won't be half bad, if he can choose the time, place, and person.

Back in West Virginia, Mamaw (was she still alive?) used to say, "Spit up and it will fall back in your face." Now, stuffing the rectory bedspread into his car, the reverend thinks he has spit in one too many local faces. He has lost control everywhere, from the belfry to the offering plate to his own little bedroom in the rectory. He has broken his covenant with God. Once again, he's been shitting in his own backyard. The time has come to move on.

On Vidalia Rogers's desk sits a note. He imagines her unlocking the church (a little surprised, perhaps, to find it empty), walking past Fellowship Hall, into the kitchen to prepare communion. She'll fill all the little glasses with grape juice, shake out oyster crackers into a basket. The choir will take their seats, watching the church fill with girls in ruffles, boys wearing white socks and loafers, women with thick, dimpled arms, men with their hair damp from Vitalis, comb marks still visible down the backs of their heads. Bessie Freeman will start up the organ, and the people will walk down the aisle, turning into pews. The choir will rise, singing, *"Praise God, from whom all bless-ings flow; Praise Him, all creatures here be-low; Praise Him a-bove ye heav'nly host; Praise Fa-ther, Son, and Ho-ly Ghost. Ahhhhh-men."*

As the reverend stands in hot sun, throwing hymnals into his car, he imagines the whole church waiting for him. He pictures Vidalia walking up to her desk, lifting the note with trembling hands:

> FROM THE DESK OF . . . Reverend T. C. Kirby
> Dear Miss Rogers,
>   I regret to inform you that a sudden, life-threatening family emergency has called me away from Limoges.
>   I don't know when—or even if—I'll be back. I hate to leave you all in a jam. I hope you will find it in your hearts to forgive me. Meanwhile, feel free to find yourselves another pastor.
>   Love One Another,
>   Reverend Kirby

He wonders how they'll ever manage without him. He thinks of the little old ladies who always promise to bake one hundred cakes for the annual picnic, then call him up crying the night before, saying City Market is closed and they are all out of sugar. They really thought he could do something about it, because the Bible told them so—loaves and fishes, water into wine.

Hell hath no fury like a pissed-off daddy, he thinks. Hell, they are worse than scorned women, and a heck of a lot stronger. All he can do is leave before Dr. LeGette hunts him down. Or maybe Sheriff Reems will come with bloodhounds and volunteers, scouring every square inch of the delta like the angry mobs in *Frankenstein*. It doesn't matter; by the time they knock on the rectory door, he'll be long gone, on his way to California.

"Before I hit the road," he thinks, "I want one last piece of Limoges." He walks into the rectory, picks up the phone, and dials three digits. Then he says, "Cordy, I've been called out of town unexpectedly. . . . No, I don't know for how long. Can you come over?"

Life Without Soul

∾

I was never trained to cook by recipes. I just put my whole self into tasting and smelling. I'd start baking in the morning. Outside I'd hear the rooster crow, hear the crickets screeching. The sun would fall through the kitchen window, hot on my arm, and the room would swell with goodness. Soon the food started talking—more sugar, pinch of flour, dash of sherry, splash of vanilla. Then I'd look up, and the sky would be orange and red. I'd cooked clear through to evening, and now it was suppertime. I was ready for anything: duck gumbo, shrimp étouffée, hot tamale pie, crawfish pie, coconut pie, delicacy, lemonade jelly roll, Jell-O divinity.

—SOPHIE DONNELL, DISCUSSING RECIPES AT HER WEDDING PARTY, CANE RIVER LAKE, NATCHITOCHES, LOUISIANA, 1930

Sophie Donnell

It's boiling hot on the LeGettes' laundry porch. I stand in front of a rotary fan, my dress whipping behind me. I lean over a deep enamel basin, jiggling soapy, wet clothes with a wire masher. The water is steaming. Miss Waldene says this is out of style, that she has a brand new Maytag, but I shrug. Say, "Go back to your sewing, and leave me and these clothes alone." Give me a basin any old day, and I'm happy.

I have a sour taste in my mouth, and I ache all over. Burr's sick with the flu, and his started the same way, only with high fever and a sore throat. I wipe sweat from my face with a towel, and when I look up, the screen door bangs open. In rushes Miss Edith. She's carrying Fanny, who's moaning and crying. Miss Edith kicks the door shut and hollers, "Hurry, lock it! Harriet's on my tail!"

I throw the latch. Few seconds later Miss Harriet runs up and rattles the door against the frame. She leans close, spread-eagle against the screen. Her body don't look human, like some kind of tree frog sticking to the leaves, oozing out jelly. Hollers, "Edith? Sophie? Everything all right in there? Anything I can do?"

"It's the bloody flux," I say. "And it's catching. You best stand back so you won't breathe it in."

"It is not," she says, but she comes loose from the screen door and walks backward down the steps. One foot slips off, and she starts to fall. Ain't got time to help. Miss Edith's already in the kitchen, yelling for me to come. Soon's I step through the door, I know something bad's done happen. The bottom of Fanny's dress all bloody. Drops spatter to the floor. Looks to me like she's been shot. Fanny, she still as a caught rabbit, the scruff of her neck tucked under Miss Edith's chin. Before I can ask a question, here come Miss Waldene running down the hall. She's holding her sewing box, using her big belly as a shelf. She been making baby clothes, and I know her mind will be swallowed whole by all this fresh blood.

"Edith?" she says and stops walking. Fanny's head starts lolling against Miss Edith's shoulder.

"Oh, my Lord!" The box falls from Miss Waldene's hands. Buttons and spools of thread roll across the floor, tinkling against the furnace register. One falls through, and I know it's lost forever.

Miss Waldene keeps shaking her head, looking from Fanny's dress to Miss Edith's hands—both are tinged red, like they been putting up beets and the pressure cooker exploded. Fanny moves her head back and forth. Her eyes slit open, and Miss Waldene rushes forward. She pushes back Fanny's bangs. "What happened? Did you fall down?"

"No, ma'am!" Fanny bursts into tears, hides her face in Edith's bosom.

"She collapsed in front of my house," Edith says, patting the child's hair. Her ponytail has come loose.

"But there's so much blood." Waldene reaches down and squeezes Fanny's leg. She lifts the dress, but the petticoat is too thick, like packed lettuce leaves. I fetch a old sheet from the linen closet and spread it on Fanny's bed.

"You can lay her out in here," I holler, then lean back and wait. Lean against the cool wall. Say, "We need towels for this child."

"Where are they?" Edith's standing in the doorway. "I'll get them."

"Don't leave me!" wails Fanny.

"Okay, dear. I'll stay. Shhhhh." Edith lays her on the bed, then sits down. Brushes back the child's bangs. "Don't cry. Please don't cry."

"I'll get them," Waldene says. She takes off running. In the hall I hear doors open and close. Then I hear her dialing on the hall phone, asking for Dr. LeGette in her trembly voice. Shrieking to his nurse, "Don't you tell *me* he can't come to the phone!"

Then she come to the door, her arms full of striped towels. Says, "Phillip's on his way. Fanny, honey? Can you talk? Can you tell us how you got hurt?" She waddles over to the bed and sits down, her big belly between her and the girl. Fanny's eyes open and her face screws up. She busts out crying, shaking her head, whipping it back and forth against the pillow.

"It can't be that bad." Waldene sets down the towels. "Did you start? Is it your monthly?"

"N-n-n-no, ma'am." Fanny hiccups, tears running into her mouth. Her lips are bleached white, two little pouches of skin.

"Then why's blood smeared to your knees?" The veins pop out on Miss Waldene's neck. "You didn't get, I mean, you weren't—"

Fanny's eyes are big and shiny. They fill, but the tears just stick there.

"Then . . . " Waldene shakes her head, looking from Fanny to Edith. "Did you cut yourself?"

"I want my d-d-d-daddy!" wails Fanny. She throws herself against Edith.

"She was attacked," Edith tells us.

Waldene whoops, clapping her hands over her mouth. She stands, weaves back and forth. Her face is real pale. "I think I'm going to be *sick*!"

"He swore he wouldn't hurt me." Fanny turns her face into the pillow and shuts her eyes. "But he did. I bled all over his mattress."

"Who?" Edith leans close. "Who said he wouldn't hurt you?"

"Oh, Miss Edith." Fanny looks up at her. "Reverend Kirby. But you can't let my daddy find out. The reverend said the blood of Jesus would come down on my head if I told."

Waldene rushes out of the room. Minute later I hear her retching in the toilet.

Fanny sniffs and wipes her eyes with the pillowcase. Now that Miss Waldene is busy vomiting, I have an idea Fanny will start jabbering. "It's my fault. I kind of egged him on."

"Shoot," I say. I'm spitting mad. "You couldn't egg on nothing."

She gives me a look. Says, "He hugged and kissed me, and I thought that was all there was to it. I liked it. Nobody ever done that to me, not ever."

"'Cause you a baby, that's why!" I say.

Edith's hand keeps smoothing Fanny's hair, sweeping down to her neck, then up, like she's pushing words up from the child's throat.

Fanny stares at her. Says, "I didn't know he would do all that other stuff."

"Of course you didn't."

"And then he put his hands in my panties." Her face screws up again, and she dabs her eyes with the sheet. "Miss Edith, once he got going, I couldn't make him stop!"

"Dear God." Edith shuts her eyes, then she moves her hand away from Fanny and bashes it against her own leg. In the bathroom the upchucking has stopped. I lean forward, look out into the hall. See Waldene stretched out on the tile floor, her arms wrapped around the base of the toilet, breathing with her mouth open.

"He said he'd never seen a girl bleed this bad," Fanny says. "I think he's scared."

"He ought to be. If he has any sense, he'll leave town." Edith cups Fanny's face in her hands. "Let's get you cleaned up before your daddy gets here, shall we?"

Dr. LeGette goes in to check Fanny and comes out cursing, ready to kill. Calls the reverend a bastard. Miss Fanny crying her eyes out. Miss Waldene crying too, saying she's going into labor. Me and Miss Edith go sit in the kitchen, listening to the ruckus. She drums her fingers on the yellow table. From the hallway we hear Dr. LeGette talking low to his baby, but I can't make out the words. My head's just a-spinning. All day I been dragging. "Think I'm coming down with that flu," I say, rubbing my neck. "Burr's been sick three days now. Got shivers and high fevers. Coughing up phlegm."

"It's all over Limoges," Edith touches my forehead, then pulls back. "You're burning up. You can't work like this. I'm driving you home."

I'm too sick to argue. Just smile and say thank you. Out in the hall, the bedroom door creaks open, and Dr. LeGette walks into the kitchen. He makes a fist and smacks it against his palm. "That son-of-a-bitch reverend is gonna be wearing stripes!"

When I get home, I find Burr lying on the floor. He's dead, I think, but when I lean down and put my ear to his chest, I hear raspy breathing. "Let's get you to bed. Come on," I tell him, pulling his arms above his head. He stirs and his eyes open to slits.

"Let go a me," he croaks, flailing his arms, batting at me. "And where you been? I wore myself out yelling for you."

"Working. You know that."

"Shit." He reaches out to grasp my wrist, but his arm flop backward, knocking against the floor.

"You're on fire, Burr." I kneel down and put his arm over my shoulder. He lean his full weight on me, pressing into my neck, and stumble to his feet. "You had anything to eat?"

"Naw," he say and coughs, spraying phlegm into my face. Then he shake out a weak laugh. "Sure hope you don't catch it."

"Already have." I steer him into the room, ease him into the bed.

"I could use a change of sheets," he complains, pressing one hand to his forehead. "And something cold to drink."

"Will water do?" I pull the quilt up to his chin.

"No, I want piss." He grimaces. "Fix me some soup while you're at it."

I go into the kitchen and bend down to remove the ash box. My knees gripe me, and my throat feels swollen. Then I walk outside to dump it in the bucket. It is a old habit because I don't make my own soap no more. I use store-bought Ivory. The cool night air feels good against my face. I wonder if I am still running a fever. If only I could just sit out here in my slip. I squat next to the bucket, taking my sweet time, looking up at the sky.

Let him sit and wait. He can't beat me into the ground for being slow. He too sick, too eat up with the flu. Way above me, the sky curves like a purplish shell, the kind Edith likes to spread out on her screen porch and draw pictures of. She brung all kinds of shells back from the ocean, where she and Mr. Zachary used to go every summer. Every year they went to a different beach. I used to get just as excited as they did. Once she bring me back a box of saltwater taffy, what Burr gobbled up, and a scalloped handkerchief, white with MYRTLE BEACH wrote in curved yellow letters. She said it was the longest drive of her life, except for the time they drove from New York. The handkerchief was the beautifullest thing I'd ever saw, except maybe for the one she brought back from Florida. It was pure white, trimmed in pink and red. The same exact shade of the azaleas behind Beaulieu Funeral Home when they bloom. If you spread it out, you'd get to see a map of Florida, long and skinny, like a man's doo-dad hanging down, only it was outlined in blue waves.

I never been outside of Louisiana except in my mind. Miss Edith told me all about it, her different beaches and how they fix the food different, and it was like I could see it. That's how I got to travel, through my ladies. I like to run my finger over the hankie, touching every city from Pensacola to Silver Springs to Tampa. There is a flamingo next to West Palm Beach, horses above Miami, and a sailfish off Daytona Beach. And these great big red crabs and sailfishes float offshore. Names I couldn't hardly pronounce till Miss Edith showed me.

In my own backyard the sun is a ripe peach hanging above the orchard, like something you'd see in Florida. It might look pretty poised over the water, staining everything orangy pink. From the house, Burr croaks out, "Sophie! Stop your lallygagging! I need me that drink!"

I stand up, rubbing my wrists like they got a low sickness, deep in the bone. I think of Mama, all crippled up in her chair, her hands drawing in crooked. I walk up to the porch, stamping my feet on the mat, and slip into the house. Then I shuffle over to the stove and bend over, fitting the ash box in its slot. I stuff corncobs into the grate, then throw in paper and a match. Smoke curls toward the ceiling, and flames spread to the cobs. I would like to nail Burr to the floor and pour kerosene on him. Throw down a match. Watch him burn, curl up like he was a paper man. Then I'd take his ashes and bury him deep.

No matter if you're sick, they's things to do. I call the chickens back in the pen and watch them trot up into their coop. Call the nanny goats and turn the mule into the pasture. Then I slog back to the house, straight to my room, and undo my hair. I slip into the bed and snuggle down into the feather mattress. The sheets cool my burning face, like I have me a sunburn. Like I've stayed too long in Florida with Miss Edith and Mr. Zachary.

All night I dream that a crow screeches out my name. This worries me because crows are bad omens. I dream of Burr's children, and they each one say, "Miss Sophie? We wouldn't never hurt Thaddeus. He got tangled up on his own."

When I wake up, I can't get out of bed. I press my hand to my forehead. I'm hot and dizzy. I throw back the covers and stumble into Burr's room. He's sleeping on his back, his legs sprawled on the quilt. They is a sick smell in here, rancid and sugary. I creep back to my bed, drag up the cool covers, and shut my eyes. All I want to do is sleep without dreaming, but my mind slips back and back and back.

What I see is this: Thaddeus holding up a string of bluegill, trying to get Burr's attention. Burr's working on a tangle in his own line. *"Daddy, look at this. Daddy, look. Look at me, look what I caught. Daddy?"*

"Burr!" I yell. "Will you turn your damn head?"

Burr glances up from the snarled tackle. He stands slowly, then slaps me so hard I taste blood. Says, "Don't you tell me what to do. Don't you call my head no damn head!"

Thaddeus runs under the porch steps, dragging his fish in the mud. Watches through the slats till we're through fighting. The big kids used to Burr and me carrying on, and his mama before me. They pitch green tomatoes like they baseballs, back and forth, back and forth, until they bust wide open.

"Sophie!" someone screams, but when I open my eyes, it's dark outside. Then I recognize the voice. Burr's calling for me, his voice weak and grainy.

"So-phie?" he rasps. "Get in here. I got gravels in my lungs, pus and gravels. It's time to call the doctor! It's time!"

"We ain't got no phone," I whisper, pulling up on my elbows. The room reels, white walls with two black windows, around and around. I slump over and shut my eyes. Seems like I have to be at Miss Vangie's at nine, only she ain't at her house no more. She's left Mr. Henry on account of his counter girl. Or maybe that, too, be a dream.

"Goddammit!" Burr growls. "Sophie!"

I pull up, let my feet dangle, and try to draw in a deep breath. My chest hurts so bad, and I'm shaking hard, like I got palsy. I ain't too sure I can make it to his room. Holding one hand against the wall for balance, I inch toward his doorway; my hair wrinkles down the front of my gown. Through his open window, the moon skims over the pines. I wonder how many days and nights we done slept through. Or maybe we already dead and this is hell—life without no soul. Me stuck with Burr for all eternity.

"I'm sick! Where you been?" His eyes are red like they holding back the heat from his brain. "Go fetch that damn doctor you work for, Dr. LeGette."

"I ain't in no shape to." I lean against the door, hugging myself. Another chill is slipping up on me.

"Goddammit, Sophie! You're just doing this to rile me."

"You don't have to scream. I hear you."

"I'll holler and howl all I goddamn please. I need me some medicine." He rubs his chest. "I can't get a deep breath no more. Feels like I've sucked in concrete. Don't you got no cough syrup?"

"Syrup?" Suddenly the room slants, and I grip the door frame to keep from falling.

"Quit acting up. Go to the goddamn kitchen where you hide everything. Go fix me something right now, or you'll be sorry." His eyes narrow and he grabs the sheet, crinkling it with his fist. "I swear you will. I won't stay sick forever."

Amen, I think, stumbling into the kitchen, blinking in the harsh yellow light. The stove has long since gone out, the noodle soup boiled down, leaving a burnt odor in the air. I don't even remember cooking it. I reach up on the shelf and run my hands over Ball jars. Beans, peaches, tomatoes, dill pickles, persimmons, quinces. The jars feel so cool, I pick up a quart of tomatoes and hold it to my face. I get so caught up in the feel that I forget what I come for. Cough medicine? I don't remember if we got any. Can't even tell where I keep the spoons or dishes, or if I have a last name.

I dig out a bottle of sassafras. Mix it with whiskey, paregoric, lemon, and vanilla. Then I pour it into a old medicine bottle and hold it up to the light. Nothing that will kill, nothing that will save.

"So-phie!" he screeches. "So-phie!"

I stagger down the hall, trying not to spill the medicine, and turn into his room. He glares at me and holds out his hand. "It's about time. Gimme that," he says, wiggling his fingers. I go over to the bed, and he grabs my nightgown, pulling down hard. With his other hand he grabs the bottle. Heat seems to blow from his body, and he smells sour and yeasty, with a faint stench of urine.

"Now you bathe me," he growls.

"No," I says, and he twists my gown. With the last of my strength, I wrench away, causing the medicine to slosh out onto the sheet.

"Now look what you done. I'll get you for this, I will." He lifts the bottle, takes a swig, and wipes his mouth. Then his eyes bug out. He coughs and sputters.

"Shit!" He spits on the floor. "What'd you give me? Poison?"

I don't answer.

"Say!"

"There's new coffins down at Beaulieu's." I step back to the wall. "Your black suit will look good against pine."

"Ain't got no suit. You too lazy to sew me one."

"I bought you one today." I'm lying, but I figure my Jesus will let it slide. When Burr gets well, though, I'll have to run fast. Run out of town and never come back. How do it come down to this? A man who sings you songs on the ukelele, then takes his pleasure out in pain?

"Yeah?" He glares at me.

"It's one-sided. A dead man's suit. Open in the back."

"Bitch." He throws the bottle. I duck, and it hits the wall behind me. The glass shatters, leaving a jagged brown stain, dripping to the baseboard. "I know what you're up to," he croaks. "Hexing, you hexing me. I ain't forgetting none of this, not ever."

I just stare. Don't say nothing.

"Now, clean that mess up. It's stinking to high heaven. I got to get me some sleep."

I'll pay for this later, but I shake my head. Say, "No." Then I lurch out of the room, leaving him to howl at the moon. I roll into bed, pulling up the quilt. My mama she sewed it before her hands went bad. After I married Burr, she give me a Star of Bethlehem, Cats-and-Mice, and Jacob's Ladder, what shows slaves rising to freedom. I close my eyes, and I am running along Cane River Lake in a white lacy dress, Burr's children skipping behind me.

Hallelujah, I say. Hallelujah.

The Undertaking

❧

I don't know of a time in the history of man where fornication rages more than today. It's a sign that the Day is approaching. But I am not your judge. I can't point my finger at any individual in this building and say you're not faithful, strong in the faith, or putting up with Satan. As far as judging the soul of a man, I'm not qualified.

—Reverend T. C. Kirby, from a sermon by the original Reverend T. C. Kirby

Summer darkness spread out like a cape, the color of aged lilacs, dropping over the Donnells' farm, over Bayou Maçon and the flat highway that led to Limoges. The stars were sewn into the night like patterns in the cloth. Miles below, a dazzle of crooked lights revealed the town. Inside houses supper dishes were washed and dried. Babies were laid into cribs. People drifted onto their porches, belching strawberry shortcake. They couldn't see their neighbors, but they heard them: Screen doors flapped on rusty hinges; children sifted through bushes playing hide-'n'-seek. The dusk was broken by flashes of orange, men lighting cigarettes, hands cupped around the flame.

Phillip LeGette and Henry Nepper walked past the Hoopers', where they saw Harriet sitting in her green kitchen, eating a wedge of chocolate layer cake. The men eased through the azalea hedge, heading toward the funeral home. Cab was waiting by the hearse, smoking a Camel. Henry looked through the rear windshield. He saw a coffin, rope, two pillowcases full of chicken feathers, a can of tar, and a gallon of cane syrup. When Phillip had told him about little Fanny, Henry had been skeptical. "But our wives think Kirby hung the moon," he'd said, shaking his head. Now he looked at everything inside the hearse. "What's all *that* for?" he asked.

"A little present for the reverend," said Phillip. "We're going to tar and feather his ass."

"That all?" Henry looked from Cab to Phillip.

"And escort him out of the parish," Cab said. "Ain't that enough?"

"What's that coffin in there for?"

"Oh, it's damaged." Cab laughed. "Calm down. We're not going to kill him."

"Then why's it in there?"

"Transportation purposes," said Phillip.

"He's not worth going to hell over," said Cab.

"Or jail," Henry said, squeezing his hands so hard his knuckles popped.

"He belongs in Angola." Cab opened the door and slid into the driver's seat. "Come on, boys. Let's go."

The hearse moved down Lincoln Avenue, turning left on Geranium. Two blocks from the church, Cab saw a petite brunette walking down the sidewalk, trailing one hand through a boxwood hedge. The woman had sturdy legs, like the cheerleaders at L.S.U. He'd recognize those legs anywhere—hell, it was Cordy King. He slumped down in his seat and pressed his foot against the accelerator. As he passed her, she turned all the way around to stare.

From the backseat, Henry was saying, "I don't know why I let you talk me into this."

"'Cause he's a raper," Phillip said. "He raped my child, that's why."

"The thing is, Phillip, he didn't rape *mine*." Henry swallowed. "He sure as hell didn't put her in the coma."

"You're saying this isn't your problem?" Phillip jerked around, staring at Henry.

"N-no," Henry stammered.

"It's a town problem, Henry. When Fanny was at the rectory today, she saw DeeDee Robichaux's girl."

"Billie?"

"She was waiting on the steps for him."

"So?" Henry laughed, but his voice was high and wavy. "She's a Baptist too."

"But Fanny said she heard Kirby tell the child to come back on Monday."

"Goddamn raper," said Cab, looking at Henry in the rearview mirror. "How old is Billie Robichaux?"

"Nine, I think."

"Goddamn raper!" Cab slapped the steering wheel.

"I still think we ought to call Reems," Henry said.

"Too late now. We're here." Cab angled the hearse into the rectory's driveway. Straight ahead Reverend Kirby was loading his black Packard sedan, trying to wedge a phonograph into the backseat. Clothes were layered in the window, studded with black shoes, choir robes, books, and paper sacks. When he saw the hearse, he dropped the phonograph; the cover snapped off its hinges.

"Where you taking off to?" asked Cab, stepping out of the hearse. Phillip got out and walked behind the reverend, eyeing the man's blue jeans, plaid shirt, and penny loafers. Very stylish for a raper, he thought. He motioned to Henry, who self-consciously shuffled to the left, forming the apex of the triangle. If the reverend ran in any direction, he was caught.

"There's been a sudden sickness in my family," T. C. Kirby said, his eyes darting from Phillip to Henry. "I was just on my way out of town."

"That sure is funny." Phillip reached in his pocket and lit a Winston. He held the cigarette between his thumb and finger, the smoke curling. "There's been one in mine, too."

"Well, I'll pray for you," Kirby said, "but first I've got to attend to family business."

"Sure, sure." Phillip waved the cigarette. "But before you go, we need you to take a little ride with us."

"Ride?" Kirby swallowed. "Well, I'd like to, I really would, but I'm already late."

"You're going to be later, preacher." Cab leaned forward and seized the reverend's arm.

"Let go of me!" Kirby tried to twist away. "Let go! You can't do this to me. I'll get you for assault and battery."

"And I'll get you for statutory rape," said Phillip.

"I didn't do it," Kirby yelled. "I didn't do nothing to nobody!"

"No?" Cab wrenched Kirby's elbow behind his back; the man dropped to his knees. Phillip hunkered down and held the cigarette's red tip close to Kirby's cheek.

"Get up and walk," Phillip said.

"This is uncalled for! What have I *done*?"

"You're a goddamn cherry popper." Cab pulled up Kirby by one arm and guided him to the back of the hearse. He glanced over at Henry. "Open that door for me. And open the casket, too."

Henry's eyes shifted back and forth, then he unlatched the door. He climbed in and lifted the casket's heavy lid, digging his fingernails into the wood. Just outside the hearse, Reverend Kirby threw up his free hand and tried to twist away from Cab.

Phillip waved the cigarette next to the reverend's cheek. "Want me to burn you?"

"No!" Kirby jerked his head backward.

"Then climb in."

"I can explain." He licked his lips. "It's all a big mixup."

"I don't want to hear it. I've been sewing up my daughter's vagina, what you tore."

"I didn't tear nobody!"

"Will you shut up and get in?" said Henry from inside the hearse. His cheeks were flushed, his heart hammered. To his horror, he was enjoying himself. This was more exciting, he thought, than an L.S.U.–Tulane game. No matter how reserved you were, when the crowd screamed for blood and victory, you were swept upward by their voices, and pretty soon you were screaming too. He'd even seen Vangie, a totally passive woman, scramble to her feet, waving her arms and yelling "Go, Tigers!"

"I'm getting tired of holding this lid open," Henry shouted.

Cab jerked Kirby's arm until he squeaked, "Okay, okay!" He walked on his toes, then climbed into the hearse on his hands and knees. He looked doubtfully at the coffin. It was lined with dark, wine-colored satin.

"Is there any air holes in here?" he said.

"Don't need any," Cab said. "Get in, boy."

As the reverend climbed into the coffin, he looked up at the men. "Are you gonna kill me? Just tell me straight out."

"*I'm* not going to," Cab said.

"Wait!" cried Kirby, looking up at Henry, perhaps sensing he was the weakest link of the trio. "If I'd known Olive was going to drink poison, I would've married her. I would've given her baby a name. I swear. Look, I'll marry her now. Just don't let those lunatics out there hurt me."

"Why, you son of a bitch," Henry said and let the lid fall.

Around midnight Burr started yelling. Sophie lay in her bed, trying to open her eyes. "I'm coughing up blood!" he screamed. "You get in here!"

All night Sophie imagined herself climbing out of bed and going to him. She pictured herself drawing water from the cistern and heating it on the stove. Then she imagined bathing his sweaty body as if he were her baby. Wiping the gummy strings from his eyes, dressing him in clean pajamas. Then she dreamed it was high summer in Natchitoches, the middle of August, and there was no relief from the heat. The corn was crow-black, and the cistern gave off a chill that smelled of metals and tasted funny against her teeth. She turned on the faucet, and water dripped slowly from the cypress barrel. When she lifted the bucket, it felt heavy, full of mud. She was six years old. She'd never heard of Burr Donnell, never heard of a place called Limoges.

She dreamed farther into the past. She was a little girl, lying under the porch swing, watching Daddy's thick shoes push away from the wood floor. Sophie scooted to the edge of the porch until her head dangled in cool night air. She watched the flat moon in a flat sky and wondered how it could stay up there without any strings. "How come the moon don't fall?" she asked her daddy.

"'Cause it ain't supposed to," Daddy said. "It lights the woods and helps lost animals find their way home."

From the other room, Burr cried her name over and over, but still Sophie dreamed on. She was bathing in Cane River Lake with Mary Annie. They found a shallow spot and lay down with their clothes on, dipping their hair into the water. Mary Annie's hair was long like their mama's, and underwater it fanned out. Sophie's hair was muddy brown, woven into a simple braid like . . . oh, like some white lady she used to know, but she couldn't see her face, much less remember her name.

Around three o'clock in the morning, Burr Donnell awakened, thinking it was August 15, 1917. He stumbled toward the kitchen, hoping he didn't run into Clynell's husband. Two mornings in a row Burr had forgotten to milk the Jerseys, and his back was still raw and oozing from the lashing. From the barn he heard the cows bawling, stamping their feet. It was raging hot, even this time of the morning, and his mouth was already parched. He kicked open the back door, thinking he could slip away from the house. Maybe he'd just creep around the barn and dip into the bayou, where it was cool and deep and dark. What Clynell's husband didn't know wouldn't hurt him.

He gave the barn a wide berth, then circled around the corn. He heard Clynell's husband rattling pails, on his way to the Jerseys. Burr ran down to the water and skidded in the mud. The full moon was on the rise, climbing up the backside of the sky. From somewhere far away he heard an owl. He eased into the water, feeling it ruffle around his chin, and floated on his back. Water filled his ears, and he heard a rushing sound and a gentle knocking, as if the fish were tapping out codes on the rocks. He washed on down the bayou, nudged south by the current. He passed under an arch of cottonwood and cypress, where crickets screamed from branches. The moon shone down on the water, reflecting stars. *When the great big river meets the little river, follow the drinking gourd.* Burr floated past a lover's lane, past a field of timothy and red clover, where a jackrabbit had dug out her nest. She rose in tall grasses, ears flicking, alarmed at the sound of human voices. Straight ahead, in a clearing, three men appeared to be chasing a giant chicken. The chicken screamed and fell into an abandoned rabbit hole. He went down screaming. Feathers wafted in night air. One of the men said, "Gotcha!"

Two startled frogs leaped into the bayou. One landed on Burr's chest, then sprang into the air. Burr heard the splash and tried to open his eyes. His body moved like a wrinkle in the water, faster now as the current swept him into Limoges. He bobbed toward the Yellow Fever Cemetery where slabs of marble and granite shone in the moonlight, like unripe crops still warm from the day's heat. His body thudded into a cypress root and got tangled in the branches; he arched his back and flipped over, facedown. He opened his mouth and breathed black water. It seemed to him that Sophie was running along the bank, her hair streaming around her shoulders like a young thing. She was singing to his children, who raced behind her, *For the old man is a-waiting to carry you to freedom/If you follow the drinking gourd.* He floated several yards, his arms trailing, then slipped beneath the surface.

Preserved Hearts

✺

TONGUE-BURNING PEPPER JELLY

18 red peppers
Cooking salt
2 1/4 lb. (4 1/2 cup) white sugar
12 oz. (1 1/2 cup) white wine vinegar

Wash the peppers. Cut in half, remove seeds and membranes. Mince peppers. Place in a bowl and sprinkle with salt. Put aside for 6 hours. Rinse the salt from peppers and drain. Place peppers in the cooking pan, and not just any pan. Use an enamel or stainless steel. Aluminum can only be used if it's been scoured, but I don't think the jelly is as good with aluminum. Here is another tip: Use the same wood spoon when you make vinegary things, as it'll absorb the flavor and might pass it on to other foods. Not everybody knows this, and now you do. Put your sugar and vinegar over peppers in cooking pan. Bring to a boil, stirring most of the time. Cook uncovered for 30–40 minutes, or until it begins to thicken. You might want to sit on a stool while you're doing this. Pour into hot clean jars and seal.

—ISRAEL ADAMS, FROM HIS RECIPE FILE, MAY 1952

Israel Adams

He's been dead a week, but she won't pick out a coffin. We still got him in the deep freeze at Beaulieu's. Got him stashed with a old Christmas turkey that somebody give Mr. Cab. "Ain't that something?" I tell Twilly. "To end up with ice creams and froze broccoli?"

"Better than to end up as fertilizer in somebody's garden," he said. "Or ate by hogs. That'd be the awfullest."

Mr. Cab said we got to talk to Sophie, make her pick out a coffin and get that man in the ground. She's had that bad flu, so I ain't rushed her. But before Dr. LeGette left town—and he tore out of here in a hurry—he said she's on the mend.

"She'll listen to you, Israel," Mr. Cab said.

"Me?"

"Yes, you."

I preen a little but hope it don't show.

"If any woman should be a widow, it's Sophie," said Mr. Cab. "But we need to get this funeral on the road. You'll go talk to her for me, won't you?"

"Yes, sir." I scratch my head. "I'll sure try my best."

I go on home to work up my nerve. I don't know why it is, but the idea of talking to her makes me feel shy. One time I saved the woman's life. I seen her beat up and bleeding, spitting out teeth. I drunk coffee with her and Twilly in the kitchen at Beaulieu's. But she was always Mr. Burr's wife. Now she just herself, alone in that rickety house. Alone and safe. If I was her, last thing I'd want be some man poking around, even if he just trying to give her a casket for free.

To soften things up I decide to bring over some food, only I won't write my name on the pan because she'll know it's mine. I go outside to the hens, shaking a can of Startena. All my chickens named after movie stars. I walk over to the little Rhode Island Red name Ava Gardner. She flies to the top of the coop and crows. Cocks her head and stares down at me with one eye, as if to say, You ain't fixing to catch me, no sir. Here lately she been crowing to beat the band. Don't know what to make of it.

"Go on, Ava!" I roll up my sleeves. "Get gone. You probably tough as shoe leather." All she good for is yolkless eggs, just little specks of yellow in the white. Doc LeGette say she probably got a hormone problem. I joke with him and say, "What you mean, whore moan? No, sir. My hen, she crows, but she don't moan. She won't have nothing to do with my rooster."

My rooster's name Frank Sinatra.

Doc LeGette just laugh and say, "Hell, fry her for supper!" He gone now, he and Misses Waldene and Fanny. Gone to Tallulah for the rest of the summer till that baby gets here. He got Dr. Bryant to look after his patients. Something big happen. Don't you tell me it ain't. They left right after the night I seen Reverend T. C. Kirby driving down the road. Feathers all over him. All the

windows rolled down and fuzz poured out of his Packard. I ask
Mr. Cab, I say, "You came and got feathers from my hens, and
now I seen Reverend Kirby tarred and feathered."

"Well, isn't that a coincidence?" he say, then clam up.

One whole week pass by, and the Baptists having fits. Trying
to preach they own sermons.

Calling up the Baptist headquarters and asking for relief.
Come to New Bethany, I think, and you see what worshipping
God all about. White folks, they too worried about how they dress
and what people's thinking to know Jesus. All the stained-glass
windows in the world won't get you to heaven any faster, but
they's pretty to look at. That's about it.

I catch me a hen name Bette Davis and wring her neck.
Always chills me a mite—maybe more than a mite—so I look the
other way best I can. When it comes time to pluck her feathers, I
can't help but sit down and be grieved. Fried up on somebody's
table is a sorry way to end up.

Now Bette Davis is crispy brown, piled up on a platter, and
you'd never know she had a name. If I wasn't in such a all-fire
hurry, I could take my time with this coffin business. Work up my
nerve and go see Miss Sophie when she ready to be seen. What I'd
do is make her some of my twenty-day pickles. By the time they's
ready, she be ready to pick out a coffin and get Mr. Burr buried
proper. But us ain't got twenty days, especially Mr. Burr.

I got plenty I could bring her 'sides this chicken. I got green-
tomato chutney. I got spice vinegar. I got quince, grape, pepper,
and crab-apple jellies. But a woman like her would have preserved everything she could get her hands on. If I give her a jar of
stewed tomatoes, she think I'm crazy. All womens know how to
put up tomatoes, but they might not know the secret: You add a
teaspoon, maybe a heap more, salt, sugar, and lemon juice.

So I rack my brain. I see Miss Sophie opening her door and
smiling at me. What's *this*? she'll say, lifting one corner of the
napkin. She'll sniff the fried chicken. Maybe she'll say thank you.
Maybe she'll pull me inside her house and start kissing me. And
maybe I am a fool. Barking up the wrong tree—one that ain't got
no squirrel. When a man's got courting on his mind, and he know
it's all one-sided, best thing he can do is pick cucumbers and turn
them into pickles. By the time they done, you either work up your
nerve or see the light. Twenty days give you time to think things
through. You can turn cucumbers into pickles, but oftentimes
you can't change the way things is. Life ain't no recipe. Some
things can't never be, no matter how hard you wish.

* * *

"All you got to do," I tell Sophie, "is show me what coffin you want. You don't even have to show me, just give me a general idea."

"A paper sack would do just fine," she said.

We're sitting in her kitchen, drinking chicory coffee from chipped white cups that's got "Morgan & Lindsay" wrote on the sides. I rest my head between my hands and glance up at her. "I can drive you over to Beaulieu's to look at the caskets."

"Huh," she said. Rolls up her eyes to the ceiling.

"Oh, come on. It's not that bad." I reach across the table and touch her arm. She so soft but got scars scattered like freckles.

"Maybe later." Sophie sighs. Then looks up sharply at me. "What's he laying in right now? The morgue?"

"No, got him in the freezer." I rub my hands over my face. I can't believe I said that, so crude like. *In the freezer,* Lord help me. Like he a roast. "Sorry, Miss Sophie."

"It's all right." She nods. "I asked."

"Well, that's where he is. And he sure can't stay froze forever."

"Israel?" She blinks. "I think I killed him."

"Oh, Miss Sophie. You did no such thing."

"It's true. He screamed and hollered for me, and I never went." She picks up her spoon and draws lines on the tablecloth, leaving thin streaks of coffee. Behind her, the screen door stands open, showing a tombstone blue sky.

"You was laying flat on your back with the flu," I say. "He drowned. He was crazy sick from fever. He just got up on his own and drowned."

"He called for me, and I didn't go." She drops the spoon and looks up at me with yellow-brown eyes. She sighs. "I used to pray he'd die. Now he has."

"You was ailing, too." I nod over at her. "Just look at you now, skin and bones."

"But I heard him calling. I just laid there."

Now it's my time to sigh. I pick up her arm and touch my finger to the scars. We ain't the same color. My finger's dark against her skin. "Lord may punish me for saying this, but maybe you better off. Mr. Burr, he can't beat you now."

"No. Guess he can't get to me now."

"Can anybody?" I say, and a smile starts in the corner of her mouth. She gets up from the table and goes over to the plate of chicken.

"Let's eat this while it's warm." She raises up on her tippy-toes and gets two plates.

"Already eat, thank you." I eye poor old Bette Davis. Taste bitter gall in my throat. Now's not the time, Lord knows it ain't, but I say, "After you eat, you think we can go pick out that coffin?"

"I'll let you know when I'm ready," she said, smacking down her plate. "I'll walk over to your house, and you can drive me over. You sure I can't get you something to eat?"

"Got any pickles?" I say, running my finger around the inside of my collar.

"No, never put up any." She reaches for a crispy thigh. "Burr didn't like sour things."

"I got some. Best they ever is. I'll give you a jar sometime. Maybe when you come over?"

"Don't hold your breath," she says and sinks her teeth into Bette Davis's thigh.

That evening the dogs start barking something awful. I go to the window and look out, and there she be, standing there in the front yard, holding a lantern. The dogs jumping all around, but she don't flinch. "Israel?" she hollers. "It's me, Sophie!"

I walk onto the porch and clap my hands. "Get down, you dogs! Go on!" They whine and curl they tails between they hind legs. "Miss Sophie? You all right?"

"Yes. I'm ready." She steps forward. "To pick out a coffin. I just now made up my mind. See, I got to thinking about Burr all stuffed into that freezer. Laying there with ice crystals in his hair." She shudders. "Letting him die is one thing. Letting him stay froze is another."

"Well, all right. All right. Let me just get my keys." I go inside where pans is boiling on the stove. I'd rigged me up a jelly bag with cheesecloth, and it's dripping grape juice into a white enamel pan. Mason jars are floating in a pail of hot water. Another set of jars is laid out on the counter, half full of pepper jelly.

Sophie opens the screen door and sticks her head inside. She looks at my kitchen, and her eyes get big. "Why didn't you tell me you were making jelly!" she cries. "Here, let me help. Let's ladle this up while your jars are still hot."

"What about the casket?"

"It can wait." She smiles and starts spooning in muddy jelly, flecked with red peppers. The air is tangy with vinegar. I screw on the lids as fast as I can. She wipes down the jars and turns them over. Then she looks all around my kitchen. I try to see it with her eyes, the shelves full of canned fruits and vegetables, all arranged by color. There's a row of tomatoes floating in quart jars like preserved hearts. I reach down and turn the jelly jars upright. If my old mama was here, she'd say what you need is always drawn to you, even if it ain't exactly what you want. You get what you ready to have.

"I never seen so many tomatoes," said Sophie. "Don't think I got a single ripe one at my house! How'd you do this, Israel?"

"Set them out early, treat them like babies. Already put up ten quarts, and summer's not even started."

"What you going to do then?" She smiles up at me.

"Used to, I give Mr. Cab my extras, but he got his own garden now. Don't know what he'll do when it comes in. Thing is, he scared to pressure-cook."

"He could freeze it, I guess."

"No, he can't," I say. "Ain't got no room." Then I clap my hand over my mouth, realizing I've done brought up something she'd just as soon forget.

"Oh, he's got some food in that freezer, all right," Sophie said. "I've seen it. So I guess Burr's been resting on butter beans."

"No, ma'am. He's resting on peas."

We start laughing, and behind us the jelly jars pop one by one.

Leaving Limoges

∾

Patient appears hot and flushed. Axillary temp—103. Some involuntary shaking observed. Eyes open and staring, but patient is not responsive. Dr. Bryant notified.

—ABIGAIL POTTER, R.N., FROM NURSE'S NOTES ON OLIVE NEPPER, MAY 1952

This is how I got here, thinks Olive.

Of the five senses, the last to leave the body is hearing. When vision fails, you will still hear the whirring of the window fan, a voice calling your name. The beating of your own heart. Morning light falls into Olive's hospital room, a wide arc that deepens by the hour. By noon her bed is washed in light. Behind her eyelids she sees gauzy pink. She remembers when she was a child, holding her palm over a flashlight, making her hand seem red and puffy. From the room across the hall, an old man keeps calling out like a goat. She wants to climb out of bed and tether him, but when she tries to move her arms, they stick to the mattress. She thinks she hears someone call out her name, "Olive? Olive, dear? Where are you, Olive?"

Her mother, maybe? Calling her home for supper. Or maybe one of the girls on Lookout Mountain, hollering out her name. She hunkers down in the dead leaves, hidden in the gully, while a girl in a brown flannel dress walks high on a ledge that shows exposed tree roots. Olive giggles, and Reverend Kirby silences her with a kiss, pressing her against the base of the tree. She does not see how anything can survive with its internal parts laid open to the elements, but the reverend assures her that anything is possible.

It is midwinter, a strange time for a church trip, but when the Lord calls (and He'd called them all the way to Signal Mountain

Baptist, Reverend Kirby had explained, to sing along with youths from sixteen other states), you generally answer. You do not play opossum with the Lord.

"I'm getting close," said Reverend Kirby. His rhythm changes, his breathing turns hot and shallow. "I'd better stop. Can't get you pregnant." He tugs out of her, cupping his handkerchief to his groin, falling back against the tree roots. Her hands are spread out on the dead leaves, palm up, and she holds her breath, waiting for him to lift the handkerchief. When finally he does, she sees that the fabric is dry.

"False alarm, I guess," said the reverend, climbing back on her.

She falls through the leaves, straight down through layers of time. It is December 25, 1946. She is ten years old, riding her bicycle, a present from Santa, up and down Cypress Street. Behind her the lake is the color of weak tea but cold as the Arctic.

"Put on a sweater!" her mama calls out, running out of the pink-and-white house. "You'll catch your death of cold! Olive!"

She falls through clouds and blue air, plunging deep into the past, until she is a fat-legged baby, her hands slapping over her mama's polished wood floor. "Da!" she shouts, peeping under a chair for the big man's legs. The big man who lifts her high carries her on his shoulders. "Da!"

"Come back here, baby," her mama said, running behind her. "Don't you go outside."

But she is too fast, her arms and legs are a blur, carrying her farther and farther away, until she is a tiny speck. The sky curves around her, and she is borne up by a thermal current, moving in circles. The delta spreads out in squares: soybeans, rice, corn, and cotton. The surface of the Mississippi glows with copper light. Sun reflects on the crooked road, shiny as the river. She sees the Galliard acreage, the square white house with the wraparound veranda. It is difficult to stay awake, but still she listens to the goat and wonders when Grandmama will call in the cotton pickers. The fields are white for miles in all directions. It is so hot an oily film hovers over the rows. She sees Papa Galliard sitting on the front veranda, rocking back and forth in a green chair. His neck is sunburned. Crickets buzz all around them.

"Bring me and Lallie something cool to drink," he hollers to one of the maids. "We're nearly parched out here. Bring us some iced tea."

Olive opens her eyes. Her lips are rough, and she could use a sip of that tea—sugary, with rounds of lemon floating in the ice cubes. It takes her a moment to realize she is in a strange room with green walls and venetian blinds drawn shut against the sun. She wonders if it is afternoon or morning. A woman with wide blue eyes sits beside the bed, reading the newspaper, tilting it toward the light.

"Tea," says Olive, and the woman drops the paper. She stares, then picks up her hand. Olive strains to look at the woman. She once knew someone with eyes that color, but she cannot remember who it was. Some boy from the delta, maybe?

"Darling, what did you say?" The woman's eyes fill. She holds Olive's hand against her cheek. "Are you in any pain? Can I get you anything?"

Olive wants to open her palm and move it all over the woman's face, as if she can puzzle out the woman's identity by touch, but her arms are heavy.

"Just tell them to hurry up with that tea," she says, or thinks she says. Behind her the cotton shimmers in the sun and the trees are so green and the goat cries out from the pasture. A few minutes later Olive closes her eyes and sees herself running across the veranda, her bare feet slapping on the gray wooden floor. She's running toward Grandmama, who holds out her arms and pulls Olive into her lap.

"Where you been, child?" says Grandmama, smoothing back Olive's damp hair. "We been waiting all this time."

The Queen of Everything

&

*From the word go, DeeDee was a bitch. DeeDee's my wife? I couldn't
do nothing right. I was always figuring her wrong—not by inches, by
miles, but she could read my mind. She'd say, "Don't tell me where
you're going. Don't tell me your problems." So when my Nash got
wrecked that time, I kept it all inside me, didn't want to worry her,
and when I got ready to take it to the service station, she saw it in my
eyes. "What have you done now?" she hollered. Hell, I couldn't shit in
the woods without her knowing about it. A man needs his privacy.
That's why I come to Korea—a full paid vacation. For free I got to go
around the world and escape a bitching woman.*

—RENNY ROBICHAUX, PFC, FIRST MARINES, KOREA, 1950

DeeDee Robichaux

When Renny found out I was going to Olive's funeral, he cut my
and Billie's new black dresses to ribbons. I'd spent two whole
days sewing them, too. So we were forced to wear matching
white-muslin frocks with navy blue rickrack on the hems. "You
can't wear white to a funeral," Butter said, and Renny sat back
and grinned, giving us the evil eye. "You look like two little
brides," he said, smirking.

When we got to Beaulieu's, cars were parked all along Lincoln
Avenue. This place used to be a mansion—whitewashed brick
with four columns and stained-glass windows like you'd see in a
church. Right behind it stood my beloved's house. Me and Billie
opened the door and walked into the vestibule. The air conditioning hit me in the face, and for a second I couldn't get my breath.

A sign over the viewing parlor said CAMELLIA ROOM. Through double doors I saw people sitting in folding chairs like they were watching TV, only they were facing flowers and a coffin.

I signed my name in the book, DeeDee Robichaux. I left off the Mrs. Renny, because that was fixing to change. "Can I sign my name, too?" asked Billie.

"Yes, baby." I peeked inside the room. Henry Nepper sat in the front row next to his hoity-toity wife, who was digging in her purse like she was trying to plant something. She was swathed in black linen, a dress I'd seen advertised in the paper. Her braids were gone, replaced by a stylish bob, and her hair seemed blonder—all the gray was gone. From the depths of her purse she pulled out a lacy handkerchief. When she dabbed her eyes, the flesh jiggled on her upper arms. Henry made no move to comfort her.

I never figured it would happen, but she left Henry. I was right there to pick up the slack, and all of his laundry, too. Which I did in a heartbeat. I was dying to get into his white-and-pink house, but he kept putting me off. This irritated me. A lot of things irritated me about Henry. He was all smiles to his customers, Mr. Rotary himself, then talked behind their backs. He called Edith Galliard the Yankee Ball Clipper. Harriet Hooper was the Wicked Witch of East Limoges. He called his own wife Dumb Bunny. While I was amused (and I'll admit I encouraged the name-calling), I wondered what he really thought about me.

After Olive died, Henry said I didn't have to come to Beaulieu's; in fact, he begged me not to. That's when I knew I had to come. I wanted him to know I had nice manners and I wasn't afraid of his wife and I wouldn't just go away at his convenience. Now I squeezed Billie's hand and guided her into the viewing room. Several people turned and stared, as if to say, White dresses! *Where's the wedding?* I smiled into their strained, puzzled faces. It wasn't like I had lots of clothes, but one day I would. That's why I didn't have any guilt at all about slipping around with Henry. If I'd had a real marriage, it might've been different, but I didn't. Even when Renny was well, he was sick. He stayed constipated, gassy, and violent. There's nothing worse than a sickly, demanding man who can't get it up. Of course, by the time they get that way, all soft and smelly, you no longer want them to.

As I guided Billie down the narrow aisle, I noticed all the flowers. Olive must've been right popular. Wreaths were arranged next to pale turquoise walls. On the largest spray, "PRECIOUS DAUGHTER" was spelled out in purple glitter. The casket itself had thick brass handles. The upper lid gaped open on its hinges, revealing tufted blue satin. Even from the aisle, I saw the curve of

Olive's forehead, the slope of her nose that was so much like Henry's I almost stumbled. For the first time I understood his loss. His pain entered my body, and it kind of felt like chest congestion, achy and tight when I tried to take a deep breath. I gripped Billie's hand, and she cried out, "*Mom*-muh, ouch!"

This got Henry's attention and everybody else's, too. He stood and rubbed his hands on his black trousers. Vangie did not look up; her face was buried in the lace hanky. Once she was hoity— but not so toity now. I walked up to the casket. Billie glided alongside me, causing several women to incline their heads and murmur. Someone in the second row was weeping, a thin colored woman in a cheap cotton dress and lace-up oxfords, probably Henry's maid or cook.

I gazed down at Olive. I'd seen her in the store a time or two, a thin, blond girl who plucked anything she wanted from the aisles and Henry never said a word. A junior hoity-toity. Her eyes, I recalled, reminded me of blue carnival glass, exactly like her mother's. I glanced down into the coffin. Olive wore a pink church dress with a Peter Pan collar; her hand was laid over a tiny white Bible, a line that Renny used to sell. A corsage of daisies and sweetheart roses was pinned to the pillow, with a card that said, "Love, Fanny."

I knew something Vangie didn't: Olive was pregnant. Months ago Henry told me. He said he'd be damned if he knew who made her that way. "Well, she didn't get pregnant on her own," I said. I'd been reading up on reproduction in *National Geographic*, and it showed these amoebas. They looked like snot globules, but after I read the articles, I decided it might be convenient—if a bit lonely—to be your own husband, wife, and child. Your own sisters, brothers, aunts, uncles, and cousins. If you wanted, you could have a whole family reunion with yourself.

"I don't know how it happened," Henry said, frowning. I could tell that he hated keeping this secret from Vangie, but she was such a ninny he had no choice. Why, if she knew Olive was pregnant, she'd probably go swallow rose poison too. Then Henry and I could marry, and I could take my rightful place as his wife, the same way Waldene nailed Dr. LeGette.

"Maybe she was raped?" I suggested helpfully.

"Maybe I don't want to discuss this anymore."

I got the hint. So I laid my head in his lap, and we just listened to birds calling out from the trees. We were in his station wagon, on his wooded property. Every now and then I'd push my head against his privates, like I was just getting comfortable. After five wiggles, he was hard against me.

Now I stared back at Olive. You couldn't tell that she was pregnant. The bottom half of the coffin was closed, and her pink dress was discreetly loose. I wondered if she really was pregnant. Like I was always telling Henry, even doctors made mistakes. And you certainly couldn't pay attention to gossip. I shuddered to think what-all was being said about me. I felt Henry's presence and glanced sideways. He was walking toward me and Billie, and he wasn't smiling. A bad sign, I thought. His eyes looked tired and red, with purple gashes beneath them.

"Hello, Mrs. Robichaux," he said, stiff-lipped.

"I'm so sorry, Henry."

He flinched, and I knew he was upset because I hadn't called him Mr. Nepper or Mr. Henry. Well, let him *be* upset. I nudged Billie, who was squirming at my elbow. We all stared down at Olive. "What a terrible loss for you, Henry," I said, saying his name a little louder than necessary.

"Yes." He cringed again. "It was a surprise."

I let that pass. Surprise was not the word I'd use. Olive had been in a poisoned coma for months. Looked to me like he'd be heartbroken, but not surprised. My child's hand suddenly felt heavy. She was barely tall enough to look inside the coffin, but what she saw was clearly making an impression. Her forehead wrinkled. I squeezed her hand, and she looked up at me with her daddy's eyes, the lashes long and stringy.

"She looks beautiful," I whispered, but I was lying. Olive looked ghastly—blue-tinged and waxy. Thin as a paper doll.

"Yes." Henry nodded. "She really does. She's in a better place. Free of pain and suffering. Free of all earthly needs."

This I didn't understand. If you took away all needs, then how could there be pleasures? You could bet your bottom dollar there'd be no sex in heaven.

"Thank you for coming, Mrs. Robichaux," he said, loud enough for everyone to hear.

"Don't mention it."

He touched my elbow, then shuffled back to Vangie. I stared at Olive for a decent interval, maybe two minutes, then I guided Billie to a seat in the third row. Two old ladies with yellowed pearls and false teeth frowned at me. They gathered up their gloves and purses. I frowned back, watching them stand and move to another row. As if they can smell Hayes Avenue, I thought, watching them settle into new chairs. I waited another decent interval, then I pinched Billie's leg and stood up. "Let's scoot, baby."

We squeezed down the aisle, wading over a tangle of feet, saying, "Sorry, sorry, sorry." But I wasn't. I didn't give a damn who I stepped on. When I reached the end of the row, I heard a woman mutter, "White trash."

"Excuse me?" I turned and scanned the row. I saw a gaunt-faced man with a black bow tie. Beside him was a lady with gray-streaked hair, cut short like a man's. The Hoopers, I thought. Next to them were three old ladies with whiskers growing from their chins. They all gazed up at me. I'd seen them before, cruising the douche aisle in the drugstore. One of them looked like the lady who baked cakes for a living.

"Did you say something?" asked the gray-haired woman.

"No, did you?" I narrowed my eyes.

The woman shook her head, and I saw that her hair was cropped off in the back, showing wrinkles on her neck. She turned to the other old ladies. "Did you hear me say anything to this *woman*?" She spit out the word like it was dirt.

They shook their heads.

"I should hope *not*," I said. "This is a funeral home, not a beauty parlor." Then I turned, pulling Billie behind me, and we walked straight out of Beaulieu's, into the warm afternoon.

I was the most miserable woman in Louisiana, living in a god-awful house with god-awful people. Renny had fallen asleep in his chair, and he smelled as if he'd messed himself again. Butter had dozed off on the sofa. A crossword puzzle book was propped over her face. The house was hot and sticky, with water bugs skating across the counters. Through the open windows, Mr. Spruel's parrot kept screeching, "Help, help!"

If I stayed here, I would scream too. I called out to Billie, and we headed down to Lake Limoges. While she ran barefoot to the water, I positioned myself on the second dock, in front of the Hoopers', where I had a good view of Henry's side door. Billie waded up to her knees and reached down to pick up smooth stones. Afternoon sun gleamed on the lake, making the waves look like crepe paper.

I'd read in the paper that Olive's funeral was at four o'clock, which seemed awful late. One by one, the neighbors returned from the cemetery, all except for Dr. LeGette and his family. They just picked up and left, and Henry—who never lied to me—swore he didn't know why. He thought it had something to do with Waldene's pregnancy. After his first wife's problems, Dr. LeGette wanted to be near the hospital in Vicksburg.

Pregnancy, I thought, rolling the word around in my mind. I watched my sweet girl, splashing in the water, backlit by orange sun, and an idea came to me, just like that. I would let myself get pregnant. It was the best medicine I could give Henry, now that he was vulnerable. A man could never turn his back on his own flesh and blood. Besides, I made pretty babies—wasn't Billie proof?

I waited for the longest time. Finally, his Rambler pulled into his driveway. He got out, walked around the car, and opened Vangie's door. She leaned hard against his forearm. When they stepped into the house and shut the door, I felt sick to my stomach. I had hoped against hope that he'd take her back to that cotton farm. I imagined them sitting at the kitchen table, his hand finally coming to rest on the small of her back, rising to touch her shiny hairdo. Friends and neighbors would walk over, carrying bowls of pretzel Jell-O salad and banana pudding. Henry would open the door, shake hands, invite them inside. They'd start talking about old times, and it would be just my luck for Henry to see his wife in an all-new light. The child was gone, but they were still parents. "It's the most powerful bond between a man and woman," he'd told me, trying to explain why we couldn't run off together.

The sun dropped behind the cypress, and the air turned blue. Lights blinked on in Henry's house, but I couldn't see him anywhere. Billie kept asking when we were going home. "I'm getting shriveled, Mama," she whined. "Please, let's go."

"Okay, sweetie." I put my arms around her. She had a fishy lake smell, and her hair hung in ringlets. As we walked slowly back to our side of town, a new idea came to me, and it was so wonderful I couldn't stop smiling. I didn't have to wait until I was pregnant, I could just pretend I was. In Henry's weakened state, he'd believe me. Then all I'd have to do was let him plant a real seed inside me. One way or the other, both of us were getting new lives.

"Why you smiling, Mama?" Billie tugged my hand.

"'Cause I'm happy." I scooped her into my arms. She was so light it frightened me. Like maybe she wasn't eating right.

"Why?" She stared at me with her daddy's eyes.

"You'll see, sweetie." I set her back down, and we started walking again. "You'll see."

That night I stole Renny's bottle of Wild Turkey and took it to my room. Then I opened all the windows and played Billie Holiday records. I sipped from the bottle and danced in my bare feet, singing, "Lover man, oh where can you be?"

From downstairs, Renny hollered, "What's all that racket?" I pirouetted twice, then turned up the volume. I didn't care what he thought. And I sincerely hoped the lyrics tormented him. They were kind of tormenting me. I put on another record, "Ain't Nobody's Business If I Do," then stretched out on the bed. Car lights swept across the ceiling, racing down the water-marked wallpaper and out the window. A dog barked. Katydids made a rasping sound like buttons rubbed together.

I had this terrible feeling that I'd never get out of Limoges. That I'd be stuck here on Hayes Avenue with Butter and Renny. I closed my eyes and thought back to the funeral home, reviewing my brief conversation with Henry. I replayed every facial movement, every wrinkle, as if I had a rolling pin in my head, going back and forth over the afternoon. Had he been trying to tell me something? He had seemed grief-stricken, to be sure, but I'd sensed something else. A new wiggle to his eyebrows, maybe. If I could get him alone, we'd be all right—unless he'd gone back to sleeping with Vangie. This thought startled me. I sat up straight, chewing a hangnail. I hadn't considered this before, Henry using his wife as a vessel of lust, but it was entirely possible. As my crazy brother used to say, "All pussies are the same in the dark."

I wondered if Henry had been sleeping with both of us all along, telling lies from both sides of his mouth, the old two-timing devil. I balled one hand into a fist and banged it against the wall. "That bastard!" I cried, wiping my eyes and banged the wall again. "I'll give him one more chance, just one more."

"What's going on up there?" Aunt Butter hollered.

"Nothing!" I yelled. "I tripped is all!"

Through the bedroom window, I looked straight into Mrs. Alice Womack's upstairs windows. Alice's middle-aged son, Ricky, pulled up the sash and stuck out his oily head.

"Turn off that nigger music," he screeched, "or I'm calling the police!"

I stood up on the bed and yelled, "It's none of your business!"

"The hell it ain't!" Ricky yelled.

I jumped off the bed and ran over to the window. "I've seen you watching me get undressed," I called out. "Maybe I should tell the police about *that*, hmmmm?"

He slammed down the window, trapping his hands. His face contorted, but I twirled around the room, laughing to myself. Ricky screamed until his mama came up and freed him.

"I'm calling," he yelled as she led him away. He held his hands in front of him, and even from this distance, I saw that his fingers were beginning to swell. I wondered how on earth he'd deliver Moon Pies. He turned back and hollered, "Calling right now."

"How will you dial?" I yelled. "With your toes?" Just in case he wasn't lying, I snapped off the record player. I hated to give in, especially to a neighbor, but I was fairly sure Henry wouldn't want any involvement with a jailbird. I'd lose him for sure.

The next morning, when I walked onto the porch to collect the mail, I saw an envelope addressed to me, with peculiar lettering, all cut out of magazines: DEeDeE RoBiChaUX. There was no stamp, which meant someone was bold enough to slip it inside the mailbox, or else paid somebody to. I ripped it open and pulled out a piece of paper, wrinkled from glue, with more crazy letters:

JEZeBeL WiNE
4 qT. FrESh RoSe pEtAls
4 gAl. bOilInG WatEr
6 lB. HonEy
4 lEMoNs
1 Qt. eGlaNtInE lEaVeS, oPtiONaL
1 oZ. YeAsT
1 mArRiEd mAN
1 TrOlLoP
1 cROcK oF LiEs

PLaCe pETaLs iN a cLEAN, wArm cERamiC CrOCK that yOu have pIcKeD oUt FRoM the dImE sToRe. PrEteNd THE vEssEl iS yOuR bODy. poUr ThE Boiling wAteR oVer PeTals, tAkING cArE nOt tO bUrN youRSelF. pLAyinG wiTh fIrE aNd oTheR hOt tHinGS cAn bE dAngErOUS. cOvER ANd let sTanD 5 DaYs. STir EVERY dAy, usInG youR fInGeRs & tOEs. StRAIn. PoUR bAck iNto cRock, BEcauSe tHaT's aLL he'S TelLinG YoU: a CRock. hE wIll nEvEr lEAve heR foR soMeOnE wHO liVES in SQualOR & whO wEARS whITe at FUNerals. ADD hONEy, sLICEd leMonS, & EglanTINE lEAVes, if YOU can FINd anY oN youR side oF tOwN. StIR Well. TaKe yEasT, pRefERabLY fRoM YoUr OwN bOdY, aNd SOfTen In 1/2 CuP luKEwaRm wAtEr. AdD YeaSt tO miXtURe, aNd bE CarEfUL NoT tO pAss aLonG aN iNfeCTIon, AS TroLLopS sO ofTen Do. CovER cROck & leT sTAnd 2 wEEks. WaIT & SEE if HE sTiLL wAnTS yOu. STraIn aGAIN & pOUR into boTTles. LEAVE boTTleS unCappeD for 3 dAyS. then CAP & cORk. Do NoT DrInk fOr aT lEasT tWo mOntHs. TiMe iMprOvEs tHE fLaVor. besT SERVEd tO tHe BiGGest WhORE iN tOWN wHiCH iS yOu dEEdee RoBIChauX.

I slipped the note into my purse, thinking I'd show Henry, to get his pity if nothing else. I needed his sperm more to make a baby, but I didn't know if he had any left. I had drained the poor man dry. Also I was utterly convinced—call it intuition—that Vangie was trying to trick him into her bed. If I were in her shoes, I would have. A man like Henry didn't grow on trees. He wasn't an EgLanTINE LeAf.

When I got to the store, he was already up in his perch, mixing cough syrups. I strolled into the stockroom and looked for a jar of grenadine, so I could get started on the lemonade. I knelt down. Then I heard footsteps, the clap of wing tips on the wooden floor. He called out, "DeeDee? Where are you, baby?"

"Over here."

He turned the corner and blinked at me. I stared back. He walked over and squatted down next to me. "How you doing?"

"Fine. You?

"Oh, so-so. Yesterday was pretty hard." He pressed his lips together and wiped his eyes with the flat of his hand. He breathed in and out. I couldn't help but wonder if he was in shock. A married man was most pliable when he was down and out. I remembered the recipe—we'd sure get a laugh out of it—but it might break the mood. I'd save it for later.

"I've missed you," he said. "I've been aching for you." He balanced on his heels, rocking back and forth, dropping one hand between his legs, massaging himself. "Listen, I just checked out front, and there's no customers. So I was thinking that we might have time for—"

"Henry," I blurted out. "I'm pregnant."

"What?" He looked a little alarmed, and I was sorry I said it. Then he glanced around to see if anyone had overheard—and he'd just said we were alone. This was a new habit, one I found insulting.

"I've got your baby inside of me, Henry." I sounded so convincing that I almost believed it.

"Have you been to a doctor?" he said.

"Dr. LeGette is out of town, remember? I don't even know Dr. Bryant. Besides, I've been through this before. I know all the symptoms."

"Oh, Lord." He leaned his head back and stared up at the cobwebbed ceiling. "I was wondering when this would happen. I mean, Vangie always told me that the mumps made me sterile, but I knew she was wrong. Golly, I'm speechless."

He pulled me into his arms, but I was the one who'd lost her tongue. The mumps? Henry? I had this terrible suspicion that Vangie was right. I thought to myself, Now you've done it, DeeDee Robichaux. Try and get out of this one. I squeezed my eyes shut, wondering if I could pass off my next period as a miscarriage.

"I'm just overjoyed! I always wanted a son," Henry said. He pulled back. "How far along are you?"

"Not very."

"I feel like celebrating. Can you leave tonight?"

"For where?"

"Well, I don't know. Maybe Las Vegas. I've heard you can get a divorce out there in six weeks." He pressed his hand to my flat stomach. "I can't have Little Henry growing up a bastard, can I?"

I laid my head on his chest so he couldn't see my face. I was afraid to speak. My thoughts were mixed up like Billie's can of Pick-Up Stix.

"Listen," he said. "You pack your bags and meet me in front of Butter's Cafe. Around four A.M."

"So soon? I mean, shouldn't we plan this out?"

"There's no need to wait, DeeDee. I'll pick you up in front of the cafe. Or is four A.M. too early?"

"No, I'll be there." I reached between his legs, rubbing the lump of flesh. His eyes rolled behind his lids. "Do you want to wait for tonight, or do you want to do it now?"

"Is it okay?" His eyes blinked open. "What about Little Henry?"

"I'm fine, Henry. Honest."

He unzipped his pants, and I leaned over, taking him in my mouth. He had a huge sexual appetite, one that sometimes left me sore-legged. I'd seen those dirty magazines he kept under his counter. A few weeks ago I sent off for a book that was advertised, but I had it mailed to D. Robichaux here at the store. When the mailman brought it, he turned it over and stared at the postmark. "Who do you know in Hollywood?" he asked me, his eyes narrowing. In Limoges, the mailmen were the worst gossips of all.

"Errol Flynn," I said, and his mouth flopped open. "We're pen pals."

Now Henry bumped against the shelves, and a bottle of grenadine toppled over, rolling back and forth, clanging against the other jars. Sometimes when I was doing this I thought, What's the use? I mean, it was boring, like eating chicken every day for a year. That was one reason I sent off for the book. Any love life could use some new recipes.

I took my time driving down Hayes Avenue, thinking, This time tomorrow I'll be gone. Each house seemed like a separate kingdom, the property lines drawn out by forsythia and crepe myrtles, the poor man's way of claiming land. I saw Mr. Spruel in the front yard, cleaning his parrot's cage with a hose pipe. I saw

Narcissa Harkey watering her hollyhocks. Next door, Santos Navarro and a dark-skinned boy hoisted a piano up the porch steps, through the front door. Mrs. Navarro held open the door with gloved hands. I saw Pernella Shaw on her porch, all stooped over, scraping leftovers into the cat's dish; the cat walked on its toes, brushing against Pernella's legs. Alice Womack stood at the edge of her driveway, hollering at two boys from Harding Avenue.

The next house, the Jacksons', was shuttered and empty-looking; Rudy and Ida May were visiting relatives in Tupelo. Tamera Mashburn's house had tomatoes rotting on the porch railing and a red douche bag pinned to the clothesline. Her toddlers stood in a wading pool, pouring out grass-flecked water with a measuring cup; inside the house parakeets flew wild through the rooms, perching on drapery rods and kitchen cabinets, the linoleum marked with green-and-white splashes, like wrinkles. And Louvenia LaCour, the retired floozy, stood on her porch talking to the Watkins man. I knew his litany by heart: lemon, caramel, vanilla, almond, peppermint extract. White, black, red pepper. Chili pepper. Allspice, cinnamon, nutmeg, ginger, cloves. Salve, liniment, toothpaste, cough syrup, Brilliantine, fly spray.

Henry had warned me not to tell Billie that I was leaving. "I know you want to tell her goodbye, but she's just a child," he said. "She's smart as the dickens, but she'll tell Butter or Renny, and they'll try and stop you." Now I walked into my little girl's room and sat in the window, watching her sleep. *I'll be back, baby. Mama's just going hunting,* I thought. Her brow creased in her sleep, as if she'd heard. I got up and walked over to her dresser, which was nothing but a strip of old kitchen cabinets we'd bought at the junk shop. I'd fixed it up with cute decals of butterflies. All her crayons were lined up on the metal drainboard. I chose red, then rummaged in the drawer until I found some drawing paper.

Billie rolled over, pulling the sheet tightly around her. She was so wise, it was hard to remember she was only nine. She could carry on a conversation like a regular adult. When I wrote the letter, though, I wrote to the part of her that was still a little girl.

Dear Billie,
When you wake up I'll be gone, but don't be sad. Just get dressed and eat your breakfast and be a good girl for your daddy and Aunt Butter. I will be back in a few weeks. Then we will have a heart to heart talk, and I will tell you some happy news. I will bring you back a souvenir, too.
I love you, Mama

I propped the note on her metal TV table, which she used for a nightstand. Then I kissed her forehead. She rolled over again and said, "Slub." Soon she'd be living like a princess on Cypress Street, and I'd be the queen of everything.

When I got back to my room, I was too excited to sleep. I brushed my hair, then wove it into a French braid. Twice I unpacked my suitcase and folded everything all over again. At a quarter to four, I crept downstairs. The door to Renny's room was slit open, but I couldn't see anything except a wedge of the metal hospital bed, the trapeze bar dangling over his chest. I held my breath, trying to remember which board in the hallway made the creaky noise. Renny was a light sleeper, and so was Butter. I half expected to see her standing next to the banister, her hair in pin-curls, squinting down at me. "You, DeeDee!" she'd cry. "Just where do you think you're going?"

The light in the living room was speckled, as if filled with television static, but I made my way past the nubby brown sofa and Butter's vinyl recliner. All the windows stood open, and the muslin curtains were stuck to the screens. Here at Butter's, noth-ing ever changed. Not the calf-roping pictures over the TV or the old cowboy hats lined up on the bookcase. This house broke my heart. I peered into the hall mirror and fingered my long braid. God, I looked awful. My hair was in knots, like something to hang me up by.

I eased open the screen door and sidestepped Billie's dog, Mrs. Happy. The dog's boyfriends came and went, but she stayed pregnant. She lifted her head from her paws and gave a disgusted snort. I stepped over her, then hurried down the steps, swinging my suitcases. The wind swept across the porch, making the old glider creak. I picked my way to the sidewalk. Hayes Avenue was deserted, and my footsteps echoed. I walked to the corner and turned right. Henry's car was parked in front of Butter's, where a faded WE'RE CLOSED sign hung in the window.

"You ready?" he said when I opened the door.

I nodded.

"Then let's go." He angled the car away from the curb. "I thought we'd spend a few nights in Monroe, just to get our bear-ings. Then we can head out to Las Vegas."

I was too excited to answer. At long last, I was leaving Hayes Avenue. Wind whooshed through the window, cool and thick, slapping against my face. He turned a corner, then circled back. As he passed Hayes Avenue again, I turned for one last look at Butter's house. When I was young, it had seemed huge, but now it seemed to shrink under the early-morning sky. The Rambler glided through the empty streets, around the Square, around the lake, then turned west on Monroe Highway.

I closed my eyes and thought of Butter turning in her sleep, one hand reaching across her empty bed. I imagined Renny sleeping on his back, the air heavy with bourbon and man-smell, his legs motionless beneath ironed rosebud sheets that I had spread earlier. Billie breathed soft as a baby, the quilt rising and falling around her shoulders. Her windows would glow violet, then blue as the sun began to climb. Butter's alarm clock would dance on three legs. She would grope for her slippers, humming to herself, thinking about making coffee and biscuits. Then she'd walk down the hall, past my room and Billie's, feeling her way down the stairs. Above her, my empty bed would wait, the linen showing the imprint of my body, as if I'd slept in plaster.

Victory Garden

❧

Head hunters of the Amazon River have an odd ritual for widows who wish to remarry. She must find a termite nest, then set it on fire. She covers it with a cloth, fashioning a crude tent, then climbs inside. She inhales smoke until she nearly suffocates. This ceremony both cleanses and frees her from the taboo associated with widowhood.

—NATIONAL GEOGRAPHIC, MAY 1952

It was the end of May, and everything was hazy-hot. Yellowjackets floated in drunken circles, as if dazed by the heat. Edith stood in her backyard, where a fifty-foot weeping willow blocked the sun. Tawny leaves drifted down. She knelt in her garden, pinching off nasturtium buds. Most people thought she was crazy, but she knew what she was doing. When she moved from New York, she had no way of buying capers. A chef in New Orleans told her she could use nasturtiums for rather tasty mock capers. He gave her a recipe, swearing her to secrecy. It required soaking the buds in a brine solution, made with 1 cup salt in 2 quarts water.

Through a gap in the azaleas she saw Cab's corn, the tassels lifting in the breeze. It was a good, deep yard, made for children, if you didn't count the ruined caskets stacked up behind the shed, or the discarded wreaths with faded bows that spelled out BELOVED MOTHER, REST IN PEACE.

For years Cypress Street had been Edith's home. It was not New York by any means, but she had slipped into the groove of small-town life, into the pleasures of seeing her neighbors live their lives: Vangie hanging out Henry's damp shirts on the clothesline; Olive and Fanny gathering pecans to throw at Harriet; even Harriet, keeping her yard immaculate and barren like

herself. Sometimes Margaret Jane and Phillip would walk over
for secret glasses of wine, holding little Fanny on their laps.
Later he brought Waldene over, showing her off to the newly
widowed Edith. In the old days, Vangie and Henry would join
them, sometimes the elder Beaulieus. Pretty soon Zachary and
Edith had a crowd on their screened porch. Harriet refused to
join them, but she turned up her record player and spied
through her venetians.

At first Edith hated Beaulieu's. In those days, Zachary wasn't
a judge—he had an office downtown over the bakery, and she
filled in as his secretary. Soon, though, she grew accustomed to
mourners threading in and out of Beaulieu's. After a while she
paid no attention to coffins being hoisted into the back of the
hearse like pieces of furniture, sideboards, and long coffee tables.

Now the quality of the neighborhood had changed. The pleasures she'd taken for granted were gone. Vangie was living at the
old Galliard place, learning to drive the Major's old stick shift.
She had not filed for a divorce, but now that Olive was gone she
had no reason to maintain the pretense of family—at least that's
what Edith hoped.

"She's sleeping with two shotguns under her mattress,"
Sophie told Edith the other day. "And she got pistols hanging
from all four posts on her mama's teester bed."

"My God." Edith rolled her eyes.

"She got dogs, she got peafowl, she got honking geese. Ain't
nobody going to get Miss Vangie." Sophie laughed.

"I've got to admire her. She's trying."

"Some people live *on* the earth, Miss Edith. Just skimming
the surface is all. And some people live *in* it. Miss Vangie's trying
to dig in, hold her own. And not let this thing with Mr. Henry
bury her."

If Henry and Vangie ever got divorced, Edith knew he'd
marry the Robichaux woman. Which would once again give her a
little girl next door, because there was no telling when Fanny
would be back. Phillip and Waldene planned to stay in Tallulah
until after the baby came. They had left so suddenly, Edith hadn't
said goodbye, but Sophie said Fanny was stronger and more dev-
ilish than anyone knew. Before the incident at First Baptist,
Fanny had been collecting hordes of mosquitoes in old mason
jars.

"Thousands of them," Sophie said, waving her hands. "To set
loose in Miss Harriet's house."

And Reverend Kirby had left town under mysterious circum-
stances, leaving the Baptists in a frenzy. Edith strongly suspected

Phillip was responsible—not that she blamed him. And strangest of all, Sophie was drunk on widowhood. She was talking about quitting all her day jobs, returning to Natchitoches. Only Harriet stayed the same—talking on her phone, cracking pecans in the hammock, spying behind her venetians. Edith wasn't religious, but even she had to admit that the Lord moved in mysterious ways. The mystery was why He had taken everyone she loved.

Through the azaleas, she saw a flash of blue—Cab squatting in the tomatoes, tying up a fallen vine. She lit a cigarette and watched him thoughtfully. She'd heard in a roundabout way (Sophie, of course) that even he might be leaving. He'd told Israel, and Israel had told Sophie, that he was thinking of selling Beaulieu's to his rival in the next parish, Mr. Johnson. Then Cab would take his money and move to Miami.

"Why Miami?" Edith had asked Sophie.

"Said it's warm in the winter."

"Yes, but he'll boil every summer."

"If he don't go there," Sophie said, "he'll go somewhere. He's got that itch. Said he's had it with Limoges."

"Haven't we all?"

"I don't know. A place can surprise you."

"It hasn't surprised me. When are you leaving?"

"When I get good and ready."

"But you'll go, won't you?" Edith held her breath. It would break her heart if Sophie nodded. Instead, she ducked her head and wouldn't answer.

"I don't understand why things have to change." Edith sighed.

"Even the Mississippi changes. That's how we got Lake Limoges. Israel said it's a oxbow."

"Everybody knows that, Sophie."

"I didn't."

"Well, you should have. You've lived here long enough."

"I come from another place where the river jumped out of its bed." She squinted up at Edith. "You sure crabby today. You need to get you a man." Sophie laughed.

"I need a man like I need a hole in my head."

"Maybe you need one of them, too." She reached over and hugged Edith. "Then I can knock some sense in."

Now Edith looked up at the sky. It was just too hot to think. If she had her druthers, she'd go around naked. Instead, she twisted her hair into a French knot and pulled on a chartreuse sheath. It was too humid for panties; she'd never been fond of wearing them, but only Zachary knew her secret. She went into the kitchen and started pickling nasturtiums.

MOCK CAPERS

When the Real Thing Just Won't Do

Gather only green nasturtium buds (yellow ones are too old and therefore useless—and so are those that have already bloomed). Place the buds in a 10% brine solution. The buds will try to float, so spread cheesecloth over them and weight down with a saucer. Let them soak 24 hours. Drain the brine. Soak the buds in cold water for 1 hour. Drain buds again. Bring vinegar to a boil in an enamel pot. Pack buds in hot, sterilized jars (pints). Cover with the boiling vinegar. Seal and process 10 minutes in a boiling-water bath. Let your "capers" stand 6 weeks, as aging improves flavor.

After the sun went down, Edith sat on the screened porch, smoking, drinking gin and tonic. Arranged on the metal table were lemons, asparagus, and carrots. A sketch pad was propped on the floor. A good drawing tip was to pick the most revealing side of your subject. Most objects had shapes that revealed identity from one angle but obscured it from another. She was a student of light and shadow. Her initial sketches were always in black and white. From her days in art school, she remembered a quote from Edouard Manet: "I search for full light and full shadow; everything else is already there."

The lights blinked on in the upstairs windows of Beaulieu's, and she saw Cab walking back and forth. Gin was the best nerve medicine on the market, and she was trying to build hers up. She loved the tang and sting of gin, the medicinal all-is-well smell. It went down like a cure, but came back poison. In general, she didn't need a man—she had her work—but now that she'd developed a yen for a particular one, it was hard to ignore him. Even if you were seven years older.

She had driven herself insane with mathematics. When she was eighty, if she were still alive, Cab would be seventy-three. So far, so good—they could live in the same nursing home. When she was sixty, he'd be fifty-three. That wasn't too bad either. They could creep around Lake Limoges for daily exercise. But when she was fifty, he'd be forty-three, and *that* scared the hell out of her. The danger was in the near, not the far: The older they got, the better.

It was the next ten years that alarmed her. She pictured him waking up and viewing her in harsh morning light, thinking he'd slept with an old woman. She took another swallow of gin and felt it move into her limbs. Until she'd made love with Cab, she'd never worried about wrinkles. She supposed she'd spurned him because he made her feel old. So she pinched off the bloom, the same way she pinched back her impatiens. In the back of her mind, she hoped the plant would bush wide, bloom its heart out. At first she accused herself of being a cradle robber. Then she began to wonder if she were trying to replace Zachary; if she let things start up with Cab, wouldn't she be doing *just* that? Men were not sugar substitutes. She wouldn't dream of using saccharine. If she couldn't get sugar, she'd stop drinking coffee.

She missed Zachary more than she could say, but she wasn't willing to spend the rest of her life in mourning. Thirty-nine was not a widowy age. If she lived in New York, she would have slept with Cab and enjoyed him to the nth degree. She had no idea why she'd lost her sense of adventure, but it was gone.

Thus, the gin: false nerve.

It was dusky dark. She walked outside, a cigarette in one hand, a fresh drink in the other. She headed toward the azaleas. All of the backyards on Cypress were flecked with lightning bugs. There had to be thousands of them, all blinking their lights to attract lovers. Edith walked slowly. She'd forgotten how pretty May nights could be in Limoges. The ice clinked in her glass like a new kind of cricket. The top of her head felt soft, as if her thoughts might swarm free.

She squeezed through the hedge and walked around the garden. Halfway to the old porch, she saw the orange glow from his cigarette. He stood up, his shoes scuffing on the plank floor.

"Edith?"

"Hi." Smoke curled up from her Pall Mall, hanging in the air like a giant corkscrew.

"Anything wrong?" he asked.

"No." She exhaled a stream of smoke. "I'm surprised you're home. Why aren't you having dinner with one of your widows?"

"Dinner was at lunch, Edith." He smiled. "I haven't had supper yet."

"I always get that mixed up." She inhaled smoke. "Show me your garden, why don't you?"

"Now?" He opened the screen door and stood on the top step. "But it's too dark."

"I have good night vision. Or did you think I was too old?" She laughed. The gin had made her fearless.

"I never said that." He walked down the steps, throwing his cigarette into a holly bush, and came over to her. In her bare feet she was a head shorter, and somehow that made her feel younger. There were ways, she was sure, of closing all gaps.

"You're the one who said it, Edith."

"I did, didn't I?"

"Maybe you should let me make up my own mind."

She lifted one eyebrow but didn't answer. "What are you trying to do, put me in my place?"

"Not unless you want to go there." He grinned. "You weren't ever too old, Edith. You just thought you were."

She turned up her face and smiled. Her chest buzzed like it was full of katydids. "Show me your goddamn corn."

"There's nothing much to see. Nothing's ripe." He reached for her glass. "What're you drinking?"

"Gin and poison. I mean, tonic."

"Yeah?" He raised the glass and took a long swallow. "Come on."

She dropped her cigarette and followed him into the corn, swishing past the long, curved stalks.

"Let me show you something. I got one ripe ear of corn. It's only yea-big." He drank the rest of the gin and set down the glass. Then he reached up, broke off an ear of corn, and peeled back the green husk. "It's so sweet, you can eat it raw."

"Who'd want to?"

"Taste it." He held it out, and she took a tiny bite. Juice spurted into her mouth, cool and sweet.

"Good, isn't it?" He took a bite and rubbed his mouth on his wrist. She reached for the corn, drawing her tongue over the kernels, and took another bite. Juice ran down her chin, but she didn't wipe it away. Even given the gin, her bravado surprised her. She felt purified, like a modern Amazon.

"No one in Murray Hill would eat raw corn," she told him.

"You're not in Murray Hill." He took the corn and pitched it. Then he put his arms around her neck and pulled her so close she felt his heart thudding. He kissed her slowly, tasting of gin, corn, tobacco. She stretched out in the weedy row, pulling up her dress, feeling dirt curve into her buttocks. He pushed down his trousers and fell to his knees. Even in the dark she could see how ready he was. He moved his hand to the small of her back. She wanted to pull him deep inside her and keep him there. Through the corn, she saw the porch light, but they were in full shadow. As her hands moved over Cab, she thought of her palette, arranged so she could find color without having to search, like a typist who never looks at her keys. They made love in colors, climbing the spectrum: sap green, Indian yellow, cadmium orange, vermilion, violet, cobalt, the tones whirring together until they resembled smoke.

Law of Gravity

Until here recently, I had a confused notion of the American Dream. I thought it meant you dreamed of cities—Atlanta one night, Birmingham the next, working your way in alphabetical order to Chicago and Dallas. E stumped me. I couldn't think of a town unless you counted Epps, just down the road, but who'd want to dream there?

My mama said her dreams were smashed all to hell. Butter said that wasn't a nice thing to say to a child, that a mother who cursed was liable to do anything. So far, DeeDee hasn't disappointed me.

—BILLIE ROBICHAUX, MAY 1952

Billie Robichaux

My daddy breaks everything in the kitchen. He tosses a bowl, and it explodes on the floor. Aunt Butter makes me sit on the porch until the tantrum passes. She puts her hands over my ears, but I still hear dishes breaking. It's all my fault for showing Mama's letter. I didn't guess my daddy would go to pieces. Next door, Mr. Spruel opens his window and hollers out, "Butter, can't you do something about that noise?"

"He's upset," Aunt Butter calls back. All around us crickets go wreep-wreep. It's hot even in the dark, but noise carries all the way down Hayes.

"Well, I can see that. You're lucky I ain't called the police." Mr. Spruel lifts his chin. "And where's DeeDee? I ain't seen her around."

"Hush up! I've got a child here." Butter's hands press down on my ears, and I hear her bones pop.

"Lord-a-mercy, she run off?" cries Mr. Spruel. A metal pan sails through the front door, rips through a hole in the screen, and thuds on the porch. Aunt Butter ignores it and starts singing "Rock of Ages." From deep inside the house my daddy lets out a wail, *"DeeDeeee!"* His wheelchair crunches over broken dishes. I start to go to him, but Aunt Butter pulls me back. "Let him cry it out." She pats my arm. "He'll feel better tomorrow."

This is her way of saying that my daddy is drunk. Ever since Mama left, he's been like this.

"That damn bitch!" He lifts the toaster and smashes it against the wall. "She's going with Henry Nepper. His goddamn store is closed. I called it up and nobody answered. Put two and two together, Butter. They've run off! I hear things, you know. Just 'cause I'm crippled don't mean I don't hear nothing!"

There's more than broken dishes in this house, things we can't glue back. I squeeze my eyes shut.

"Don't listen to your daddy. He's talking nonsense," Butter says. "It's not good for children to hear grown-ups talk. Let's you and me walk over to City Market for some groceries."

"No." I grip the sides of the swing and hold tight.

"Billie!"

"Where is my mama?"

"I don't know."

"Yes, you do."

"I don't, either. Nobody does."

"Somebody's got to."

"You got that note. She said she'd be back."

"But what if she likes where she is?"

"She'll be back. Anyhow, it's too soon to worry."

Me, I'm not so sure.

After Daddy goes to sleep, we sweep up the kitchen. "Watch your feet, honey," says Butter. "Get you some shoes on."

We fill eight grocery sacks with the last of her Fiesta dishes. We keep the dented pans, though. The walls are so nicked and scuffed it looks like people have been dancing on them with spurs and pointy high heels.

"I sure hate for you to grow up this way," Butter says, herding me back to the porch.

"I don' care." We sit down in the glider.

"Well, I do. This ain't normal. My daddy never broke a dish in his life, except on accident."

I don't know what to say. If I agree with her, then I'm siding against my own daddy. See, I remember how he used to be, so sweet-eyed and cheerful. He is a man who needs his legs the way some people need brains, like being smart in arithmetic. Take Mr.

Hawley at City Market, the way he adds up my Coca-Cola bottles for refund. Adds it up in his head. He's never wrong, either. Why, if you took that away and made him count on his fingers, it would break his heart.

My daddy don't give a flip about addition. He just needs to sit down on the commode instead of messing himself like a baby. If my mama would only play rook with him, he would be happy. Or if she'd just hold his hand.

"Aunt Butter?"

"What, baby?"

"Why's my daddy throw things all the time?"

"'Cause he's frustrated. 'Cause he's lost his manhood."

"No, he hasn't. Just his legs."

"Same thing, baby." We rock back and forth a few minutes.

"Aunt Butter?"

"Yes?"

"Is my mama coming back?"

"Why, sure. She wouldn't leave you for the world."

"Then where is she?"

"We done went over this, Billie. I don't know. She must've had her reasons. I know she loves you, sugar."

"But where do you *think* she went?"

"Oh, I reckon someplace quiet so she could get hold of herself."

"Why's that?"

"Well, sometimes a woman needs time to herself. Your mama's no different from nobody else."

"And we don't give her time for that?"

"Law, you'd wear the horns off a billy goat. Don't worry so much!" She pinches my chest. "Even Jesus took time off, now and then. I know what we can do. Let's sing hymns. It'll make us feel better."

She belts out "Jacob's Ladder." Singing and praying, these are Butter's favorite things. I've been trying to pray for Mama, but every time I go to the Baptist church, nobody's home. Just yesterday I knocked on the rectory, and an old man with thick glasses came to the door. Told me he was a fill-in preacher, that Reverend Kirby had left town.

"Why?" I couldn't believe it. He'd always been so nice. He told me he had a guaranteed way to get action from the Lord. "I'll teach you a whole new way of praying," he'd promised. "And your mama, too."

"Think it was a family emergency," said the old fill-in.

"Will he be back?"

"Child, I don't think so."

My face must've caved in, because the fill-in said, "Child, let my Brenda fetch you some nice hot gingerbread. She just made a pan."

A wrinkled woman came to the door, clutching a dishcloth. I caught a whiff of cake, and my stomach growled. She wrapped a hunk in a paper napkin, and I walked back home, feeling the heat from the gingerbread seep into my hands. What I needed was prayer, but food was awful good, too.

Now Mr. Spruel sticks his head out the window and sings,

It's time to say good night,
it's time to good night.
Hi-ho the merry-o,
it's time to say good night.

"Oh, hush." Butter laughs. "Come over and join us, you old fool."

"Can't." His face is tiny and hard-boned. "Mrs. Spruel would tan my hide."

"Mrs. Spruel has been dead forty years," says Aunt Butter. "So you either hush or sing with us."

"Can we sing 'In the Garden'? It was Mrs. Spruel's favorite."

"Why, sure." Butter smiles. His face disappears from the window. A minute later he walks up our porch steps, waving like he ain't seen us in years.

"Have a seat." Butter points to a wood rocker. "I'd offer you some tea, but all my drinking glasses is broke."

"I heard." He sits down, cocking his head toward our dark house. "Guess he ran out of things to throw? Or maybe he don't like your cooking, Butter."

"Huh," Butter says.

"He ought to be accountable."

"A *cannibal*?" I say, jumping out of the swing.

"No, no!" Mr. Spruel laughs. He explains the word. "I just meant he ought to replace them dishes or else not throw them in the first place."

Butter pulls me back to the swing, wrapping her arms around me. I wait till they start singing, then I slide out of her arms and jump off the porch. Mrs. Happy and two of her middle-aged puppies trot after me. I stretch out in the grass, feeling the dew seep into my shirt; the dogs turn their heads from side to side, trying to figure me out. I feel extra safe outside, with the night washing down, dark as my mama's hair. I look up at the sky and make the same wish on every star.

Love Is a Crooked Road

(With Potholes)

❧

I'd like to make one thing clear: I don't go off with men for the hell of it. It just looks that way. I have my reasons: Love is one, pain is another. See, when I go too long without any loving, I get this awful burning pain when I pee. One time I thought I was dying, and I went to see Dr. LeGette. He told me it was from too much intercourse. Then he wanted to know if I'd been having too much. "Ha, just the opposite," I told him. Later I went to the library in Tallulah and looked it up in a urinology book. I decided that I needed regular love to keep the hole open, the same way you keep an earring in a newly pierced ear. A fourteen-karat-gold post, not the cheap kind that turns you green. Some men are like earrings, only they'll turn your insides green. You have to find the ones who are pure gold. And this is what my running off is all about.

—DeeDee Robichaux, from a letter to Tamera Mashburn, postmarked Canyon, Texas, June 6, 1952

An aerial view of the Texas Panhandle shows grain elevators, feedlots packed with Herefords and the occasional longhorn, green wavy acres of mesquite, and back roads thick with prairie dust—all strung up by a rope of highway. It's flat, treeless land, sweeping down into the Lone Star State. In the distance is the future—dirty streaks in the sky like pencil marks: Somewhere in New Mexico it is raining.

Every few hours, a turquoise station wagon pulled off the

road, and Henry Nepper climbed out to inspect his radiator. The Texas heat frightened DeeDee, too. She kept a red-plaid Thermos under her seat, the ice cubes melted into puppy teeth. They stopped for gas on Route 60 near Canyon. Inside the store, jars were packed with whole jalapeño peppers, onions, and tomatoes. An RC Cola thermometer hovered at ninety-nine degrees. In the back room, men with dirty fingernails shot pool. The balls cracked and scattered over green felt.

"I just don't like it," she whispered to Henry, shaking her head. "What if we break down? We'll die of thirst."

"You're right. Let's try another road." He unfolded a map and traced his finger over a red line, small as a capillary. Their journey had already cut a jagged seam across Texas, as if they were traveling at night without headlights. In east Texas they stayed at an old woman's Victorian, where each room was named after a season. They chose Autumn, an orange room with rocking chairs and a brass bed. The triple windows looked out into an oak tree the old lady swore was five hundred years old. ("She ought to know," Henry joked when the woman left.) It was here that Henry gave her a gingerbread pig; DeeDee produced a book wrapped in brown paper. "Your early Christmas present," she told him, smiling as he ripped the string. The book was illustrated with love-making positions that boggled his mind. And they'd tried every single one. His main concern was Little Henry, but she assured him the baby was fine. "Snug as a bug" is the way she put it, imagining a worm hiding in cabbage.

"Where'd you find something like this?" he'd asked, trying not to sound suspicious.

"Ordered it from one of those dirty magazines you keep in your office."

DeeDee pulled the sheet around her breasts, and Henry tugged it down.

"Don't," he said. "I want to look at you."

She shrugged and licked grease from her fingers. There was a bottle of Beaujolais on the dresser, next to a beeswax candle and two silver goblets. Henry had brought these things from home, sneaking them from the china cabinet as if his wife still lived with him. Which only proved that you could take the man out of the marriage, but you couldn't take the marriage out of the man.

At another place near Dallas, they stayed in a room where a velvet painting of a bullfighter hung over the bed, and in the morning they ate *huevos rancheros* with potatoes and refried beans. "We'll never get to Las Vegas, will we?" DeeDee drew up on one knee, puckering the sheet, so that he had a full view of her upper thigh. She was worried that she'd have her period before they reached Nevada. Six weeks was a long time to carry a phantom baby.

"Sure we will, sweetie. Texas is bigger than I thought."

They drove with all the windows rolled down, listening to Bob Willis on WRR. Eleven miles outside of Grand Saline, Henry swerved to miss a dead armadillo, slinging DeeDee against the window.

"You don't have to wreck us," she cried, slapping his arm.

"Couldn't help it, baby." He kept his eyes on the road. DeeDee turned and stared; the armadillo's delicate feet stuck straight up, as if it were praying. This was the third one they'd seen today. She huddled against the door and watched the road. The sheer size of the sky diminished her. By the time they rolled into the Blue Swallow Motor Court at Caddo Lake, she was asleep, curled up like a shrimp.

Later, Henry brought take-out food in little white boxes—slabs of corn bread topped with roast beef; mashed potatoes; pinto beans; corn; biscuits to mop up gravy; buttermilk pie. DeeDee sat cross-legged on the bed and nibbled a biscuit. "How'd we end up in *east* Texas?" she said. "We already *been* here."

"I just drove," he said, but it seemed to him that a compass was imbedded in his brain, pointing east.

"Did you *ever*." She narrowed her eyes. "If I didn't know better, I'd say you did this on purpose. That you're trying to sneak us back to Limoges."

"Look, it's your fault. You were sleeping on the map. Didn't want to wake you, darling." He pulled up on his elbow and grabbed her toes. He didn't like to think of Nepper's Drugs, because he was being more than irresponsible—it would probably bankrupt him, all closed up like that, what with Miss Byrd working at the Majestic. She was probably going around town saying Mr. Henry had gone crazy. He'd never closed the store except when Olive died. People wouldn't know what to think, and that would be especially true of Vangie. Or maybe she'd be glad. She could get him on desertion, and he wouldn't get a dime out of that store. Not that he deserved it.

Earlier, when he'd been driving east, he'd thought of Vangie's swinging pageboy, the way the light turned her hair the color of Olive's. Any other woman would have kicked him into the street, thrown his underwear and socks into the driveway. Instead, she'd left *him*, which was almost a smite. He was not looking forward to the divorce, even though he'd never been to Nevada. In his own small way, he fought change. He liked his socks in the same drawer, his brown shoes lined up under his brown suits. He had lived in the same house his whole married life, just around the corner from where he was raised.

"Are we going to live in your house?" DeeDee ran one finger down his spine. He shivered. Sometimes she was clairvoyant.

"I haven't thought that far." He arched his back. "She'll want it."

"So do I."

"I'll buy us something prettier. Anyway, by law it's half hers. You wouldn't like it there, DeeDee. There's nothing but a pile of gossips on Cypress Street."

"Gossips don't bother me."

"Maybe not now, but they will later. When Billie doesn't get invited to birthday parties and mother-daughter teas. You know all that goes on in Limoges, don't you?"

"Not firsthand." She lifted one shoulder, barely an inch. "You trying to talk me out of this?"

"Oh, honey. I'm sorry, but you need to know. If we could live on an island, we'd be fine. You know how Limoges is. It'll take people a couple of years to get over this." He pushed his hand up her leg, then leaned over and kissed the inside of her knee.

"Over what?" She shoved his hand away.

"Why, the scandal."

"Is that what we are?"

"I'm afraid so, sweetheart."

"Hmmmm, it sure doesn't feel like it."

"Well, it is. And you might as well prepare Billie. She won't be getting many invitations to birthday parties."

"What do parties have to do with us?"

"They'll hurt Billie's feelings. And yours, too."

"I doubt it. She feels like I do about society things. I could care less about the cream de la cream of Limoges."

"No, it's *crème de la crème*," Henry corrected.

"Well, what*ever*." She lowered her face between her knees so he wouldn't see her blushing. After a minute she looked up. "You know what? Those biddies can go to hell. We don't need parties."

"Well, I don't know," he said. "Parties are nice. I always enjoyed the ones at Edith's."

DeeDee jerked her knee into his arm.

"What'd you do that for?" He rubbed his elbow.

"'Parties are nice,'" she mimicked. She threw the biscuit against the wall, where it clunked and left a greasy stain. "Hell, you'll probably expect me to go to church and sit in the amen row with your customers, the ones with oodles of babies."

"I won't." He slid his hand under her leg. "But we really ought to find a church home."

"What's that?" She made a face.

"Just where we'll worship. We've got to somewhere. We can't ignore the whole town."

"I do it now."

"You just think you do. It's easy to ignore from the outside. Anyway, I'll bet you've got friends over on Hayes Avenue."

"That trashy place?" She rolled her eyes. "I'll *never* set foot over there again. Listen, honey, when we get back to Limoges, can we start looking at houses?"

"We'd best wait until Vangie and I divide the property."

"Don't make me wait *too* long, Henry." She reached for him, sliding her greasy hand around his testicles, feeling the soft, springy hairs. She threw back the sheet and pushed her face between his legs, drawing one of the sacs into her mouth. Henry grabbed her head and pulled her against him.

"Who needs parties?" he thought, his ambivalence dissipating. "Who needs a church home? I'll have my own personal sideshow every night of the week."

Around seven o'clock they dressed for supper. They stepped out of the room, into warm air that smelled of barbecue, draft beer, and burned corn-bread fritters. The aromas emanated from a squatty, cement-block diner. "Let's don't eat *there*," DeeDee said.

"Why not?"

"'Cause it looks like it's been farted on," she said.

"DeeDee! What a thing to say!"

"Well, it's true."

"How would *you* know?" He frowned. "I really wish you wouldn't say things like that in front of me."

"You never cared before."

"You never said things like that, either." He sighed. "I want to keep you on a pedestal."

"I don't like high places."

"Then don't talk like trash."

DeeDee's mouth opened. She shook her head, too furious to speak. Henry started walking, one hand resting on the small of his back, fingers splayed toward his hips. He didn't even realize what he'd said. He's better than Renny, though, she thought. "He may hurt my feelings, but he's got money and he loves me and all his male parts work—well, nearly work."

A mosquito buzzed close to DeeDee's ear, and she slapped it away. "Damn these bugs! They should make citronella perfume."

"That's good!" Henry laughed and hugged her. "See? You don't have to be common. You're smart as a whistle."

"A whistle is smart?"

"This one is." He squeezed her bottom. They walked out to the turquoise Rambler and got inside. He stuck the key into the ignition, then fingered the horseshoe chain. "I saw a diner over on the highway. It had a great big catfish sign out front. You want to try it?" He reached across the seat and touched her breast. "Or can we have one more quickie?"

"I sure hope all these quickies add up to a longie." She laughed.

"They're not *so* fast, are they?" His forehead wrinkled.

"You said it first." She opened the door, sticking out her foot, but he pulled her back.

"Hey, where you going?"

"Back to the room." She grinned. "For the quickie."

"Let's do it here."

"Here?" She looked around the *U*-shaped motor court. All the pink doors were shut. The blue neon arrow streaked back and forth, above a sign that blinked V CAN Y. "Won't somebody see us?"

"Nah. We're parked way over here." He was already unzipping his pants, and his penis speared up. He reached for her. "Come on, it's dark. Nobody'll see. And that book said to pick new places to have intercourse."

"I don't know. I'd feel so naked." She wrinkled her nose. "You know?"

"Come on, DeeDee. One for the road." He felt between his legs, squeezing himself.

"Oh, all right." She leaned over, taking him in her mouth, thinking how many times a day he handled himself, dressing, bathing, urinating, scratching. To her, it was a foreign object. It aroused her to imagine his big hands circling himself, jiggling the same way he shook elixirs at the pharmacy, up and down, the bones clicking in his wrist. Just yesterday he was in the shower, and when she pulled aside the plastic curtain, he turned, and she saw his erection peeping between his soapy fist.

"What are you *doing*, Henry?" she cried.

The soap slipped from his hands and clunked against the tub. Hot water buzzed down, plastering his hair against his forehead. He grinned and stared down at his long, wrinkled toes. "You caught me."

"But you've got me for that." Her eyebrows came together, and the back of her throat burned. She wasn't about to let him see her cry. So she peeled off her clothes and got inside the shower.

"Sometimes I just like it simple," he explained.

"Masturbation is about as simple as you can get, Henry. It's almost like one of those amoebas I read about."

"It's not fun, especially." He sounded apologetic.

"Then why bother?"

"It's quick and it's clean."

"How?"

"Well, my nuts get to aching? So I do it, and the shower washes everything down the drain."

She stood under the hot, spiky water, and tears rolled down her cheeks. Once she thought he craved her. Now she realized he just craved. For the first time she wondered if Henry might be warped. Or maybe she was deformed on the inside, incapable of love, with a cleft in her heart like a cleft lip.

"It's that damn book. It's got me worked up," Henry said, standing under the nozzle, tilting back his head, letting water spray into his mouth.

"How can a book do that?" She knelt, grasped the soap, and lathered up her hands. Then she reached for him. "I'm the real thing, Henry."

Now he pulled her arm and said, "Lay down, baby, so I can do you." He pressed her into the seat, and she wrapped her arms around his neck. Fumbling between her legs, he hooked her panties to the side and entered her with short, quick thrusts. She lifted her legs, pushing the balls of her feet against the window, angling herself so that he could batter against her. She pushed against him, then swayed back, feeling the tip of his penis against her vulva. It was like swinging, she thought. From a high tree, the same rhythm and pull of gravity, only faster.

"You're so *big*, Henry," she whispered, thinking of Chapter 11 in the brown-wrapped book, titled "Talking Dirty."

"Yeah?" As he moved inside her, he couldn't help but think of the old days with Vangie, when he couldn't seem to last. Not that it was all his fault.

"You've got the biggest one I've *ever* seen," she whispered. Then she said other words, and he pulsed inside her.

"Now it's my turn," she said, thumping her pelvis against him in a bone-jarring rhythm. He was afraid she'd dislodge Little Henry. He felt his penis bend as he wondered how many lover-boys she'd had. If he was the biggest, who was the smallest? He imagined a row of men, all with different-sized erections, parading in front of her. She commanded the men to lie down, then she straddled them one at a time, testing for fit. As she stood up, she pointed at him, "I'll take *this* one." He hated the notion of any other man entering her. It was difficult enough to justify Billie—when the child lagged around the drugstore, he'd catch himself thinking, *She's Renny's semen, Renny ejaculated inside of my DeeDee, buried himself to the hilt.* He went as far as to imagine fluid spurting from Renny, at the mouth of DeeDee's womb.

She wrapped her arms around his waist, digging her hands into his buttocks, pulling him against her. "Hen-ry," she said, breathing in the first syllable of his name, exhaling the second. He waited until she shuddered and her arms fell loose over her head, curling against the chrome door handle. Then he lifted up on his elbows. "DeeDee?"

"Yeah?"

"How many men you been with?"

"Why?" She shot him a look, then straightened her panties. "I ought to ask you the same question."

"Haven't been with any men, DeeDee."

"Well, *okay*. Two men, you and Renny."

"Only two?" He looked skeptical.

"Why? Don't you believe me?" She narrowed her eyes, then scooted across the seat, next to the door. She glanced out the window. The parking lot was still empty.

"Actually, no."

"Why?"

"Because of what you said." Henry started the engine and backed out of the parking lot. He pulled onto the highway and looked at her. "Don't you even want to know what you said?"

She ignored him and rolled down her window. Watery air poured into the car. The round dials glowed green, and from the radio, Eddie Fisher was singing "I'm Yours." She felt her temper building—a sort of tingling at the base of her skull, seeping to her throat. It was none of his business about Jackson Brussard or the one-eyed jeweler and his son. With all her heart, she was convinced that what Henry Nepper didn't know wouldn't hurt *her*.

"Well, you said I had the biggest cock you'd ever known."

"I did not say that word," she snapped. "I did not say *cock*."

"That's what you meant."

"I was only using suggestions from the book." She turned back to the window. Clearly, this man was no Jackson Brussard. Clearly, she'd sold herself short—she had run off with a man who slept with his mouth open and played with himself in the shower. Now that they were away from Limoges, he *looked* and acted different—slit-eyed and rumpled, vicious until he'd had his second cup of coffee.

"You got all that from the book?" Henry said hopefully. He felt perspiration drip down his neck. "I mean, you acted like you'd been through all kinds of men."

She ignored him and shoved herself against her door. Henry shook his head. The old silent treatment. His mama was an expert, and Vangie wasn't half-bad. He hated pouty women. It amazed him that he had chosen another woman with the same talent. "I sure can pick 'em," he muttered. She turned slowly, her eyes narrowed. The wind whipped her hair behind her.

"What did you just say?" She leaned forward.

"Oh, DeeDee, don't do this. I used to get enough of this at home. Anyhow, I can't help being jealous. I hate the idea of you with another man." He reached across the seat, brushing his fingers against her shoulder. She squirmed away, but he grabbed a handful of her dress, squeezing her leg.

"I was just trying to *arouse* you." She spit out the word. Her head was full of new phrases, thanks to the book. "You sure didn't need that, did you?"

"No." He glanced away from the road. "I'm Ready Freddy."

"You can say that again. In fact, soon as we get back to the motor court, I'm reading Chapter 12." She watched him sideways.

"What's that? 'More Dirty Talk'?"

"No, 'Premature Ejaculation.'"

"I don't have that problem." He stared, then nudged her leg. "Do I?"

She stared, one eyebrow raised.

"It's not *my* fault."

"No?"

"You could be more ladylike and not have to come fifty-eleven times. Maybe then I could hold back."

"Nothing's *ever* your fault!" She grabbed his hand and slung it into the dash so hard, the radio dial cracked. The red button swept back and forth, stopping on a Harmony, Texas, station where a preacher gasped out, "Brother, are you saved?"

"Goddamn," Henry groaned. "My hand's broke."

"I'm glad."

"Why, I ought to put you out on the road."

"You wouldn't dare."

"Don't tempt me."

"What about Little Henry?" She smirked.

He cradled his hand in his lap, then shifted his eyes at her. "If he's anything like you, keep him."

"Maybe I lied." She tossed her head back. "Maybe there *isn't* a little Henry."

"Are you lying?"

"What if I am?"

"I hope to God you are." His foot mashed the accelerator, and they sped around a curve, past a rusted sign that said CADDO CREEK.

"Well, ha ha! There *isn't* no baby!" She hollered. "And there probably won't ever be, between your premature ejaculations and your mumps. Vangie was right: I'll bet you're sterile, Henry!"

"You sound like somebody from Hayes Avenue." His voice was cold.

"Maybe that's 'cause I am."

"That's where I'll leave you, too." His upper lip curled. "We're going straight back to Limoges."

"I don't care. I don't need you. I'll find somebody else."

"I hope you do." Henry tried to lift his hand, then winced. "I just pray Vangie'll take me back."

"Bastard!" DeeDee reached across the seat and slapped him hard, knocking his head against the side window. With a little cry, she balled up her fists and pummeled him. Henry threw up his good hand to block a slap to his temple. The car veered down the road, headlights moving diagonally, shining through a patch of fog. Straight ahead was a green metal bridge.

"Are you . . . " the preacher's voice faded, replaced by static. The Rambler slammed into the green rail and burst through, scattering metal fragments. DeeDee's door swung open, then snapped shut. The car seemed to hang in the air. Henry wasn't certain whether the steering wheel had flown loose or he had fallen forward. Then the car thudded into the water, causing the hood to fling up. The steering wheel struck his chest with such force it left a halfmoon indentation.

"God!" DeeDee screamed. "Oh, God!"

She saw something white jutting through her right thigh. Realizing it was bone, she threw her head back and screamed. Black water gushed into the car, covering her feet, then her knees, slowly gurgling up to her waist. She stopped yelling and looked down. Dozens of fragrant, slimy lily pads skidded into the car.

"We'll drown," she screeched. The pain was making her dizzy, nauseated. "My leg, oh, my leg!"

Henry was slumped over the wheel. Water flowed into the car, rising up to their chests. She whimpered and shook Henry's arm. He flopped facedown, splashing her.

"Henry?" She pulled him up, grimacing with pain, and tried to pin him against the seat. He slumped back into the water. Outside the car, water was level with the windows. Crickets sang from the weedy banks. Her leg throbbed. She inhaled, bit her lip, and grabbed Henry's collar, heaving him over the steering wheel. Water streamed down his head, pattering all around him.

"You're not dead," she cried. "You're just knocked out is all."

She groped for the handle and tried to pull herself through the window. Pain ripped through her thigh as if her leg were detaching at the hip. She let go of the handle and collapsed against the door, leaning her head out the window. "Help!" she screamed. "Oh, God, is anybody out there? Can anybody hear me?"

The shrilling snapped off. After a moment, the peepers started up again. A bullfrog burped out a flat, sour note. Something made a rattling sound, like beads in a tin box. A snake? she wondered, picturing cottonmouths and water moccasins skimming through the creek. From the road, headlights slapped across the woods, sweeping over the blacktop highway. A Ford pickup rattled over the bridge, whooshing past the torn railing.

"Help me!" DeeDee screamed, smacking her hands against the water, sending ripples toward her fractured leg. She threw back her head, sucking in air. Then she heard another sound, the hum of an engine in reverse. She glanced around and saw the truck backing up, onto the bridge, until it was even with the gap. Two colored men got out of the car and stared through the torn metal.

"Down here!" she called, waving one arm.

"Hold on, miss," yelled the tall man.

"I'm hurt bad!" she screamed.

"It's all right, miss," said the other. "Please don't scream. We gone get you out of that mess in a heartbeat."

Five Thousand Mosquitoes

∾

The doctors in Texas are begging me to come fetch DeeDee, 'cause she's throwing food and calling them names. She has broke her leg to pieces in a car wreck that killed Mr. Henry. Mr. Spruel has offered to drive me down. While we're in Texas, I just hope I am fortunate enough to find fresh poblano peppers. Then I can make rajas. Wash 6 poblano peppers. Put them on a pan and broil on high, taking care not to scorch. Turn on all sides, then remove from the oven. Wrap in damp cloth to cool down, then put in plastic bread bag and tie up. Steam 20 minutes. Remove seeds and membranes. Slice in long strips and sauté in oil. It seems crazy that something this hot can be tempting and delicious. Even so, many cooks think they ain't worth the bother for a recipe that only serves four to six.

—BUTTER DEWITT, OVERHEARD AT HER CAFE, JUNE 8, 1952

Sophie Donnell

On my way to Miss Edith's, I see Limoges in a whole different way. It strikes me that downtown is a lot like Natchitoches—crepe myrtles, crooked streets, lacy wrought iron. A place where pepper pods are strung up and the houses are built off the ground. I wonder if the cottages here are made of bousillage walls—Spanish moss, deer hair, and mud. Ours was like that back home. I hum to myself, sing praises to my Jesus. When I get to Miss Edith's, I almost fall out in a dead faint.

Mr. Cab Beaulieu sitting at the kitchen table, drinking coffee and eating buttered toast. I don't open my mouth. Just take off my hat and set it on the counter, acting like he ain't there. Acting like they both ain't barefoot. Miss Edith sits down next to him and rubs the back of his wrist, her fingernails parting the dark hairs. "We should take your car out to Vangie's place," she say. "Mine's been acting up. I don't trust it."

"If you don't mind riding in a hearse." He smiles.

"No." She pinches his arm.

"You might as well get used to it." His eyes flick over to me. I'm staring with my mouth wide open, one hand on my hip.

"I didn't hear you come in," Edith say. She don't even have the sense to blush.

"Then you must be deaf." I march over to the counter and pour me a cup of coffee. "Can I hitch a ride with you?" I ask. "Me and Miss Vangie going for a practice drive this evening."

"You haven't heard?" Edith sits up straight, sucking in her cheeks.

"Heard what?" I lift the cup, sip coffee.

"What, you firing me?"

"No, no!" Edith shakes her head. "It's Henry, Henry Nepper. He was killed last night."

"Say what?" My hand jerks, sloshing coffee. It drips down my arm. I set down the cup and reach for a dishrag. The only reason I know about Mr. Henry's mystery trip is because he asked Israel to feed and water his dogs. Soon as he left town, Miss Vangie drive up in her daddy's old car and steal the dogs. Israel started to take off after her. "Let her go," I said. "She needs them dogs worse than he do. Let her go."

"It's true," Cab say. "They're shipping his body back home tomorrow."

"How'd he die?" I say, trying to feature Mr. Henry dead. "His heart give out?"

"Car wreck." Miss Edith winds her arm around Mr. Cab. "Went off a bridge in Texas."

"Killed him outright," Cab say.

"That woman was with him." Edith grimaces. "DeeDee Robichaux. She survived. She's in a hospital down there. I heard her aunt's gone down to get her." She pauses, rubbing the bridge of her nose. "And now we've got to tell Vangie. I don't want her hearing it on the phone. That's what I told Sheriff Reems when he came over here. He's letting us tell her. I'm just praying that Harriet doesn't get to her first."

"It's early yet," I say. "Maybe she ain't heard."

"Maybe." Cab touches the back of Edith's neck, lifting her hair with one finger.

"You leave Miss Harriet to me." I pick up my hat and turn toward the door. I can't help but wonder why everybody tries to protect Miss Vangie from the truth, yet even I'm guilty. It's her husband dead, not ours. But white folks especially like to coddle they women. If you protect too much, it seem to me you just turn them back into little girls. Yet here I go, here I go.

"What you going to do to Miss Harriet, Sophie?" Cab laughs. "Sit on her?"

"I got my ways. If you leaving, you'd best hurry."

"Just let me get my shoes on." Cab reaches under the table. "Won't take us long. I'm a pretty fast driver."

"Yes, but you've got a slow car." Edith leans over and kisses him square on the lips.

"You be careful," I say. "Don't need no more funerals around here. No offense, Mr. Cab."

"You're right, Sophie." He puts one arm around Edith, his fingers touching the edge of her breast. "We all got to stay alive and well so we can help each other."

"Amen," I say.

I walk out of Edith's shady yard into the Neppers' ankle-deep grass. The house has a sad, caved-in look. The roses is shaggy, full of dried-up blossoms, the ground beneath messy with petals. I curve around the forsythia and look up at Harriet's house. The windows all pushed open, but the Ethel Merman records ain't playing, which I take as a good sign. I open the back door and step inside. Miss Harriet standing at the counter, wearing a frilly pink robe, pouring a cup of coffee.

"Miss Harriet?" I say.

"Ahhhh!" She throws the cup into the air, slinging coffee on the wall. The cup smashes on the floor. She whirls around, one hand rising to her throat. When she sees me, her mouth makes a little *O*.

"Oh, my Lord!" she cries. "It's *you*. You scared the life out of me, girl. Don't *ever* sneak up on me again, or I'll have your hide!"

"Yes, ma'am."

"And what're you *doing* here, anyway?" She steps over the spilled coffee and broken cup. "You're supposed to be at Edith's today."

"She give me the day off. So I thought I'd come over here."

"Well, you thought wrong. I don't need you." She flicks one hand at the floor. "At least, I *didn't*."

"I'll just mop that up for you."

"Please do." Harriet pulls out a green chair and sits down. She twists her head like a parakeet and stares at me, raising one chubby finger. Says, "And fix me another cup while you're at it. I'm shaking like I'm froze. Then you can go."

"You sure? I won't charge you for today," I say.

"Why?" Her eyes narrow.

"Because you got it coming to you. I mean, you overpaid me last week."

"I did *not*."

"Yes ma'am, you did. You give me a five-dollar bill instead of a one."

"I'd never do that," she says, but she don't look convinced. "Then why'd you take all this time to tell me, hmmmm?" She taps her fingers on the table.

"You know I can't hardly read." I stick one hand behind my back and cross my fingers. Truth be told, I can read good as her. "I just tucked that money in my bra, same as always," I say. "Then I stuck it in my Clabber Girl can. So when I bought me some soda crackers at City Market, I handed them your dollar, and they give me all this change. They told me it was a five. So I figure you got it coming."

"And a good bit more than just today." Harriet nods. "I'd be ashamed if I couldn't make change for a dollar."

"Yes, ma'am."

"So why didn't Edith need you?"

"Oh, she's got that bad vomiting virus?"

"Don't tell me something else is going round."

"Sure is, and Miss Edith, she was scared I'd catch it. Mr. Cab got it, too."

"My Lord." Harriet slaps one hand to her face. "If the Le-Gettes were home, I'd be surrounded by bloody flux and now this."

"You just go upstairs and lay down and rest. I'll clean up. Get your beauty sleep."

"I think I will." She smiles. "I'm just wore out."

"Do you good," I say, squatting down, picking up the broken cup.

Miss Harriet gets up from the table. Says, "I got me a bowl of shrimp in the icebox, and you know what? I've got a taste for gumbo. Fix me a pot like you always do, Sophie."

"Yes, ma'am."

"You are such a sweetheart, Sophie. Don't forget my coffee, now." She waddles out of the room. I wait until I hear her climbing the stairs. Over my head, the floorboards creak, followed by the box spring as Miss Harriet arranges herself on the bed, humming to herself. Then I open the drawer, looking for scissors and electrical tape. I gather it up and creep into the living room.

The black telephone sits on a marble table, surrounded by a leather address book, doodle pad, and jar of butterscotch candies. I lift the cord and follow it behind the table, under the slipcovers, to a little box next to the floorboard. When I move the davenport, I uncover a rat's nest of cut-up magazines—*Saturday Evening Post, Christian Science Monitor, McCall's*—and a Sears, Roebuck catalog. All the pages are chewed and cut up. I lean over and poke

the catalog with the scissors. "Paper dolls for Waynetta Dawn?" I
wonder. But I ain't seen that child in weeks. I pick up the telephone cord and snip it in half. After I tape the ends together, I sit
on my haunches. From a distance, the cord looks fine. I shove the
davenport back into place, over the papers—I ain't cleaning it
up—and walk back into the kitchen.

"Sophie?" hollers Miss Harriet. "Are you bringing my coffee
this year, or do I have to fetch it my own self?"

"No, you stay put," I call out. "I'm coming right now."

I fix her coffee like she likes it, with three spoons of sugar and
a slug of cream. Then I carry it up. "Don't forget my gumbo," she
says, taking the cup with both hands.

"Fixing to start the roux right now," I tell her, then go back
downstairs. On my way back to the kitchen, I gather up all the
Ethel Merman records. I open the oven, shove in the records,
turn on the heat. Then I stand back, watching the records curl.
Jerk them out before they get to smelling bad.

I still got more to do. I prop open the door, then go outside, to
the LeGettes' yard. Behind the crepe myrtles are two quart jars,
say Ball on the sides. I hold them up to the light. They just full of
Miss Fanny's dead mosquitoes. A few is still alive, buzzing against
the glass. On the jar, Miss Fanny has wrote "5,000 mosquitoes."

I put the jars in my apron and hurry back to Miss Harriet's to
make the gumbo. First, I start chopping onions. Then I make a
roux. Women in my family grew up knowing how to make all kinds
of gumbo. Today, I make seafood, Natchitoches style. #1. Take 2 T.
bacon drippings and about 2 T. flour and stir until it's the color of a
copper penny. Always have as much (or more) fat as flour. Be sure
all signs of whiteness are gone. If it gets burnt, you got to throw it
out and start over. #2. Sauté your onions, garlic, parsley, celery,
green onions. Five thousand mosquitoes are optional. Cook until
onions are crystal clear and celery is limp. #3. Add water and seasonings—Tabasco, bay leaves, peppers, salt. Cook 2 hours. #4. Peel
and devein shrimps. Add to pot, with 1 t. lemon juice. Cook
another 30 minutes. Some people adds okra, but I don't. #5. Add 2
pints oysters and their juice. You can add crab claws, too. Cook 15
minutes more. Add 3 T. fresh filé. #6. Serve over hot rice, with
hunks of French bread. Serves 12 generously.

I still ain't through. I open a drawer and take out a sheet of
paper that say *From the Desk of Leonard Hooper*. In my fanciest
handwriting, I scribble out, *I quit. Sincerely, Sophie Donnell*. Then
I go straight out the back door, and I keep on walking, all the way
around the azaleas, all the way to the back door of Beaulieu's,
where Israel Adams is waiting.

Hallelujah.

Eggs in Purgatory

From the kitchen of Edith Galliard

3 T. olive oil
1/2 small onion, minced
1 1/2 lbs. fresh tomatoes, peeled, seeded, & chopped
2 T. torn, fresh basil leaves
2 T. parsley, minced
Salt and freshly ground pepper
4 large eggs
4 1/3-inch-thick slices Italian bread
6 T. freshly grated Parmesan cheese (1 oz.)

Heat 3 T. oil in skillet. Add onion and sauté until soft, stirring occasionally (about 6 minutes). Add tomatoes. Bring to simmer. Mix in basil, parsley, salt and pepper. Increase heat to high and cook until almost no liquid remains in pan, stirring frequently, about 15 minutes. Press the back of a large spoon into the tomato mixture, dividing it into four sections. Make sure they are evenly apart. Using the spoon, form little wells. Carefully break 1 egg into each well. Season eggs with salt and pepper. Cover pan and cook over low heat until eggs are soft-poached, about 6 minutes. Meanwhile, preheat broiler. Brush both sides of bread with oil. Place on baking sheet. Broil bread until golden brown on both sides. Sprinkle cheese over eggs. Divide toast between shallow bowls. Gently spoon eggs and sauce over toast.

Serves 4.

Epilogue:

Still Life with Tombstone

❧

The bigger the town, the harder it is to ruin your name. A small town can wreck a person in a single day. In Limoges it takes about fifteen minutes. Then you're ruined, you're a strumpet, the town floozy. You're the woman who single-handedly shut down the only drugstore in town. People will overlook a lot, but just cut off their penicillin and banana splits, and see how fast your name turns to mud.

—DeeDee Robichaux, Parish Hospital, after throwing contents of breakfast tray at Nurse Abigail Potter, June 9, 1952

Henry Nepper was buried in the Galliard family plot, in the center of the cemetery between the Confederates and yellow fever victims. Vangie stood next to the mound of black soil, thinking it resembled a heap of crumbled cookies, the kind she used in key lime pie. Wreaths and sprays were bunched together with handwritten notes from friends. Scattered about were curved marble stones, generations of dead Galliards. Everyone had left except Edith and Cab, who stood under a live oak, their hands joined.

"It's sickening hot," Vangie said to herself, wiping her neck with a Kleenex. The sun pushed against her as she leaned over to straighten a wreath from Rotary. *Henry, we'll miss you,* was scribbled on the card. She had half expected DeeDee Robichaux to send something, even though she'd been transferred to Parish Hospital—in traction, she'd heard. With a shattered leg.

Two days ago, as Vangie sat at her mother's old sewing

machine, Cab and Edith had driven up the long road with the news that Henry had died instantly in a car wreck. Though she had loved and buried many people, including her own child, Vangie had never planned a funeral. And here she was, organizing Henry's. Life, she decided, was like cleaning out a messy refrigerator: It overwhelmed if you tried to do it all at once. Better to take it one shelf at a time. She chose a cherry coffin with brass handles, ordered roses and bachelor's buttons for the spray, and wrote down a list of hymns for the organist at First Baptist. Over Edith's protests, she'd driven herself to the monument lot. She'd had a time deciding on the headstone. The salesman confused her by suggesting inscriptions.

"Blessed Husband and Father?" he asked.

Vangie shook her head.

"How about Blessed Are the Dead Which Die in the Lord?"

"No." She sighed. "He didn't exactly die in the Lord, if you get my drift."

The man scratched his head. "Loved by all who knew him?"

"No."

"Precious Memories?"

"Absolutely not!"

"Well, how about, After Life's Fitful Fever He Sleeps Well?"

She had almost decided on a simple square of marble, which would blend nicely with Olive's. Then the salesman suggested a paired stone.

"Paired?" she said.

"His and hers," he said. "It's thrifty. Buying ahead saves time and money in the long run."

She stared at a long slab of granite, trying to imagine the eternal equivalent of a double bed:

Nepper

Henry Eugene	Vangie Louise
Born March 23, 1908	Born March 26, 1912
Died June 8, 1952	Died

Now that she thought about it, Went Out with a Bang would have worked best. Oh, if only epigraphs were more truthful: Made Good Biscuits; Mean As a Snake; Sometimes He Would, Sometimes He Wouldn't. She Flew the Coop.

"Made up your mind, Mrs. Nepper?" asked the salesman.

"Almost," she said. No matter what she put on the marker, Henry needed one of his own, not a double. She wanted to bury him next to his mama and daddy, but all the plots were filled. The ground was just packed with deceased Neppers. Finally, she bought a sunny plot near Olive.

Now she looked over at Edith and Cab. "You go on," she called out. "I'll walk home."

"In this heat?" Edith stepped out of the shade, still holding Cab's hand. "Sweetie, you'll dehydrate in this heat."

"I won't stay long. I just want to be alone for a bit." She watched Cab and Edith walk to the hearse. Then she looked up at the sky. The clouds were shaped like markers, and way off in the distance she thought she saw a red plane. She glanced back at the grave. The wake itself had been tense, with curious Limogeans she'd never seen before creeping up to the casket. Henry had looked, well, like Henry. Cab had fixed a natural-looking smile, and his coloring was ruddy. They said he'd cracked the windshield, but she couldn't find a mark on him.

Vangie heard footsteps, someone running down the gravel path. She turned, thinking Edith had returned, but it was just a skinny redheaded girl running toward her, running over generations of dead Limogeans. She stepped on a flat stone that said MA, then stepped on PA. She walked up to Vangie, twirling one pigtail. "It's me, Billie Robichaux. You remember me, Mrs. Nepper?"

"Why, I sure do." She held out her hand to hug the child. Billie hesitated, then looped her wiry arms around Vangie's waist. A scent of bananas and peanut butter wafted up. The part in the child's hair was poignantly crooked, the scalp radiantly white.

"I heard about Mr. Henry." Billie turned up her face. "I'm so sorry, Mrs. Nepper. He was with my mama, you know that?"

Vangie nodded.

"They ran off. Aunt Butter had to fetch Mama from Texas."

"I heard." Vangie touched the child's head and swallowed. "How is your mama?"

"Oh, awful bad!" Billie broke away and walked over to the edge of the grave. "The doctor said she'd walk with a limp for the rest of her life, but she called him a goddamn liar." She slapped her fingers over her mouth. "I didn't meant to cuss. I was just saying it like she did."

"I suppose I might've, too." Vangie smiled.

"My mama says a lot of things. You're supposed to be twelve years old to visit at Parish Hospital, but the nurses let me anyhow." She walked on her toes across the graves. After a long time she whistled and pointed to a marker. "Look here. This one was born in 1844. She's been dead a whole hundred and eight years. Can you feature it?"

"Billie, did you add that up in your head?"

"Yessum. And look over here. There's more." She held out her hand, and Vangie took it. They walked past the huge Confederate marker, where the flag snapped in the hot wind. They walked past a whole family of Brittons, past stones that said DADDIE. Some of the markers were covered with black moss; others looked rusty, crawling with ants, with blurred inscriptions, as if someone had sandpapered the letters.

Billie knelt in front of a small, halfmoon marker that spelled out OUR BABY. "Alice Maude," Billie read. "Born January 30, 1824. Died August 21, 1824. She sure didn't live long."

"Back in those days they didn't," said Vangie, standing behind her.

"She's been here, let's see, a whole one hundred and twenty-eight years."

"A garden of bones," said Vangie.

"And dead people, too." Billie stood up and rubbed her nose. "Why did my mama have to be in Mr. Henry's car?"

"I think you should ask your family, Billie."

"I did." She lifted her shoulders. "Daddy said it was a love snarl, but Butter—she's my aunt? She said they was friends."

"I guess they were."

"Are you mad at us?"

"Oh, no!" Vangie shook her head.

"My daddy said you would be. He's been crying awful bad. He can't get to the hospital to see Mama cause he's crippled? He got blown up by a hand grenade. Like this." She touched her fingers together, then pulled them apart. "When she ran off, he broke every last thing in our kitchen. Just threw it against the wall. So Aunt Butter had to buy all new? She bought plastic this time. Will that break, Mrs. Nepper?" Billie's eyes filled, but the tears just stayed there and didn't spill over.

"Come here, sugar." Vangie knelt down. "Your mama is alive. And she'll come home to you."

"Our home ain't regular."

"Don't know many that is."

"You don't?" Billie wiped her eyes.

"I sure don't."

Billie considered this a minute. Then she looked up. "Aunt Butter tries real hard. She fixed me a lemonade stand, but it was so hot all the ice melted. I walked to town, just to see for myself if Nepper's Drugs was closed. And you know what? The mayor, Mr. Chenier, was out on the sidewalk trying to fry a egg? Then I went by your house, but this mean lady came and chased me off."

"Oh, honey. I've moved."

"Where to?"

"A farm. I've got dogs and geese. Even a pair of peafowl."

"Pear of pee foul? What's that."

"Peacocks, darling," Vangie said. "Peacocks."

"I ain't never seen any of them. All we got is chickens." She dragged one sneaker through the grass. "Can I come see you sometimes? My mama said I can't work for hire, but there ain't no harm in just visiting, is there?"

"Not a bit." Vangie smiled and pulled Billie's pigtail. "I'd like that a lot. You just call me, the number's one forty four. And if your daddy says it's all right, I'll pick you up. Anytime."

"I can help you put flowers on Mr. Henry's grave, too." Billie tilted back her head, looking into the trees. "This is the biggest durn cemetery I ever saw, ain't it?"

"It sure is."

"My daddy says there's dead Yankees buried here."

"I never knew that." Vangie tried not to laugh as the child took off running, rolling into a cartwheel. In her mind's eye, Vangie turned with her. The sun darted from behind a cloud and beamed down on the granite markers. A rabbit hopped over a flat stone that said MY WIFE, past a marker that was shaped into a point, like a sheared-off steeple.

"Mrs. Nepper!" called out Billie. "Here's a dead Robichaux! Ain't that something? Daddy said we don't have no kinfolk up here." She turned another cartwheel, then landed upright and spun into a circle, clapping her hands. "Come on, Mrs. Nepper! Come with me!"

A sparrow, startled by the noise, flew away from the live oak and swooped toward the entrance, under the arch of wrought iron. It flew higher, over the cemetery, where Billie and Vangie walked between the headstones, together yet separate, like pearls divided by a length of string. The child reached up and took Vangie's hand. Above them a red plane sputtered, drawing out a *V*.

The plane drifted over Geranium Street, throwing shadows over the heat-waved road, over houses snug and colorful as carnival beads. It passed over Delphinium, where DeeDee Robichaux lay in her hospital bed, dreaming of nothing, then it blew toward Cypress Street, where Edith led Cab into her kitchen and shut the door. Two houses over, Harriet sat at her dining table, eating mosquito soup, licking the spoon. She looked out the window just as Phillip LeGette pulled into his driveway, parking under the chinaberry tree. He smiled over at Waldene, who was smiling down at her new baby daughter. In the back seat, Fanny rolled her eyes and stuck out her tongue.

High over the lake, the little red plane drew out V's, one after the other, filling the sky. All over Limoges people sat on their porches, cracking pecans and fussing about the heat. All over Limoges women rocked in gliders, fanning themselves and drinking tea. Some looked up at the sky, others called out to babies who were digging to China with tarnished silver spoons. Most everyone settled back in their chairs, gossiping about the dead and the living. From far away a child's laughter rang out, and the people nearest the cemetery leaned toward the road, straining to see past the markers and wrought-iron fence. The laughter rose up again, but whether the voice was real or imagined, or something carried by the wind, they couldn't have said.

Index to Recipes

~

Author's Note

You won't find Limoges, Louisiana, on any map, but it's a lot like my birthplace, Lake Providence, in the northeast corner of the state. In 1953, my father managed the local dime store, Morgan & Lindsay; when my mother was pregnant with me the planters' wives brought her everything from yellow roses to maternity clothes. Although Limoges is fictional, the area's generosity is real. During the last three years, many friends eased the gestation of this novel with committed attention, suggestions, silence, hymns, hot apple pie with rum sauce, and *lagniappe*.

I'd especially like to thank Wendi Leigh Welch, a Natchitoches native, for keeping watch; Robert ("le sheriff") Riffle for botanical nomenclature; Hank Nuwer for hilarious margin comments; John L. Myers and Margaret J. Campbell for readings, recipes, and graveyard tours; Peg Lynch for helping me over molehills; Diana Gabaldon for helping me over mountains; Janet McConnaughey and Sherry Kirksey for maps, phone books, and sources; Don Weston and Eloise Edwards (L.S.U. Agricultural Center, East Carroll Parish) for patiently and colorfully answering my questions; Angie Dorman for putting me in touch with Annie Noggles, cropduster extraordinaire; Amy Upchurch and Mary Williams, two great librarians, for allowing me to smuggle out old newspapers.

I owe a warm debt of gratitude to some Manhattan miracle workers: Ellen Levine, Gladys Justin Carr, Ari Hoogenboom, Cynthia Barrett, and Paul Olsewski. Also, long overdue thanks to Lucie Prinz and Virginia Kidd—their encouraging letters always seemed to arrive at the right time; and to Donovan Webster, an author and gentleman, wherever you are.